LOVOA'S CHALLENGE

EMMA K BLACKER

2QT Limited (Publishing)

First Edition published 2017 by

2QT Limited (Publishing)
Unit 5 Commercial Courtyard
Duke Street
Settle
North Yorkshire
BD24 9RH

Cover design:Robbie Associates Ltd.
Cover images: shutterstock.com

Printed in the UK by Lightning Source

A CIP catalogue record for this book is available
from the British Library

ISBN 978-1-912014-78-1

Titles in the Lismarian Series

Hannoki's Will
Lovoa's Challenge

Still to come...
Mesrra's Power

Prologue

DAVID wandered around his home, trailing his fingers over various surfaces – a table, a chair, a picture frame – and with his eyes closed he remembered Elen. Everything here reminded him of her. She was gone. She was not coming back.

'Dad, it's time.' David turned around to see his daughter standing in the doorway. Reluctantly he walked towards her and took her arm, and together they left for Elen's funeral.

⁂

'I want to go back to Lismar,' David said as he sat drinking whisky with Mark Yoland after the funeral.

'You know that is not possible, the planet is now protected, and what about your family?'

'My children are now adults, they don't need me, but the Lismarians do.'

'No, they don't, the culprits have either been caught and executed, fled Federation space in fear of a similar fate should they ever return, or committed suicide out of shame. It's over.'

'No, it's buried. We never caught the true criminals. Theron Gallo and Petro Diaz disappeared into unknown space. How can anyone guarantee that the trade won't start again once you and I are gone?'

'There are no guarantees in life David, you know that.'

'That is why I want to go back. To prepare them as best I can should anyone try to restart the bloody trade.'

'You can't affect their development David. They need to find their own way from now on.'

'I don't think my being there would cause them any further damage. I have already spent months on the planet.'

'If I were able to get you to Lismar, what then? The border is still monitored – you can't go back and forth as you see fit.'

'I plan to go there and stay.'

'You won't survive long on the surface.'

'You seriously think I don't know that? I got cancer from the suns after only a few months. I have tried for years to track Gallo and Diaz but uncharted space is just too big. What the Lismarian wings can offer is so valuable. I won't let them be harvested again.'

'I should be able to get you there, but you will never be able to return. We can't leave a shuttle there and the planet is too far away, even for your impressive range, to call for help if you need it.'

'I don't care.'

⁕

Prela stood watching as a shuttle slowly landed on Hannoki's Peak, a mountain named after her great-grandfather. She had picked up the telepathic message asking for permission to come down a short time ago. The caller, David, had been trying to contact her grandfather, Milkoy, but he had died some time ago and the mantle of first protector had passed to her and her mate. She knew who David was, her grandfather had shown her everything after she had mated and he knew she would be taking his place.

She had been shocked to discover that her people had been killed so their skins could be used as clothing and their wings to make other things. She had never truly understood that. David was a human who had helped stop the attacks, he had built the machine that had been used by her grandfather and great-grandfather to protect their people, and would be used by her if the traders ever returned. Milkoy had never expected David to return to Lismar as the planet had made him sick, though that had not stopped him missing his friend, so she had been surprised when she had heard a strong alien mind calling in their own language, and now he was coming back, and she was scared as to what this could mean. They had remained prepared. She had been told that humans lived a lot longer than her own kind, so it was important that the knowledge of how to defeat the traders was not lost. The strongest couples had been made protectors and had been put in charge of collectives distributed across the land, where others had congregated for protection. Prela, like her father, still tested the machine on occasion, passing energy to the others to direct it where needed so they would never again be subject to a tortuous death.

The shuttle landed, the hatch slid open and a male walked out into the bright sunlight.

'David, I am First Protector Prela and granddaughter of Milkoy. Welcome back to Lismar.'

⁜

'Are you sure you want to stay?' Mark asked him as they stood together by the shuttle. They had landed two days ago and had been warmly welcomed by Prela and her mate. David discovered that she knew everything that her grandfather had known, so he had explained to her what had happened since he had left Lismar and that he had come back because of his fears of the trade restarting. Prela was happy for David to stay, though she felt it best if he stayed on Hannoki's Peak, away from the general population. She was as concerned as Mark about the impact his presence would have on the people.

'I am sure.'

'What do you want me to tell your children?' asked Mark.

'They know what I intended to do. We have already said our goodbyes. The only thing that needs to be considered is an explanation for my absence. I agreed with them that if I decided to stay, they would stage a shuttle accident and announce my death.'

'That is very final.'

'It's the way it has to be. I stayed for Elen and the children, but I always wanted to come back here. My family know that.'

'I'll miss you, but I understand.'

'Thank you. When you see my family, reassure them that I'm happy and I love them.'

'I'll tell them. Goodbye and good luck.'

Chapter 1

On Lismar, 75 years after Hannoki

JERA sat next to her mate, Neron, listening to his breathing as it became more and more laboured. She had felt him getting weaker for some time, had known when the suns were no longer enough to stop the effects of old age. She had warned the protectors a few days ago that she felt their time was limited and that they would need to appoint a new first protector, but it was only now she felt some of them arrive. She knew that she should get up and greet them, but she was so tired and did not want to part from Neron, even for a moment, so she stayed and held his hand and waited.

'Jera?' he said, so quietly she could barely hear him.

'I am here,' she said, squeezing his hand, hoping he could feel her.

'The protectors?'

'They've arrived. Do you want to see them?' she replied.

'No, I'm too tired now. I'm sorry, I cannot keep going. I wanted you to live so much longer.'

'I have lived long enough,' she responded, crying. 'It's time for you to rest now.'

'They will come again, do they know that they will come again?' he said, getting upset. As he had grown weaker, Neron had become more and more obsessed with the traders' return.

'I know, I have told them many times,' she said and kissed his hand.

'Good, they understand that though it has been so long, they will still come, they will come.'

'They know, I have told them,' she repeated.

'Good,' he said, then took a deep breath and shook, then nothing. The hand in Jera's grip went limp. Crying, she climbed into the bed next to him and, with tears running down her face, also breathed her last.

⁜

'There is no point in having first protectors,' Geslan said.

This had been an ongoing discussion since the health of Neron had started to deteriorate; Jera had spoken to them all several times over the last few weeks, arguing that they needed to find a couple to replace them before they died. When no decision had been made, she had pressed the importance of appointing another couple. She had been unable to put any names forward as both she and her mate had withdrawn from society a long time ago, so she did not know who could take the position. Since the message had come about Neron's collapse, the argument had become heated, as time was clearly running out.

'But the traders may return,' Ovrra countered.

'They are not coming back. If they ever did exist, it has been generations beyond counting. I do not know how many times I need to say this to make you all understand, they are not coming back.'

'You can't say that for sure.'

'This is not something we can say for sure on either side,' Herra said. 'We have been going over this since Neron started to weaken. Personally, I don't think the traders are ever going to come back but I will also concede that I can't prove that they won't. I don't think that this should be a discussion over whether they will or will not come back; it should be a discussion on whether we keep the rank of first protectors or not.'

'But what is the point of having them if the traders won't be returning?' Geslan asked.

'None of us has authority over each other, but the first protectors have seniority, and there have been occasions when they have been needed to resolve a dispute.'

'They have not been needed for that for years,' Geslan scoffed.

'Yes, but when Derun took over his father's collective and claimed that you had stolen land from him, you didn't complain when the first protectors became involved and agreed with you,' came the retort from Herra.

'We also hold the position of protector due to our strength, a strength that is needed to protect the people when the traders return. If you are saying, Geslan, that the traders are not coming back, then we have no right to hold our positions and should return to being equal, as it was in Hannoki's day,' Ovrra pointed out.

They all sat in silence for a moment as this fact sank in. Their control and social power were all reliant on the traders' return. They might not like first protectors dictating to them, but accepting them was a necessity if they wanted to hold their positions.

'Fine, but if another first protector is appointed, who would it be?' Geslan asked.

'Essac asked to mate with Bahia a few days ago,' Herra said, breaking the silence.

'They are both the strongest in their families so, in theory, they could claim ownership of both collectives, giving them a great advantage over all of us.'

'I never took either of them to be so mercenary.'

'They're not, it's a love match. Individually, they are stronger than us, they would lose nothing in mating. I think they could easily be convinced to become first protectors.'

'Do you think their families would agree to it?'

'I don't think that they could refuse, the position goes to the strongest mated couple.'

'A lot of the protectors are not here and they will not be happy that we have made this decision without them.'

'There are enough of us here, if we are all in agreement, to sway the vote.'

'If they don't like it, then they should have been here. The next first protectors should have been chosen earlier so that Jera and Neron could have shared everything they knew.'

'Why are they not here?'

'Because they no longer care or have respect for the first protectors.'

'Possibly,' Geslan said. 'Does everyone else agree?' he asked the room, and everyone gave their agreement.

'Then I think we should talk to Essac and Bahia immediately, there may still be time...' Geslan said, but before he could say any more he gripped the table and took a sharp breath, and everyone else around the room was affected.

'They have died,' Herra said.

'Hannoki save us if the traders ever return.'

✳

They all stood around the pyre. Although it was normally traditional to bury the bodies of the dead, the first protectors were always burnt on the mountain top. Some said the tradition started with Hannoki. The fires were lit and they stood in silence as the flames consumed the two bodies. The remaining ashes would be thrown into the wind and carried away.

✳

The following day Geslan stood with the others, ready to take flight. 'We are agreed then? We fly to Hesrun's collective to tell them of our proposal for his son and Bahia.'

'Just so,' Herra said and the others also acknowledged. 'Are you going to tell him we are coming?'

'I will communicate with him en route, but let us not waste any more time,' and he jumped off the side with the others following close behind him. Together they soared through the air, the descent so much easier with the wind behind them. It did not seem to take them any time at all until they were clear of the mountain range.

'*Hesrun,*' Geslan called with his mind.

'*What is it, Geslan?*' the reply came.

'*The first protectors are dead. I'm on my way to your collective, there is something I need to discuss with you.*'

'*Geslan, this is not a good time; can you not just tell me what it is that you want?*'

'*The timing is perfect, and if you had honoured the first protectors and attended them, I would not now have to come to you.*'

'*Very well,*' Hesrun replied resignedly, '*I will see you soon.*'

It was not long before Geslan and the other protectors saw the collective in front of them. As they circled they could see Hesrun waiting for them on the battlements and felt his surprise at seeing so many of them.

'Welcome Geslan, welcome everyone,' Hesrun said after they had all landed. 'Would you like to come in? I'm intrigued as to what brings you all here.'

As they settled themselves in one of the living areas, Hesrun asked, 'When did they pass?'

'You didn't feel them?'

'No, I assume I was too far away.'

'They passed yesterday morning and were burned that evening.'

'And you wait until now to tell me? I would have come.'

'You got the message the same as everyone else that their death was imminent. If you chose not to attend, that was down to you.'

'I'm sorry, of course it is not your responsibility to keep me updated. I would have been there but I could not afford to leave here at the moment. What is it that was so urgent that you all had to come straight here?'

'We hear that your son wishes to mate with Bahia.'

'You are right, that's why I could not leave here.'

'Because your neighbours are very unhappy with the match?' Herra asked.

'Not just them – both mine and Berren's other children are against it.'

'I thought it would greatly benefit both families?'

'The problem is, Essac is a second son and Bahia is the youngest, but they are both the strongest by far in our families. If they never mated or mated anyone weaker, then it would not be a problem, but together! They would retain their strength and could then control both collectives over the rest of their families, and the older children do not want to lose out to them.'

'Then perhaps what we have come to suggest will find favour with you,' Geslan said.

'Neron and Jera had no children and we are all agreed that there is still a need for a first protector,' Herra said.

'Really? You are all agreed on that? I thought that when they passed it would be a natural closure as they had no powerful children to demand the right of the title – anyway, the traders are not coming back.'

'We're mixed in our opinions on whether the traders will return but we do recognise the need to have someone who has authority over us for when the inevitable disputes between us happen,' Geslan said.

'You are considering Essac and Bahia as first protectors?' When he saw the nod of agreement, he continued, 'They are also both very easy-going and not likely to interfere with the running of the collectives, and as first protectors, they can't hold a collective themselves, so it would stop the arguments that are going on now. You are all agreed with this?'

'Everyone here is, but the others who were not present at the death have not been asked,' Geslan stated.

'We are close to a majority,' Herra pointed out. 'If you, Essac and Bahia agree, then we would only need a few others to agree and I don't see that as a problem.'

'I like this idea. Let me call Essac and see what his views are,' Hesrun said. '*Essac*,' he called.

'*Yes Father.*'

'*I need you to join me.*'

'*I'm coming.*'

It was not long before Essac came into the room. He paused briefly at the door, surprised at how many protectors there were.

'Come in Essac,' his father said. 'The first protectors have died and there has been some discussion on who should take their place. The suggestion at the moment is you and Bahia, after you have mated, obviously.'

'Why us?'

'It's a position that goes to the strongest couple, which would be you. What do you think?'

'It's something I had never considered – I knew we would be the strongest in our families and surrounding collectives, but the strongest altogether?'

'We believe so, we haven't heard of another couple who would be stronger than you.'

'I'll need to talk to Bahia about this. When will you need an answer?'

'As soon as possible.'

'Then if I may be excused, I'll go and talk to Bahia.'

'You may go,' his father said and Essac left the room.

'Do you think he will take it?' Herra asked Hesrun.

'I don't know, he is not keen on taking authority. Both he and Bahia do not understand why their brothers and sisters are upset over their mating as they have no interest in taking over the collectives.'

'Then they sound like the perfect choice since they are not interested in ruling.'

'Indeed.'

⁕

'*Bahia,*' Essac called to her.

'*I'm here,*' she replied.

'*Are you alone? Can we talk?*'

'*Yes, I'm trying to keep away from my family at the moment.*'

'*I know the feeling,*' Essac said, '*but I have received an interesting proposal which may resolve the problems we are having with our families.*'

'*What proposal could possibly change the feelings of our brothers and sisters?*'

'*That we take the position of first protectors.*'

'*You are joking? I thought they were not going to be replaced, and anyway, the first protectors would have to die first.*'

'*They have.*'

'*When?*'

'*I don't know, I forgot to ask, but it must have been recent because a lot of the other protectors are here talking with father, and I don't think they are joking.*'

'*It could be a great opportunity,*' Bahia said.

'*Would it? It is an obsolete role.*'

'*Only because it was allowed to be.*'

'*So are you saying you want to accept?*'

'*I think we should, do you not agree?*'

'*I will let them know.*'

Once Bahia and Essac had agreed to take the rank of first protectors, all the arguments among their families ended and no further opposition was put forward. They stood now on the battlements, hand in hand, while behind them their families stood in support of them. They looked at each other and smiled, when they came back they would be a mated couple and would be going to Hannoki's Peak to start their lives together as first protectors. They were excited about what they could do, what they could achieve. They smiled at each other and together they jumped off the battlements.

Chapter 2

Two years later.

THREE couples stood in front of the steward. They had applied for permission to try for a child and they now awaited the decision.

'Do you honestly think you can support a child?' the steward asked them. Every month the peasants were allowed to request permission to mate, and Protector Jeka thought it was necessary to control the population on his collective. The steward had the task of keeping all the records, not just on who had children and how many but also of any deaths. Protector Jeka wanted to know the exact number of peasants who lived and worked on his land.

'Control is imperative,' he always said. 'If we let them breed as they wish, we would be overrun within a year,' which was why these people were in front of him now.

'Yes sir,' Fesrun replied as he stood nervously next to his mate, Mesrra.

'You have never been given permission before,' he said. 'My records show you have no children.'

'Yes sir, this is the first time we have asked.'

'Why are you asking now?'

'We have been mated now for a year sir, we believe it's time to start a family, with your permission.'

The steward nodded at the information and made a note on the paper in front of him before moving on to the other couples and asking them the same questions.

He knew what the answer would be to all three of them, he had had their details before they had approached him, but he would not make it that easy for them. Once he was done with his questions, he made them wait while he pretended to ponder the question before giving them his answer. Yes, they could all try for a child today.

❋

They all stood outside the steward's home waiting to take to the skies.

'You all came to me asking permission for the same thing, permission to have a child. I have been generous and granted it to all of you. I must, however, remind you that should the mating today not result in conception, then you must return and ask me again. Is this understood?' As he watched them nod in understanding, he continued, 'Though you have all been given this wonderful opportunity today, whatever the outcome you are all expected to work tomorrow.' The three couples again nodded. 'Then I wish you all the best,' and he stood away from them. The couples looked at each other and then one after another they took to the sky.

Once Fesrun and Mesrra had gained some height, they flew away from the other couples, not wanting to accidentally collide with them. Once they were happy that there was enough distance between them and the others, they started to mate and lit up the sky around them.

❋

Their mating was explosive. As soon as they began, the skies started to light up with all the colours of a rainbow. They travelled for miles, twisting and turning together, their two bodies fusing to create a new life, with everyone below watching them. Finally they landed, exhausted, to lie on the hard ground. It had been explained to them what would happen and they thought that they were prepared for it, but nothing could have prepared them for the energy they had produced, they could not have believed it possible. As the shock began to subside, Fesrun pulled himself up onto his elbow and looked at his mate. She turned her head to look at him. He met her eyes for a moment and smiled before running his gaze over the rest of her body, looking for changes, trying to see if their joining had been successful. His eyes stopped at her stomach where he could already see the baby beginning to develop. Tentatively he put his hand out and placed it over Mesrra's stomach.

'He's going to be a strong one,' Fesrun observed.

Mesrra placed her hand over her mate's and replied, 'It might be a she.'

Fesrun looked into her eyes and asked, 'Does it matter either way?'

'No, it doesn't.'

As the wonder and shock began to wear off, they began to take in their surroundings. They were no longer on Jeka's collective, that much they knew as they could see the mountains rising up on the horizon, but they were unable to say where they were, the only indication of direction they had was the trail they had left in the sky.

'We should try and get back while there is still a trail, of sorts, to follow,' Mesrra said as she struggled to get to her feet. Exhausted, she swayed for a moment before she was able to steady herself by placing her hand on her mate's shoulder, but she could imagine the overseer's wrath if they were not back in time for their day's work.

'We can't go back,' Fesrun said slowly, not moving from where he still sat on the floor. 'They will know that our child will be strong once it's born; they will try to make sure you lose it before it can become a threat.'

'What do you mean? Of course we have to go back, we

have nowhere else to go.'

He gently took hold of the hand that rested on his shoulder, and she felt reassurance in his grasp. 'Protector Jeka will not let us keep our child,' he repeated.

'Of course he will, the laws...' she started, but stopped as she saw Fesrun shake his head in denial.

'The protector has broken so many rules, why not this one? The old laws are more likely to guarantee that our child will be killed or taken away from us. If our child, once mated, is stronger than any of Protector Jeka's offspring, he or she should become protector in their place. Can you honestly imagine him allowing that?' he asked her gently, tightening his grip on her hand so she could not pull away from him. 'And even if our child did not take over as protector, he or she would be strong enough to challenge the system of the collective – either way, our child would be a threat.'

Fesrun watched Mesrra as his argument slowly sank in, and saw the panic that came with understanding.

'But we can't just leave, what would we do? Where would we go?'

'That, I'm afraid, I don't know, but we must keep away from Protector Jeka or any other protector until our child is old enough to store its own energy. When that happens, he or she will be too old for them to harm without broadcasting it to everyone.'

'We have to go back and pack.'

'No!' he replied forcefully, 'it won't take him long to find out whose mating had taken place. If we return now, he will be waiting for us.'

'But everything we have, our whole lives, are there,' she protested.

'No,' Fesrun denied, standing up and taking his mate gently in his arms, 'our whole life is here – you, me and our child, what more do we need?'

She shook her head, trying to fight his logic, scared at the idea of having to start out with nothing.

'What is it that we have left behind? An old cabin that would not have survived another storm, mats worn thin with age and cracked bowls? Nothing that cannot be replaced, but could we replace our child?'

⁑

Protector Jeka stood looking out of the window as the sky lit up above his collective. He heard a sound behind him and turned to see his mate, Kisa, enter the room. She walked across and stood next to him and looked out of the window.

'It looks as if the first protectors are going to have a second child,' she said. 'I'm surprised, they only had their little boy a short while ago.'

'No, the mating started here; it's not the first protectors.'

'Then who?'

'I don't know,' he said and called out to a servant to bring the captain of the guard to him. While they waited, they watched in silence as the couple moved away from the collective. There was a knock on the door.

'Enter!'

'My Protector, you asked for me?' his captain said.

'I want you to find out who that couple is, and when you do I want them brought to me.'

'Yes, my Protector,' and he turned around to go.

'Use whatever means you feel necessary, but I want that couple, even if that means you have to bring all recently mated couples to me and have to rip the collective apart in the process.'

'Of course, my Protector,' and he left the room. Waiting outside for him were two of his men and he sent them to get a troop together and meet him at the steward's home. He would know who had permission to mate today, and if it was a couple who did not, then they would have to do as the protector advised and tear the collective apart to find who was missing.

⁜

Bahia felt the hum of energy first. Initially confused as to what was creating it, she opened her mind up and searched for the source, and smiled when she realised that a couple had risen to mate. She walked out onto the balcony and looked down. In the distance she could see the different colours lighting up the normally white clouds. As she watched, the colours got brighter and brighter as the couple got nearer to them.

'Who do you think it is?' Essac asked, having come up behind her.

'I don't know. I hadn't realised that any of the protector's children had planned on mating. Whoever it is, they are creating the same amount of energy as we did. I don't know who would be strong enough to do that.'

'It could be anyone. Normally, strong children come to strong parents, but it is not always the way.'

'Whoever it is will have a powerful child, but if they are not from a protector's family, they will be hunted down,' she said, looking at the now vivid colours. She closed her eyes and again sent her mind out to see if she recognised the couple. She felt Essac's hand on her shoulder giving her strength as she searched. She felt the couple, they were so overwhelmed by what they were experiencing that Bahia gasped at the raw emotion. She took a deep breath and closed her mind before opening her eyes. 'They are in the throes of the mating flight but they are shocked and overwhelmed. Neither of their minds are familiar, so I don't think that they are from a protector's family,' she informed Essac.

'Then every protector is going to be out looking for

them.'

'It looks like they are settling down.'

'Can you sense where?'

'I'm not sure. Near the junction, and if not, then on Osvai's collective, I think. It's hard to say from here.'

'I will try to find them. If they are not from a protector's family, I'll bring them back here,' he reassured her and turned and left the room, leaving her standing on the balcony, watching as the last of the colours faded from the sky.

When the sky had finally returned to normal, she turned and went back into the room to where her son lay, and bent down and lifted her baby into her arms, needing the reassurance of having him close to her. He woke up and protested at being removed from his nice warm bed but quickly quieted when he recognised his mother's arms. 'Ssssh, my little one, let us just hope that your father is in time to save the other couple's baby.' Yet no amount of wishing would alter reality. She knew that the child's chances of survival were small if the parents were not from a protector's family; everyone would know what the colours in the sky meant, and any protector who found them would dispose of the child and separate the parents to make sure they would never mate again and create another powerful child. Years ago such actions would have been unthinkable, but with changes in society, and their predecessors having been happy to remain divorced from everything that was happening below them, now meant that the authority of the first protectors had declined to such an extent that they were generally considered a joke. Both Bahia and Essac knew why they had been given the position: it got them out of the way. If Essac challenged them over the baby, Bahia was worried that he would not be able to stand up to them. As far as they were concerned, he no longer had any authority over them, which was unfortunately now true in practice, if not in theory. In an outright confrontation, Essac would be the stronger, but such an action could lead to an outright revolt of all the other protectors, and they could not deal with that.

Since they had become first protectors they had tried to make a difference but so far they had been unsuccessful. She prayed that their son, Solvan, would be able to change things for he promised to be stronger than anyone had been in generations. For now, the only thing Essac could do was try to get to the family before a protector did and bring them here so they would be safe. She did not know what the outcome would be, but she feared the worst. Essac had been too late the last time there had been a strong mating – it had not been as powerful as this one, but strong enough to have been considered a threat to the local protector. The parents had hidden and had been successful for a while, but they had been hunted down and the child had been killed about an hour after it had been born. The parents had been saved and now worked here, for them. They had had another child, but it was not strong.

Solvan had fallen asleep again in her arms, so she returned him to his cot and then went back out onto the balcony and looked down, as if desperate to see anything, but she was too far away and just had to wait for Essac to return to her.

⁜

Essac jumped off the side of Hannoki's Peak with his wings outstretched. He caught the currents that swirled around the mountain, finding the ones that would push him towards Osvai's collective and the junction. The junction was an area of land that came under the jurisdiction of the first protectors and, other than the forest and the mountains where they lived, it was the only section of land over which they had control. It had been necessary for the previous first protectors to take control of it as it bordered three collectives and a bitter dispute had broken out over ownership, with no one willing to concede it to anyone else. Essac hoped he would find the couple there, on his land and not on another protector's. As he glided down the mountain the forest below became clearer and more defined. It was one of the few places where trees and a large range of vegetation grew in such abandon, watered by the streams that flowed down the mountain range. The water supply was limited everywhere else, which reduced the type of crops that could be grown, although the winter months were easier as it was cooler and the rains put moisture into the ground. As he flew he scanned the thick canopy of branches and leaves but could see nothing through them, so had no way of knowing whether the couple had landed nearby and sought refuge.

As he approached he flew low, as close as he could to the treetops, and slowed down, trying to see or sense anything from the forest, but with no luck. As he cleared the edge he sped up again and started to circle around the area, looking for any trace of them, but there was nothing, not of the couple or anyone else. With a sinking heart he headed towards Osvai's collective and hoped that no one else had found them first. He prayed to Hannoki that if they remained free, they had realised the danger in going back to their collective because their protector would either have seen, or been told that a powerful mating had started on his land.

They cannot have got this far, he thought as he flew further and further into the collective. They would have been exhausted and most probably on foot. He stopped and turned back towards the forest. From the sky he could see for miles across the flat, barren land of Osvai's collective and, other than a handful of derelict cabins, he saw nothing. He cast his mind out to each of these places but knew without stopping to look at each one that they were as empty as they seemed. The collective had declined over the last year as, like the previous first protectors, Osvai had fallen ill and his two powerful children were arguing over who would take control after he and his mate had passed. These arguments meant that no one was managing the workers. It could be possible that they had met other workers who had taken them in as runaways from another collective, not realising what they had done, but he thought it highly unlikely. The only place he could think they had gone was into the forest, so he turned and flew back to have another look, sure that he had missed something. As he returned he felt the winds pick up. He looked up and saw clouds rapidly moving across the sky, and he realised with a sinking heart that he would have to return home otherwise the increasing winds would make it impossible for some time. He hoped that the couple had found somewhere they could shelter until the winds had passed.

Chapter 3

THE steward had seen the sky light up shortly after the three couples took flight and his heart sank. He hoped that the couple were far enough away for Protector Jeka not to have seen it and realised the significance. Shaking, he headed back home and started to get all the records together in case the protector demanded to know who had mated today. It was not long before there was a loud hammering on the door and a demand to be let in. Taking a deep breath, he opened the door to the captain of the guard.

'Protector Jeka sent us,' he was informed. 'He wants to know who that couple was.'

'I thought you might be coming,' he said and indicated the table where he had placed the records, picked up the top one and handed it to the captain. 'This is the list of the three couples who were given permission to mate today. None of them were powerful – one couple already have a child who also has no power and it was the first time for the other two. There was no reason to believe that any of them would create a powerful child.'

'We need to check these three couples and, if need be, find out if anyone else might have mated without permission.'

'I will compile a list of everyone who has been denied permission.'

'Thank you, we will check these first,' the captain said. 'If we need to, we will come back for the other names.'

'I have this for you as well,' the steward said and started

to unroll a larger document. 'This is the complete map of the collective and here, here and here are where the three couples live.' He pointed out the relevant sections of the map. 'Here are copies of those sections, which would be easier for you to take,' and he passed them over.

'Thank you,' the captain said as he took them. 'I'll let you know if we need the list and return these to you when we are done.'

The steward sagged in relief when they left, glad that he had not been dragged off by the guards. Pulling himself together, he started to put the names together.

✣

The captain looked at the sections of maps that the steward had given to him as he waited for the rest of the guards to arrive. The three couples were in different sections of the collective so he briefed his guards and split them into even groups, making sure that their strengths were evenly balanced. He went with the group that was going to the couple who already had a child as they lived in the area where there were most workers and, with a small child involved, their visit was most likely to cause unrest.

He arrived at the address and pounded on the door, demanding that they be admitted or the door would be smashed in. The door was opened almost immediately by a male.

'I'm looking for Ireln and Parra,' said the captain.

'I'm Ireln, my mate is inside,' he said and opened the door wide so the captain could see a female sitting at the table holding a young child. As he walked in she stood up and placed the child on the floor. As she did so, it was clear that they had not been successful in their attempt to have a second child. 'Is there a problem?' Ireln asked as the guard stopped at the doorway.

'You are Parra?' he asked the female.

'Yes sir,' she replied.

'It was you who rose to mate today, not another couple?'

'No sir, it was myself and Ireln. Other than my daughter, there are no other people living here.'

'We will need to check that is the case,' he said and indicated to his men to move forward and search.

'If you explain what is wrong, we might be able to help you,' Ireln said.

'I do not explain the protector's business,' he replied, and watched while his men worked.

'There is no one else here,' one of the guards confirmed, as he walked out of their home.

'Then we will leave you,' the captain said to the couple and turned and left. Once outside, he communicated with the other two groups. One informed him that they had secured the couple, their mating had been successful and asked where the captain wanted to take them. '*Take them to the dungeons and place them in separate cells. Protector Jeka can decide what to do with them when he is ready.*'

'*Yes sir.*'

The second team had more worrying news: no one was there. Cursing, the captain took to the skies and flew to join them, landing next to the leader of this group.

'We have searched their place, such as it is, and the others are now talking to the neighbours,' he informed his captain, who nodded his understanding and went into the cabin. It was obvious when he walked in that the cabin had already been searched, and that the few possessions they owned still seemed to be there, so they had not packed and left.

'Make sure the men search the surrounding cabins as well – knowing what they have done, they might be seeking shelter elsewhere.'

The captain walked out of the cabin and looked around at all the other homes. The missing couple would know that they would be sought. If they had returned to the collective, they could be hiding anywhere. He knew that if it had been him and his mate, he would not have returned and would have found somewhere to hide, somewhere he could protect his mate and child, but would they?

Already he could hear sounds of discontent as the men searched the surrounding properties. How far should he go? He knew that this could cause its own problems.

'Check all the cabins in this section for them,' he said. 'I will head back to inform Protector Jeka of the situation and see how he wishes to proceed.'

'Of course, captain,' the team leader said and watched as he took to the skies. It would be so much easier if the protector would permit telepathic communication, he thought, but he only permitted it within his family and other protectors, he did not want his mind polluted with those beneath him.

⁜

Protector Jeka was furious when he heard the news.

'I told you to use any means,' he yelled at the captain, 'any means! Bring me that couple!'

'What do you want us to tell the people, they will be angry at our treatment towards them.'

'Do you think I care what they think? They have no right to know my business – offer them no explanation.'

'Tensions were rising among the couple's neighbours. If we continue across the whole collective, the people could cause us problems.'

'Then deal with them. I do not care if the peasants are not happy, rip their homes apart if you need to.'

'Yes, my Protector,' replied the captain and he turned

and left. He went out to the barracks to gather as many men as he could for the task. He was standing with them, ready to leave, when he felt it, the wind had picked up suddenly. His heart sank: a wind storm was the last thing that he needed now.

⁜

Mesrra and Fesrun felt the wind rising on their heated skin and they knew what it meant. They had walked to the forest and kept to the tree line. They did not know where they were and could only guess at the direction of Protector Jeka's collective from the trail of colours in the sky. The forest could offer them somewhere to hide while they decided what to do next. They knew nothing of the collectives in this area or of the protectors who ran them, but they feared that they would be sought. The wind picked up quickly and was making walking difficult. The branches of the first trees they reached were thrashing about, the leaves that had been ripped from them joining with the debris being whipped up from the floor, making it hard to see.

'We have to get out of here,' Mesrra shouted, but even as she said it, it was clear that this was not going to be easy as she could see very little in front of her. She stumbled and put her hands out in front of her to try and break her fall, but her hands went through the ground and she continued to fall through the earth. She screamed. Fesrun tried to grab hold of her but the ground gave way under his feet and they fell together.

'Mesrra!' he called out after they had landed with a thud a short way down.

'I'm here,' she said, opening her eyes. Light came though from the hole above them and she could see that they had fallen into a small cavern. 'Are you all right?' she asked him as she cautiously made her way the few feet towards him.

'I'm fine – and you and our baby?'

'We're fine,' she replied. 'It looks like we have found our shelter from the storm.'

'There must have been easier ways, but it will do.' After carefully looking around them, they found a space to settle down and drifted off to sleep listening to the sound of the storm above them.

Mesrra awoke to the sun shining down on her. She gently eased herself away from her still-sleeping mate and scrambled out of the cavern. The wind storm had stopped and the suns were now shining bright in the sky. Mesrra found a break in the foliage and spread her wings to open as much of her body as possible to the rays. That was how Fesrun found her a short time later. He stood still and stared at her in wonder, taking in the different sheen of her skin now that she was pregnant. She felt his presence and turned to smile at him before folding her wings back.

'We should remember this place,' she said, 'in case we need to come back here.'

'Where do you think we should go? We don't know this place.'

'We need to find out, find out if there is a collective we can go to. We need to talk to other workers before we can make any sort of plan.'

'I think you just came up with one,' he said.

＋

The damage the wind storm had caused in the forest was obvious. Branches littered the floor and the occasional tree that had been too old or too young to withstand the force of the wind had fallen, forcing them to scramble over the ground with difficulty. Once at the edge they looked out, the suns so much brighter out of the shade of the trees. They looked out at the flat land in front of them and, holding hands, they took a deep breath and walked out, going straight ahead.

'Why is there nothing here?' Mesrra said. 'This soil is better than on our collective.'

'I know, I would have thought this was prime land.'

'Over there,' Mesrra said, pointing to their right. Fesrun turned and saw a group of people coming towards them. As they got closer, it looked like a family group. 'Are you ready?' Mesrra said as they got close enough to talk.

'No time like the present,' he replied, then shouted, 'greetings!'

'Greetings.' The senior member of the group came forward, while the others, a couple with several young children, held back. They all looked nervous. The senior male had different markings from the others but the similarities were still there. Fesrun wondered if he was the grandfather.

'Where are you heading?' Fesrun asked.

'Why? What is our business to you?'

'Nothing,' Fesrun replied, surprised by the hostile response. 'We are new and were wondering who the protectors are. We do not know the area.'

'You've left your collective?' the old man asked.

'Yes,' he said after a pause.

'Don't worry, I won't ask you why. If you're looking for another collective to work on, then don't come here,' he said, 'the conditions are bad and getting worse. We're leaving our collective.'

'Where is it you are heading?'

'The land near the forest,' and he pointed in the direction from which they had just come. 'No protector owns it, the first protectors apparently have the rights there, but the soil is good and unused, and since they do nothing with it, we were going to try and farm it ourselves.'

'Hannoki – you are joking.'

'Why not? The protectors will not be able to do anything to us and why would the first protectors care – they don't use it. We will not claim ownership, we will simply work it to feed ourselves.'

Fesrun thought about this, turned to look at Mesrra and saw that she was thinking the same thing. If they were living outside a collective, living on their own, then it would be easier to hide their child when it was born. If they set their home up near the forest, they would always have somewhere to shelter if needed. They knew how to build, every worker did on Protector Jeka's land as they had to make their own homes and maintain them. They had no tools but the family in front of them did – could they help each other? Borrow their tools in return for labour?

'Can we join you?' Fesrun asked. The old man smiled and nodded.

Chapter 4

THE phone was ringing. Cal looked and saw that it was his father again. With frustration he answered it as it was clear his father was not going to stop trying to get hold of him.

'Cal,' his father said when his son finally answered, 'I know you are back on Europa. I need to see you, there is something we need to talk about,' he said, getting straight to the point.

'I don't know when that will be,' Cal replied, 'I'm here for business, not pleasure, and I just have too much to do. What is it you wish to discuss?'

'I'll only talk about it in person, Cal. I'm not asking you to come round for a social visit, I'm asking because I need you and I don't know who else I can trust.'

'Are you in trouble?'

'I don't know,' he replied honestly.

'I'll be round tonight,' Cal said.

⁜

Cal's father cut the connection, leaned back in his chair and took a deep breath. Was he doing the right thing bringing his son in on this? He had been sickened by what he had found out while doing his research. He thought it had all been consigned to history but then he had heard rumours that had worried him. Perhaps the history was not as buried as he had thought it was, but did he really believe that there was a mass conspiracy or had he just been in politics for too long?

There was a knock on the door. 'Come in!' he shouted.

'Head Chairman, the car is ready,' he was informed.

'Thank you,' he said, then stood up and collected his case before walking out of his office. He climbed into the car parked outside his home. 'Good morning Adam,' he said to the driver.

'Good morning sir. Are we going to the central office?'

'Yes please Adam,' he replied. 'How is your family?' he asked as the car started up.

'They are well sir, thank you,' Adam replied as he programmed the destination into the car and it pulled onto the road. The head chairman pulled his computer out of his case and logged on to continue his investigation. For several minutes he worked in silence, used to the daily commute.

Adam pulled onto the main highway and picked up speed. Suddenly the peace was broken by the sound of grinding metal.

⁂

It was on every channel, on every screen, on every planet in the Federation of Worlds: the head chairman was dead, killed in a road traffic accident. Silence had fallen as people heard the news. How could such a thing have happened? 'Surely there had been safety measures in place that should have prevented this?' many people were asking each other. Assurances were given that a full investigation would be made into the tragedy, and if there had been any negligence or any other form of foul play then the people responsible would be punished under the full weight of the law. The deputy chairman addressed the people, telling them that even through this difficult time, the running of the government would go on as normal; that he and the rest of the board were in full agreement: there would be stability, there would be continuity.

※

'It's done,' the voice said over a secured channel.

'So I've heard,' came the reply. 'Your payment is on its way.' The man leaned forward and broke the connection.

'Things are moving quickly,' a new voice said. A woman had entered the room near the end of the conversation. Walking up to the man sitting in front of the console, she slipped her hands onto his shoulders and began to caress him. 'Finally,' she whispered in his ear, 'the old man has gone.'

'Mmm,' he murmured, taking one of her hands off his shoulders, moving it to his mouth and kissing it, 'but there are still a few loose ends.'

'Which could have been avoided by killing him quietly. Suicide, an induced heart attack or stroke, they are all much cleaner ways to kill someone.'

'I know, but our employers wanted a public death.'

'Do you want me to dispense with the technician?'

He tugged her so she fell onto his lap. 'You read my mind,' he said and tried to kiss her but she pulled away.

'Always,' she said, smiling, and moved to stand up. He grabbed her and held her tight.

'Where do you think you are going?' he asked, annoyed.

'I thought you wanted the technician dead?'

He laughed and let her go. 'You really do enjoy your work,' he said.

'That's why you love me so,' she said, kissed him teasingly and slipped off his knee.

※

Cal Everson turned the screen off in frustration, sick of hearing the same news again and again, sick of hearing various so-called expert opinions of what had happened to his father. The only thing Cal was interested in was the result of the investigation. He had wanted to be involved in it, had argued that with his expertise he was one of the best-qualified people to lead it, but he had been refused. Cal had been furious with the decision, they had said he was too close to it, he would not be objective when looking at the evidence. Not objective! He always had to be objective with a father in high politics, he had never been blind to what his father was. Now he was left on the outside, waiting for the results of an investigation into a death everyone was already calling an accident – but how could it be? He knew what security measures were on the car, he had designed and installed them himself. His father should never have died in a crash, and he was being told to wait on someone else's report. His frustration was simmering.

'Sir,' Jane Keyworth, his PA, said. Cal did not acknowledge her, but he knew he was being unreasonable towards her. She had worked for him for the last five years, always exceeding his expectations quietly and efficiently. None of his foul temper was her fault; there was just no one else he could take it out on. He heard a scraping sound and, curious, turned around and saw her placing a tray with coffee and a sandwich on his desk. Something inside him cracked, because no matter how awful he had been since he got the call telling him his father had died, she was still silently looking after him.

'I should have been there, this is my fault.'

'No, it's not,' she replied.

'He knew there was something wrong, and I didn't take him seriously.'

'I know when he called you, I put the call through to you, remember? He died fifteen minutes later, so you would not have got to him if you had gone straight there.'

'But he tried to call before and I always put him off.'

'You always put your father off, but when he had

something important to say, he left me a message to make sure that you *did* call him back. This time he didn't do that; you had no reason to think anything was wrong.'

'I should have known,' he said.

'I never knew you were telepathic,' she said.

'I'm not.'

'Then how could you have known? If he truly believed his life was in danger, he would have known what precautions to take and he would have told you instead of telling you something vague.'

'So are you blaming my father for being careless?' he snapped at her. Even as he said it he knew he was being unreasonable.

'No, I'm saying that maybe he did *not* know,' and she calmly left the room.

Cal sighed, angry with himself for the way he had spoken to her. He was never the easiest person to work for and Jane had been with him the longest. He hit the communicator.

'Yes sir,' she answered.

'When the report comes through, can you bring it to me,' and ended the communication, cursing his lack of backbone for not saying sorry and cringing at his repeat of the request – of course Jane would bring it through immediately.

Sitting in her office, Jane smiled to herself at the repeat request. She knew her boss too well. He was a pain at times, most of the time if she was honest, but she loved the challenge of working for him which was why she was still there. She also understood the need to blame someone, anyone, when you lose a loved one. She could take his anger if it helped him to deal with his father's death, but only for now. She would give him a few days to get his head straight, then help him with it if need be.

As if someone was listening, a provisional report came

through to her and her heart sank. She knew how long these reports took and this was too soon, and for all his repeated requests to see it, Cal would know it was too soon as well. She transferred the file to Cal's computer, and took a deep breath before entering his office, smiling as she saw him picking at the food she had left him. Well, at least he was eating something.

'Jane,' he said, looking up as she came in.

'I have transferred the report to your secure account.' Call pushed the sandwich away and opened the file. His brow furrowed as he realised what he was looking at. Jane stood in silence as he read what was in front of him, expecting the reaction.

'This is it?' he questioned.

'It's all that they have sent through so far. They said it was the interim report.'

'If the full report says twice as much as this one, it will still be nothing,' he said, 'but you already know that.'

'I skimmed it before I came through,' she admitted.

'I can't believe this is all they sent you.' He pushed the computer across the desk and leaned back in his chair. 'It answers nothing. It as good as says that this was a random accident and could not have been avoided, that the shield in the car was insufficient to have withstood the collision and the other car's guidance system had failed. Who do they think they are trying to fool? I know what my father's security was, I know what sort of impact the regulation shields could take and I know the strength of the one I put in his car. This,' and he waved at the screen, 'does not even let me know if he was using the car to which I added extra protection.' He slammed his fist down on the desk, stood up and turned his back on her.

'What do you plan to do about it?' she asked him.

'What can I do? They won't let me investigate.'

'When has someone telling you that you can't do something ever stopped you? Just because you can't officially investigate, does that stop you making your own enquiries?'

'No,' he said after a moment, 'Jane?'

'Yes sir.'

'I need you to make some calls.'

*

Cal went to the morgue to see his father. When he had made the request, he had been told that it was not necessary, that his father's identity had been confirmed through DNA. It took him a while to make them understand that he needed to see him, needed to pay his last respects, and finally they had agreed. Now he was sitting outside in his car looking at the bland building in front of him.

'You don't have to do this,' Jane said, sitting next to him. They had come straight from a meeting. He had told Jane that he would go in alone and would not be long, but now he doubted himself. He had not seen his father in so long. Did he want his last memory of him to be laid out in the morgue?

'Yes, I do,' he said, 'I need to do this,' and he took a deep breath. Jane grabbed his hand and squeezed it briefly, but when she went to let it go, he kept hold of it.

'Come in with me?' he asked and she nodded and opened the car door. He kept hold of her hand as they walked into the building. Jane just being there gave him the strength he needed to walk in.

They were led to a cold white room by a member of staff, where there was a table with a white shrouded shape. The man walked to the table and went to pull the cloth back.

'Wait!' Cal said. The man stopped and looked up. 'Can

you leave us?' The man nodded and without a word he turned and left, closing the door quietly behind him. Cal didn't want a stranger here, didn't want a stranger seeing any weakness he might show. Jane squeezed his hand, trying to give him some reassurance and support. He returned the pressure briefly before letting her go and walked forward towards the table alone. He paused in front of it, pulled the sheet away and, taking a deep breath, looked down onto the burnt face of his father. It had been cleaned up; the gash running down one side of his face had been stitched so that it did not gape open. With a shaking hand he reached out and touched the other side of his father's lifeless face, but quickly snatched his hand back, surprised at how cold and hard it was.

'I will find out what happened Father, I swear.' Abruptly he turned and stormed out, grabbing hold of Jane and dragging her out behind him. He did not stop once he was out of the room, but kept on going down the corridors and out to the car. He opened the car door and pushed Jane inside before going around to the other side and climbing in next to her. Without saying anything he sent the car to his apartment. Pulling up outside the housing block, he scrambled out of the car and was around the other side just as Jane climbed out. He took hold of her arm and pulled her inside, ignoring the doorman, and across the entrance hall to the elevators where one was standing open, waiting for them. Within seconds it was taking them up to the penthouse. As soon as the doors opened again, he was out and unlocking the door. Jane followed him. He took hold of her again and led her across the lounge and into his bedroom. Then, for the first time since they left the morgue, he spoke. 'I need you Jane,' he said simply, stroking her face with unsteady hands.

'I need you too.'

Cal swung the bedroom door closed.

*

Something was chasing him in the dark. No matter where he tried to run, it hounded him, always close on his heels. Occasionally he got a glimpse of the thing. It was hideously burnt. He turned and tried to face it, to fight it, but his movements were restricted and he could not hit out. He began to panic – it was going to get him as it had got his father. It was here! It grabbed hold of him in an embrace and again he tried to lash out, but his arms were pinned to his sides.

'Cal, wake up,' a voice shouted in his ear.

Suddenly the shadows dispersed. He was breathing heavily and sweating, being held tightly by a very female form. As sanity started to return he realised where he was, knew who was holding him so tight and the familiar smell of her reassured him that he was safe. He turned and the arms released the tight grip. 'Jane?' he whispered.

'Yes,' she replied and he kissed her, drowning his pain in her.

Cal awoke slowly and experienced a feeling of peace that he had not known since he had received word of his father's death. He stretched and turned onto his side and saw Jane lying next to him, still asleep, and last night came back to him. He smiled to himself. She had made everything seem all right for a while. As he lay there he started thinking over everything about the circumstances of his father's death, and for the first time he was seeing all the events with a clear head, he was seeing all the inconsistencies that were being discounted as if there was a desperate need for it to be written off as an unfortunate accident. The question was – why? If someone had made a mistake, why the determination to cover it up? What was it that his father had wanted to tell him?

Jane stirred next to him, breaking his train of thought. He looked down at her and watched as she opened her eyes.

'Good morning,' he said. She groaned in protest and tried to burrow under the covers to get away from the light coming in through the windows.

'Come on sleepy head, it's time to get up. We have a lot of work to do, you and I.' As he spoke he pulled the cover down until Jane's head was again exposed. She mumbled a protest and tried to reclaim the cover. 'Are you always such a grouch in the morning?' he asked, amused.

Hearing the levity in his voice, she blinked once, then again, and looked at him in surprise. Over the course of the night, some of the strain and anguish had eased from his face. 'You're feeling better,' she stated, looking at him.

'Yes,' he replied and smiled back at her.

A smile spread across her face. 'I'm glad,' she said, before swinging her legs over the side of the bed. She bent down and picked up his discarded shirt and pulled it on before getting up and walking towards the door, avoiding his hands as he tried to grab hold of her.

'Where are you going?' he protested as she walked into the bathroom.

'I thought you said we had work to do,' she retorted and he laughed as he rolled off the bed and followed her.

*

'I think we have a problem,' she said, walking towards the man seated behind the desk.

'What's happened?' he said, looking up from what he was working on.

'The pup wants to look at the crashed car.'

He paused in what he was doing and looked up at her. 'That can't be allowed.'

'Do you want me to handle it personally?'

'Of course,' she turned to leave, 'but try not to kill him. For him to die now so close to his father's death would raise questions that I don't want asked. The head chairman's death has been written off as an accident; for his son to die so soon afterwards would raise suspicions.'

'Suicide?' she questioned.

'Cal is well known, too many people would find it hard to believe and I can't take the risk.'

'So what do you want me to do?'

'Be imaginative,' he said and returned to his work.

⁜

'Damn them,' she said, hitting the button to disconnect the call.

'Is there a problem Jane?' She jumped, so caught up in her own frustration that she had not realised she was no longer alone. She turned and saw Cal standing by the door. 'Sorry, I didn't mean to frighten you.' He walked further into the room and stopped by her desk.

'It's all right.' She sighed, leaned back in her chair and rubbed the back of her neck in frustration. 'I was just cut off again.'

'Cut off?'

'I've been trying to get you an appointment to see your father's car so you can examine it, but I can't.'

'What do you mean, you can't? I've heard you sweet-talk the hardest businessmen.'

'Be that as it may, I can't sweet-talk a recording.'

'You haven't talked to anyone?' he asked, confused.

'Sure, and they either tell me I have got the wrong department and transfer me to a recording or I get disconnected, like just now.'

'Who have you been trying to talk to?' he asked.

'Everyone,' she replied and listed the various

government departments she had spoken to, including the people involved in the investigation. 'I've even tried the office of the deputy chairman but I couldn't get through.'

'That makes no sense,' he said.

'Tell me about it,' Jane said. 'I have never encountered such obstruction.'

Cal was silent for a moment. 'I was expecting to be asked to look at my father's car. Yes, I know,' he said when Jane started to say something, 'I know I was refused permission to be part of the investigation team, but I'm still the leading expert on the shielding technology and, as such, I was expecting to be asked for my opinion,' he said. 'I'm surprised they won't take your call.'

'I honestly don't know what to tell you. I've tried everyone I can think of but I'm just not getting anywhere.'

'Strange,' he said, and after a pause, 'keep trying for the rest of the day and if you have any success, let me know immediately.'

'Of course, but what then?'

'I'm going to see if any of my contacts will help. If, between the two of us, we have no success, then we might just have to invite ourselves.'

'I don't understand? If they won't talk to us, how do we invite ourselves?'

'Jane, Jane, use your imagination,' he said and walked into his office, laughing.

Chapter 5

'ARE you sure you know what you're doing?' Jane whispered as they stood outside the security hanger. She glanced nervously around her as Cal stood next to her, working on the door lock.

'I don't remember you being so faint-hearted in the past.'

'I don't remember ever breaking and entering before.'

'Good point.'

'I thought so,' she muttered to herself. 'Are you sure this is going to work? I mean, we still have time, we could leave,' she suggested hopefully, but as if in reply, the solid metal doors in front of her slid open.

'You were saying?'

'What about the alarms?'

'I opened the door with the correct security code so the alarms won't activate.'

'What about any other security measures, cameras, monitors, etc?'

'This is a warehouse, why would there be any other security?'

'Because of what's in here? Like your father's car.'

'When the examination was apparently completed, it was moved here for holding. I guess they thought no one would be interested in it now.'

'So you are assuming there is nothing else?'

'No, I checked out the security of this place before we came.'

'Have you done this before?' she questioned

suspiciously.

'No, why do you ask?'

'You know how to get in and not only did you think to check but you were also able to access information that I would have thought was classified as limited access.'

'I designed the system so knowing how to get the code was easy. As for checking the security, you're right, it is not accessible to the public. I do have access to the database with the information on it because of the work I do,' he explained. 'Now come on, we don't have much time,' he said and began to walk through the open doors. Jane watched him for a moment before she followed him. Inside she had expected one large room but instead there were several rooms, all with closed, locked doors.

'Where do we start?' she asked, imagining having to check every room.

'Room A6,' he replied casually before walking down the corridor to a door at the end. He paused in front of it for a moment before connecting his hand-held computer. This one only took him moments before the door popped.

'You make this seem so easy,' Jane said.

'It is for me, but it wouldn't be for anyone else.'

'Won't they realise that you've broken in?'

'If they check the records they would see that the room had been accessed by someone but not who. Don't worry, this won't come back to us.'

'Oh, I so hope that you are right.'

'Have some faith Jane,' he said as he pushed the door the rest of the way open and walked in.

Jane silently followed him into the room. The lights came on with their movement and she saw in front of her the mangled wreck of a black car. Cal just stopped walking and looked at it. Jane reached out and put her hand on his shoulder and squeezed it, not knowing what to say to him. This damage should never have happened, not to this car or any car with the safety features that existed now. So how *did* this happen? Cal squeezed her hand in acknowledgement, walked towards the car and circled it, every now and then stopping to look at something. Jane stood there and watched him and saw him getting more and more angry as he looked at the car.

'They have not examined the car,' Cal said, breaking the silence.

'How do you know?'

'The security systems, the specialist shield technology is in the car, the panels that would have to be removed to get to them have not been touched.'

'Are you sure it's the right car?'

'The identity plates are my father's,' he said. 'I'm going to do my own examination.'

'Won't that be detected?' Jane asked him.

'Possibly. I'll try and put it back together again but with the damage I will have to break parts off to get to what I want to look at. If someone comes back to have a further look, then yes, they would know someone has looked,' he admitted. 'If you want to leave now and deny all knowledge of this, then do so now.'

'Is there an office in this place?' Jane asked.

'Yes, why?' he asked.

'Well, if you can get me into it, I can do a bit of investigation of my own while I'm here,' she offered.

Cal led her out of the room and through another door, which again he managed to open in moments. Inside was a small, cramped room, in the middle of which was a desk with a computer. 'Will you be all right in here?' he asked.

'I am now in my element, you go back to yours,' she said.

'Thank you Jane,' he said and turned and left before she could say anything.

‘How is it going?’ she asked him as she heard him come into the office.

‘I have looked at that car and it is not my father’s.’

‘Are you sure? You said that it has your father’s identity plates.’

‘Yes, the plates are definitely his, but it is not his car. This car has, without doubt, been swapped with another.’

‘How do you know that?’ she asked.

‘There is no shielding technology in that car,’ he said. ‘I’m not just talking about the specialist equipment that my company has developed for high-profile people, but there are not even the basic safety measures that you would expect to be in every car bought today. My father had no hope of survival when that collision happened.’ Sighing, he ran a hand through his hair, ‘Anyone looking at the car would have seen that immediately, so how come the report says it was a system failure?’

‘While you’ve been looking at the car, I’ve been doing my own investigation. How what I found out connects with your father’s death I’m not sure, but it does go some way to explaining how that car is not your father’s.’

‘Go on,’ Cal said.

‘Michael Felham, the new head of your father’s personal transport and one of the members of the team on the official investigation, has disappeared,’ Jane informed him. ‘At first I thought he must have realised he had made an error and tried to cover it up and, while he still could, has left. With what you have just told me, he must have known the cars were switched – it would have been impossible for him not to know what to look for.’

‘We need to check his financial records, see if he was paid off.’

‘I’ve already done that, he has a large amount of debt but other than his wage, nothing else has been paid in.

He has also made no transactions since he went missing.'

'Could he have been paid to swap the cars and then cover it up, then fled in fear before being paid?'

'Or been killed?' Jane supplied.

'Or been killed,' he repeated. 'You mentioned that Michael was the new head of transport – when did he take over? Do you know what happened to the previous person?'

'I looked,' Jane said. 'Michael took the post only two weeks before your father's death. The previous person also went missing.'

'How much do we know about him?'

'Nothing at the moment, I haven't had the time to look into him yet,' she apologised.

'Can you keep looking?' he asked her. 'Find out everything you can about both of them.'

'Of course,' she said and started work on the computer again.

'Can you do this elsewhere?'

'Yes,' she confirmed.

'Then let's leave here now, I'm starting to suspect that someone had my father killed. This place is giving me bad feelings.'

Jane switched the computer off and stood up, and together they left, making sure everything was switched off and locked up.

⁜

He woke and reached for Jane but only found a cold, empty bed. He opened his eyes but the room was dark and he could only see the digital clock showing the time. Cal groaned when he saw it was just after 2.00am. He sat up and remembered last night, how the realisation that his father's death had been planned had left him drowning his sorrows in her. She had been keen and eager, but where was she now? Then in the silence of the night he heard it, the muffled sobs coming from the next room – is that what woke him? Cal swung his legs out of bed, walked silently to the door and listened. He frowned as he heard the sound again. It was definitely someone crying, and the only other person here was Jane. What would have caused her to cry like this? Slowly he opened the door but the adjoining room was also dark. 'Lights,' he said and they came on. Cal saw her then, sitting curled up on one of the chairs, crying as if her heart was broken. As the lights came on she buried her face in the pillow she had been holding. Cal paused, he did not like to see her in such pain and was unsure what to do. Jane had always been so strong, stronger than him. He walked into the room and crouched down in front of her. She didn't look up so he reached out and took hold of one of the hands holding the pillow tightly to her face. She resisted at first and tried to pull away but Cal was firm as he took her hand in his. Still holding her hand, he eased the pillow out of the other hand and dropped it onto the floor before picking her up and sitting on the chair with her on his lap. At first she remained remarkably stiff, then suddenly she made a choking sound, collapsed into his arms and totally broke down while he just held her and tried to soothe her.

'They slaughtered them,' she choked as she started to calm down, 'like we used to kill cattle.'

'Who killed who?' he asked, confused, but got no reply. Jane had fallen into an exhausted sleep. Gently he picked her up and carried her to bed, where he hoped she would now sleep peacefully.

⁜

'Good morning,' said a voice from the doorway. Cal opened his eyes and turned his head towards the door and saw Jane standing there with two cups in her hand.

'Good morning, I thought you would have slept longer.'

'It's 10.00am,' Jane pointed out. 'I'm sorry I disturbed you last night.' Her head was bent downwards so her hair hung forward and he could not see her face clearly.

'Have you had breakfast yet?' he asked her, trying to ease her embarrassment.

'Only coffee,' she replied, looking down at the drinks in her hands.

'Then give me five minutes to shower and I will cook you up a storm,' he said, and was relieved when he saw Jane lift her head and smile and felt some of the tension ease out of the room. Cal took the second drink from her and drank from it before heading into the bathroom.

An hour later they sat together over the table having finished a cooked breakfast. In a relaxed silence, they cleared the dishes and sat down in the living room with fresh coffee.

'So, what happened last night? What made you so upset?' he asked suddenly and watched as Jane tensed up at the questions.

'I couldn't sleep so I thought I would start looking into the two missing technicians, and the more I looked, the more I discovered.'

'What did you find out?'

'I think I know why your father was killed,' she said.

'Don't mess with me,' he warned.

'I'm not,' she said, hurt that he would think that, 'though how I got there is not straightforward.'

'I trust what you say Jane. I need to know what happened.'

She took a deep breath. 'As I said earlier, I couldn't sleep so I continued working on the missing technicians. The previous head technician, Henry Blaski, was, from everything I can discover, a good, hardworking man. His accounts are in good order, he was married with children and yet he just suddenly went missing. There is no trace of him anywhere, he has not accessed his accounts, but his disappearance led to Michael Felham taking his place, a man who has a serious gambling problem and is in debt, not just to legitimate lenders but I think, looking at some of the withdrawals made, also to off-book people as well.'

'You keep referring to Henry in the past tense.'

'Yes, I found out where he is: his body is in the morgue. The time of death is when he was reported missing. I think that either Henry refused to be bought or they couldn't risk approaching him, which meant that he had to be killed so he could be replaced by someone who could be bought.'

'But you said that no money was paid into Michael's account.'

'True, but I wouldn't be surprised if his body shows up soon as well. From what I've found, Michael is very unreliable, he could not be trusted to keep quiet.'

Cal was silent as the news sank in. 'So Henry was murdered so my father could be killed in a car crash which was made to look like an accident,' he said slowly. 'Is that what you are saying?'

'Yes, that is what I believe,' she said.

'But who would go to so much trouble to make it look like an accident? Who wanted him dead so much?' he asked.

'I don't know who is behind this, they are either extremely good at covering their tracks on the computers or they haven't been using them.'

'But the reason?' he prompted. 'Jane?' he questioned when she did not respond.

'Promise not to be mad.'

'Mad about what?'

'How I got the information.'

'If you can give me the answers I need, then I don't care about how you got it,' he said.

'We'll see,' she said, looking sceptical, 'but here goes. Someone went to a lot of trouble to have your father killed and have it look like an accident. Why? No matter how he died, there would always be an investigation or enquiry, there would always be a media frenzy, so why an accident and not an assassination? Was it because of who wanted him dead or was it to do with what your father was working on? If he had been assassinated, then the government would be frozen, no bills, treaties, nothing could be passed until the investigation had finished and a new vote had taken place.'

'However, if the head chairman dies of accidental or natural causes, the deputy takes over and the running of government continues as normal. Yes Jane, I know the law,' Cal cut in.

'So, that being the case, I started to look into your father and what he had been working on. Your father was working on a new trade deal which would have improved the time of the transport routes to the new colony, Maia. A lot of research was put into it, but the interesting part is that what made this such a great deal was changing the regulation in an area of space which is at present restricted. If ships could go into it and not have to go around it, this would save a significant amount in travelling time. Your father looked into why it had been restricted and was going to propose the area be reduced to allow ships to travel through most of it.'

'Why would he do that? Areas of space are normally restricted because they are dangerous. I can't believe he would endanger ships like that, and if there were safety concerns around this area, the Federation of Worlds Navy has the final authority on where ships can and can't go.'

'The space is restricted not because it is dangerous but because of a planet within it.'

'But planets which are hazardous or are inhabited by people with no or limited technology are flagged and a wide berth is taken around them, but the whole area of space is not put out of bounds.'

'Unless, due to the history of the planet, our ancestors did not want anyone to know it was there,' Jane said and smiled at the look of bemusement on Cal's face. She pulled her computer towards her, logged on and pulled up some old pictures of women wearing stunning coats and dresses. 'The planet is inhabited by a race we have named the Lismarians. They were discovered over eighty years ago. Unfortunately, the records are patchy but it seems that their discovery was not officially declared; instead they were killed and skinned. These clothes,' and Jane pointed at the screen, 'are made from living, sentient beings.'

'Good God,' Cal said, looking horrified.

'Tests done on their wings revealed that they are thin, lightweight and extremely strong. Several businesses found good use for them and made a fortune. The illegal trade finally finished when the origin of the material was discovered, the pirates supplying the wings and skins were all put to death and the matter was hushed up. The area of space was restricted so no one could return, and the public was told that the company producing the clothing had failed due to supply problems. More significant, however, were the businesses that used the wings: they all collapsed very quickly as they were not able to synthesize anything even close to the weight-to-strength ratio, and we still haven't.'

'You think that they might want to restart the trade?'

'No, I think they might already have restarted the

trade. When he investigated, your father noticed that there was evidence of space travel in the area and he had completed a draft to the FWN to patrol the region, though he died before it was submitted.'

'Can you say for certain that this is happening?'

'Your father thought it was.'

'How were you able to find this out?'

'I got the information from your father's files,' Jane admitted.

'I have gone through his computer, I found none of this on it.'

'You know when I said please don't be mad?' Jane said and Cal nodded. 'Your father had sealed files on his computer which I kind of hacked into.'

'You what?'

'Well, I thought that anything sealed would be important.'

'Were there any more?' he asked.

'A few, but I haven't been able to get into them yet.'

'Keep looking.'

'I will, but what do we do now?'

'On the face of it, we need to accept the official report and not ask any more questions. No one knows we broke in to look at the car. Would anyone be aware of your searches through my father's computer?'

'If they were looking for them and were better than me, then maybe.'

'So it is possible?'

'It is possible but unlikely, why?'

'A great deal of planning went into killing my father and making it look like an accident. So far we have found everything out through non-official channels,' Jane snorted at the diplomatic statement, 'and we need to keep it that way. If whoever is behind this finds out we are looking into it, we might also die in an accident.'

'What do we do with the information we have?'

'I have an idea, but I need to think on this. Just see what else you can find for now.'

Chapter 6

GILCAN stood out on the balcony and looked over the land. At one time, he would have known how many peasants worked here, but not now. Over the last few years, extreme discontent had started to spread through all the collectives and people were leaving. Some were trying to set up on their own, finding small patches of land that were not controlled by a protector due to arguments over ownership, some were going to other collectives. His mate, Pesline, liked to think that she had been managing it with her steward since they had mated, but her unpredictable decisions normally meant that the steward came to him for final and more sensible advice and then left him with the job of trying to make her understand why his way was better. He was normally successful, especially if he twisted things to make it look as if it had originally been her idea, because she always had to have the final say. The collective had been her father's and she had been the stronger, but only slightly, when they had mated, a fact that she never let him forget.

Now there was another issue over which they were arguing. The first protectors had been to see him and had wanted to examine his battlements. He had been expecting them for the last week or so as he had heard complaints from the other protectors about what they saw as their lies and interference. The first protectors had been saying that the traders were returning and everyone had to be ready to defend themselves. Of course they were not returning, everyone knew that. Previous generations had used the same rumour to control the peasants, using the fear to keep them obedient, but it had been a while since that ploy had worked, which was why the movement of the workers was now becoming a problem – no one believed it. The first protectors must be out of touch with everything below them if they thought that they could get their power and authority back with that story. What other reason would they have for saying the traders are back – they did not have a collective to hold together and the timing of this was seen as suspicious now that Solvan had come of age. He would not be able to take over his parents' position until mated, but with his strength he could choose his mate and still be strong enough to take over from his parents.

For all of that, Gilcan had been impressed with Solvan when he had visited. They had stood together on the battlements, and he had had to admit that he had never been up here before and had not realised how bad a state they were in. Pesline had made a poor excuse not to join them so he had been at liberty to ask any questions he wanted, without her interfering.

'Why do you think they are coming back now?' he had asked.

'I can feel them,' Solvan had replied.

'For how long? How do you know it was them?'

'You are the first to ask me that,' he said. 'I was raised to know what to expect when the traders returned so when, two weeks ago, I started to feel a hostility towards us, I started to contact all of the protectors to warn them.'

'But how did you know it is the traders and the feelings aren't from something else?'

'As I said, I was brought up on the old accounts of the first protectors and what they experienced, so I knew what I felt was alien,' Solvan had said. 'That is when we started to communicate with the protectors about the coming threat, but a few days ago everything became even more necessary, which is when I started visiting.'

'A few days ago I felt a stabbing pain,' Gilcan said, also remembering old accounts told to him as a child.

'Yes?' Solvan prompted.

'I thought nothing of it, it was irritating but nothing more...' he paused as the realisation now set in, 'but it was, wasn't it?'

'The pain was the death of a family living independently near Protector Tesrun's collective.'

'But he is a considerable distance away, I couldn't have felt a peasant's death from here.'

'Normally not, but they were not just killed, they were skinned alive. That extensive pain would have carried, no matter how strong a person was.'

Gilcan paled, 'Are you sure?'

'Oh yes, I can see and feel so much more than you,' Solvan said, 'enough to know which area the farm was in and, after a brief search, find it and the dead bodies.'

'What did the other protectors say when you told them?' Gilcan asked.

'They accused me of lying to them.'

'Surely you could have shown them what you saw and felt?'

'Only if they were willing to open their minds up to it, which they weren't,' Solvan said. 'You are the first of the protectors to actually listen to what I say.'

'I confess my feelings are mixed. Pesline certainly believes the traders will never return, which is an influence, but I have my doubts, which are sufficient to make me want to know how to rebuild the battlements and what I would need to do if I need to defend my collective.'

'If you don't have them, we have copies of all the plans of all the collectives. I can find yours and lend them to you to help with the repairs,' Solvan said, 'and I can explain what the accounts say of what you and Pesline need to do when the traders attack.'

'Pesline does not believe and will refuse to listen. Just tell me.'

And explain he had. Pesline had been furious when she had found out that he had listened and encouraged Solvan, and had not understood that he had shared his fears. He had ordered men to start rebuilding the battlements and when she had found out, had stopped it.

'You're being foolish,' she had spat at him, her revulsion easy to feel.

'I knew what I felt before he came,' he had argued back.

'Your imagination was just playing on you from the rumours and what the other protectors have been saying.'

'No, it's more than that.'

'No it's not, you are just being deceived by the first protector and every twinge you feel fuels this foolishness.'

'No, I don't believe that.'

'If they ever truly existed, they do not exist now,' Pesline said. 'The battlements are in ruins because they have not been needed, and with the peasants leaving, I won't countenance the expense of repairing them on a whim.'

'Since you feel so strongly on the matter, I'm surprised that you did not say so to Solvan while he was here.'

'I had important business to attend to on the collective that could not wait,' she tried to justify.

'I'm sure you did,' he replied sarcastically, knowing the truth she would not say aloud.

So now he looked out on the collective and wondered what their fate would be.

⁜

It had started as a mild irritation. If he had not been thinking so much about the conversation he had had with Solvan, he probably would not have even registered what it was. It built quickly to a cold, oppressive feeling that sent fear through him.

'*Pesline*,' he called to her.

'*What do you want? I'm busy.*'

'*Do you feel that? The traders are coming.*'

'*Don't be ridiculous, the traders are not coming back and now you are imagining things because I let you indulge in that foolishness with Solvan.*'

'*I told you, it's not foolishness and they are coming, if not to our collective, then close by.*'

'*I will not argue with you in this way. Stay where you are,*' and she shut off the communication.

Gilcan started to get restless and pace the floor. He should be going to the battlements and getting ready but he needed Pesline with him and he knew she would not go there unless forced, so he had to wait for her.

'Father...' Gilcan turned at his name and saw his eldest son as he burst into the room, breathless and radiating fear. Before Gilcan could respond, Cardoc came forward, grabbed his father and dragged him out onto the balcony. 'Look,' he said, pointing up at the sky, 'what is that?'

Gilcan looked up and could not believe what he was seeing. He did not know what the traders looked like, not even Solvan did, but what he was seeing had to be them – who else could it be? In front of him, coming down from the sky, was a huge, shining object which left a burning trail behind it. He concentrated his mind towards it and was glad of the hold his son still had on him. He pulled his mind back and took a deep breath to get control of himself again and he knew he had to get to the battlements now if he was going to save the collective. He pulled out of Cardoc's grip and headed out of the room. He was about to call out his mate's name when she appeared at the door in front of him.

'We have to go,' he said.

'Where? What's happening?'

'The traders are here, we need to go to the battlements,' Gilcan informed her. He was aware that she replied but did not hear her over the mental call.

'*Gilcan,*' Solvan called out to him.

'*Here.*'

'*The traders are coming to you. Will you be ready?*'

'*We are on the way to the battlements now,*' he replied.

'Gilcan, did you hear what I said? We have to leave here now.'

'No, I know what to do, Solvan told me, but we need to get to the battlements now.' When she made no move to leave, he grabbed her and dragged her from the room.

Pesline snapped when she felt herself being hauled down the corridor. Cardoc followed, looking shocked. Gilcan was insane, she thought, risking their lives for the peasants. Who was he kidding? 'Gilcan stop!' she shouted and tried to pull out of his grip, but he didn't even break step. 'Stop, stop!' She was begging now, thinking she was going to her death. They passed a room and she reached out and took hold of the doorframe, forcing him to stop. He pried her fingers loose and continued to pull her down the corridor. Pesline cursed and tried to hit out at him, but he was expecting it and blocked the blow. Only her mate, out of all the other protectors, wanted to do the right thing. She looked around for anything that could stop him and saw her son following them.

'*Help me,*' she pleaded with her son in desperation when she realised she could not stop her mate on her own.

'*How? I don't want to hurt you?*'

'*Feed me more energy so I can use it against him.*'

Cardoc drew energy into himself and then came forward and took hold of his mother's hand, feeding it into her. It only took a moment and Gilcan was so driven he did not notice what they were doing until it was too late. With the extra strength her son had given her, she added her own to it and used it to hit Gilcan again and he crumpled, unconscious, at her feet. Cardoc ran forward and helped his mother to pull him up off the floor.

'Where are we going to go?' he asked her.

'The basement,' she replied.

'But there is no way out from there.'

'Yes there is, just trust me,' and together they carried him down the corridor and to the staircase.

'*Get the children and meet us in the basement immediately,*' she ordered the servant in charge of her other children, knowing her order would be obeyed without question.

By the time they had carried him to the basement they were both out of breath. She was relieved to see that her other children were already waiting for her there, along with several other servants.

'What are we doing here?' Cardoc panted. 'You must be mistaken, we can't get out from here.'

'No, there are tunnels which start here,' she said, then walked to a pile of cases and started to move them one by one from the wall.

'Will someone help me,' she snapped and Cardoc and the servants came forward. 'Not you,' she said, pointing at one of the servants, 'find us some torches, we are going to need them, and the rest work at clearing the cases.'

Behind the cases was an old door. Pesline grabbed hold of the handle and tried to open it but it was either locked or warped with age.

'Stand back,' Cardoc said.

'Be careful how much you use, there will be no sunlight where we are going,' Pesline said. He nodded his understanding and sent a small blast at the door, enough to create a hole big enough for them to climb through.

The servants carried Gilcan through the door, and on the other side was a passageway. The darkness meant that little could be seen. The servant she had sent for the torches returned and some light was shed, but not enough, and it was with great unease that they all moved forward.

'What are these tunnels?' Cardoc asked his mother as they made their way through them.

'I don't know where they came from but I used to play here with my brother as a child.'

'I didn't know you have a brother – why have you never mentioned him before?'

'I no longer have, that is why the tunnels were sealed,' she said, making it clear she did not want to discuss it any further.

Pesline hoped that she could remember the route correctly. It had been so long since she had been down here and she could only hope they did not get too lost, but it was the only way she could think of to get out of the collective without being seen by the traders. Pesline told her son to follow the main passageway and ignore the narrow side tunnels. It was cold and dark, the torches that Cardoc and the servant at the rear carried cast little light and created huge shadows on the walls. Unused to being closed in and without any sunlight, feelings of panic began to settle on everyone, especially the younger children, who huddled together for comfort, but as they reached out to their mother for reassurance they were rejected as old memories came back to her. The main passageway suddenly split in two and Cardoc turned to look at his mother for directions.

'Look on the wall, there should be an engraved marking indicating which way to go.'

Cardoc held the light to the wall, but the uneven surface and the poor light made it impossible to see any markings, if indeed there were any. He ran his hand against the rock face and after a moment felt the straight indentation.

'It's this way,' he said and they started to walk.

It happened suddenly, a loud, crashing sound that echoed through the tunnel, followed by a blast that knocked them all off their feet and swept in dust and gravel, making them cough and struggle for breath. The whole tunnel seemed to shake with whatever had hit it, and rocks began to fall from the ceiling. The children could be heard screaming with what little breath they had left. Pesline grabbed at her son in the darkness and, as the torches went out, she felt his hand take hers then knew no more.

❋

'We need to find out if anything is going on in that area of space,' Cal said in frustration.

'I know, but the only people who would know would be the FWN. I have looked at their databases and they are just not paying any attention to that area of space that I can see. Space is huge and they don't consider that section important,' Jane replied.

Cal sighed in frustration and ran his hand through his hair. 'There is someone I can talk to.'

'You mention this now?' Jane said in annoyance. 'After I have been looking at things I should not be looking at.'

'Drop the offended act, you've enjoyed the challenge.'

'True, but you have still not answered the question.'

'I didn't want to bring in anyone else unless I had to.'

'Who is it you want to talk to?'

'His name is Admiral Johnson. He was an old school friend of my father ... and is my godfather,' he added as an afterthought.

'Would he know what's going on?'

'Probably not, but he does have the authority and connections to order a discreet investigation, without questions being asked.'

'How well do you know him? Well enough to trust him with your life?'

'I guess we're about to find out.'

It took him a while but finally he was put through to the admiral.

'Cal, I was going to call you. I was sorry to hear about your father, he was a good friend.'

'Thank you, Admiral.'

'Admiral? How formal.' He paused as if expecting Cal to say something. When he didn't, he continued, 'Why do I get the impression this is not a social call?'

'I'm afraid that it isn't. I need a quiet favour from you.'

'OK, this could be interesting. I'm listening, but I won't make you any promises.'

'I need a certain area of space investigated.' He passed on the co-ordinates.

'I assume you know that is a restricted area?'

'Yes sir.'

'And I don't suppose you want to tell me why you want the section checked out?'

'No, I'm afraid I can't. Please, you'll just have to trust me, for old times' sake.'

For a while he said nothing, then, 'I can't give you any promises, but I will see what I can do for you.'

'Thank you sir, I would greatly appreciate anything you can do for me.'

✳

Pesline awoke in agony. She felt as though she were being skinned alive again and again and there was nothing she could do to stop it. It was hard to tell if the screams she heard were in her head or her own and her family's, and she wished she could fall back into unconsciousness.

Slowly it began to ease off and she was able to think again. She opened her eyes but it was so dark that she could not see. She pushed herself up into a sitting position and groaned as everything hurt and the air was still full of dust and grit. Finally, the mental onslaught subsided enough that she was able to block out the rest, and she held her aching head in her hands, trying to process everything that had just happened.

She started to hear other sounds around her and realised that she was not the only one who was conscious. She rolled onto her hands and knees and crawled towards the whimpering she could hear, and her hands encountered something warm and alive. It jerked briefly at the contact, but Pesline held on. 'Ssh, it's me,' she whispered.

The whimpering stopped. 'Mother?'

'Yes.'

'Where are you? What happened?' another voice asked.

'I'm not sure, just stay where you are until I know everyone is all right.'

'*Showing such concern for others? Are you sure you're feeling all right?*' Gilcan spoke directly into his mate's mind.

'*I had no other choice.*'

'*There was another way, the right way. But you were just too cowardly to trust in it.*'

'*There was no guarantee that it would work, we could all have been killed.*'

'*And this is better?*' he asked, disgusted. '*They are all dead. WE WERE SUPPOSED TO PROTECT THEM.*'

'*I'm not discussing this with you now,*' and she shut her mind off from his. She stretched out to locate the others, starting at the back. The servant who had been at the rear was dead, her mind was blank. Lying underneath her was Gilcan and she moved away from him quickly. On either side and slightly on top of him were the other two servants, the ones who had been carrying him. One of them was slowly regaining his senses. The other, however, was barely hanging on to life but without the sun could not heal and Pesline did not think he would last too much longer. In front of them were their children. They were now all conscious and all scared, clinging to each other, some even now unable to block out what was happening on the collective. Selma, her eldest daughter, was hiding her own feelings from her siblings and was trying to reassure them, telling them that Mother and Cardoc would get them out safely. Finally she turned to her eldest. He was lying next to her, awake, but his mind was still reeling from the cries of the peasants.

'Cardoc,' she said, giving him a shake.

'I'm all right,' he replied, pulling himself up so he was sitting. 'The others?' he asked.

'One of the servants is dead, another will soon join him, the others will be all right.' Then she added, 'And your father is awake.'

'What did he have to say to all of this? No, let me guess, that we should have stayed and tried to do something.'

'*That's right, and if you must have this conversation, don't have it aloud – the children are already upset, they don't need to hear this as well. Oh, and Devi has just passed away,*' said his father.

'I don't need to hear this, we need to get out of here,' Cardoc said, dismissing his father's words as if he had not heard them. He eased himself to his feet using the tunnel wall as support, before taking hold of his mother's hand and pulling her to her feet as well.

'How do we get out of here now?' Pesline asked. 'The

torches have gone out.' The lack of light was making her panic.

'Come on children, stand up,' Gilcan said. A rustling sound from behind them indicated their father pulling himself to his feet. 'Come on all of you, up now.' They reacted to the authority in his voice and slowly disengaged themselves from the huddle they had created and stood up. 'Now, all of you stand in a line and everyone hold hands so you form a chain. Whoever is at the front, take Cardoc's hand, he will take your mother's, so as she leads us out of the tunnels we can all stay together.'

'Why do I have to lead?' Pesline asked.

'You are the only one who has been here before and you need to do something to stop you from panicking,' was the terse reply, *'so stop complaining and lead us out of here, and whatever you do, don't let go of Cardoc's hand.'*

Their progress was slow. Someone stumbled and fell every few metres because of all the fallen rocks, but at Gilcan's direction, no one ever let go of anyone's hand. Pesline used her free hand to trace the wall of the passage. Every now and then they came across a side tunnel, so at these points she had to run her hand over the surface until her fingers encountered the markings cut into the rock and she knew it was all right to carry on. Eventually the air became fresher and a slight breeze could be felt moving around the passage, then turning a corner, the exit could be seen. Everyone let go of each other's hands and hurried towards the light as quickly as they could.

Clambering out into the sunlight, everyone stretched out their wings and tried to brush off the dirt that covered them as best they could. Gilcan looked about him as he walked out, supporting the last servant at the rear. The tunnels had led them out at the bottom of the hill where the castle had been. The castle had sat on the edge of the collective, overlooking everything in front of it, so they had come out behind the collective. As he looked up at it, all he could see was a jagged top. He sat down on a nearby rock and looked at his family. Pesline was still shaking, but now out of the cave, was fast regaining her composure. Of his children, he could not tell what was dirt and what was bruising, though looking at them, he doubted any had suffered serious harm, as all stood straight, accepting the healing energy of the sun. The person who caused him most concern was the servant, Geric. He and Devi had shielded Gilcan from the worst of the blast. His back had been lacerated by the force of the grit as it had flown down the passageway. Now he was out in the sun, he just sat to one side, too exhausted to do anything else.

Gilcan moved towards Geric, put his hand under his arm and pulled. 'Get up!' he said, forcing the servant to stand and reveal more of himself to the sun. After a while Gilcan felt the servant take more of his own weight and, satisfied that Geric would be all right for now, Gilcan moved towards his mate, who now appeared to be feeling more like herself. He pulled her slightly aside, so they would not be overheard.

'So now what do you plan for us?' he asked.

'We go back, the traders will have gone.'

'You must be joking? If I'm not mistaken, that explosion was the castle being destroyed and the traders will have killed all the peasants, so what do we have to go back to?'

'But why would the traders have destroyed the castle?'

'Where is your mind? Or did you hear nothing that First Protector Solvan said? It was the energy that they sent for us to direct towards the traders that destroyed the castle. The traders just skinned everyone alive.'

'Oh Hannoki,' she said as her legs gave way and she sank to the floor.

'After what you did, I don't ever want to hear you swear on his name again,' Gilcan snapped before turning from his mate and walking away.

'Where are you going?' she called after him.

'To see what the collective looks like,' he replied and continued on his way. The children looked shocked as he walked past them, but he just smiled his reassurance to them as he went. Cardoc looked towards his mother, before following his father around to the other side of the cliff. The pathway was uneven and several times they had to resort to scrambling over loose rocks. Flying would have been easier but they were afraid of drawing any attention if the traders were still there. As they got higher, the dust and grit got thicker, then suddenly they were at the top of the cliff. The wind whipped around them, sending the dirt at them with stinging force. The top of the cliff was jagged and narrow, and looking down they saw a crater where the castle used to stand. The rock and soil round the edges was still moving, settling itself down into its new position.

'Oh Hannoki, no!' Cardoc breathed out when he saw the destruction of his home.

'Save your prayers for them,' his father replied, pointing to what little could be seen of the collective.

His people were all dead, he knew that. They must have been herded into numerous groups before they had been killed and now there were just large piles of bodies. Gilcan could see the traders, from this distance he could not tell exactly what they looked like, but they were tall and the sun glinted off them.

Even as they watched, the few remaining traders climbed aboard the large, strange vehicle they had seen come from the sky. It suddenly seemed to come to life, fire appeared from behind it and then it took off into the sky with a near-deafening roar and disappeared.

'And you wanted to tangle with them?' Cardoc stated. 'Mother was right, you are misguided,' and he turned and left his father.

Reaching the bottom of the cliff again, Gilcan arrived as Cardoc had just finished telling his mother what he had seen.

'You see, I was right,' she stated when she saw Gilcan. 'If we had stayed, we would all be dead.'

'No, we would have destroyed them and everyone would still be alive.'

'You have no way of knowing that,' she said in contempt.

'We should have tried.'

'Based on what Solvan told you he had read in old documents? I didn't like our chances.' Gilcan did not reply, he just looked at her with so much disgust that she dared not say any more.

After a while, she asked tentatively, 'Have you come up with any ideas of where we can go now?'

'To Ovato.'

'Your brother? But you dislike each other.'

'You seemed to get along fine with him!' he said, looking at her. 'Besides, you have no family left other than me and the children, and Ovato is the only family I have left. Where else would you suggest we go?' and when she made no reply, 'I thought so.'

Chapter 7

SHE was filled with a sense of hate and darkness. She tried to fight it, to push it away, but it remained and grew stronger and stronger and started to engulf her. She felt that it would choke her and she clawed at it. In desperation, she knew that she had to escape from it, but no matter what she did, she had no success.

Lovoa woke up with a start, drenched in a cold sweat and shaking uncontrollably. When she realised she was safe at home, on her own mat, she started to relax. The nights were the worst, the dreams took such a strong hold of her that she could not escape when asleep, but the feeling was always there, haunting her continuously. She knew there would be no point in trying to sleep any more, the first of the suns would be rising soon.

The morning brought her no peace, but it never did these days. Even in the heat of the rising suns, she felt cold. She did not need much sleep, not compared to her parents, but she still felt exhausted all the time. She got up and went into the small communal room of their cabin and splashed water onto her face in the hope that it would help to clear her mind, but it did not. At least, she thought, she had not been plagued with one of those other dreams tonight. It had only happened twice and she had woken up screaming, convinced she was being skinned alive. She had terrified her parents on those nights; they had not known what to do or how to console her as she clung to them. She had not dared tell them about all the other times, when she had been awake and it had been like living the nightmare.

'Did you sleep well?' her mother asked as she walked into the room.

Lovoa looked up from where she was preparing breakfast. 'Yes mother,' she replied.

Mesrra looked at her daughter and noticed the sunken eyes, and her heart sank as she knew her daughter was still suffering so much. 'Lovoa?' her mother pressed, concerned.

'I'm fine,' she tried to reassure her, but she could feel her mother's worry, felt she did not believe her. 'Mother, I'm fine,' she repeated and then walked towards her and kissed her cheek. 'It was another bad dream, nothing more.'

'I don't like these dreams of yours...'

'Why?' Lovoa cut over her. 'Dreams are dreams Mother, they will pass in time. Now sit and eat and stop worrying,' she said as she placed the food on the table.

'But...' Mesrra started to say.

'Leave her alone Mesrra,' Fesrun said as he came into the room and sat at the table. 'Good morning Lovoa.'

'Good morning Father,' she replied and the conversation ended as breakfast was eaten in silence, though Lovoa did sense that her mother was unhappy with her father over getting her to drop the subject. Lovoa often wondered if her parents knew how much she could read from them.

⁜

Lovoa was in the barn packing the harvest into bags and then stacking them neatly against the wall. It was physically hard and monotonous labour, but the only farm task her parents allowed her to do. One of the bags slipped as she placed it at the top and it fell, pulling the rest down with it and they all landed at her feet.

Restacking everything felt like it was just an impossible task and, upset, she sat on the floor, trying to get her energy together to restart the task. She had never felt so tired and frustrated, the little sleep she would normally have had been replaced by a constant cold, alien feeling that had made rest impossible for the last two weeks. As soon as she fell asleep, a feeling of horror would overtake her and she would wake cold and shaking, and that was if she was lucky. She was now scared to sleep, no matter how badly she felt she needed it. She had thought that had been bad enough but now there was the feeling of being skinned and the occasional stabbing pain that followed it. The first time it had happened, she was scared that something more serious was wrong and had thought about talking to her parents, but she could not cause them to worry about her, so when they asked, she told them everything was fine, but they knew she was lying. It had been years since they could read her, so as it continued she had remined silent because she did not want to worry them and she did not want them to lie to her. They looked at her as if they thought she was suffering, though, and did not believe her when she told them everything was fine.

Then she felt it, not the mild, irritating stabbing pain she had felt before, this was so much worse. She bent over with the pain as she felt that she was being stripped of her skin again and again. Mixed in with the bombardment of pain were the flashes of huge, shining things. She had images of groups of people standing in terror and, watching what she was feeling, these things were walking from group to group, skinning them alive. She had no idea what they were or how they connected to what she was feeling now. She had no idea how to stop what she was feeling. She tried to block it, the way she blocked her parents when they tried to intrude on her mind, but it did not work. She lay there writhing in agony, screaming.

'Lovoa!' Mesrra shouted as she heard her daughter scream. She dropped her tools and ran for the barn, closely followed by her mate. They had not seen or felt Protector Buxus arrive – could they have missed him, could he have found her?

When they arrived at the barn they found her alone, twisting and turning on the floor, tearing at her hair.

'Lovoa!' Mesrra called to her, but got no response. 'Fesrun?' She looked pleadingly at her mate, not knowing what to do.

'We can't move her while she is like this,' he said and together they sat and tried to give her what comfort they could. Mesrra tried to read her daughter's mind, but she just hit a block. Even in her pain, Lovoa was careful to prevent anyone else feeling it as well; she was protecting them. As she started to relax, Fesrun picked her up, carried her into their home and placed her onto her mat. She was still semi-comatose, but she recognised her own bed and relaxed into it.

'Should we not have her out in the sunlight?' Mesrra asked.

'We can't, Protector Buxus keeps coming around unexpectedly, what if he was to see her? Anyway, there is plenty of light coming in through the windows,' and they both sat there and watched as slowly she relaxed completely and slept.

⁕

Lovoa woke slowly. Weak sunlight came in through her windows. Had she managed to sleep through the night? She did not even remember going to bed. She turned and saw her mother sleeping next to her and her memory started to come back to her, but she felt nothing now, whatever had caused it was gone. She tried to get up quietly so as not to wake her mother but was not successful.

'Lovoa,' she said as she stirred.

'Yes Mother,' she replied, and they looked at each other for a moment before Mesrra took her daughter in her arms and hugged her.

'You scared us. What happened yesterday?'

'I don't know; I just got overwhelmed.'

'What by?' When she did not answer immediately, her mother continued, 'I know you have been lying to me when you said everything is fine, but that needs to stop now. Tell me what happened.'

Lovoa looked at her mother in silence for a few moments before finally replying, 'I felt as if I was being skinned alive again and again, and I could not stop it.'

Mesrra just looked at her daughter. She had her own thoughts about it, and started to ask further questions, but Lovoa spoke over her.

'I can't talk about it now, I left the barn in a mess yesterday,' and she stood up, having immediately regretted telling her mother the truth.

'Leave it for now. I'm worried, I want to know more about what you have been feeling.'

'Not now, please,' Lovoa begged, 'I need to clear my head.'

⚜

Lovoa felt her muscles pull painfully as she lifted the nearest sack as she started to restack yesterday's work, giving her some masochistic pleasure. It felt good to be physically working, it reminded her that no matter how many dead, skinned bodies filled her mind, she was still alive. She had asked if she could work in the field today so she could be in the sun but had been told no.

'What if Protector Buxus decided to visit?' her mother had said, so she was in the barn working as usual.

Her parents had never let her meet anyone, not even some of the other independent farmers, and as far as she knew, no one else knew she existed. She had tried asking them why, and had been told that it was dangerous being independent and that if anything went wrong, she would still have a chance to be free if she wanted to be. She did not believe them.

A noise outside caught her attention and she dropped the sack. Cautiously she opened the barn door a crack and looked out, just in time to see Protector Buxus approach through the sky and land next to her parents. He was their so-called local protector. They were independent and officially under no protector, yet he liked to pretend that he oversaw them. She knew that he had forced a few of the other farmers to move onto his collective. His visit was not surprising, he had arrived as usual with his entourage and was acting as though Lovoa's parents were little better than the dirt that they worked. From the barn, she could not hear what was passing between him and her parents and she was too scared to try and read any of their minds in case they picked up on it. His visits were becoming more frequent and from what she had overheard from her parents in the evenings, he wanted them to leave but for some reason he was not resorting to the very forceful tactics that he had used on the other farmers. They had wondered why and had thought themselves either lucky or too small to concern him that much. They were sure he did not know about her, but with each farm that failed, life was getting harder as they had fewer neighbours with whom they could trade.

Protector Buxus did not stay for long and he was not even out of sight before her parents returned to work. Knowing that she could not go out and talk to them, she returned to her stacking. She was going to have to wait until later to see if there were any questions her parents would be willing to answer. She was worried about what they would do when they could no longer hold out against the pressure Protector Buxus was placing on them. Would her parents even take her with them? They never let her out, they would not be able to hide her on a collective, so they either had to admit to her existence or tell her to go and survive on her own. She sighed and slammed another sack into place. In a few days the last of the harvest would be in and a new crop would need planting – the cycle never ended.

'Lovoa?'

Startled, she turned to see her mother standing at the door and smiled at her. She had been so absorbed with her thoughts that she had not been paying attention to who was near.

'Are you willing to talk now Lovoa?' her mother asked as she walked into the barn, not willing to let yesterday pass without an explanation.

'Not really.'

'We just want to help you if we can.'

'I know, maybe I'm just worried about the farm.'

'There are always problems with the farm, but this is new. Please, Lovoa, tell me what is wrong,' Mesrra pleaded.

'Can we talk tonight? When we have time and father is there.'

'I will hold you to that,' Mesrra said and gave her daughter a brief hug before going back out into the field.

❉

Lovoa was in their cabin preparing food for her parents when they returned. She set the table in silence and placed the meal in front of them as they settled down to eat, and no one said anything until the table was cleared.

'What's wrong Lovoa,' her father asked her. 'What happened yesterday?'

'I don't know what happened, only what I felt,' Lovoa started. 'It felt like I was being skinned alive again and again. The pain was almost unbearable and I could do nothing to stop it. I have no idea how long it lasted, I don't remember when it finished or how I got to bed.'

'It lasted for hours. I don't know if the pain eased off or whether you were just too exhausted. We carried you from the barn and put you to bed,' her father said.

'I think yesterday was the worst, but I don't think it was the first time. I know something has been troubling you for a while now, no matter how often you tell me you are fine,' her mother said.

'I have had this feeling for the last two weeks. It's like nothing I have ever felt before, cold and dark and, more than that, it has been continual. I have been blocking it out as best I could while I was awake, but at night when I sleep it crowds in on me and gives me nightmares so I cannot sleep for long. I didn't think it could get worse until I started to get the odd stabbing pain and these flashes, which I didn't understand until yesterday.' After she had finished talking there was silence and when her parents did not speak, she asked, 'Do you know what is wrong with me?'

'I think I might know. Have you ever heard about traders or why we have collectives?' asked her mother.

'No.'

'We were both raised with stories of the traders – everyone we have ever known has been – but we were told that if they ever did exist, they were not coming back. We decided not to pass these stories on to you as we didn't think there was any truth in them and they were very disturbing.'

Her father continued, 'The stories said that when they came, they skinned everyone alive. Hannoki was the first to find a way to defend against them and lost his life on the mountain peak that now has his name. His son, Milkoy, and his mate became the original first protectors. Being so much stronger than everyone else, they could sense when the traders came were coming and would warn the protectors to be ready to defend their collectives. The collectives exist so that people are grouped together, which made them easier to defend.'

'And you think they are back because I felt like I was being skinned alive?'

'Yes, and because today Protector Buxus came to our farm to inform us that the first protectors have been telling all the protectors that the traders are coming back,' added Fesrun.

'But why me? Why don't you feel this as well?'

'You are different, Lovoa, special.'

'Is that why you kept me away from everyone else?' Lovoa asked.

'We needed to protect you while you were still too young.'

'How am I different?'

'You are strong – we have known you would be from the moment we landed after our mating flight,' her mother said.

'What do you mean by that? I'm not strong, father is stronger than me.'

'We are not talking about your physical strength, Lovoa. You are stronger in other ways.'

'I don't understand what you are talking about, and how would you know, anyway? You never let me do anything to prove what I can and can't do.'

'We could not allow anyone else to find out about you,' Mesrra argued.

'Were you ever going to tell me?'

'Of course, but we always planned to tell you when the time was right.'

'So you have waited until now to tell me, when I'm starting to suffer because I'm different – you had no right,' Lovoa said and stood up.

'Please,' Mesrra said, 'we had to protect you and hiding you was the only way we could think to do it.'

'I understand that you needed to protect me, but you should have told me everything as soon as I was old enough and then I would understand what is happening now.'

'You don't understand,' her mother said, upset.

'You are right, I don't, and please don't bother to explain it to me tonight,' and she went into her room.

Lovoa was so angry with her parents, she paced up and down in the small space. How could they know she was strong? What did they mean, anyway? She sighed and sat down on her mat. She had so many questions going around in her head but she knew that if she went back out there now, she would just argue with them again. She would wait until the morning, she decided, when she was calmer. It would also give her the chance to think of the questions for which she really needed the answers first.

※

'That didn't go well,' Mesrra stated.

'Did you ever think that it would? Maybe Lovoa was right and we should have told her when she was old enough.'

'I know, I think a part of me was hoping that we would never have to.'

'We would've had to tell her sooner or later, you know that. She knows no one except us, she has no knowledge

of society. If anything happened to us, she would be lost,'
Fesrun said.

'We have not been fair on her, have we?'

'No, I don't think we have.'

'So what do we do now?'

They sat in silence for a while, thinking. 'The only
thing I can think of doing is going to Protector Buxus,'
Fesrun said finally.

'Are you mad, after we have spent so long hiding her
from him and all of the other protectors, you just want to
hand her over?'

'She is too old now for him just to kill her – it would
be felt.'

'I do not trust him.'

'Neither do I, but if the traders are back, Lovoa's
strength might be vital. Have you considered that there
might come a time when she must learn to use her
strength without becoming a danger to herself or those
around her?'

'We never needed any training for what we can do.'

'We can only do a fraction of what Lovoa should be
able to achieve. How could we possibly comprehend
what she needs?'

'Can we think about it before we decide anything?'

'I wasn't suggesting that we do anything tonight or
even tomorrow, I was just pointing out a possibility and
what needs to be considered.'

'We must discuss it with Lovoa before we do anything.'

✢

Lovoa sat in her room and even though she could not
hear what her parents were talking about, she could
sense their feelings. She felt their remorse over the
argument at first and then later their realisation that they
might lose her in the near future. She heard them go to

bed, still undecided on what they would do. She knew that nothing would be decided tonight, but tomorrow when she talked to them again she hoped that whatever they had been talking about after she had left the room would come up. If not, how would she raise it? Too much was going through her mind for her to make sense of it tonight, so she lay down and closed her eyes, and hoped for a little sleep before the inevitable nightmares started again.

Chapter 8

SOLVAN inhaled sharply as the alien feeling that had been in his head continually for the last two weeks suddenly started to build rapidly and became much more focused.

'I think they are coming,' he told his parents. They were all standing around a table covered with old documents, studying everything that any first protector had ever written.

'Are you sure? You have never picked them up until it was too late before,' his father said.

'I know, but it's strong this time. There must be more of them for me to feel them like this.'

'If there were more of them, they could be ready to attack a collective,' Essac said. 'Do you know where they are heading?'

'Give me a minute,' Solvan said and he closed his eyes and sent his mind out. The moment he touched on them he recoiled in disgust. 'They are coming down west of here.'

'We need to get to the power base.' They all went up the carved stone staircase to the plateau at the top of the mountain. In the corner was the machine. Neither Essac nor Bahia had ever been told how it worked, had never met the previous first protectors and had never been trained in the role that they had taken on, so they had had to work it all out for themselves. The machine was like nothing they had ever seen before. There were two chairs next to each other and three panels, a large one in the middle and a smaller one on the outside arm of each chair.

'Do you know what you're doing?' Solvan asked his parents as they took a chair each.

'We think so,' Bahia said as she rested one hand on the large, central panel and the other on the smaller side panel.

'I still think you should let me try,' Solvan argued.

'The instructions were clear,' Essac said, 'it takes a balanced couple to operate.'

'In other words, a mated couple.'

'Exactly.'

'It looks like they are heading to Gilcan's collective,' Solvan said.

'You spoke to him recently, will he be ready?'

'Yes,' Solvan said, 'give me a moment. '*Gilcan!*' he called out.

'*Here.*'

'*The traders are coming to you; will you be ready?*'

'*We are on our way to the battlements now.*'

'Gilcan said they will be ready.'

'Good, because if he does not divert the energy, his castle will be destroyed.'

With their hands on the panels, Bahia and Essac started to draw in the energy around them and when they could hold no more, released it into the machine and sent it towards Gilcan.

'No!' Bahia shouted out. 'He didn't catch it.'

'Solvan, where are you going?' Essac asked as his son started to run to the side of the mountain.

'To Gilcan's, I have to do something,' but before he could jump off the side, he collapsed onto the floor, as did his parents, and they all knew it was too late.

⁂

'Solvan,' his mother said as he walked into the room later that day. He was still shaking and unable to completely control his feelings so his skin had taken on a slightly reddish tinge. Bahia stood up from where she was sitting next to her mate and walked towards him. She reached out to her son, pushed him into the nearest chair and slowly began rubbing the back of his neck, trying to ease the inner turmoil she could feel. When Bahia felt that he had better control over his feelings, she stopped and returned to the chair she had just vacated.

'I take it you went to Gilcan's collective,' Essac said.

'Yes, when I was able to block out what I was feeling, I thought that if I got there in time, I might be able to save a few at least, but I could see I was too late as I approached. As I got close I saw something big and dark flying off in the distance, leaving a white trail. I didn't get too close but it moved very fast and it still felt as though I had been hit as it passed – I nearly fell from the sky. I have never seen or felt anything like it before. As I got close to the collective, I could see that there were piles in the outer fields, so I landed and saw that they were made up of the workers' bodies. They had all been skinned and stripped of their wings. I couldn't sense anyone still alive nearby as I started to make my way further in. It was the same in all of the fields, I couldn't find anyone left alive, anywhere.' Solvan took another deep breath. 'It will be impossible to identify any of them.'

'How many are dead?' Bahia asked.

'I don't know, the way the bodies were piled makes it hard to estimate. Over a thousand I would guess, but Gilcan and Pesline would have a better idea.'

'I see,' said Essac. As Solvan had talked, the images had come so vividly to his mind that he had caught a glimpse of what Solvan had seen. 'You said the castle was destroyed, do you know what happened to Gilcan and his family?'

'Before I left I did a last circuit around the collective and saw Gilcan and his family heading, I'm assuming, to Ovato's collective, though how they got out Hannoki only knows,' Solvan added bitterly.

'I don't understand how this happened. You said that out of everyone, Gilcan was the only one willing to listen and learn.'

'He said he was willing, he even said he was going to the battlements. Why would he say that knowing his castle would be destroyed when he was not there to control the energy?'

'Do you honestly think Gilcan could have deceived you? I doubt there is anyone alive who is capable of that,' Bahia said.

'If I had been rudely intrusive, you are probably right. I did feel division in him over the issue of the traders, but Pesline wouldn't listen to me at all and Gilcan said that she firmly believed that the traders were never going to return. Either of these views could account for what I felt from him. I should have looked further.'

'You did what you could Solvan, and you had every reason to believe that Gilcan would do his duty as a protector.'

'It will be interesting to see how the other protectors will now feel, whether they will finally listen to me and do their duty to the collectives, as written in the laws of Milkoy.'

⁂

Solvan stood out on the balcony and looked down. He could not see anything on the ground, he was too high up, but watching the few clouds move in the wind helped to calm him. Until today, the traders had been attacking the small, independent farms. These attacks had always happened so quickly that the first he had known about them was as they were happening. As soon as he knew of an attack, he had gone to each location, only to arrive too late to save anyone, so he buried the skinned bodies because he knew no one else would. He could not tell the ages of the dead, but he knew that the traders did not worry about killing children, judging by the size of some of the bodies. There had even been a baby among the dead, too young yet to have wings, but they had still taken what skin they could off the very small body. He had wanted to lay the baby with its parents but had no way of knowing who they were, so he had put everyone in the same grave and placed the baby next to a couple who had been nearest to the tiny body, thinking that the parents would have been trying to protect their child, but having seen how the traders had dumped the dead on Gilcan's collective, he was no longer sure he had been right.

He had tried to get the protectors to see the reality through him, to see and feel what he had. He had even left the family killed outside Protector Tesrun's collective while he went to speak with the protector and his family and had tried to get them to go to the farm to see for themselves, but they would not. All he ever got was, 'The traders do not exist any more.' He knew all their explanations for what they had felt; they just were not able to accept the truth. After the family had refused to look at the bodies, he had gone back and buried them.

'Why will they not listen?' he had fumed at his parents when he had returned from Tesrun's collective.

'If the traders are coming back, some of the protectors could lose their collectives,' Essac said. 'They have been ignoring the laws for the last few generations, and many of the collectives have not been passed to the strongest mated couple.'

'Of course they have,' Solvan said.

'No, they haven't, they have been passing the collectives to the strongest mated couple within the family. The law says that the collective must go to the strongest, regardless of family or birth, and if this were enforced, there may be current protectors who would lose their position.'

'It's also why so many collectives are in trouble at the moment,' Bahia carried on after Essac finished, 'everyone now wants what they consider to be theirs by right.'

Knowing this had helped Solvan to see the politics more clearly, but it had not helped him argue with the protectors and had only increased his frustration. Only Gilcan had seemed to listen, and look what had happened. Thinking about Gilcan, and how he had been able to save himself and his family, made him so angry. Could they not see that when the traders came, they would not have a collective any more? Would they all listen now?

Solvan supposed that the traders had gone to the small farms first to see what would happen, to see if they would be attacked as they had been in the past, and when they were not, they then went to the smallest collective. It was still a big jump for the traders, the largest family had consisted of only ten people, to a collective of over a thousand. How many traders had been needed to skin so many people? A lot more than for a family, so was that why he had been able to sense them so much earlier? There was just so much he still did not understand, despite the hours he had spent reading the old accounts left by previous first protectors.

The irony was that if the protectors would not start to defend their collectives, the small, independent farms were now probably a safer place to be. Why would the traders bother with a family when they could attack a collective? Some of the collectives would be very easy targets. When he had visited Ovato, the immense hatred and hostility coming from the workers had been obvious, so he knew it would only be a matter of time before the collective revolted. Solvan had tried to warn Ovato about that as well, but he had refused to listen on both counts, asking what he knew about running a collective which, of course, neither he nor his parents ever had.

Solvan went back inside to his parents. 'I'm going to visit the other protectors again to see if they have changed their minds now.'

'Wait Solvan,' Essac said, 'we need to consider another problem.'

'What problem could be bigger than getting the protectors to see sense?'

'Being able to use the power base.'

'You and mother did just fine, I don't see what the problem is.'

'We are not as strong as you, you knew the traders were coming before us. Using the power base was extremely draining. If there had been more, we would not have recovered in time.'

'I can't use it. Every account says it needs two to operate it.' His parents made no response, but Solvan realised what they were thinking. 'You want me to mate so I can use it instead of you.'

'You would probably lose some strength but you would still be more powerful than us. You could offer more protection to the people.'

'Who would you suggest?'

'Erle is the most powerful known female.'

'Buxus's daughter?' Solvan said. 'I don't recall seeing her when I paid her father a visit.'

'She is not as powerful as you,' Essac warned.

'How do we know I would not lose the strength to

sense the traders in enough time to stop them if I mate with her?'

'I share that same concern, but we were exhausted after using it. If there were more than one attack, then you and your mate could do the second blast. We still felt them before they landed, just not as soon as you,' Bahia said.

'Fine, I will meet her, but I make no promises to you,' Solvan said. He could understand his parents' concerns, he could feel that they were much more exhausted than they were admitting.

⁜

'*Buxus*,' Essac called.

'*Yes, First Protector*,' he responded, his annoyance tangible in his tone.

'*I am on my way over with Solvan as we speak.*'

'*With respect, First Protector, I have already heard what you have to say about the traders and my battlements.*' Essac winced, knowing what his son would say to that after all he had witnessed and felt.

'*Be that as it may, that is not the main reason for our visit on this occasion. Solvan wishes to meet Erle.*'

Then, after a stunned pause, '*Then you are both most welcome.*'

⁜

'*Erle!*' She heard her father yell both mentally and verbally, making her wince with the volume of it. '*Where are you?*'

'What have you done to upset your father?' Misca asked.

'Nothing Mother, I swear,' she replied. Misca just grunted, not convinced by that.

Erle closed her eyes and concentrated, '*I'm on the balcony with Mother,*' she told her father. She half

91

expected him to order her to his office in response but he didn't, he just acknowledged her answer. She was just about to voice her confusion to her mother when Buxus walked out to join them.

'What's so important that you have to yell so loudly?' his irritated mate asked him.

'First Protector Essac has just contacted me; he and Solvan are en route here and should arrive very shortly.'

'What's that to us?' Misca asked.

'They are coming here so Solvan can meet Erle.'

'Why would he want to meet me?'

'I don't know. He is powerful and, as far as I know, you are the most powerful unmated female. Certainly none of the other protectors' daughters that I know are as strong as you. Essac didn't spell it out, but I can guess why he wants to meet you.'

'You think First Protector Essac is proposing a match between Erle and Solvan?' Misca asked in excitement.

'Why else would he request the meeting? Personally, I can't think of any other reason, can you?'

'If he is coming here to propose a mating, won't I have a say in it?' Erle asked, annoyed.

'No,' both of her parents said.

'I thought you said that the first protectors were obsolete and should have given up the rank years ago when Neron and Jera died.'

'So I did, it is not the rank or position that concerns me, but to be mated to Solvan,' he said, as if this explained everything, yet she still did not understand, could not grasp her parents' excitement over the match.

'Why are you so reluctant? Have you ever seen Solvan?' Misca asked her daughter.

'No, I saw First Protector Essac when he was last here. I couldn't see anything exceptional about him.'

'My dear,' Misca said, glad that she thought she now

understood the root of her daughter's reluctance, 'Solvan is so much more powerful than his parents. His patterning extends all over his body and is very intricate; to mate with him would make you so much more powerful, more powerful than your brothers, even us,' she said, indicating herself and her mate.

'He's really that powerful? You have seen him?'

'Only briefly. When First Protector Essac paid us a visit, Solvan was with him, but he only stayed briefly before, I believe, going on to another collective,' Essac said.

'My daughter, the strongest mated female on Lismar,' Misca said. 'Ooh, I like the sound of that.'

'So do I Mother, but what about the traders?' she asked after a moment.

'Myth, that is all,' Buxus said as if it were not important, 'but if the first protectors want to believe it, who are we to correct them when they want Erle? By the time they realise their mistake, you will be mated and it will be too late – we will have become the most powerful family.' He moved towards his daughter and took her arm, 'But enough of this, he is coming here now and we must be ready for him when he arrives.'

His mate shrieked, 'Why did you not say so sooner?' She grabbed her daughter, pulled her out of Buxus's hold and ran out of the room with her, heading for the private chambers. Buxus was left standing there on his own. He knew better than to get involved with women's business; he just hoped it would not take them too long.

⁑

Buxus stood alone on the battlements waiting for the first protectors while the females were getting ready. First Protector Essac had not given a time for his arrival, but he had said he was on his way which meant he could be here at any moment, so he stood looking towards the mountains waiting for any sign of them. When he saw two marks in the sky, he knew they were coming.

'*Erle! Misca!*' Buxus called to them, '*they're coming, come to the battlements at once!*'

'*We're on our way,*' the reply came.

It was not long before they joined him and turned to look towards the mountains where by now the two marks could definitely be identified as the First Protectors Essac and Solvan flying next to each other in perfect formation. Buxus and his family were transfixed by the ease with which they caught the air currents as they neared.

'I suppose they need to be good at flying if they keep having to go up and down that mountain of theirs,' Erle said, nervous.

'Just wait Erle, if all goes well, you will soon be flying as easily as them,' Buxus whispered to his daughter as he squeezed her shoulder reassuringly.

※

Solvan could see Buxus standing on the battlements, with whom he assumed to be his mate and Erle, awaiting his approach, although he was not yet close enough to distinguish their markings. He could, however, see that no repairs had been carried out on this side of the battlements since his last, all-too-brief, visit.

As he got close to the castle he took Buxus and his family by surprise by suddenly turning left and circling them. His father, who had been expecting Solvan to do exactly that, followed him, keeping their flying formation tight. They both flew around the battlements so they could see whether Buxus had conducted any repairs at all. Solvan was annoyed but unsurprised when he saw they were in exactly the same condition.

As he came full circle, he saw that Buxus and his family had turned to watch him as he flew back around. He glided up to them and landed a few feet away, his father beside him.

'First Protectors, we are honoured to have you here,' Buxus said as soon as they had landed. Solvan's brows rose at that, remembering clearly the reception he had received last time. 'You have met my mate, Misca, of course.'

'Of course, how are you Misca?'

'I'm well, thank you First Protector,' she replied.

'May I introduce you to my daughter, Erle,' Buxus said, indicating the female Solvan did not already know.

'A pleasure to meet you,' Solvan said, bowing slightly to her in acknowledgement.

'First Protector Essac, it's an honour to meet you again,' Buxus said. 'Now, if you and Protector Solvan would like to come down into the castle, we can have some refreshment.' Solvan looked at them. Misca was just standing there with an almost fanatical glint in her eye, Buxus was bending over backwards to be pleasing, probably for the first time in his life, and Erle, though she said nothing, had a supremely confident expression on her face. She returned Solvan's assessing look with one of possessiveness. Solvan pressed gently on her mind and he was not surprised, but extremely irritated, to find that she already considered their mating to be a done deal.

'Thank you,' Essac said and together they went inside.

Once they were settled and drinks had been passed around, Solvan said, 'I hope you are planning to repair your battlements soon, Buxus.'

'As I told your father previously, the traders are not coming back so why would I need to spend my time and resources rebuilding the battlements?'

'I suggest you go and visit Gilcan's collective, did you not feel what happened there?'

'*Now is not the time,*' his father said.

'*It is always the time.*'

'*You need Erle.*'

'*Not as much as she wants me, or can you not feel what she is broadcasting?*'

'*Point taken.*'

'I don't know how much you felt the other day, and I don't know how you explain what you did feel, but while Erle and I get to know each other better, go to Gilcan's collective or send someone if you can't be bothered to go yourself.'

'What do you think I'll find there?'

'A dead collective, and you'll see what will happen to your collective when the traders come.'

Buxus was silent, thinking over what Solvan had said.

'What do you mean, "get to know"?' Misca asked, breaking the silence.

'No offence, but if Erle and I are to mate, it's only wise that we get to know each other well first – we might find that we are not compatible and then where would we be?' Solvan felt the annoyance of both mother and daughter at his suggestion. They had taken the suggestion of a mating as definite; Erle was very confident that as the most powerful female available, she was the only option. There were always other options.

'How do you plan to get to know my daughter?' Gilcan asked.

'I know a place we can go and talk, get a feel for each other,' Solvan said.

'Then go and get acquainted,' Gilcan said.

Standing back on the battlements a few minutes later, ready to take flight, they were all surprised when Essac joined them.

'*I don't need a chaperon.*'

'*No, but I don't trust you not to try and ruin this.*'

'*I know my duty, Father.*'

'Does your father have to come?' Erle asked and she reached out and put her hand on his arm.

'Appearances must be maintained,' he replied, annoyed at the contact. 'Are you ready for this?' and he jumped off the battlements into the air. Taking a deep breath, Erle followed him and together they headed back towards the mountains.

'What did he mean about Gilcan's collective?' Misca asked.

'After what we felt the other day, I fear I know, but I'll send someone to make sure.'

Chapter 9

LOVOA had woken again in the night and had lain awake for a while before, frustrated, she got up and prepared the breakfast for her parents and left it on the side before going out to the barn to work. She was aware of when her parents woke up and left the cabin. She expected them to come and find her, but they did not, probably assuming that as she had left early, she wanted more time on her own.

Lovoa was just finishing stacking the sacks a few hours later when her mother came in. 'Your father and I need to go over to Relson's farm. Will you be all right on your own for a few hours?'

'Of course,' she replied.

'Remember to keep out of sight.'

'I know mother. I've nearly finished here, is there anything else you need me to do?'

'No, but we'll talk again tonight when we get back.' Lovoa nodded her head and without saying anything else, her mother left.

Lovoa tidied everything up and went back into the cabin. Everything was clean so there was nothing to do in here either. She went to pour some water into a bowl so that she could wash off the dirt from the barn, but she paused and looked out at the forest next to their farm and, after making sure that her parents were well en route to the Relson's farm, she grabbed her cloak and left. She knew the forest well, some of her earliest memories were of being in there with her parents, and they had always made sure she knew where she could hide if she needed to and how not to get lost.

When she was older, she had explored on her own and found some beautiful, peaceful places and had started to go there every chance she got. At first her parents had been fine with it, and had given her a cloak she could cover herself with, just in case there was anyone else nearby to see her patterning and identify her. In the end, she supposed, it was her own fault for going too often and for not telling them exactly when and where she was going, because now she was only allowed to go if she told them first, but the temptation to go now while both suns were out was overwhelming. Her parents would not be back for hours, and she would make sure she was home before them, so they would never know.

At first the vegetation was light but slowly grew more and more dense the further she walked until only patches of sunlight made it through the leaves. The change in temperature was noticeable once she was in the forest, the air was so much cooler and had a different feel and smell to it. Having grown up next to the forest, she was used to it and had been surprised when her parents had told her that there were no trees where they had been raised and until they had left their collective, they had never seen one before. The forest grew all the way around the Hannoki mountain range, where there were streams which ran down from the mountains and natural springs where the ground had cracked. That was where she was heading now, where she could wash the dirt off her body and sit and listen to the sound of the forest.

It was that sound of running water she heard first. She smiled to herself, knowing she was near her sanctuary. Lovoa headed towards it and found the small stream which she followed against the current a short way. Looking ahead as she went, she could see more sunlight coming through the trees in front of her and she knew she was near her clearing. The trees stopped at the edge of a pool of water, allowing the bright mid-day suns to shine down unhindered, and the ground under her feet became soft and covered in a green, furry plant. She had asked her parents once what it was but they did not know, they did not know any of the plants. A small stream flowed into the pool, her parents had said that is what kept it filled, but Lovoa did not think so. She liked to dive down, completely submerging herself, and when she did she could see and feel water coming from the rocks at the bottom.

Stripping off her cloak, she carefully stepped in. The water was cold as it lapped around her lower legs. She waded in further until the water was up to her waist and started to scrub the dirt from her arms and face. As the grime washed away, an elaborate patterning was revealed, a beautiful but complex design that covered her entire body, from the end of her toes to the tips of her long, graceful fingers. Her parents had the same patterning on their bodies, of course, but it was nowhere near as extensive or as dense as her own. As the grime was washed off by the water, the sun made her skin shimmer as she absorbed the energy from the rays. The feeling exhilarated her and made her feel strong, easing the pain in her stiff muscles. Suddenly she dived under the water, needing to feel clean all over. The slight current tugged at her hair and pulled at the dirt there. After a while, she surfaced, waded out of the pool and went to sit on a tree stump just at the water's edge, letting her wings fall behind her and her feet dangle just clear of the water. As she rested, she allowed the sun to restore her low energy levels. She loved this area, here she could fully open herself up to the sun.

Right in front of her was Hannoki's Peak, by far the

highest of the mountains in the range that had the same name. Her parents said that name when they were surprised or angry. She had asked them what it meant and they had said it was the name of an important person but gave no more details. She wondered now if he had anything to do with these traders they had tried to tell her about last night.

Shadows passing overhead startled Lovoa out of her thoughts. Looking up, she expected to see birds moving in the branches, but instead she saw three people circling above the trees. Quickly Lovoa grabbed her cloak. She thought about running, but if they were circling around they might notice the vegetation moving and investigate, so she hid in the nearby undergrowth so that if they looked down they would not see her. Looking up again, she prayed for them to keep going and pass her by, but her heart sank as she realised that they had started to descend. Lovoa could see that there were two males and a female. The younger male landed at the edge of the pool first with such grace that the water barely rippled around his legs, and the other two closely followed him. The female was unsteady as she landed and stumbled into the younger male, and he grabbed her and steadied her and let her go again straightaway. Lovoa's lips twitched slightly as the female had tried to take hold of his hand as he held her briefly, but had not been quick enough. She wondered if the poor landing had been deliberate.

A niggling thought at the back of Lovoa's mind warned her to slip away into the forest, but curiosity kept her hiding in the undergrowth, watching the trio. She had never met anyone other than her parents and she wanted to see why they were here. They all had a lot more markings than her parents did, and the design of the older male covered a great deal of his body but started to thin out below his elbows and knees. The other two were younger. The male had a patterning as intricate as her own and his covered his entire body, as did Lovoa's. His patterning was the same as the older man, making them father and son. The female was the least impressive of the group. Her white hair fell to the small of her back, her skin was neither as elaborately nor as extensively marked as the father and son's, but there was something about her that was familiar, which was disturbing as no one should be familiar to her. Lovoa took an instant dislike to the female's possessive manner towards the younger male, and by the way he kept trying to avoid contact, she guessed that he did too. The older male went to the tree stump she had just vacated, giving them a little space.

'So, now we are here, what do you want to do?' Lovoa heard the female ask.

'I think it's important I know a bit about you.'

'Why?' She sounded like she was complaining. 'Once we mate, we'll know everything about each other.' The male turned his back to where Lovoa was hiding and she could not hear what he said in reply.

Lovoa started to feel anxiety and resentment. It began gradually so it took her a while to recognise the emotions, but why should she feel this way towards them? Surely not because they had come to her favourite spot! No, she realised, she felt nothing towards them other than curiosity, which meant that these were not her emotions. They were quickly getting stronger and stronger and Lovoa tentatively reached out her mind and found that they were coming from the younger male. Curiosity got the better of her and she tried to ascertain the root of his turmoil. She felt he was divided between what he knew he should do, though it was abhorrent to him, and what he wanted to do, but she could not discern what the problem was.

⁂

After a short time, Solvan stopped what he was saying to Erle.

'You were saying?' Erle prompted.

'Give me a moment,' he said and then turned and waded to where his father was sitting.

'What's wrong, Solvan?' his father asked, alert to his son's sudden change in mood. With the ease of long practice, Solvan closed his mind off completely and he found her hiding somewhere very nearby. Her mind was strong and shielding reasonably well, but still he wondered how he had not felt her as soon as they had landed. Who was she though? Not a protector's daughter, he was sure from her curiosity in them, but definitely another option to Erle.

'Everything is all right,' Solvan replied out loud, then added, '*Someone is here,*' to his father's mind so neither the female or Erle could hear. He turned his head one way, then another, trying to locate the intruder's position.

'Solvan,' Erle called, coming out of the water to join them. 'Come back in,' she said, taking his arm and trying to pull him back into the pool with her.

'Give me a minute Erle,' he said and removed her hand from his arm. He could feel her annoyance that she was not getting his full attention. Solvan was silently cursing, he was going to have to do something to get this female out of hiding and could think of no way to do it without Erle seeing, so why try and hide it from her?

'She's confused,' he said to his father. 'She can see us, but she is shielding reasonably well and I can't quite locate her. I just know she is near enough to be able to see us.'

'What are you talking about, can't it wait until later,

Solvan?' Erle complained, but Solvan ignored her.

✳

Lovoa realised too late that as she could sense him, he could sense her. He was standing still, scanning the vegetation as if he was looking for something, looking for her. What she felt from him now was curiosity and the desire to find her. She should have left earlier; she could not be found.

Lovoa's curiosity was quickly giving way to fear as she realised that he could feel her, was looking for her. All of a sudden she felt that she had to go, now! Easing her way backwards as carefully as she could, she winced as the leaves moved and a twig snapped. A sudden splashing sound made Lovoa look up. Through the foliage she could see the girl floundering in the water and the younger male moving quickly towards her. In sheer panic, Lovoa gave up trying to leave quietly and turned to run, but too late! He grabbed at her through the branches, catching hold of her wrist, and tried to drag her out. Startled, Lovoa tried to get free, she twisted and turned in his grip, bruising her wrist, but to no avail.

'Let me go, I'm sorry,' she begged. In response, he tightened his grip and pulled harder. Lovoa made one last push in sheer desperation; she felt something surge through her, leaving a tingling feeling across her skin. She stumbled backwards and fell into a bush, stunned at being free. She staggered briefly as she stood up and began running through the forest, trying to put as much distance between them as possible, before he could recover and begin to chase her.

Lovoa ignored the branches that ripped at her cloak and skin. She knew he was chasing her, she could hear him as he pushed his way through the foliage. Gradually, though, the sounds faded as she put more distance between them, until all she could hear was her own jagged breathing. She came to a stumbling halt and tried to get her breath back. Behind her there was no sound of pursuit and, gasping in relief, she turned to face the direction from which she had just come, but realised that he did not need to see her to be able to follow, her path through the forest was clear. Slowly this time, Lovoa picked her way through the bushes, but still she could not shake the feeling that he was behind her, catching her up. Eventually she broke out of the undergrowth into an area of less dense vegetation. From here she could again run without making her direction too obvious, but she knew he was still there. It occurred to her then that if she knew where he was, could he feel her in the same way? That no matter how cautious she was, he would still be able to follow her.

Lovoa stopped and concentrated. Yes, now she was focusing, he was clear in her head. He knew where she was, he could feel her as she could feel him, and he was desperate to catch her. It did not matter how far she ran, he would get her. Lovoa started to panic, how could she ever get away from him? If she blocked him so she could not feel him, would he still be able to feel her? She had been able to stop her parents from reading her for years but had still always been able to sense them. She wished they had told her more last night. She wished she had listened to them and not come into the forest. She took a deep breath and concentrated, put the barriers in place that she used around her parents and then pushed his mind out. Lovoa felt vulnerable not knowing where he was, not knowing if he was going to come up behind her at any moment. She went back into the heavy vegetation, curled up with her back to a tree and watched for him, hoping that if he could not sense her, she was well enough hidden that he would not see her. She pulled her cloak tight around her as if it would help to protect her, and realised with surprise that she missed his mind in hers. Was she really that lonely? She thought, chiding herself for a fool.

Lovoa heard him only moments before he appeared a few metres in front of her. From where she was hiding she could see him approach. He wasn't running and from the way he was gasping, running was not a usual exercise for him. He stopped right in front of her and she held her breath, scared he would detect even the slightest movement. He seemed to stand there forever, looking around, then he looked straight at where she was and Lovoa cursed herself, knowing that she should have moved further away, but his gaze moved on and he walked away. Slowly she let the air out of her lungs before taking another deep breath. She didn't move after he had gone, instead she remained hidden and did not allow herself to think. She did not know how long she stayed hidden. Slowly, other things began to make themselves felt, like the cramps forming in her legs. Gradually she stood up and sighed in relief as the muscles in her legs straightened themselves out. When she looked around, there was still no sign of him, so she began to walk back home. She kept to the heavy vegetation where possible so she could hide in it if need be, though it was slower going.

As she made her way home, she constantly paused to see if there was any sound that could indicate him following her as she dare not check with her mind in case he found her again. She did not even want to check to see if her parents were home yet. If they were back and had found her gone, they would be so worried. Normally when she was caught out she would have let them know she was all right and then face their anger when she got home, but she had no idea if he would feel it as well and

then he would know where she lived. When would she be
able to open her mind again? From how far away would
he be able to sense her? When would he stop looking for
her? She had no answers to any of these questions and
wondered whether her parents would. She was going to
have to tell them everything, she realised. Oh Hannoki,
she was going to be in so much trouble.

Lovoa was angry with herself for getting into trouble
so spectacularly, but also with him. It was not as if she
had done anything wrong, she had as much right to be
in the forest as he had. Was it because she had been
watching him? She could understand him being annoyed
over that. Perhaps he had wanted to give her a lesson
in manners, but would that justify him pushing over the
female he was with to get to her? Or chasing her through
the forest? She did not think so.

Had he been doing something he should not have
been doing? Again she dismissed the idea, nothing she
had seen seemed wrong and none of them had been
concerned at being seen. She had not felt anger from
him, she realised, and surely he would have been angry
if this had been the case. She paused, confused, and
thought for the first time about what she had felt from
him. He had not wanted to be at the pool, and he had
a problem for which he did not like any of the possible
solutions had been her first impression of him, then
surprise, curiosity and a very strong desire to get hold
of her, but not why. She sighed and continued walking,
there was nothing she could do now other than get home
without being caught.

The sunlight started to come through stronger and
the foliage became less dense and she knew she was
nearly home. Her parents were home, and even through
the barriers she had put into place she could feel their
panic at finding her gone. She just stopped herself from

reaching out to reassure them, she would be home soon, then she could explain everything to them, including why she could not let them know she was all right.

Lovoa was at the edge of the forest and could see home. She was relieved that she had made it back and was about to leave the forest's edge when she saw Protector Buxus talking to her parents outside the barn. Her heart sank, this was not a good day she thought as she turned and walked back into the forest to wait for him to go. Why was he back again so soon? He had been there only yesterday. She would have to stay close as she would not be able to sense when he left and did not want her parents to worry about her absence for any longer than they had to. Lovoa honestly did not know if the day could get any worse, between the trio at the pool, being chased and now Protector Buxus, what more could possibly go wrong? Protector Buxus, Lovoa thought, *that* is why she thought the female looked familiar, she had the same markings as Protector Buxus. Lovoa could only hope that the other female had not got a good enough look at her to describe her to her father. If she had, at least he was at the farm now. After he left she would get the chance to explain everything to her parents and they could leave before his daughter got home and told him what had happened. Thank Hannoki for small blessings.

Chapter 10

'SOLVAN?' asked his father, as his son's tense frame began to relax.

'Everything's all right,' Solvan replied reassuringly, before he lunged forward, grabbed hold of the hiding female's wrist and tried to pull her out. She staggered forward slightly, off balance, and he saw the extensive patterning running to her fingertips. Solvan felt a moment of elation for here was another option, followed by confusion – how had his parents not known of her existence? Then he felt himself being thrown backwards, and the hand he had used to hold the girl felt as if it was burning and his head was spinning.

'Solvan!' both his father and Erle shouted in surprise. He pushed himself up slightly, shaking his head to try and clear it, and looked towards where the girl had been in time to see her pick herself up, stagger slightly then begin to run through the forest without even looking back. Solvan wondered whether she had even realised what she had done as his father arrived at his side and helped him to his feet.

'Are you all right?' he asked, concerned.

'I'm fine, look after Erle,' he replied before he took off after the girl, leaving his shocked father and a furious Erle behind.

Without explaining to his father or even acknowledging Erle, he ran after the girl. He lost sight of her after only a few moments but he could clearly see the trail of broken branches that she had left behind that anyone could follow. After a while the trail became much less obvious, then ended altogether. He did not need a trail though, he could feel her panic and could follow that. He did not need to push himself so hard, he knew that she could be miles away and he would still know where she was. She might be strong but she was unaware of how she was broadcasting to him.

Solvan realised his error too late, she was starting to work it out as her mind closed off to him. He started to run towards her as fast as he could but he was too late and could no longer feel her. He cursed Hannoki and made his way to where he last knew her to be; he did not know where else to go to try to pick up her trail.

He stood in the last location at which he had sensed her and looked over at the vegetation, but he saw nothing. He scanned with his mind to see if he could pick anything up from her, but there was nothing. He could not believe it, he had never encountered anyone who could remain closed to him when he was determined to find them. He had thought that she had not had any training, but now he was not so sure. He had so many questions about her.

Frustrated, he moved on, scanning with both his eyes and mind, but he could find nothing, no cracks in her mind and no broken branches to mark which direction she had taken.

He had searched for the female for some time and when he finally admitted to himself that he would not be able to find her this way, he realised he was very lost in the forest. Solvan always flew everywhere so he was used to seeing everything from high up and had no concept of direction from ground level. Without being able to see very far because of the trees, he no longer knew where he was. He reached out with his mind and found his father.

'*Solvan,*' his father said when he felt his son's touch,

'are you all right? Where are you?'

'I'm fine,' he said. 'I lost her somewhere in the forest and now I have no idea where I am. I'm going to have to follow your mind back to the pool.'

'Hurry back, Erle is getting impatient.' Solvan felt his father's irritation with her.

'I'm on my way back now. If she is so bad, why did you not take her back to her father?'

'I suggested it but she refused to go back.'

'I'll come as quickly as I can,' Solvan said, resigned to an argument that he neither wanted nor had time for, but no matter how tempted he might be, he could not leave his father to deal with Erle alone.

Solvan looked above him and doubted that he would be able to fly up and through the trees, the branchs were thick and interlacing. Taking a frustrated breath, he headed back through the vegetation in the most direct route back to his father. He hated walking, flying was so much easier, quicker and less painful he thought as he was scratched by the branches. It seemed to take so much longer to get back to the pool.

Finally, Solvan could see more sunlight coming through the trees and he knew he was near the pool. The strength of his father's mind confirmed it and he hurried forward. The trees ended in front of him and as he walked out into the clearing he saw his father sitting on the tree stump and Erle pacing up and down, her anger clear. She heard him as he arrived and spun around and glared at him. She was struggling to maintain control, and he was sure that if she were pushed any further, her skin would turn red.

Erle stormed up to him. 'Was that really necessary?' she snapped. 'You brought me here to get to know me better, then ran off. How dare you! This was your idea.'

Solvan did not reply. He knew that other than a

grovelling apology, which he was not prepared to give, anything he said to her would just result in an argument, so he just stared at her.

'Well?' she challenged when she got no response.

'I don't have to justify myself to you,' he said.

Erle was at first taken aback that anyone would talk to her in that manner and was about to demand proper respect, but realised just in time to whom she was talking. Solvan was so much more powerful than her and she wanted his strength, which she could only get through mating with him. Angering him would not get her what she wanted.

'I am sorry, I was just very disappointed that our time together was interrupted,' she said in a placatory tone, trying to undo any damage her bad temper might have done. She was worried, though, about Solvan's unpredictable behaviour and what aspects of his personality she would take on once they mated. Worried that she would make matters worse, she moved away to try and calm herself down.

What had happened? They had been together in the water 'getting to know each other' as Solvan had insisted before the mating, when all of a sudden she had seen him struggling with a female with extensive patterning, so much more extensive and detailed than her own that she could not believe what she was seeing. Who was she? How was she able to be so close to her father's collective without him knowing anything about her? The struggle had not lasted long before Solvan had been thrown back and the female had run away. Erle had been glad to see her go, but then Solvan had picked himself up and followed her into the forest and Erle could have screamed in frustration. This girl would be a threat. Erle knew that her position as Solvan's mate had been, as far as she was concerned, guaranteed because she was the strongest female and he wanted to mate.

Essac walked up to his son. He had stood back during the small confrontation with Erle and his heart had sunk: it was clear that the two were not well matched and a mating between them would be disastrous.

'That was quite a shock she gave you,' he said, indicating his son's hand, and Solvan lifted his arm to look at it. Spreading all the way from the tips of his fingers, across the whole palm and just touching his wrist were angry red burn marks where he had gripped the girl's wrist and she had channelled energy to push him away. Cautiously he balled his fist and felt the burns smart slightly. He had been so focused on trying to catch her that he had not noticed them.

'It's nothing to worry about, the suns will heal it quickly enough.' He shrugged as if to dismiss the injuries to his hand. 'I think she was as surprised as I was at what happened, I don't think she knows what she is capable of doing. I must find her as soon as possible.'

'I know you must, but what about Erle?'

'If she is ready to go, I'll take her back to her father and make my excuses. If she refuses, then all the better and she can stay here and return when she is ready, but I will not delay because she wants to be stubborn,' he said and turned away from his father and went towards Erle.

'I'll take you back to your father now,' he said simply.

'What about our arrangement?' she asked.

'I'll let you know, but you need to go back now.'

'And if I refuse to do so until we are mated? My father does expect it.'

'Do you think I care what your father expects? He is not my superior, I am his. If you refuse to leave here, that is up to you, but I'm leaving and truthfully it would suit me better if I didn't have to take you back to your father.' Solvan turned away, he did not want to stand there and argue with her.

'You can take me back to my father.' Erle was furious with Solvan, how dare he treat her like this? She was the daughter of a protector, but at least if he escorted her home she could save some face with her family. She joined Solvan and Essac in the pool and together they took to the skies again. The trip back to Protector Buxus could have been quicker but as they flew, Solvan scanned the forest below, hoping for a glimpse of the girl, but the trees grew too thickly throughout most of the forest for anything to be seen on the ground.

The forest receded, then stopped to reveal field after field, first of the independent farms then those belonging to Protector Buxus. The workers could be seen slaving away on the last of the year's harvest. There was no point in scanning for her now, Solvan realised. He doubted she could have got this far on foot and if she had, it would have been easy for her to have either taken flight or hidden in one of the many storage huts at the edges of the fields. In the distance, Protector Buxus's castle could be seen and Solvan turned his head to look behind him to where Erle was flying next to his father. He could feel that she had not calmed down. Turning to look ahead of him again, he could see the castle more clearly. He contemplated going faster, but decided against it since Erle was not a good flyer and it would be unwise to arrive at her home ahead of her and embarrass her, at least no more than she was already embarrassing herself since she seemed unable to get a grip of her emotions.

As the trio circled the castle, Solvan could hear a bell ring within. He grimaced, they had been seen. They approached the battlements from which they had originally departed and went to land, Solvan first, gracefully and lightly, followed by Essac and Erle. Having years of experience, Essac dropped down as gracefully as his son, without having to take a single step forward to balance himself. Erle, unfortunately, stumbled as she landed and had to take a step forward.

Buxus had heard the ringing and knew that his daughter was returning. He was worried, he had expected them to be gone for much longer. He just hoped that Erle had heeded his warning and watched her tongue and her thoughts in front of the first protector. Leaving the accounts he had been working on lying on the table, he made his way up to the battlements to meet them. As he walked out he could see that the group had already landed. What the first protector and his son were thinking he had no idea, but one look at his daughter and his heart sank. She was furious, leaking emotion both physically and mentally and to such an extent that Buxus found his temper starting to rise with his disgust for her. This was not good, something had gone seriously wrong. He could not believe his daughter's bad manners in broadcasting her emotions as if she were a common peasant, and when he found that his own emotions were becoming entangled with hers, he quickly had to block off his daughter's thoughts.

Solvan stepped forward towards Protector Buxus. 'My apologies, Protector Buxus, for returning so soon, but something urgent has arisen that I must attend to.' At the end of this statement, Protector Buxus felt Erle's fury rise. He tried to give her a mental nudge to get her to calm down but it was either ignored or she was too furious to notice it.

'Of course,' Protector Buxus replied, feeling it best to get them away while Erle was so furious and hoping that she had not ruined everything. 'I fully understand, you must have so many responsibilities at the moment. Will you return soon?' he asked.

'Alas, I can't answer that at the moment. I will let you

know shortly how things will be between Erle and myself,' Solvan said, 'but my father and I must leave now. Goodbye Protector Buxus, Erle.' Erle made no response at all so Solvan turned and walked towards the battlements then paused briefly to wait for his father to make his farewells and join him. Essac did not keep him waiting long, and together they jumped off the battlements and began to fly back towards the forest and the mountains.

The pair flew in silence all the way back, each lost in his own thoughts. As they reached the foot of the Hannoki range, they began to fly higher through the wind to the peak. Solvan had always found it exhilarating but he knew many struggled with the flight and it was not long before the smooth stone landing surface could be seen, sheltered from the wind by a natural crevice.

'Would you like to explain to me what happened in the forest?' Essac asked as he landed next to his son.

'I think I found a different option. As to precisely what happened, I'm not sure. The female was strong, much stronger than Erle, but I have no idea who she was.'

'How do you plan to find her?'

'I was in her mind in the forest, before she cut me out. I'm hoping that she might drop her guard a little when she thinks she is safe and I can get in again.'

'And if she doesn't?'

'When I was in her mind, I did pick up that she considers herself a peasant and fears the protector. That being the case, I'll look at the nearest independent farms first – no protector would be unaware of someone as powerful as her on their collective.'

'There are lots of independent farms along the border with the forest. Do you even know where you were when you lost her?' Essac asked.

'No, but I can't leave it, not until I have tried to find her.'

'What about Erle?' Essac called after him. 'Time is

running out, how long are you going to wait?'

'Though I dread the thought of taking on any of Erle's traits, I havn't forgotten my responsibilities, Father,' Solvan replied before walking off, leaving Essac standing in the corridor.

Essac sighed in frustration. He had a fairly good idea who this female was, he had searched for her for long enough but had never found her. He now feared that Solvan would spend too long looking for her and neglect what had to be done. At least if he went with him, he could steer him away from looking in areas he had already searched and hopefully save some time. With that thought in his mind, he ran after his son.

'Solvan!' he shouted as he came in sight. Solvan stopped and turned at the sound of his father's voice. 'I will help you look for her.' Solvan looked at his father for a moment and then nodded his consent.

⁜

Erle and her father had left the battlements and were now inside, and Misca had joined them, drawn by the fury Erle was broadcasting. 'What happened?' Protector Buxus demanded. 'Because there had better be an excellent reason why you are displaying such bad manners. I could have felt your anger from the other side of the collective.'

'It's not my bad manners that are the problem,' Erle retorted.

'Really? I got the impression that Solvan could not have left any quicker even if he had tried. That he did not even push me over the subject of Gilcan's collective was remarkable.'

'Give her a chance to explain, for Hannoki's sake,' his mate said. 'The fault could all be the first protector's.'

'Regardless of who was at fault, the first protectors

were not showing their emotions so clearly,' Buxus snapped.

'Erle, what happened?' her mother asked.

'We went to this clearing in the forest. It was very pretty and had a pool with enough water to immerse yourself in. At first I thought everything would be fine but very soon he left me and went to talk with his father. I don't know what they were talking about, but it looked as if something was wrong. I went up to him but he ignored me, and the next thing I knew I was pushed back. Of course I'm furious at being shown so little respect.'

'He assaulted you? Why?' Misca asked, shocked.

'I'll not suffer the insult, neither will the other protectors when they hear of this!' Buxus shouted. Now he was angry – no one had the right to assault his daughter.

'It wasn't deliberate,' Erle admitted, 'he went to grab at some female who was watching us and I was standing next to him.'

'Who was she? Some independent farmer? What did she have to say for herself?' Buxus asked.

'Where was she hiding?' her mother asked.

'I don't know who she was, but I don't think she is a farmer.'

'Why not?'

'Because she was very powerful. She was in the bushes and I think Solvan must have sensed her there. He grabbed hold of her and started to pull her out into the clearing. I didn't get a good look at her because she was wearing a cloak, but I did see her arm and her patterning covered her hands.'

'That's impossible,' Misca said, 'you must be mistaken. There is no female that powerful. Trust me, we would have known if one had been conceived: the first protectors' mating flight lit up the sky, it's not something that can be hidden.'

'I know what I saw,' Erle argued.

'Fine, I'm sure you know what you saw, but what did she have to say for herself? Where is she now?'

'Nothing and I don't know. She threw Solvan off and ran into the forest. Solvan followed her but came back a while later, on his own. I don't think he found her, and I think that is why he wanted to get back here as quickly as possible, so he can go back and look for her.'

'Hannoki!' Buxus cursed.

'Impossible,' Misca said.

'No, it's not,' Buxus said, and both mother and daughter looked at him in surprise.

'Do you know who she is?' his mate demanded.

'I think so,' he admitted. 'Can you describe any of her patterning?'

'No, I didn't get a good enough look.'

'Who do you think she is?' Misca asked.

'The daughter of peasants,' Buxus replied.

'You have let a powerful female live on our collective – are you mad?' his mate shouted at him. 'How could you?'

'I don't know for sure, I caught only a glimpse some time ago and it was not on my collective.'

'What do you plan to do about it?'

'Go and see the family,' he replied.

'And if she is there?'

'If I'm right and she is there, I'll worry about what I will do then.'

'I'll come with you,' Misca said.

'No, you are too angry and this visit needs a cool head. I will go alone,' and as a man used to having his orders obeyed, he went back up to the battlements, leaving his mate and daughter below to discuss Solvan's actions and his own.

Buxus stood on the battlements and cursed his luck as he took to the skies. As he had said, he had a very good idea who this female was. Some years ago, he had gone to visit Fesrun and his mate with the aim of forcing them off their farm and onto his collective. They had not been at home and he had sent his men to tear their cabin apart as a message to them and others. Buxus had wanted them to be the first to leave as they had been one of the first to start. He had wandered to the barn as he had wanted to destroy their harvest himself, but inside he had seen more than he had expected: a child playing. He had been surprised as he had not known they had a child, no one had ever mentioned it before, but as his eyes got used to the darker interior, he saw her markings. He had never seen anyone as strong as she was and he was afraid, so he had very quietly withdrawn before she knew he was there.

He could not decide what to do about her. She was too old for him to just kill her, and he had no idea of what she was capable of, so he had gone to the cabin and ordered his men back to the castle. He had thought about it for days: he could not kill her, but if he acknowledged her existence, there could be a call for her to have his collective once mated, and at that time he had no sons. In the end, he had decided to do nothing and pretend he had never seen her. The girl's parents had kept her hidden since birth and they seemed determined to keep it that way. He had remained cautious, though, and had not used force as he had with the other farmers, and had waited to see what would happen.

If the girl was the same one that had been chased by Solvan, then she was likely to be upset and if she was not trained, it would make her very unpredictable. He had not wanted to take any men with him in case she saw it as a threat, and he wanted to be able to talk to them sensibly. As he arrived he saw Fesrun and Mesrra coming out of the cabin. They looked up and saw him, and stopped and waited for him to land. This was going to be a difficult conversation, he thought.

✱

Fesrun and Mesrra returned home and went into their cabin. On finding it empty, they were not initially worried as Lovoa was normally in the barn, but when they could not find her in there either, they began to worry. When Mesrra returned to the cabin, she went into her daughter's room to see if she had left anything that would indicate where she was or if anything was missing, and realised that her cloak had gone. Mesrra tried calling to her daughter but found that she had closed her mind.

'Maybe she just needed some time alone,' Mesrra said.

'She would have been alone here.'

'She wouldn't have seen it that way. We'll just have to wait for her to come back.'

'I hate it when she does this,' Fesrun said. 'She gave her word she would not do this again.'

'I know,' Mesrra said, then after a moment. 'Do you feel that?'

'Protector Buxus, damn him. His timing could not be worse,' and together they went outside and watched him approach.

'I have never seen him come on his own before,' Mesrra said.

'Lovoa,' Fesrun said with a sinking feeling.

'We don't know that,' Mesrra said, and then Protector Buxus landed in front of them.

'Protector Buxus,' Fesrun said.

'Fesrun, Mesrra, I have come to speak to your daughter,' he said, getting straight to the reason for his visit.

'Our daughter, Protector Buxus? I feel that you have been misinformed for we have never been blessed with children,' said Mesrra as calmly as possible. Her mind was reeling with shock – she had no idea that the protector knew about Lovoa, and for how long he had known.

'Let us not play this game. I know you have a daughter of great power, I have seen her myself, but I have let you try and hide her from me as it suited me to do so. Now, however, it does not and I will speak with your daughter – immediately.'

Realising that there was no point in denying it any further, they glanced at each other.

'I don't know where she is, Protector Buxus. I don't think she is anywhere on the farm at the moment,' Mesrra confessed. Protector Buxus was furious, he had been so sure that she would have returned to her home by now, but these peasants could always be lying about her not having returned.

'Then you will not mind if I have a look around.' he stated and without waiting for a reply, he walked into the cabin. He had never been inside it before, or in any of his peasants' homes, for that matter. It was small, only three rooms in total, a general room and two sleeping rooms. He smiled to himself – if he or any of his men had ever come in here it would have been clear that there was another member of their family, but no one ever had, they saw it as beneath them to go inside instead of getting them to come out. It took very little time to search and the only other building was the barn, but again it took only moments to ascertain that she was not there. He tried searching with his mind but there was nothing. It did not surprise him: one thing he knew she had always been able to do well was shield her mind.

When he came out he saw them both watching him anxiously. He could take them back to his collective and make their daughter come to him, he thought, but she would either come angry, thinking her parents needed to be saved, or she might not come at all since she had always been taught to hide.

'If she is not here, where would she be?' he asked them.

'We don't know, my Protector, she should be on the farm,' Mesrra replied.

'Has she ever left before when she was not supposed to?'

'She used to,' Mesrra admitted.

'Where did she normally go?'

'She wanders into the forest. I don't know where she goes, when she gets back she just says she went for a walk,' Fesrun answered.

'So she has no special place she likes to go?' He pushed harder.

'Not that she has ever told us, no, my Protector.'

'Told you!' he exclaimed in disbelief. 'What sort of parents are you that your daughter needs to tell you things, why do you not know?'

'Our daughter is stronger than us, and we have not been able to read her since she was very young,' Mesrra said, trying to defend herself.

'Would you not follow her if you cannot read her? How can you let her wander on her own?'

'We need to work on the farm, we can't watch her all the time and she can look after herself,' Mesrra said, shaking, not quite able to believe that she was challenging him.

Protector Buxus felt himself having to bite his tongue to stop himself saying what he wanted to say. He knew that what they were saying was the truth. How could he expect them to be able to read their daughter when he could not?

'I take it you don't know when she is due back.'

'No, my Protector,' Fesrun said.

'When she finally returns home, I need you to bring her to the castle straightaway, do you understand?'

'My Protector,' Fesrun said, 'please forgive my curiosity, but how long have you known about Lovoa and what do you want with her?'

He paused for a moment, what to tell them that they would believe?

'I have known about her for years. I came here once when you were away and saw her playing in the barn. As to what I want with her, I would have thought with a daughter as powerful as yours, you would know that the traders are returning.'

'We suspected that they were back,' Fesrun confirmed.

'Then you understand why she would be needed.'

'Yes, my Protector, we will bring her to you as soon as she returns,' they promised.

Protector Buxus accepted that he would have to take their word for it but he was worried about Lovoa. Had she seen Erle and recognised her as his daughter? Was she afraid or angry at being chased? He supposed he would just have to wait and see. With all these thoughts in his mind, he took flight and headed home, ignoring the dark, alien feeling that suddenly increased in strength. He had told Lovoa's parents that she was needed for help with the traders as he thought they would accept that, especially if they had heard rumours from other peasants, but he was waiting for his messenger to return from Gilcan's collective before he decided whether he believed they were back or not.

Fesrun and Mesrra stood together outside the cabin and watched as Protector Buxus flew away. They were just turning to go back into the cabin when they felt a rush of hot wind. Fesrun grabbed at his mate's arm and pointed upwards. 'Look at that,' he said.

Mesrra turned to look at where her mate was pointing and she could see a bright line in the sky.

'What is it?' she asked.

'I don't know, there was a bright ball in front of it, which went behind our cabin.'

'Do you want to go and have a look?'

'No, it was probably just a falling rock, it just seemed to come very close to us.' They continued to look at the bright line for a moment but it was quickly dispersing into the air. Mesrra left him watching the sky. Falling rocks were not uncommon, but never had one come so close that she had felt the air move as it passed. She went into the cabin and started wiping down the already clean surfaces, her hands shaking as she did so.

'Mesrra, what is it?' Fesrun asked, having come into the cabin and seen how upset she was.

'How can you ask that? How could he know about our little girl?'

'Not so little now.'

'Don't get flippant with me. You know what I mean, we were always so careful and yet he just happened to see her.'

'I don't understand why you are so upset. We were discussing taking Lovoa to Protector Buxus anyway. That he knows about her already, well surely that is a good thing? It means less explaining. It means that he has known for a long time and has done nothing to harm her.'

'I know that it should be, but I just got the feeling from him that he was furious, that he does not mean us any good.'

'It could just be that he is angry that he needs a peasant's strength to defend against the traders, but when Lovoa returns we will talk to her, ask her if anything happened in the forest that we should know about.'

'Maybe,' Mesrra conceded, 'but promise me that we will do nothing without first getting Lovoa's agreement.'

Fesrun laughed. 'I don't think it would be possible to

make Lovoa do anything she does not want to do, so I won't worry about that.' He took hold of her hand and he could feel it still shaking so he pulled her towards him so he could hold her. Mesrra went willingly into his arms and held him, resting her head on his shoulder.

'I just wish everything could be simple again. I look into the future and I can't see what I am supposed to be doing any more.'

'Things will sort themselves out again, you will see,' Fesrun replied. 'What was that?' he said, letting Mesrra go.

'What is it?'

'I thought I heard something outside.'

'I didn't hear anything; do you think it could be Lovoa?'

'Possibly, but more likely Protector Buxus has sent some men to wait for Lovoa's return. Stay here and I will go and see.'

Fesrun begun to walk towards the door but as he approached it, it exploded open, the force sending him backwards into the table, breaking it. Mesrra screamed as she saw her mate collide with the table and crumple onto the floor. She was about to go to him when she saw what was coming in through the hole they had created. Two entered and they were wingless, with a skin like nothing she had ever seen, grey and solid. She could not see their faces, she did not even know if they had faces, there was only a flat, dark surface where a face should be. Mesrra didn't get the chance to notice more as the pair moved forward. They first went to Fesrun, grabbed him by the arms and shook him roughly, making him groan.

'Stop it!' Mesrra screamed at them, and picking up a cup, threw it at them. One of them said something to the other, but she didn't understand what had been said, and the second one came towards her. Realising too late it was after her, Mesrra tried to escape by going around him, but found that for all their size, they were still quick and he was able to grab hold of her arm with enough force to make her cry out in pain, but he did not lessen his grip. The other one picked Fesrun up off the floor as if he were a rag and carried him outside. Mesrra was dragged out just behind, kicking and screaming. Fesrun was dropped onto the floor at the feet of another one of these things and he tried to struggle up, starting to recover from his fall, only to be pushed back down by a huge foot.

'Where is the other one?' one of the grey men asked.

'There were only these two in that shack,' replied the one still holding Mesrra.

'Well?' he asked of the rest who were returning from searching the rest of the farm.

'There is no one else here, it must have left already.'

'Fuck it, what a waste of a trip. I wouldn't have bothered landing for just these two.'

'What do you want us to do with them?' the one holding Mesrra asked.

'A feisty little thing, isn't she?' the leader said. He went up and took hold of her face to look at her properly. 'Do you want her?' he asked the captor.

'Only her skin and wings,' he replied.

'Then I suggest you get on with it so we can go and look for a better catch.'

'With pleasure.'

With that, the leader turned around and headed away behind the farm where the shuttle had landed.

⁂

Lovoa walked further into the forest and shuddered, she wanted to get far enough in so if anyone should come looking, she would not be too easy to find. She had been so relieved to have got home that seeing Protector Buxus had upset her more than it should. With her mind so tightly closed off, she had not been able to sense him. If she had arrived home any sooner, she would have been seen.

Lovoa tried to pull her now tattered cloak around herself, but it did not help. It was not because she was cold that she could not stop shaking, it was the shock of what had happened at the pool and the unease of a second visit from Protector Buxus in one day.

Suddenly she felt terrified and she hurt. She looked around her but could see nothing, could hear nothing, so she checked herself but there were no injuries that she could see. What was going on? Slowly she relaxed the block around her mind and the feelings intensified and left her gasping at the intensity of them. Her parents!

No! Not them! She started to run back as quickly as she could, cursing herself for having walked so far away when her parents needed her. Oh Hannoki, let her get back to them in time.

Their thoughts were only of terror and Lovoa could not tell what was happening. If Protector Buxus was hurting them, she would make him sorry she promised herself. She was nearly there, she could see the brighter light ahead of her where the trees started to thin but before she could get there she heard a scream – her mother's? Her father's? Hers? She did not know as she collapsed onto the floor, feeling as if her skin was slowly being removed from her body, from her feet first, and there was nothing she could do to stop it. She tried to put the blocks around her mind back in place but she could not concentrate with the absolute agony that was wrecking her body.

Chapter 11

'SOLVAN! Slow down!' called his father. They had gone back to the forest, first to the area where Solvan had lost the girl but she was long gone. Since then they had been searching nearby to try and find some indication of which direction she had taken. Essac was not convinced, to him everything looked the same, dark and gloomy, but Solvan was determined and was marching on ahead, resolved to cover as much ground as possible in his hunt for this girl. Essac was following as best he could.

Solvan stopped and turned to see his father walking some distance behind him. He thought that he moved badly on his feet but his father was clearly struggling more.

'We have to find her quickly,' Solvan said when Essac finally joined him. 'I can do this on my own if you want to go back home.'

'No, I'm all right. I just don't feel that walking through the forest is the best way to find her, there are too many places to hide.'

'How would you suggest I try to find her? She has put mental shields up that I can't get through so I'm unable to locate her the way I would anyone else. She ran away from me, scared, so she won't come forward on her own.'

'No, but I have been giving it some thought. She can't be living in the forest as there is nowhere to grow anything. If she is hiding in here, she knows what she is doing or you would have found her previously. I think you need to start looking at the independent farms and collectives that border the forest.'

'She could be hiding here and others could be supplying her with food. I don't know anything about plants, but she might be able to survive on the vegetation here. She certainly wouldn't need to eat much.'

'I doubt it. She must have parents, and possibly other family members, they can't all be living in here. We need to be looking outside the forest.'

Solvan was silent for a moment. 'You don't want me searching in here,' he stated.

'I just think it would be a waste of time.'

'You seem very adamant about someone you know nothing about, or is there something you are not telling me?'

Essac made no reply.

'Father?' Solvan prodded.

'If she is who I think she is, I know that shortly after you were born I searched this area for her parents and could find no trace of them,' he said finally.

'Excuse me! You knew she existed and you never told me. You wanted me to mate with Erle when there was another option?' Solvan was furious.

'I didn't know she was another option – I didn't even know she was a she or if she had even survived,' Essac said.

Solvan took a deep breath to get control of the emotions that were turning turbulent inside him. 'I think you had better explain.'

'When you were only a few months old, your mother and I witnessed a mating flight. It was as explosive as when your mother and I created you. The couple landed near to what is now Protector Buxus's collective but at the time it was in dispute. Protector Osvai was dying and several of his family members were fighting for control. I went in search of the couple but a storm moved in and destroyed any trail they had left behind. When the storm had passed, I continued to look for them but with no luck. I thought that they may have tried to live in the forest or had entered the collective and hidden the child, but I was never able to find out. I searched this forest extensively for months but found no trace of them. I watched over the collectives near the forest to see if there was even a hint of a new couple joining – it was not as if I could ask, that would have put them at risk – so over the years I have payed closer attention to Buxus's collective in case I could catch a trace of the child's existence, but I never have until today.'

'You kept this from me? Why?'

'Not all children conceived survive, so we had no idea whether the baby was ever born, but seeing her today, I can't think who else she could be.'

'Why did you aaaahhhh!' cried Solvan, suddenly pitching forward in agony. Essac moved forward to try to catch his son but was too late, and Solvan fell to the floor, gasping for breath. He lay there for only a moment before he slowly began to pick himself up off the floor. Essac reached out and grabbed his arm to help him to his feet. Once up, Solvan leaned against a tree, pale and gasping slightly for breath. Essac had never seen anything like it before.

'What happened?'

'I think,' Solvan gasped 'that it came through her.'

'She has been hurt?'

'I'm not sure, there was a feeling of overwhelming pain, but for some reason I don't think it was hers.'

'It would have to be someone close to her, though, for it to affect you both so much and not me,' Essac said as Solvan pushed himself away from the tree to stand without support, though swaying a little. 'But I now know where she is,' he said, and began to walk past his father towards the forest's boundaries.

'Solvan!' Essac shouted after his son, but he did not reply. With a sigh he followed and it did not take him long to catch up. Whatever had happened, Solvan had not recovered from it. He was walking using the trees as supports. 'Solvan, this is ridiculous, you need to rest. Tell me where to find her and I will bring her back to our home.'

'No. I need to find her, need to know she is all right.'

'Lean on me then, it will be easier,' Essac said, holding his arm out to his son. Solvan looked at it for a moment before taking it.

Essac had never seen his son like this before. Solvan was so much stronger than everyone else, he had become used to thinking of him as indestructible. Seeing him suffering now, Essac was unsure what to do.

Solvan placed most of his weight on his father. He knew he should listen to him, go and rest and let him look, but he saw time getting away from him and he felt so close to her at the moment, so close.

Essac was so lost in his own thoughts that when Solvan stumbled again he went down to the ground, taking Essac with him. Solvan just lay there this time, not moving. Essac crouched down next to him to see if he was all right, and found that he was just unconscious. Essac moved to stand up again when he noticed something and crouched down again to have a closer look at his son's hand. He picked it up carefully and saw that the burns the girl had given him when she had escaped were healing quickly, as expected, but what was very odd was that the patterning on his hand had changed slightly, had taken on some of her pattern traits. Essac was mystified, he had only ever heard of this happening once before. He needed to talk to Bahia, and Solvan needed to rest. Essac carefully pulled his son into his arms and stood up. Solvan was heavy, a dead weight. This was not going to be a good flight home, Essac realised.

⁂

Lovoa lay on the ground, shaking uncontrollably as the last of the wracking pain subsided, leaving her drained and exhausted. She pulled herself up onto her hands and knees, looked around her and realised that it was darker. One of the suns must have set but she would not know for sure until she was out of the forest. She carefully pushed herself into a sitting position and leaned against the trunk of a tree. As she moved, her vision blurred slightly and she was filled with the desire to just stay where she was until everything settled, but she knew she could not, knew she had to get home to her parents. She opened her mind up and searched for them, trying to find out what had happened, but found nothing. She had never been unable to feel them and their lack left an emptiness within her.

Her parents!

Frantically she pushed out harder and stronger with her mind, not caring for the moment that the male might find her, but there was nothing, her parents' minds were gone. Lovoa got cautiously to her feet, her whole body aching in the aftermath, her head spinning and her vision blurred. She took several deep breaths to steady herself before walking in the direction of her home. She staggered as she started to walk and was glad of the close-growing trees to help support her. As she moved, her eyesight started to clear and her balance returned, allowing her to move faster, without the need for support. The trees began to recede and she knew with relief that she was nearly home.

Lovoa ran out of the security of the forest and across the open field towards home, not even thinking about any dangers that might still be there. As she ran past the barn she could see their cabin. At first she thought the door was open but as she got closer she could see that a large hole now replaced it. Lovoa could not think what could have caused that damage or why? She started to run as quickly as she could, screaming her parents' names as loud as she could, both verbally and mentally, but her calls were met with silence. She arrived at the cabin and stopped at the doorway. She shouted again, and still getting no reply, she walked in. With one of the suns having set, the light coming in was limited and she could not see well. Her eyes adjusted to the reduced light quickly and as the shadows became objects, she could see the damage in the room and was horrified. The table was smashed, the chairs had all been knocked over and there were cups and plates on the floor where they had been knocked off the side. Carefully she walked across the room to check the bedrooms. They were untidy, as if they had been searched, but there was no damage. Whatever had happened was confined to the general room. Lovoa felt a glimmer of hope: her parents were not here so maybe they had gone somewhere too far away for her to sense them. Protector Buxus could have taken them, she realised, but she would have to check the barn first to make sure they were not there.

Lovoa left the cabin and had just started to walk towards the barn when something caught her eye, something was lying on the ground behind the cabin. 'Mother! Father!' she called again as she walked around the side. She heard a clunking sound and whispers she could not understand in response to her call. She opened her mind again but still could not feel her parents. Instead she felt intense darkness and alien feelings, the same as she had been feeling for the last two weeks, but greatly intensified. She stopped, knowing what she was experiencing was wrong and dangerous. Her parents were not here, she knew that, and no good was going to come of her staying here. She started to back away when something grabbed her from behind. She struggled but her arms were pinned to her sides by a strong band of what looked like arms but were larger than anything she had seen before and were grey and smooth. She kicked out and her feet encountered something very solid. Whatever held her made a noise like a laugh, and picking her up off her feet, it carried her to behind the cabin. What she saw there horrified her and she stopped fighting, too shocked by what was in front of her.

Two bodies were lying in pools of blood, and neither of them had any wings or skin left on their bodies. There was nothing left that anyone would have been able to identify them by, but Lovoa knew who they were and now she knew why she had felt as if she had been skinned alive and why she could no longer feel them. The bodies belonged to her parents. Her nightmares came back to her, the flashes of images that had haunted her for two weeks had all been real. How many had these things killed? These were traders, she realised. This is what her parents had been trying to tell her yesterday. She started to struggle again, kicking and screaming, but the thing's grasp just tightened around her in response. She heard it say something that she could not understand, and when it got a response, she looked up and saw that there were more of them. She had not noticed them before as her whole attention had been taken up by the dead bodies in front of her. Further away was a large, shining object and another of these things walked out and came towards them. It sounded as if they were talking to each other, but the sounds were strange to her.

'What an amazing specimen ensign, where did you find it?' the lieutenant asked.

'It was just coming out of the cabin.'

'I thought you said you'd searched it?'

'I did, I think she just got here.'

He walked forward and with one hand grabbed Lovoa by her head, while with the other pulled her hair way from her face so he could see her clearly. 'I don't think I have seen any of them so beautifully marked, she alone will earn us a fortune.'

Lovoa tried to pull her head away from the hard, cold grip, but could not. She did not need to understand what they were saying to know that they were talking about her and that she was about to end up the same way as her parents.

'Ensign, since you found her, would you please do the honours?' the lieutenant said.

'With pleasure boss,' and he let go of Lovoa. As her feet touched the ground again, he pushed her so she fell and landed next to her parents' bodies, her hands in their blood. She lifted her eyes from her soaked hands and turned and saw that the thing had something in his hand now and was coming towards her. He said something else, and it sounded as if the others were laughing at the comment. Anger overtook her feelings of fear. She was nothing to them, she realised. This thing had enjoyed killing her parents and was going to enjoy killing her while the others watched for entertainment. Out of instinct she started to pull in energy from the sun, the way she always did when she was hurt, hungry or tired, because it made her feel strong and now she needed to fight.

The thing was coming closer and she shouted, 'No!' in denial of what he was going to do. She put her hand up as if to stop him, but the gesture was full of the pain and anger channelling through her, and all the energy she had pulled into herself was released and hit the thing. She saw it fall and she scrambled to her feet and started to run, once clear of the buildings, she spread her wings and flew towards the forest, convinced that the others would be chasing her. In her panicked flight, she did not look where she was going. She should have stopped flying and started to run again once she reached the first trees, but she did not, and she hit a tree and fell to the ground. She pushed herself to her hands and feet and continued to stumble through the forest and did not stop until she found the hole in the ground her parents had shown her as a child, with instructions to come here and hide if told to do so. She climbed in and collapsed onto the floor, shaking and shocked. She kept listening for any sounds that she had been followed, but there was nothing and after a while even their alien presence began to recede and she fell into an exhausted sleep.

∗

The lieutenant had not believed his luck when that girl had shown up. He had been dreading going back to the main ship with those two skins and explaining why they had landed to begin with when they were only meant to be scouting the area for their next targets. He had gone back out to see what was taking so long and seen her in the ensign's arms. He had been on several raids but had never seen anyone like her, and the boss was going to be very happy with the skin.

He stood there with the rest of his men and she was pushed into the blood of the other two.

'Ready to join the others?' he asked jokingly as he approached her, but then she shouted and put her hand up. A burst of something came out of her hand and hit the ensign and he crumpled to the ground. She scrambled to her feet and ran away. After a stunned moment, the others started to follow her.

'Stop!' he shouted.

'She's getting away,' they protested but obeyed the order.

'Do you want to end up the same way?' he asked them and pointed to the body.

Lying where he had fallen, the ensign was clearly dead and in two halves, but inspecting the body they realised that the blast had not ripped him in half as it appeared from a distance, but had disintegrated the majority of his torso, leaving only his head, arms, upper chest and legs. There was no blood because the heat of whatever had hit him had sealed the wounds and melted the material of his suit. The lieutenant did not know at what temperature the suits would melt but he knew they were built to withstand extreme heat.

'Christ!' his men cursed.

'What did she do?' None of them had ever seen anything like it before.

'Get him on board, we are leaving now.'

'You want to bring him back?'

'The captain is going to want to see this, and I don't want to be here in case she decides to come back, do you?' he questioned.

The others quickly picked up the body parts and carried them back onto the shuttle. The doors closed and they headed back to the main ship. The captain was not going to like this.

When they got back to the ship, the captain most certainly did not like it. 'Explain to me what the fuck you thought you were doing?' he demanded.

'While we were scanning the area, we saw a male with impressive markings. I thought it would be a good opportunity to get a valuable skin, so we landed, but when we got to the location, he had left and there were only two left. We decided to take the skins since we were there. We had skinned them and were about to leave when a young female arrived, and she had the most amazing skin I have ever seen.'

'Yet you haven't brought her skin back with you.'

'We were going to, but she did something and killed Edwards. I had his body brought back for you to see.'

'Explain further.'

'She was on the floor. Edwards was about to skin her when she let off this blast, then she was running away and Edwards was dead and in two pieces. His torso had been disintegrated, the skin cauterised and his suit melted. I ordered my men not to chase her as I thought she would kill everyone else who got close and it was important to get back to report to you.'

'Where is the body now?'

'It's still in the shuttle, I didn't know where to put it.'

'I want to see it now, and get the doctor to meet us there.' Together they went back to the shuttle, where the doctor was already waiting for them. They went in and let the doctor examine the remains.

'You said that one of these people did this?' the doctor asked.

'Yes,' the lieutenant said.

'What do you think, doctor?' the captain asked.

'It's not just the wound that has been cauterised, his whole body has been cooked with the heat of whatever killed him. If that was not bad enough, the material of the suit has melted. I have dealt with bodies killed in many different ways, from fire fights on planets, bombs and ships that have exploded, but I have never seen the suits melt in this way. The temperature needed would be phenomenal.'

'Thank you, doctor.' the captain said, then to his lieutenant, 'Call in the other shuttles. As soon as they are in, we will leave, drop off the skins we have and then rethink our tactics.'

'Yes sir. Can I ask why the sudden change of plans over a death?'

'Read the old logs, it looks like these people are starting to remember how they used to defend themselves.'

⚹

Bahia felt when her son started to regain consciousness and went up to his room. She knocked and when told to come in, she opened the door and saw him sitting on the bed with his head in his hands. As she walked in he looked up at her and smiled reassuringly.

'How are you feeling?'

'Better, I think,' he replied.

'How much do you remember?'

'Everything. Unfortunately. I am sorry Mother.'

'You have nothing to apologise for, you were just doing what you thought was right.'

'I'm not so sure Father understands.'

'Trust me, he does. Will I see you in the living room shortly?' she asked and he nodded acknowledgement.

Solvan sighed as his mother left his room and rubbed his face in frustration. He had regained his senses as his father had arrived back home. He had been furious with him for bringing him back and had wanted to leave straightaway, but without the physical support from his father, he had just collapsed again. He assumed his parents had put him to bed, as he certainly could not remember how he had got here. He had never been so overwhelmed before and he could only imagine that it had come from her. His heart twisted over what must have happened to her for him to be overpowered by it. It was reassuring to know that she was still alive from the waves of emotion he was feeling. He got up and went down to join his parents. He was embarrassed when he saw his father sitting at the table and he went and sat down next to him.

'Good morning, Solvan. How are you feeling?'

'Better, thank you. I'm sorry about yesterday, I should never have spoken to you as I did.'

'It's all right, you were feeling a lot of emotions, and most of them were not yours.'

'It doesn't feel all right,' he said.

Essac laid a reassuring hand on his son's shoulder. 'You are so used to being able to block everything that this is new to you. If you had not been so strong, you would have learnt long ago how to manage this. We have all been there,' Essac reassured him. Solvan covered his father's hand and squeezed it in silent acceptance of what he could not voice. 'What do you think happened?'

'I think her parents were killed, she was frantic over them.'

'That would explain a lot. You are of similar strength and have already created a connection, which is rare. What do you plan to do?'

'Try and find her. She opened up her mind and gave away her location. If I leave now, she might still be there.'

Chapter 12

AS Lovoa started to regain consciousness, she became aware of a dull, throbbing pain. She lay still and wondered what had happened, everything seemed so blurred in her mind. The throbbing became annoying and she started to turn over to lie on her back, thinking that it might help. As she moved the pain became sharp and excruciating, forcing her to go back onto her stomach. Her hands clenched the ground beneath her in reaction. Slowly the pain returned to its persistent throbbing and she started to notice where she was. She was lying on the floor in the hole her parents had shown her years ago and not in her bed as she had originally thought. She remembered being chased through the forest – had she fallen?

Cautiously she began to move as she needed to see how she had injured herself and get back into the sunlight so she could heal. The pain was worst in her wing she realised, but she would not be able to see anything down here. Carefully, she climbed out of the hole, taking care not to knock her back in any way. Once out in the limited sunlight, she took off her cloak and turned her head to see her wing, but it had folded against her back. Slowly she began to open it out, and by the time it was fully extended, she was shaking with the effort and the pain in her back. Now that she could see it, she sighed with relief: there was no damage to her wing. She could just make out bruising across her back around the wing joint, but could not see it well enough to assess the injury. Checking herself through the dirt that covered her, she could find nothing more than cuts and more bruising. Slowly she folded her wings back behind her, the last thing she wanted was to knock them any further and cause more damage. How she was going to explain everything to her parents she did not know. She reached out with her mind to tell them to stop panicking, she was coming home, but found nothing.

All the events she could not quite remember suddenly became crystal clear and she was overwhelmed by grief and loneliness. She sank back down to the floor and held her head in her hands as she cried for their loss.

How long she sat there she did not know, but she knew she could not stay there forever. She thought about going back to the farm, if only to collect a few things she might need and bury her parents, but then she remembered those things. She had been lucky to escape alive and with her skin intact, but would they be waiting for her to come back? She could not take the risk and would not be able to honour her parents' bodies as she should.

She was so tired that she thought about staying a little longer, to sleep, to mourn, but the light was increasing, which raised the question again of how long she had been unconscious. When she had been attacked, the first sun was descending. Now was the time for her to move, she knew, when she could use the sun to heal and give her the strength she so desperately needed, but where could she go?

Could she set up a farm on her own as her parents had? It could not be too hard to find a patch of land, maybe move into one of the cabins that had belonged to a family that had moved onto Protector Buxus's collective. No, it would not be possible, she realised. Her family had struggled and there had been three of them, and the next planting cycle was due and she had nothing to plant and nothing to exchange to get it. She also knew that she would make herself easy to find and attract the attention of the protectors. No, she could not set up a farm on her own, but what else to do?

She had overheard her parents talking about unrest at Protector Ovato's collective. They had commented that if some of his workers became independent farmers, they would replace the ones Protector Buxus had forced onto his collective. If her parents had thought that workers could leave without being noticed, could she join one? Her parents said that she was different, special, which is why she had been hidden, but she had not understood what they had meant. If she went to Protector Ovato's collective, then she was sure she would be far enough away from anyone who had known them and she would be safe. She put her cloak back on and slowly made her way out of the forest, taking a different route to her normal one as she did not want to come out anywhere near the farm. In her mind, she said goodbye to her parents and asked them to forgive her. The suns were up as she left the relative safety of the forest. She sighed her relief and seeing and sensing no one near, she took off her cloak and let the suns' rays fall on her skin. It would have been better if she had not been so filthy from lying on the floor, most of her skin was covered with dirt, but there was not much she could do about it at the moment. She headed in what she hoped was the direction of Protector Ovato's collective. She decided that if she felt anyone close, she would put her cloak on, just in case.

*

Solvan saw the farm from a distance as he flew towards it. From the sky it looked peaceful, there was no one in the fields in front of the cabin. Wary because he was sure the distress he had felt had come from here, he circled around before landing. As the rear of the property come into view, his heart sank. There on the ground, several metres behind the cabin, were the burn marks that he had seen at every trader attack and he prayed to Hannoki that she had not been here. He felt nothing dark and alien nearby and was as sure as he could be that they had left. He landed behind the cabin and saw the two skinned bodies. As with all the others, it was impossible to identify the remains but he was sure they had been the girl's parents. He walked away from them, wanting to search the cabin and the surrounding area to see if she was still here, hiding, hurt. He could not sense her again but he had to believe that she was alive and just blocking him out. He was convinced that as he had felt her pain so clearly, he would feel her death.

There were two small burn marks on the grass nearby with a strange substance mixed in with it that he could not explain. He went around and into the cabin and saw the struggle that must have taken place, the smashed table and broken cups and plates on the floor. He checked the other rooms, but she was not there. He walked back out and looked towards the forest. If she had been here, he knew that she would have escaped back there. He thought about going in to the forest to try and track her, but though he had not been successful last time, maybe this time she had not been as careful, as she had been careless when she had first run from him. It could wait a short while he decided. He knew that she would not come back here if she had seen this. Her parents needed to be buried and not left out to rot, so he went and searched for the tools which every farmer had for the fields in order to dig their graves. He had buried every other farmer, and had asked his father to try and organise people to go to Gilcan's collective to arrange the mass burials as best he could. He could not leave these two people who had cared for, and meant so much to, the girl just because he was desperate to find her.

✳

The sun helped Lovoa to shake off some of her weariness but did nothing for her grief. As she saw cabins and cultivated fields, she put the cloak back on with reluctance, as a lifetime's habit of covering up, of hiding, took over. She thought her actions silly as she was going to try to join a collective and work with others, and she would not be able to hide any more.

Lovoa had started walking in what she thought was the right direction from overheard conversations, but as the suns rose higher and higher in the sky, all she saw were the occasional independent farms. She saw a few people working in the fields, and they would look up and watch her pass, worried that she might cause them problems. One or two were curious as to why she was covered up while the suns were out and Lovoa noticed that no one else was. She fingered the cloak and thought about taking it off again, but could not bear to do it, not yet. Perhaps when she had been among other people more she would consider it. Her legs started to ache, she had never walked so far before and if she chose to fly, then the cloak would have to be removed. Flying had come easily to her, she had taught herself, much to her parents' amazement and horror, while they were in the fields. They had returned one day to see her happily gliding around the cabin and barn. They had yelled at her as she could be seen for a considerable distance, so she had never really had the chance to see how far she could go.

The first of the suns had started to descend when Lovoa decided she needed to ask if she was going the right way. She had been under the impression that Protector Ovato's collective was the next nearest to

Protector Buxus's, so surely she should have reached it by now?

She decided to approach the next workers she saw in a field. She pulled the hood further down over her face and wrapped the cloak tighter around herself in a defensive gesture. They looked at her with suspicion as she went towards them but waited to find out what she wanted.

'Hello,' she greeted them, 'can you help me?'

At her question they relaxed slightly, but were still doubtful of her intentions.

'What do you want?' the male replied, stepping forward.

'Am I going the right way for Protector Ovato's collective? I didn't think it was far away, but I have been walking a long time.'

'You are going in the right direction. You should reach the outer fields in about a half day's walk, but it's not a good place to be at the moment,' he warned her.

'Why?' she asked, hopeful that they may know more than her parents had.

'The protector is treating everyone badly, too much work and not enough food.'

'Thank you,' Lovoa said and started walking towards the collective. Half a day's walk, she thought to herself. She would do well to try and find somewhere to spend the night so she would have the next day to try and find someone who would be able to help her find a place to sleep and work on a field. She walked for a while longer. As she got closer, she started to encounter fields which were barren and cabins which needed repair. If they had been abandoned, perhaps she could stay in one of them overnight, she thought. Tired and sore, she came to another one. Cautiously, she sent her mind out and sensed no one. She went to the cabin and pushed the door open, shouting to make absolutely sure it was empty.

As expected, there was no reply. Opening the door, she saw the layer of dirt that had settled over everything and she knew beyond all doubt that it had been abandoned. She closed the door behind her and took off her cloak. She checked all the storage areas hoping that some food had been left behind, but there was nothing. She sighed and resigned herself to being hungry. There wasn't even any water to wash the dirt off herself. She was so filthy she could barely see the markings on her arms and legs, and she could only assume that her face was as dirty. Cloak or no cloak, she was not going to benefit from the suns' rays until she was clean. She searched the rest of the cabin and found a bed, at least she was going to have a reasonably comfortable night's sleep, and she settled down for the evening.

⚜

Eventually he was told that the messenger had returned. 'Do not just stand there, show him in!' Protector Buxus snapped at the servant. A few moments later, another male walked in. 'Well! What did you find out?'

'I am sorry, my Protector, but Protector Gilcan's collective has been destroyed.'

'What did the survivors say happened?'

'There were no survivors, Protector,' the messenger said. 'There were people there who had been sent by the first protectors to bury the dead, but they said they had found no one alive.'

'There were thousands on that collective,' Protector Buxus stated.

'Yes, Protector, there were piles and piles of bodies stacked in every field.'

'Still?'

'They are trying to bury them as quickly as possible, but there are just so many.'

'Protector Gilcan?' he asked.

'There was no sign of him, his castle was destroyed.'

'You may go.' As the messenger left, Buxus got up and paced his room. After a while he sent for his steward.

'I want you to find the plans for the battlements and get them repaired as quickly as possible. Warn all the men that the traders have returned. Get them to the independent farms and get those people here even if they have to be dragged kicking and screaming from their land,' he ordered when the steward arrived.

'Yes, Protector,' he replied.

'Get some people together, volunteers, to go to Protector Gilcan's collective and help bury the dead.'

'Yes, Protector. How many dead are there?'

'The whole collective.'

'I will arrange it straightaway.'

Protector Buxus continued to pace for a while longer after the steward left before leaving the room and walking up to the battlements. Mesrra and Fesrun had not got back to him and what he had just been told made it imperative that he got his hands on their daughter. He had gone there first to protect his daughter's interests, but now he was looking at protecting his collective – she could defend his land, she could mate with his son and improve his family's strength.

He jumped off the battlements and flew to the farm. It occurred to him too late that they might have fled, but what he saw when he got there was worse, he landed and stood by the grave. He had no way of knowing how many bodies were in it, but he thought that he would have felt her passing if she had died. He knew that she was not going to come to him, for if she had planned to, she would already have arrived. Now he would have to try and find her.

⁂

Lovoa woke after sleeping surprisingly well. For the first time in weeks she had had a dreamless sleep, the nightmares and the continual alien feeling had gone, bringing with it a great sense of relief. The suns were starting to rise again and she was hungry and thirsty. It was time for her to be moving on, she knew, as there was nothing in the cabin to alleviate her need. Even through the dirt the suns would help, but not if she wore the cloak, so she wrapped it up, relying on the dirt to cover her, and with a feeling of regret, she left the safety of the cabin.

Even with the limited amount of sun she could take in, she felt better being outside and was able to suppress the worst of her hunger and thirst. As the suns climbed higher in the sky, she started to see more people. Some were walking away from the collective, and a few people stopped and warned her not to continue, that she would regret it if she did, but she only saw her chance to work and get the few things she needed to survive.

Lovoa kept on walking and as the first sun reached its peak, she arrived at the first of the collective's fields. As she walked further into the collective, she saw more cabins, similar to the one she had lived in with her parents, and huge fields that spread further than the eye could see. She had never imagined one person could own so much. Now she was here she realised that she did not know how they were run or who she needed to approach. She could see people in the fields but she had expected more. She thought about approaching the workers directly because surely they must know who oversaw them, but even with the blocks in place around her mind she could still sense their desperation and starvation. The cabins she could see were all in need of repair, some had even collapsed and the shells left to decay. Maybe the independent farmer had been right when he had warned her not to come here, but where else could she go?

She decided to keep going. It might be that things would be better as she got closer to the centre, but nothing changed, still only a few people in each field and, strangely, most were elderly or children – where was everyone else?

A line of black smoke started to rise up a short distance in front of her. The people in the fields saw it as well and Lovoa could feel their fear but knew that she would not be able to discern its cause unless she opened her mind up, which she was not prepared to do yet. Something was on fire, but in the dry conditions of summer, fires were not unusual and could spread quickly. Whoever was in charge would be organising the workers to put out the fire. If she helped, someone might help her in return, so she quickened her pace towards the source of the smoke.

It was not long before she started to smell the smoke, felt it sting her eyes and catch in the back of her throat as she breathed. It was quickly becoming thick and black and as the wind blew towards her, it filled the air. Whatever was burning was not under control. As she got closer to the fire, the cabins were built very close together. She had hoped the conditions of them would be better, but they were not, and even through the smoke she could see that most of them needed to be rebuilt; surely people were not forced to live in such conditions. It was not just what she could see, but also smell. Even over the acidic smoke she could smell dirt and rot. She used her cloak to try and cover her nose to block the smell out, feeling sick from the intensity of it. She could see no one, they must all be trying to put the fire out. If it got totally out of control, it would consume all of the cabins she was passing. She soon heard the sounds of a crowd, so she followed the sound as she could no longer see where the smoke was coming from over the tops of the cabins – it now just filled the air.

The noise got louder and louder, and the smoke so thick she was struggling through it. They must be near to getting it under control, she thought, as she turned the corner.

A large building was alight and she could feel the heat of the flames coming from it. A large crowd surrounded it and none of them were trying to put it out. A section of the building collapsed and the crowd cheered. Shocked, Lovoa stopped. She had never seen so many people in her life, they filled the space between herself and the burning building. What was going on here? Why was no one putting the fire out?

She saw a second group of people approach the crowd and a fight broke out between them. A rush of anger washed over her. At first she was confused as to why they were feeling like this and by the sheer intensity of their emotions hitting her shields, wave after wave. They hated their protector and were tired of being hungry and living in homes that were in poor condition, which they had neither the time nor the means to fix themselves.

Lovoa relaxed her shields slightly, as curiosity and the need to know more of what was going on outweighed her fear of being found by the male from the pool. She doubted that he would be able to distinguish her mind from everyone else's here. She got a rush of thoughts and emotions and, concentrating, she was able to pick up more personal details. One young man was angry because the protector had taken his father away as punishment for falling behind in his work and he had not been seen since. Another was angry because he had lost two of his children to starvation as he had not had the means to feed them as the taxes were too high.

The fire had not been an accident, she realised, it had been started deliberately to hurt the person they saw as directly responsible for their pain and suffering. They could not get to the protector, so they had attacked the person in charge of running the collective, the one who took pleasure in enforcing his orders and showed no leniency.

The feelings started to make Lovoa's head ache, she was being bombarded with so much emotion and she was not used to it. She started to take deep breaths, fought for control and slowly managed to mute the thoughts and feelings and became more aware of where she was. As she had been concentrating, she had left her hiding place and walked towards the crowd, but this was the last place she wanted to be as the mood of the crowd was getting more and more violent.

Lovoa saw that the guards were moving away from the crowd. What were they doing? Retreating or waiting for reinforcements?

A tingling sensation caused Lovoa to shiver. What was that? All of a sudden, the man in front of her fell to the floor, groaning in agony. She paused, wondering what to do, then as she bent to help him, the tingling feeling came again. Looking around her, she saw the blast come from the castle and hit another peasant, who collapsed. The blasts came again and again, and when she looked up to the nearby fortifications, Lovoa saw a large male with several others standing behind him. As she watched, others joined him and also started attacking. As the blasts came, the crowd began to panic and ran away from the danger. Lovoa did not move quickly enough and was pushed to the floor by the retreating crowd. Once down, she was constantly knocked and kicked by the panicking people. She felt their fear and their suspicions that anyone who was left would be removed by the waiting guards. Every time someone else was hit, the panic increased and screams could clearly be heard.

Then Lovoa saw her through the legs of the running peasants, a child on the floor. She was lying curled up on the ground and people did not see her and were tripping over her. Some turned back to see what had nearly caused them to fall but none stayed to help her up. Was she even alive? Lovoa thought for a moment, and then, as if in answer to the silent question, the child moved, pulling her limbs even tighter into herself, if that was even possible.

Lovoa gave up trying to get up off the ground, and instead, on her hands and knees, she forced her way through the crowd, not caring if she caused others to fall over her. They could fend for themselves; the young girl could not. People were being knocked off their feet all around her and the tingling feeling was irritating her mind. Finally, Lovoa reached the girl and put her hand on her shoulder. With the contact, the girl's absolute fear washed over her for a second until she was able to block it out. She could feel the girl shaking under her touch.

'I have come to help you,' Lovoa shouted but got no response. It was doubtful whether the girl had even heard her over the noise of the crowd. Lovoa grabbed her and pulled her up so she had to look at her. She was met with a very thin, dirty, tear-streaked face. The girl fell into her arms easily, as if she had instinctively recognised her best chance of survival and escaping the fleeing crowd. As Lovoa held her tightly and began to force herself to her feet, more than ready to leave as quickly as possible, the tingling came again, but this time stronger, more focused, focused at her. It gave her the second's warning she needed to turn and see a blast coming straight for her. She put up her free arm as if to ward off the blast and imagined a barrier in front of her. She felt the same tingling in her arm as she had before, with the male at the pool and with those things that had killed her parents. The blast stopped just inches away from her arm, then a second one came, then a third, each one more powerful than the last. Then came one that was not short and sharp like the others had been, but was continual and battered at her quickly and poorly created shield. Lovoa felt more than one mind attacking her, and knew that her shield was wavering and would fail soon. She did not know how to strengthen it or even how she had made it to start with, and with the child clinging to her, she feared that when she lost the barrier, the force of the attack would kill them. Lovoa was determined that the child should not be hurt, she was too young and nothing that had happened today or in the days, weeks, leading up to this would have been her fault in any way. Anger built up in her, and with one mental push she let the barrier go and pushed out, as she had done at the clearing. The attack stopped. Exhausted, Lovoa stood up and turned to leave, but she felt the tingling too late and collapsed onto the floor.

⁕

The peasants had been protesting outside for the last few hours. At first Protector Ovato had been annoyed by the protests. He had ordered his guard to break them up and had thought no more of it, but as attempts were made to suppress the group, more and more peasants had joined in and fought back against his men. His captain had come to him trying to make excuses for the ongoing disorder, telling him that there were more peasants than they had anticipated. Ovato did not understand the problem. He told the captain that if there were more peasants, use more men to break them up, use any means available on them. He thought that would be the end of the matter.

The last report infuriated him. They had set the steward's residence on fire and the crowd was not letting anyone close to extinguish it. How had his guards let it get this far? He had ordered his captain to just finish it and said he did not care how he did it, but he could feel the exhilaration of the group as the building burned. They felt secure in their numbers and were not concerned about his men stopping them. Where had they acquired the confidence to defy him? He felt their joy and heard their shouts of success as part of the steward's home fell down. The guards tried again to break them up but were easily rebuffed.

He did not need this now; he already had enough to deal with, with Gilcan and his family showing up at his collective a few days before. Gilcan did not seem to be happy about having to ask for help from him, and probably would not have done so if it were not for his younger children, who were in shock. Pesline had been hysterical when she had arrived, screaming that the traders had arrived and begging and pleading for his help and protection. He had tried to tell her she was being ridiculous and had been paying too much attention to the first protectors, but she would not listen and started screaming at him, telling him her home had been destroyed and that they had nearly all been killed. She had told him of the day it had happened and Ovato had remembered the pain he had suffered and started to have his doubts. He would have someone go and look to see what had happened at the collective, but he had decided to take them in on his own terms. Pesline and Cardoc had not been a problem but Gilcan had immediately started to tell everyone about the traders and how they would all die if Ovato did not do his duty. It had upset so many of his people that Gilcan was now restricted to the rooms his family had been allocated

and was not allowed to leave unless one of his guards
went with him. It was bad enough that the peasants were
now revolting outside; if he was not careful, they would
be revolting inside as well, courtesy of Gilcan.

He demanded that the captain come before him again
to explain how he had let things get as far as he had.

'You are a fool,' Protector Ovato shouted, 'you should
have stopped this at the beginning; you should have
made it clear that to defy me would be punished with
extreme force.'

'It took time to get the men together. There was nothing
we could do, they outnumbered us from the start,' said
the captain, trying to justify himself.

'I do not want your pathetic excuses for your
incompetence!' Ovato shouted as he paced the room
in frustration. His guard either could not or would not
finish the revolt. 'Inform Protector Pesline and Cardoc
to join me on the battlements. I will finish this myself,'
he decided and stormed out of the room, leaving the
captain to follow his orders.

Ovato could hear the peasants as he approached the
battlements, and as he opened the door the noise was
overwhelming and the heat of the fire extreme. If it were
not put out, he knew it could easily spread to his castle.
How the peasants could stand so close to it he did not
know. Looking down, he was surprised by how many
had gathered – were any left in the fields?

Not bothering to wait for Pesline or Cardoc to arrive,
he gathered his energy together and fired on the
peasants below. They were standing so close together
that he did not need to aim: he was guaranteed to hit
someone. He had got off two more shots before Pesline
and Cardoc arrived. They came and stood next to him
on the battlements and looked down on the chaos. The
peasants had started to realise what was happening and

the mass had started to disperse rapidly. People were running in every direction, as fast as they could.

'Well, are you planning on helping me, or are you just going to stand there?' he snapped as he let off another energy blast. He felt, rather than saw, Pesline and Cardoc gather their energy together to join him in assaulting the peasants. He smiled when he heard Cardoc laugh as he hit a peasant directly and sent him sprawling in the dirt, clearly taking pleasure from the fear and pain they were causing to those below them. He was a boy after his own heart, for all of his father's twisted ideals.

They were just sending the blasts down randomly when suddenly Ovato encountered a resistance; his blast had hit a shield. He gathered his energy and sent a second blast, then a third, each one stronger than the last, and all of them were blocked. Who was down there who could do that? He tried to see who it was, but he was too far away. All he could make out was two people huddled on the floor. He gathered everything he had and sent out the energy, not as a blast but as a constant stream. He was going to break that shield. He again hit the resistance.

'Help me,' he instructed Pesline and Cardoc. They turned and saw what was happening. They stopped their assault and each placed a hand on Ovato and put their energy into him. Too late he felt the retaliation as the energy was sent back at him – the last thing he remembered was flying backwards and hitting a wall with force.

Cardoc saw the returning energy a second before it hit. He let go of Ovato and had started to step back as it hit and he watched as Ovato was thrown backwards. Cardoc went to the edge of the battlements and saw the pair on the floor stagger to their feet and turn and leave. He gathered the last of his strength and sent a last blast down, and saw with satisfaction that they collapsed onto the floor and did not move. He would leave it to the guards to collect them.

✳

'Ayne!' Kesli screamed as she saw the young child go down. She had been searching frantically for both her daughter and mate ever since she had felt his pain. She knew they were still alive but nothing more, then suddenly she saw her daughter knocked to the floor by the panicking crowd a few metres in front of her and she was helpless. She tried to push through the crowd to get to her, but everyone was going in the opposite direction and would not let her through. Then she saw someone else reach her daughter. 'Please, please let them be trying to help her,' she thought, then, as if seeing it in slow motion, she saw Protector Ovato send an energy beam down towards her daughter and the stranger. She knew from witnessing the people who had been hit groaning in pain on the floor that the blasts were not strong enough to kill an adult, but what if it hit her child? Would it kill Ayne? Just as she thought the blast would hit them, a shield appeared around her daughter and the stranger. Kesli looked on in amazement. Who could possibly be strong enough to defy the protector? The blast was followed by a second and then a third, and each one was blocked by this person. Kesli felt relief and again started to force her way through the crowd, but then another blast came, but this one was different. It was a constant stream and seemed to last a lifetime to Kesli, but then it ended abruptly as the attack stopped. Kesli could not see the protector on the battlements any more. She had no idea what had just happened but she could not believe that the attack had finally stopped as she saw the stranger struggling to her feet, holding her little girl, but then one last blast came through and hit the stranger on the back and sent them sprawling on the ground. Kesli finally broke through the crowd and ran to her daughter. The stranger was lying on the floor with her daughter underneath. In a panicked moment, Kesli wondered if they had both been killed, but when she rolled the body over, there was her daughter curled in a ball and crying and she thanked Hannoki that she was safe as she gathered her up in her arms.

After she had calmed her daughter down slightly and assured herself that other than a few bruises, she was unhurt, she turned to her daughter's saviour. Surely he must be dead, but as she examined the body, she could not believe what she saw: a small, filthy and battered girl, and everything about her, other than her strength, screamed peasant.

'Kesli?' She turned and saw her mate as he struggled through the crowd. He looked ill and held his side.

'We can't leave her, she ... she...'

'I know, I saw,' he replied, brushing the hair off the girl's face. 'We'll take her home, try and hide her.' Kesli nodded in agreement.

⁕

Many of the guards saw what had happened and, like everyone else, had a lot of questions concerning who that person was. The person who had defied the protector was so covered in dirt that it had been impossible to identify any markings. However, one of the guards recognised the female who had run to the pair after they collapsed and had grabbed the young child. He had tried to tell his senior officer but was not able to due to the chaos all around them, so he had watched them and saw that she was joined by her mate and a few others, and they had carried the unconscious person away. He could not stop them now, but he knew where they were likely to take the stranger.

⚜

Essac soon had reason to be grateful that he had not gone with his son on his search for the girl. He got the occasional updates from Solvan but none were very hopeful, especially when he reported that he believed her parents had been killed by the traders. Essac was with his mate, going through all the old documents, when he began to get irritable. At first he ignored it, thinking it was just the situation that was getting to him. He sighed and rubbed his neck, trying to ease the building tension, then noticed that Bahia was doing exactly the same thing. He met her eyes over the table and he realised that there was more to what they were both feeling. Essac sat up straight, took a deep breath and began to concentrate, clearing his mind to see if he could locate the place from where the feelings were coming.

'Ovato, damn him!' he said with force, hitting the table.

'What is he up to?' Bahia asked.

'Hannoki only knows. It feels like he is letting out bursts of energy at something, but I have not detected any traders.'

'Neither have I,' replied Bahia. She moved to sit next to him, took his hands in her own and filtered her own energy into him. Essac again closed his eyes and concentrated on Ovato. With the extra strength, he could see further and more clearly, he felt his mind fly free and he could see outside his mountain and surrounding area.

'Damn him,' Essac cursed again as he saw what was happening. He saw the fire and the peasants gathering around it en mass and Ovato firing at them from the battlements.

'What is it? What is he doing?' Bahia asked.

'It looks like his peasants are revolting, a building is on fire and they are all around it. He has started firing at them.'

'Oh Hannoki,' Bahia whispered, 'how could he? Is he killing them?'

'I could not tell. He had better not be or he will not hear the end of it. I had better go and deal with it' he said, letting go of Bahia's hands and getting to his feet.

'No,' Bahia said, halting him, 'send Solvan.'

'He will not go, he is looking for the girl.'

'No, Solvan would be better at dealing with this.' She smiled, shrugged, 'He's getting nowhere trying to find her; he needs a new challenge to focus him.'

'And?' he enquired. 'I know you too well, what else is on your mind?'

'It did occur to me that if I was looking for somewhere to hide, that collective might be a good place to go. She can't go home, and she could see the forest as too dangerous as that is where she encountered Solvan. Ovato's collective is large and disorganised and near to her home, who would look for her there?'

Essac just looked at his mate for a moment and knew that she was serious. 'I will contact him.'

Chapter 13

AFTER burying the bodies, Solvan went and searched the forest in the hope that the girl had left a trail he could follow, and though he had seen broken branches, he had no way of knowing when this had occurred or what had caused it, and it had led to nothing. She seemed to know the area well and would know where she could hide, so he had returned to the farm. Now he stood by the cabin and opened up his mind. He had no real hope of finding her this way, she seemed to have spent her whole life hiding from people, both mentally and physically, and with her strength he would not be able to find her unless she wanted to be found, but he could think of nothing else to do. He was sure that she would not approach a collective and he could not see how she could set up an independent farm on her own, without any support from others. The only option he thought she had was to return here and collect as many supplies as possible, and to return to wherever she was, which is why he was here now.

He felt it as a slight distortion in his mind. At first he did not recognise what he was feeling, but when he concentrated on the source, he realised that someone was letting out bursts of energy. What was going on? He was about to contact his father when he heard his father's voice in his mind.

'*Solvan!*'

'*I was just going to call you. Do you know what's happening?*'

'Ovato is attacking his workers. It appears that they have set fire to a building and are protesting. The guards have tried to break it up but they are too heavily outnumbered.'

'Hannoki curse him,' Solvan swore.

'Are you able to go there and deal with this? You are nearer and though it's of little use without the protectors' support, I'm reluctant to leave the power base in case there is another attack.'

'That will not be a problem, I will be more than happy to deal with Ovato,' Solvan said, furious that he could behave this way against his people.

'Thank you – will you keep me informed?'

'Of course,' and with that Solvan broke the connection.

He had spoken to Ovato about the traders a few days ago. Ovato had been the most arrogant and obstinate of all the protectors, refusing even to consider that the return of the traders was a possibility, and had tried to order him off his collective. Solvan had felt the tension among the workers and had tried to warn Ovato that he would need to look at how he treated his people if he did not want to lose them. Solvan had thought he was warning him against his workers leaving for another collective or setting up as independents, but a revolt like this was unprecedented, and for Ovato to be attacking those he was supposed to protect...

Solvan took to the air, determined to deal with Ovato as quickly as possible. He must be stopped and taught how to do his duty, and replaced if necessary. He was frustrated at having to break off his search but he understood his parents' reluctance to leave the mountain top in case the traders attacked again, and Ovato had to be dealt with immediately.

Now that he understood what he was feeling, Solvan felt other minds joining the attack against the workers and assumed that either other members of Gilcan's family were assisting or that Gilcan had arrived to help with the attack. This only added to his foul mood – if Gilcan was helping, then obviously he was not only content with killing all of his own workers, but was also attacking workers from another collective.

He felt the change from short blasts to a long, constant blast. He concentrated on this and could tell that Ovato had met resistance. Solvan smiled to himself as he felt the other minds joining to help. Ovato could not defeat this person on his own, so who was that strong? Then the obvious answer came, it had to be his girl, it could be no one else. Just as he realised this, he felt her retaliation and recognised her mind, and everything stopped. Solvan laughed to himself as Ovato had unwittingly given him the knowledge he wanted. He increased his pace – he had to get to her before Ovato and his men did. Ovato would not take the knowledge of her existence well, let alone her actions against him.

╬

Lovoa slowly became aware of her surroundings. She smelt dirt, not the foul stench of the filth near the burning building, but from the fields; it smelt like home. She stretched and felt a rough material under her, and knew that she was not at home. Her head ached and it seemed to take forever for her to gather her thoughts. With an effort, she opened her eyes and looked about her and saw that the style of the room was the same as hers had been, but nothing else was familiar. Where was she?

She pushed herself into a sitting position, wincing as her whole body ached. She remembered the fire and the crowd around it. She remembered the panic and the little girl, and then the attack on her. What had happened after that?

Lovoa saw that there was only a small, shuttered

window that did not let much light into the room. She thought that was strange as she was used to large, open windows that took up much of the wall to allow the winds to blow through during a storm, reducing damage to the cabin. From what she could see, she was sitting on a filthy, very worn mat placed on the floor, and there was a second one lying next to her, which was in the same poor state. She assumed that these must be what passed for their beds, as she could see nothing else in the room. A noise came from next door. Lovoa turned her head towards the doorway, which was covered with a rug, just as it was pushed aside and someone came through it. A woman walked in, paused and smiled when she saw Lovoa sitting up on the mat. Lovoa could not see her clearly as there was only a weak light coming through from the room behind, but she could tell that she was extremely thin. As she walked into the room and knelt next to her, Lovoa could see her better. She could not tell how old she was, but guessed that she was young, probably not much older than herself, but harsh living had aged her well before her time. In her hand was a bowl, which she held out to Lovoa.

'Please, eat,' she said. As Lovoa reached out and took the bowl from her, she saw that it was small and cracked around the edges, and in it was a thin liquid. Tentatively, Lovoa tried it. It was cold and slightly grainy, and she did not recognise what it was, but her stomach reacted immediately to the food and she realised how hungry she was. How long had it been since she had last eaten? Lovoa could not remember. She ate it all quickly – too quickly, she realised, as her stomach protested slightly – and handed the bowl back. She did not like to ask for more, even though she desperately wanted to, as it was clear that this stranger had so little. As soon as Lovoa had handed back the bowl, the stranger jumped nervously to her feet and moved quickly towards the door.

'Wait!' Lovoa said, and the woman stopped and turned back, her brow creasing in worry as if she had been caught doing something wrong. 'Who are you? Where am I?' she asked, indicating the room in which she found herself.

Lovoa could see her visibly relax and relief flood her face. Surely she could not be scared of her? Yet Lovoa was too well mannered to look into the woman's mind for the answers.

'My name is Kesli. You are in my home and that of my family.'

'But how did I get here? I don't remember anything after...' She stopped as she realised that she could not remember what had happened after she had retaliated to the blasts that had been fired down on her.

'After you resisted Protector Ovato,' Kesli finished for her. There was considerable awe in her voice. Lovoa could only look at her in astonishment. 'My mate and I brought you here after you collapsed.' Looking at Lovoa's still-blank expression, she asked, 'You really don't remember anything?' and when Lovoa shook her head, she went on to explain further. 'Protector Ovato was punishing us for defying him. He started to attack and he would have killed my daughter if you hadn't saved her. Her name is Ayne. Afterwards, however, you collapsed and the attacks stopped. I don't know everything else that happened, it was hard to see through the crowd. Bringing you here was the least we could do; you needed to be hidden from the protector's men as he will be furious with you.' Kesli finished talking and just looked at Lovoa, unsure what to say or do next.

Lovoa thought about what she had said. There had to be more to it as she hurt far too much. Something else had happened, something Kesli either had not seen or did not want to say. Little light was coming into the room, so she pulled herself to her feet, stood up and took a few steps to the window and opened the shutter, but it had not been stopping the light getting in. There was no light as both suns had set and it could be a few hours or so until the first one started to rise and she could get some relief for her painful muscles. She swayed briefly at the thought and Kesli rushed forward to support her.

'You must lie down,' Kesli insisted as she tried to lead Lovoa back to the mat. Lovoa shook her head, she was frustrated with everything that had happened and wanted to be up and moving, not resting where her thoughts would play on her mind.

'I don't need to rest, I need the sun. How long is it until the first sun rises?'

'There will be no sun for another two hours.'

'You mentioned a mate and daughter, where are they?' The mats in the room indicated that the small family slept here together.

'We wanted to make sure that you were able to rest.'

Lovoa looked towards the doorway, but everything beyond it was hidden from view by the rug, so she walked past Kesli and towards the adjoining room.

'Please,' Kesli begged as Lovoa lifted the rug and walked into the neighbouring room. She saw Kesli's mate sitting at the table with a small child cradled in his arms. He looked up when he saw Lovoa and his mate.

'Why are they not in bed?'

'We were waiting for you to wake,' as if the simple explanation was enough. Lovoa's heart twisted inside her that they had given up the most basic needs for her. She walked to the child and gently laid her hand on her head. The child stirred under Lovoa's touch, but did not wake. She seemed no worse for wear after her experience as she lay in the comfort and security of her father's arms.

Lovoa raised her eyes from the child and looked at the father. He looked as exhausted as his mate and there was clear bruising on his face, which showed that he, like his daughter, had not escaped the riot unscathed. An image flashed through her mind of herself tripping over someone during the chaos, and then she recognised him as that man. She had felt guilty for not being quick enough to help him, but now she was glad that she had not because otherwise she would not have been in time to save the daughter.

'Take her next door and put her to bed,' she said, unable to bear the way these people had put her needs over their own and well aware that they now needed the sleep much more than she did. He looked at her in surprise.

'There is no need mistress, we are all right where we are,' but everything about him belied that statement, from the greyish tinge of his skin to the slump of his body, it was as if he no longer had the strength to sit up straight.

'You are uncomfortable and tired. I don't need to sleep any more and you have already done more for me than I could ever have expected.' Her words were pleasant but there was an underlying edge of authority, which they quickly picked up.

He looked at her for a moment, surprised; the command had certainly been there but had been issued in a calm and quiet voice. They had always been used to orders being shouted or threats given, yet spoken like this, he found himself standing up before he realised what he was doing.

'Thank you.' He bowed respectfully, then turned and left the room, carrying his daughter, and his mate followed him.

For a moment Lovoa stared at the doorway through which her hosts had just passed, before turning away and looking out of the window. They were nervous of her, yet what had she done to warrant that? She had saved their daughter and they, in turn, had sheltered her from the protector's guards. They had taken the greater risk, for if they were discovered, there would be reprisals, but there was more to it than that, they showed her a level of respect that she did not deserve. She looked down at her hands and gently traced the markings that were visable through the dirt. Other than the male at the pool, she had not seen anyone with such extensive patterning. Was it important? She had never thought to question why her parents had less than her, and she had had no one else to compare to until now. Yet what was so special about her? She was a peasant and had nothing in common with the great protector. All these questions kept going around and around in her head. She sat down, raised a hand and started to rub her forehead as if she could rub the problems away.

'Are you all right?' Lovoa turned and realised that Kesli was looking at her, a worried and confused expression on her face.

'I'm fine. I thought you had gone with your mate to sleep.'

'That was kind of you, letting them go to get some rest,' she said, inclining her head slightly in respect.

'Don't you wish to sleep too?' Lovoa asked.

'It's not necessary,' Kesli said, though Lovoa could see the same lines of exhaustion on her face as on her mate's.

'You look as exhausted as your mate. Go and sleep, you will be glad of it later.' When Lovoa saw her hesitation, she added, 'Don't worry about me, I can look after myself until morning, it's only an hour or so away.'

'Of course, I didn't mean to imply ... that is...'

'I understand, go and sleep while you can.'

Kesli gave a shy smile and left.

Finally left alone, Lovoa stood up and walked around

the kitchen. She came to the window and opened the shutter but it was still too dark to see out. She turned and looked at the rest of the general living area. Going through their storage areas, she found that there was surprisingly little, just enough for this family to have another full meal. How could they cope as a family? She was still hungry after all that had happened, and the little that Kesli had given her was not enough to make up for the last few days with no food, especially since the cloak and dirt had prevented her from taking in the sun as she would have done back at her parents' farm, although she needed so little compared to her parents and, she assumed, Kesli and her family. She thought about all the sacks of food that she had left behind and wondered if she had made the right decision not to have gone back for some of it.

Her parents. She still felt empty at their loss but she had to push it back, she just had to, though she doubted the image of her parents' bodies would ever leave her. She hoped that the memories that would abide would be of happier times, of when they were alive, not as she had last seen them. With a ruthlessness that she was quickly learning, she pushed the images away because her own survival should be the most important thing on her mind right now. She would grieve when she was safe. After a while she turned back to the stool, moved it so she would be able to catch the first rays of sun in the morning and sat down, and for the first time in what seemed like an eternity, she felt she could relax for an hour or so.

✳

Solvan saw the rising smoke as he reached the outskirts of the collective, and was surprised that the fire was still burning. He thought about going straight to Ovato to demand to know what he thought he had been doing by allowing it to continue for so long, then thought better of it. She had been at the fire, he had felt that, and it was worth checking to see if there was any trace of her there first. As he got closer, the smoke got thicker and darker, forcing him to land and walk because he could not see well enough. Walking slowed him and he grew more and more impatient. Workers were running past him and as they knocked into him, he felt their pain and fear. Solvan could not understand how Ovato had ignored what was happening on his collective.

When he finally arrived at the burning house he could see that the fire was nowhere near the blaze it must have been and was now reduced to hot, smouldering remains giving off a lot of smoke. With only a handful of guards around trying to put it out, Solvan guessed that it would burn itself out in another hour or so. He stood in front of it and thought about leaving it alone as it was unlikely that the heat from it would start any other fires now. Instead of wasting his time and energy on it, he decided that he should be looking for the girl and dealing with Ovato. He turned to leave and as he did so he scanned the surrounding area and saw several bodies lying on the floor. Some were groaning and twitching on the ground, others were so still. None of the people were being helped by the guards, and those not working on the fire were dragging the bodies onto carts, and he assumed they were removing the dead. Solvan walked to the nearest body and the moment he touched it he felt nothing and knew it was too late. Gently he turned it over and saw the wide-eyed stare of a young female. He knew that there was nothing he could do for her. She had been killed either by the blast or by being trampled after she had fallen. Either way, Ovato was to blame.

Solvan wondered how many other people had died here today. Anger burned through his veins at the way these people had been treated. He started to walk from one body to another, most were dead or too seriously injured to be helped. He saw movement to the side and saw two people run towards one of the groaning bodies and started to drag it away before the guards saw. Ovato had been told how bad things were, had been warned of the discontent, but Solvan had never imagined that things could ever have gone this far. To his left he saw that a female had also come out of hiding and was trying to support a semiconscious male, either her mate or her brother he would guess by their markings. He saw one of the guards approach them and, with a clenched fist, hit the female in the face, sending her sprawling in the dirt. He bent and said something to her that Solvan could not hear and she cried hysterically on the ground. When she had fallen, the male she had been helping had also collapsed, unable to take his own weight, and two more guards arrived, took hold of him and tried to drag him off. The female grabbed at one of the guard's legs to try and stop him but he just kicked her in the face until she let go. Solvan thought that if he did not do something now, none of the people who had survived the attack would be seen again, they would be taken away by the guards and that would be the end of them.

Solvan stood up and started to walk towards the guards who were dragging the male away, determined to stop them, when a loud, cracking sound came from behind him. He turned and saw a handful of the guards running away from the smouldering shell of the building. They had not been treating it as a priority and now it looked as if it was about to collapse on several struggling workers, who would not be able to save themselves. A few guards were now trying to stop it but they could not avert the collapse and he knew he had to put that fire out now and stabilise the building. There were several ways in which he could have accomplished it but, partly in annoyance at their incompetence but mainly feeling the need to make a very clear point, he decided to make it memorable. He relaxed himself and drew the energy in from around him. He felt himself expand with the power, but with the ease of long practice, he kept it under control, then suddenly discharged it in the direction of the burning house, and watched in satisfaction as the flames were engulfed in light and suddenly went out. Solvan knew that his method had not only been extremely effective in putting the fire out, but had also been visually spectacular. When he had drawn the energy in, he had seemed to grow in stature and his form had shimmered, making him look like some mystical being.

Those who were near enough to see through the smoke saw the light from the energy and that the house which had been on fire one moment was a cold ruin the next. The guards who had been trying to put out the fire stopped and stared in amazement, not sure what had just happened. They had been fighting the fire for what seemed like hours, with no real success, but this one individual had extinguished it in a matter of seconds. Their gaze moved from the ruin to Solvan, but they could not see him properly through the smoke because he was covered in ash, as were all who had been close to the fire. Solvan looked around him and saw that some of the guards were just staring at him, not sure what to do or say. He ignored them and turned his attention back to the guard who had been kicking the female in the face. She had let go of her loved one and now lay sobbing and bleeding on the ground as the guard was dragging him off, seemingly unaware of what had just occurred.

Solvan walked up to the guard and grabbed hold of him. 'Where is Ovato?' he demanded. He was in no mood for pleasantries and any sympathy he may have had for the guards had faded and died after seeing what they were doing to people who could not defend themselves. The guard snapped himself out of his shock at being stopped, dropped the peasant's arm and sneered at Solvan, seeing only a filthy peasant in front of him who had dared to grab hold of him and challenge him. He tried to wrench his arm away.

'How dare you touch me? I will have you beaten,' he snarled.

'You can try,' Solvan said, almost amused, 'but you won't get very far.' The guard just stared at Solvan for a moment as if he could not quite believe what he was hearing. 'While you're thinking about what you will try to do to me, you can tell me where Ovato is, since he is obviously not where he needs to be.'

'You should show proper respect to the great Protector Ovato,' the guard spat in reply, trying to draw himself to his full height in Solvan's grip, but he was still several inches shorter than this stranger.

Solvan was not impressed. 'Ovato,' Solvan said, deliberately missing out the title, 'shows no respect to me or his people, so why should I show him any respect?'

The guard raised his free arm and went to strike Solvan, who saw it coming, grabbed his wrist and twisted it sharply, taking the guard to his knees. The others saw what was happening and approached the pair.

'I will have you beaten to death,' the guard was screaming.

'Be quiet you fool,' one of the other guards said. 'He does not know, he must not have seen,' he stammered to Solvan.

'Do you know who I am?' he asked the newcomer.

'No,' he admitted, 'but you put out the fire, you must be a protector.'

Solvan felt his temper stretched to its limit. 'I am

Solvan, son of the first protectors,' he stated in a cold tone, more frightening that any explosive display of emotion could ever have been. He let go of the guard's arm and looked around to see the reaction to his words.

For a moment the guard on the floor just stared up at him, disbelieving. No one had seen the first protectors take an interest in the collectives for generations. He had actually thought that they no longer existed, regardless of what other people had been saying recently. What was it his colleague had said? He had put out the fire? Slowly he turned his head and saw the cold ruin of the steward's house where a few minutes ago it had been burning hot, and he was filled with dread. 'My Lord Protector, I ... I ... I...' He did not know what he could say that would save his life after striking Solvan.

'First Protector,' the other guard said, 'forgive us, we were not expecting you to come. We had no idea you were expected, and the dirt!' He stumbled and grew nervous, worried at the criticism, but as he spoke, Solvan looked at himself and saw the dirt and ash that now covered his markings.

'Stop!' Solvan said as the man tried to apologise. 'Just take me to Ovato at once, and get me a cloth so I can wipe the ash away.'

'Of course, immediately,' he replied and Solvan realised that the man was terrified of him, which made him wonder what Ovato would have done to them. The other guard was still on his feet, white and shaking. Solvan could feel his fear and as he reached out and touched the man's head, he realised that he expected to be executed for his behaviour. All Solvan's anger at him eased off.

'We will consider this a great misunderstanding, and no more will be said about it this time, but you will not get a second chance,' Solvan informed him. The guard looked up at him as if he could not believe his ears and as the meaning of his words sank in, he started to cry because he was not going to die today.

'But,' Solvan cut over the guard's profuse thanks, 'you must stop assaulting the people. Let their friends and family take them away in peace.'

'Protector Ovato gave orders that they had to be taken to the cells to be punished for their defiance.'

'They have been punished enough. You are to follow my orders and tell the families they can take away their loved ones, with no repercussions.'

⚜

'Why is my head aching so much?' Ovato thought as he woke up. He opened his eyes and was surprised to find that the room was filled with light. He started to push himself up into a sitting position and stopped as his whole body protested at the movement.

'Gently,' his mate said, coming to the bed and helping him to lie back down. Ovato turned his head and saw not just Welra but also Pesline, Cardoc and Gilcan. Gilcan? Why was he here and not confined to his room? Something was very wrong.

'What happened? What are you all doing here, especially him?'

'You do not remember?' Pesline asked.

'Would I ask if I did?' he snapped.

'What is the last thing that you remember?' his mate asked him. 'Then we will know where to explain from.'

'The peasants were causing a disturbance and I told the captain of the guard to deal with it. I don't know after that.'

'The guard could not get control of the peasants and they set fire to the steward's house. You went up to the battlements and started to try to subdue them. Pesline and Cardoc joined you in attempting to disperse them, and one of them hit you back,' Welra explained. Ovato just lay there for a moment, rubbing his temples as he thought about what he had just been told. He did not think it was possible.

'Help me sit up,' he demanded after a moment.

'Is that wise?' Welra questioned.

'I will not have you speak to me as if I'm an incompetent invalid, help me up,' he snapped. Welra sighed, used to her mate's behaviour, leaned over and helped him to sit up and rested him against the wall. The sunlight streamed in through the window and covered him. He sat in silence with his eyes closed for a while as he absorbed the sun.

'You have explained why I'm here, but not why you are all here with me, especially him,' he said, nodding towards Gilcan.

'What do you mean? Where else would we be?' Pesline demanded. 'We are here because you needed us and Gilcan is here in case we need him.'

'Why would we need him? He sympathises with them,' he said in absolute contempt. 'You should all be trying to find the person who attacked me, not standing around in here. Have you even started to look?'

'Not yet, but...' Pesline started to explain how both she and Cardoc had also been drained by the attack but Ovato cut over her, not prepared to hear what she had to say.

'Why not? Did I not take you into my home when you had nowhere else to go?' he shouted at her.

'But Ovato,' she tried to explain again, 'we tried ...'

'I don't wish to hear your excuses Pesline.'

She took a deep breath and said, 'My Protector,' trying a different tactic, 'this is your collective. I would not presume to impose my orders on your people.' She was furious, both she and her son had been left drained and disorientated by the attack to the extent that the servants had had to drag them off the battlements to safety. If they had not been helping Ovato to block the attack, Pesline was sure it would have killed him, it had been so powerful. She had tried to explain but he did not want to hear what had happened. Pesline wondered if now he had had a chance to take in the sun, he remembered what had happened and was preventing her from explaining because he did not want to be in debt to her and Cardoc. So, she had decided to adopt a stance that he could not so easily dismiss, that she had no right to give orders to his people, and he knew it.

Ovato looked at her and she saw his eyes narrow in annoyance. 'I am undoubtedly surrounded by fools,' he muttered under his breath as he tried to swing his legs over the side of the bed, intending to rise.

'You shouldn't get up just yet,' his mate said.

'Are you daring to tell me what I should or should not do?'

'Of course not, but you need more time to regain your strength.'

'I don't need time, I'm fine,' he retorted as he finally managed to sit on the edge of the bed, 'and get me the captain of the guard. If you're not looking for the peasant who attacked me, it is to be hoped my people had the sense to do so.' He paused as if the effort of sitting up had been too great before continuing, 'Has the fire even been put out yet?' he asked as an afterthought.

'The guards are working on it at this moment,' Pesline said.

'Why have you not seen to it?' he snapped. Pesline took a deep breath, trying to get hold of her emotions before answering him. She knew he did not care about the fire, he could have dealt with it himself when it had been started, but he had just chosen not to. She felt there was no point in trying to explain to him that after the hit, she had not had the strength to put it out. She took another breath, about to answer him, when she felt it, as did Ovato and everyone else in the room. They all paused as they felt the surge of power, and as one they held their breath.

'It was him,' Ovato said to the still room. When no one moved, 'Well, what are you doing just standing there, go and find him and bring him to me,' he screamed, while trying to pull himself up. He stood for a moment before falling back onto the bed, shaking. As a result, a few moments of chaos reigned as the people were torn between helping Ovato and obeying his orders. 'Pesline, take your mate and son and go and find him before he escapes again. He cannot be allowed to remain out there.'

'Of course,' Pesline said and she went to the door with Cardoc behind her, but Gilcan remained where he was. 'Gilcan, we must go.'

'Must we? You need my help to hunt down a peasant?'

'You would disobey me? Here, in front of everyone?' she asked.

'You are not my master, and I have made my thoughts clear.'

'You are refusing to follow my orders, Gilcan?' Ovato said.

'You are not my protector, Ovato, you have no authority to give me orders,' Gilcan replied.

'Am I not? Where is your collective now? You have come here looking for shelter, saying that you have lost everything. You will obey me or you and your family will leave here.'

'Gilcan, please,' Pesline begged.

'Fine,' he finally conceded, 'but only because the younger children need somewhere to stay,' he said, making it clear that they were his only consideration. A smile twitched his lips as he saw Ovato turn a reddish shade. He was furious and could not hide it. 'Are you all right, Ovato?' he asked, knowing that the question would annoy him further.

Ovato clenched his fists and glared at Gilcan, wishing he had the strength to remove the smile from his brother's face.

'Ovato?' Pesline said, terrified that Gilcan had pushed him too far, but neither Ovato nor Gilcan paid her any attention as they glared at each other. The tension in the room continued to increase, and no one knew quite what to do to break the deadlock.

Knock knock!

Before any reply could be given, the door swung open. Without taking his eyes off Gilcan, Ovato shouted, 'Unless you're here to tell me you have that peasant, GET OUT!' Ovato heard the door slam shut and thought that the person had left until he heard a voice.

'Now that was not very polite of you, Ovato,' the softly spoken voice said.

'You will address me as Protector or I will have you skinned,' he shouted back, still not looking at the newcomer, too intent on his power struggle with Gilcan.

'I would like to see you try, Ovato,' the intruder said. Though his voice remained even, there was a great deal of menace in his tone. 'Though I don't think you will have much luck in skinning me, I should warn you that I am very fond of my skin.' He paused and looked around the assembled company, he had everyone's attention now, and he knew it. He felt a certain amount of satisfaction when Ovato's head snapped in his direction and he just stared unbelievingly at him. 'You know, Ovato,' Solvan said, deliberately missing out his title, 'you probably would have been better occupied putting out that fire than harming your dependants. Anyway, I have just done it for you so you need not worry about inconveniencing yourself any further.'

'You?' Ovato hissed.

'Me what?' Solvan asked with feigned innocence.

'The power surge just now,' he replied before he could stop himself.

'You shock me, Ovato, that you even felt it,' Solvan said insultingly, 'but who did you think it was? From what I have seen, your guards are quite incapable.'

'I ... do not know,' he stammered, not wanting Solvan to know about the peasant.

'Indeed,' was all Solvan said, yet he remained standing, staring at Ovato, until Ovato began to feel uneasy. He abruptly turned his attention to the others in the room. 'Well Gilcan, Pesline, it is good to see you all looking so ... alive.' His voice was as hard as steel. 'Have you seen your collective recently? I have. It has been – well, how can I say this? – reduced to rubble and all your people skinned and dumped into piles to rot. You really should have taken my advice.' There was so much hatred in his voice that Pesline shivered in fear. How could she ever have thought that Solvan was not a threat to them? 'My father has organised people to bury the dead for you, as we felt that someone needed to show the bodies the necessary respect.'

Suddenly Solvan changed tack and turned his attention back to Ovato. 'You must be wondering why I have come here so unexpectedly,' he said in such a laid-back tone, almost as if this were a casual visit, that Ovato was thrown mentally off balance yet again.

'Of course,' Ovato replied, at a loss for what to say or how to act. When Solvan had previously visited, Ovato had at first been wary of his strength but had then decided that he was just a boy acting on his parents' instructions and had no real idea of how to lead or of what he could do. Now he was regretting that assumption.

'I have come back to make sure you are prepared for the traders so you can defend yourselves when they decide to attack you. I know I have already examined your battlements and told you what needs to be done, and now I need to make sure the repairs are underway.'

'But the traders are not coming here, they would not dare.'

'Then you are a fool, they destroyed Gilcan's collective with sickening ease,' he said, waving his hand in Gilcan's direction, 'because he chose to run and not defend what he had sworn to protect when he became protector. They will destroy you as easily if you are not prepared, and from what I have seen so far, this collective will be just another simple harvest for them.'

'How dare you say this to me?'

'Easily, Ovato, because it is the truth, and as son of the first protectors, I need you to understand that. It is also my right to replace you if you refuse to fulfil your duties as a protector,' he snapped and then walked right up to the bed and pushed Ovato so he was again lying down. Ovato tried to pull himself up but could not with Solvan's hand against his chest, pinning him down. Solvan continued, 'I will replace you with someone who is competent and will not save his or her own skin by running away like a coward.'

Solvan watched as Ovato's anger increased, suppressing what little common sense he had, until he had reached the point where he was ready to fire at Solvan with every shred of energy he had left. 'You are welcome to try it Ovato, but I feel I should warn you that it would not get you very far, because I can hit you so much harder.' Shock at what he had so nearly done, and that Solvan had seen it so clearly, caused Ovato's temper to cool and be immediately replaced by cold dread. Ovato was used to being surrounded by people to whom he was superior and could bully; he was not used to dealing with people like Solvan.

'*You cannot deal with me, only obey me,*' Solvan whispered in Ovato's mind, so quietly that Ovato wondered if he had really heard it.

Looking at Solvan, he realised that he had no choice but to obey him if he wanted to keep his lands, but Solvan would pay for this later, so he had better watch his back, he thought.

He hated Solvan for interfering with his collective. He was no fool, though, and realised that there was probably more to Solvan's arrival than a desire to make sure that everything was ready for the traders' arrival. He knew he had seen the fire, but had he known about it before he had arrived? Had Solvan felt it when he, Cardoc and Pesline had attacked the peasants and if he had, he would know that there was someone very powerful somewhere on his collective. Could he be here looking for him?

Chapter 14

LOVOA stood in the middle of a vast field with clusters of cabins around the edges. At first she thought she was on Protector Ovato's collective, but everything was in a better state of repair. Slowly she started to walk through the fields and it was not long before she saw the first pile of bodies. Horrified, she turned away. The bodies were in a large pile on the ground, discarded as waste and decomposing in the heat of the sun. No one had protected them and there was no one left to care for the remains. The further she walked, the larger and more frequent the mounds of bodies became. Was there anyone left alive here? She could not sense anything, but still she searched, not wanting to believe that no one had survived. Finally, she saw strange markings on the ground as if it had been on fire, but they formed a distinct pattern and were isolated. She then looked up and saw the ruins of a castle. It had been destroyed completely, the rock broken and jagged. What had happened? How had she got here? Is this what had happened when she had felt the crippling pain the day before her parents had died?

She felt it then, a tingling feeling that went down her spine. Someone was watching her. She turned around and saw him standing in the field behind her.

'Come to me,' he said. She hesitated, unsure if he could be trusted. When she did not move, he walked slowly towards her and there was something about him that was familiar.

'Please, we can help each other, we can defeat the people who did this, who killed your parents. You just need to trust me.' He was right in front of her now and she could see the pattern on him. He was the male from the forest pool. How had he got into her head? She so wanted to trust him.

'Will you come?' he asked again and held out his hand to her.

'Yes,' she replied, following her instinct. 'I am...'

⌗

Lovoa woke with a start and looked around at her surroundings, temporarily disorientated, and realised that she was no longer in the field surrounded by the piles of dead bodies, but instead was sitting at the table in Kesli's kitchen. The suns had started to rise and the light was shining on her back, causing her to wake up.

It had been so real while she slept, she had honestly thought she was standing in that field even though she had never seen it before. And the male, how had he got into her dreams? Even though she had only seen him briefly in the forest, she had recognised him as soon as she had seen him clearly. He had asked her to come to him and trust him, but she knew she had no reason to. She had feared him in the forest, feared being caught, but as he stood there in front of her, asking her to trust him, her instinct told her that she could, and she had been about to tell him where she was when the sun had woken her.

Lovoa stood up in frustration and cursed that she had woken too soon. Her muscles had stiffened from sleeping in such an awkward position, and slowly she stretched as best she could in the confines of the small room. She tried to extend her wings but stopped as they brushed against one of the walls, so she folded them back. Then she looked outside, as she was desperate to be in the sun, but the old concerns of always having to hide still caused her to be wary. She sighed in annoyance with herself, these are the people with whom she wanted to live and work, and after yesterday she thought most people would have a good idea of who she was and of what she was capable. She took a deep breath and walked outside into the sun, and it felt glorious, even through the dirt that covered her she could feel the heat and energy, and she had never realised how much the cloak had blocked. After standing there taking in the suns' rays for a few minutes, Lovoa carefully extended her wings and turned her head to inspect them as best she could for any further damage. She was relieved when she saw there was none, and even the bruising from a few days ago when she had hit the tree was a lot less painful. It now covered a greater area but was only a muted yellow and green colour instead of the angry, vivid colour it had been before. She touched it gently and could detect no lasting damage or pain. Sighing with relief, she folded her wings back behind her, thinking that a few hours in the sunlight and all the bruising would be gone.

Lovoa remained outside, taking in the sun. After a while she saw and heard families moving around in the nearby cabins. One family, then another, started to leave. Some paused when they saw her and began to whisper among themselves. Lovoa heard a noise behind her and turned around to see Kesli's mate walk out behind her. Seeing her, he paused, smiled tentatively and then bowed awkwardly, obviously not knowing how to behave towards her.

'Where are you going?' Lovoa asked him.

'To the fields to work, we have much to catch up on after yesterday.'

'You would still work for your protector after what

happened yesterday?'

'Of course, how else would we be able to feed ourselves?'

'Even after the way you and the others were treated by the guards and the protector, after they nearly killed your daughter?' she asked, bemused that he seemed just to accept the situation.

'We were in the wrong, we should've been in the fields working. We can only hope that if we work hard and catch up on the work, then he will treat us leniently.'

'If you were to hand me in, he would be thankful,' Lovoa pointed out, though as she offered the solution, she hoped that he would not take her up on it.

'That is very likely, but without you I would no longer have a daughter and that is unthinkable,' he replied. 'I need to go to work' he said, looking at the other farmers who were already moving off towards the fields and Lovoa realised that he would not go until she had said that he could.

'Of course, have a good day,' she said, not knowing what else to say to him, and he turned and ran off to catch up with the others. She pondered over how on the one hand he could be worried about what the protector would think about the revolt yesterday and his need to protect his family, yet on the other, not take the obvious solution and tell the protector where to find her. Was he keeping her hidden from a sense of morality or out of fear of her?

Lovoa stood outside for a while longer, wondering what to do; she knew she could not stay here for long, but where to go? Instinct told her that she could trust the male in her dreams but she did not know why as she had been so scared of him, but going to him was not an option as she had no idea where he was or who he was. Everything had become so complicated.

She turned and went back inside. If her mate was up, then Kesli might also be awake by now, but as she entered the cabin there was no sign of her in the kitchen. She went to the rest area and listened, and when she heard nothing, she pulled the hanging back from the doorway as quietly as she could and saw Kesli still sleeping, with Ayne cradled in her arms. Lovoa smiled at the image they created and quietly left so as not to disturb them, as she knew that Kesli had not had much sleep last night.

They would be hungry when they awoke, she thought, and her own stomach made itself felt with the thought of something to eat. She started to look around the kitchen for food so that Kesli would not have to worry about preparing anything when she woke up. She had always made her parents' food and she felt it was the least she could do in return for hiding her. She found so little in the storage areas, she was amazed that they could survive on it. She would have to be careful about what she made as she had no idea how long the little food that they had was meant to last. She looked at what was in front of her and realised that no matter how much she wanted to eat, she was not going to – she could not take food away from this family. She had always needed a lot less to eat than her parents and in bad years had gone for days without food. It was very unpleasant, even painful, but a lot easier for her. Her parents had not been able to get as much energy from the suns as her, and she wondered if it would be the same for Kesli and her family. For the first time, she was angry with her parents for never explaining anything to her, anything about herself and how others lived outside their farm.

Lovoa managed to put a meal together for Kesli and Ayne using as little as possible, and was about to pick it up and take it in to Kesli when she heard a voice behind her.

'You shouldn't have.' Turning, Lovoa saw that Kesli was behind her, and in her arms, and still so trustingly asleep, was Ayne.

'It's all right, I was careful and used as little as possible,' Lovoa assured her.

Kesli looked at her, bemused, and said, 'No, you should not be cooking for us.'

'Why not?'

'You are a protector, it's wrong; you should have woken me to cook for you.'

'You needed to sleep. I'm no protector and I should decide what is right and what is not.'

'But...' Kesli started to argue.

'You would argue with me?' Lovoa asked, but when she saw the terrified expression on Kesli's face, regretted the jest. 'I'm sorry. I'm not a protector and I do not know why you keep calling me one. I grew up on an independent farm with my parents and when I became old enough, I always cooked for them, so please sit and eat.'

Reluctantly, Kesli sat down at the table and accepted the food placed before her. Slowly she ate it, but she never took her eyes from Lovoa.

'Do I scare you so much?' Lovoa asked at last, noticing her unease.

'Slightly, but you confuse me more.'

'How? I'll not be angry at anything you tell me,' she promised.

Kesli took a deep breath. 'You are as powerful as any protector, you defeated Protector Ovato, yet you don't behave like one,' she said.

'I'm a farmer like you, I have never been anything else. What is it about me that makes you think I should be a protector?'

'You have a lot of markings, more than the protector and his family, so I just assumed.' When Lovoa looked confused, she continued, 'If you have a lot of markings, you are normally of high rank. I thought everyone knew that, did your parents not explain that to you?'

'No,' Lovoa said and slowly sat down next to Kesli. 'I'm beginning to realise that there is a lot they did not explain to me.'

'You could not ask them now?' Kesli asked tentatively.

'No, they died a few days ago,' Lovoa replied after a pause.

'I'm sorry. How did they die?' The question was out before Kesli could stop it, and from the look on Lovoa's face, she wished she had not said anything.

'I believe my parents were killed by the traders,' she replied eventually.

'But they do not exist, they are only stories, our protector has always said so.'

'If they don't exist, then I don't know what I killed. I came home to find two skinned bodies on the ground. I was attacked and managed to kill one of them before getting away. They were nothing like us. If they were not the traders, they were something just as bad.'

⁂

Solvan was pacing up and down in the chambers that had been allocated to him, trying to get rid of his frustration and anger. Everywhere he went there was someone there, to help him, to make sure he did not get lost, to see to his needs, were among the excuses that were used, until he had finally had enough and retreated behind the closed door of his room so he could think in peace about how he was going to get time alone to search.

To make matters worse, Solvan suspected that Ovato did not believe that checking the battlements and investigating the uprising was the main reason he was here. Ovato would know there was someone very strong on his collective. No one but he could have defended against Ovato so strongly, if somewhat clumsily, so Ovato would also assume that if Solvan had felt his attack on the workers, he would also have felt the retaliation. Which he had, and he needed to find her badly.

Not being able to do anything else for the moment, Solvan climbed onto the bed and closed his eyes for a rest. He had not intended to fall asleep, but he was just so exhausted after chasing the traders and the girl that he drifted off to sleep. His dreams turned, as they often did, to Gilcan's collective as he had seen it after the traders' visit. He knew that by now many of the bodies would have been buried but he could not get them out of his mind. He was walking through the fields among the piles of bodies when he saw her standing there. She had let down her defences and had somehow drifted into his dream.

'Come to me,' he called, afraid she would leave before he could reach her. She stopped and looked at him, and he had walked slowly towards her and asked her to help him and to trust him. She had paused and considered what he asked, and had started to tell him something before she disappeared. She had woken up he guessed, but she had let her guard down and he knew where she was.

⚏

'*How is it going?*' Essac asked of his son later that day. He had tried to communicate a few times but each time he had sensed that his son was with others and had withdrawn. Even as he asked, he could feel Solvan's frustration with his situation.

'*Badly,*' Solvan said, confirming his father's suspicions. '*I lost my temper with Ovato and threatened him in front of his mate, Gilcan and Pesline. He will not quickly forgive me for embarrassing him,*' he said before going on to explain everything that had happened. *'It has at least forced him to admit that I have authority over him and he cannot now easily disregard me while I am here.'*

'*That's true. I wouldn't worry about it too much, though. Ovato would never have assisted you, whether you gave him reason to or not.*'

'*I suppose you're right. At least our roles have now been clearly defined.*'

'*How is the search for the girl going?*'

'*I know where she is, I just haven't had the chance to collect her yet.*'

'*How did you find her?*'

'*You could say she found me. I fell asleep and was dreaming of what I saw on Gilcan's collective and then there she was. How she got into my dreams I do not know, but her guard was down and I knew where she was. I haven't been able to get there because everywhere I go, there is someone there to "help" me, and even when I walked out of the room a moment ago, someone was hovering.*'

'*Why is he doing that?*'

'*Ovato knows about the girl, or he at least knows there is someone very strong on his collective. By the time I got here, Ovato's attack on his people had stopped in a very unexpected way. I don't know all the details, only the information the guards had, but someone had knocked Ovato unconscious, and he was still in bed recovering when I got here. I would bet anything that he suspects she is my main reason for being here, hence the constant supervision, and at the moment I'm reluctant to lead them all to her. I don't trust Ovato's family or servants and I don't want to have to fight them all.*'

'*Is that a possibility?*'

'*I'm not sure. Ovato is not popular with any of his people but he is greatly feared, so they may feel that they have to do as he orders because of the possible repercussions if they do not,'* **Solvan said.** *'These people don't remember a fair protector and, from what I can gather, Ovato is as bad as his father was. As a result, they associate power and authority with fear and pain, and will all take a lot of convincing otherwise, and as perverse as it sounds, they might trust him more because I am much more powerful than him.'*

'So what do you plan to do? It's only a matter of time before the traders attack again, so you cannot wait too long.'

'I know. I think we have some time, though, as that dark feeling has gone for the moment.'

'Are you saying the traders have left?'

'No, I think we have a reprieve, they will be back. I will try to gain some support and if I can get to the battlements alone, I can easily fly to her. Even if someone is with me, I'm hoping that Ovato and his family's skills in the air are as good as Erle's. If that is the case, I can easily lose them.'

'Why not just fly out of the window of your room?' **Essac questioned.**

'I think Ovato thought I might do just that. There are narrow slits in the wall of my room, certainly not big enough for me to climb through.'

'You are joking!' **Essac exclaimed.**

'No, they are just big enough to let the light in.'

'You could make yourself a bigger hole.'

'Don't think I have not thought of that and, if necessary, it's still a possibility.'

There was a knock on the door and as soon as it opened, Brelsa, Ovato's eldest daughter, walked in.

'I have company again, I will contact you later,' **Solvan told his father. He cut the connection and turned to face Brelsa.**

'I believe it is considered polite to wait to be invited in,' he said, wiping the smile off her face.

'I'm sorry,' she said, 'I only wanted to see if you needed anything. I could show you the castle if you like,' she walked further into the room and stopped right in front of him, smiling, 'or anything else you might want to see.'

Solvan felt his anger rising again. He had thought Erle was bad but Brelsa could possibly be worse.

'I need to see the battlements,' he said, wondering if she would actually take him there.

⚜

'My Protector,' the captain of the guard said, 'one of the men has information we believe you want.' The captain had argued first with the household servants and then the protector's family until finally he had got to see his protector. He was kneeling on the floor, his guard behind him, praying that the information was worth what he thought it was. If not, they were both due a severe punishment for disobeying the protector's mate.

'Why do you think you have any information I want to hear?' Protector Ovato said irritably. His head still ached and his mood was extremely black.

'I did tell them to leave,' his mate said, 'but they were adamant that the information they hold is of the utmost importance, and they would not listen to my command.'

'What do you have to say?' Ovato asked his captain.

'Is that all you have got to say? They disobeyed me. Me! I want to see them punished,' Welra shouted.

'I am in no mood for an argument. The captain obviously has something he thinks I should know, and if he has not, then I will punish him. What is your information? And I warn you, it had better be very good for you to have disobeyed Protector Welra.'

'My Protector, this guard has the information, he told

me directly, and we've been trying to see you ever since.'

'Yes, yes, if you do not get around to telling me soon, I will have you thrown into the cells. Tell me.'

'My Protector,' the guard said, his voice shaking, 'I know where the girl is.'

'What girl?' Protector Ovato said irritably.

'The girl who assaulted you during the peasants' uprising,' he clarified.

'It was a girl? You saw her?' Ovato's mind was running with the possibilities. He was sure the first protector was aware of the peasant, but for it to be a female? Did he know?

'Yes Protector, she was thin and dirty, but definitely a female,' the guard responded.

'Tell me what you saw.'

'There was a lot of smoke from the fire and the peasants were running everywhere, but then an area cleared and in the centre was the girl with a very young child. The energy was streaming off her. I tried to get closer but I couldn't get through because of the crowd. Then it stopped and she collapsed on top of the child. A female went to her, turned her over and picked up the child – which had the same markings – and they were joined shortly by her mate who, with the help of some others, carried her away. I recognised the markings of the parents and I believe the girl was taken to their cabin.'

'And you only tell me now?' Ovato said, pulling himself up, furious over the delay.

'My ... my Protector,' the guard stammered, 'we've been trying to tell you.' He was shaking.

'My Protector,' the captain of the guard said, 'we couldn't have hoped to capture her without taking a large number of men, thereby disobeying your commands to regain control of the peasants.'

'*And you tried to stop them from talking to me!*' Ovato

turned and mentally berated his mate.

'*You were unwell,*' she tried to defend herself.

'*Did you even ask them why they were so desperate to see me?*' He did not wait for her response. 'Take what men you need and do anything you consider necessary to bring her to me,' he ordered.

'Yes, my Protector,' both men said and turned and left as quickly as they could.

⁂

Lovoa was sitting outside, next to Kesli, and had Ayne curled on her knees, since the child had just climbed up and made herself comfortable before her mother had been able to stop her. Kesli had protested but Lovoa assured her it was fine.

'A lot of children are going with their parents,' Lovoa observed as she watched others run towards the fields, most with children.

'Yes, it's normal.'

'Do you normally work in the fields as well?'

'Yes.'

'Then why do you not go to work and take Ayne with you? Who looks after the children when you do?'

'If they are old enough, they help us, even if only with small tasks like carrying tools or seeds. The really young ones like Ayne are all kept together and we take it in turns to look after them.'

'And today?' Lovoa prompted.

'Ayne is scared and sore after yesterday, and I couldn't make sure she was all right if I were in the field working all day.'

'Is that why you don't want me to look after her? Because you don't know if I could look after her properly?'

Kesli laughed, looking at her daughter happily clinging to Lovoa. 'No, Ayne knows you will look after her no matter what – that's why she clings to you so tightly. I've not seen her this trusting with anyone who is not family before,' she confessed.

'Then I'm honoured,' Lovoa said and stroked the child's hair. In response, Ayne moved even closer to her. 'Then go, I can see you are anxious about remaining here. I will take good care of her for you and I'll have food cooked for when you return,' Lovoa assured her and eventually Kesli left, running towards the fields to join her mate.

Ayne watched her mother leave, and for a moment Lovoa was worried that she might be upset without either of her parents near, but Ayne did not seem bothered by their absence, so Lovoa guessed she was used to being without them.

'Now, what to do with you?' Lovoa asked Ayne, not really expecting a reply. Having never been around any child, she was not sure how to amuse her. Ayne looked at her when she spoke. 'I don't suppose you know what you want to do?' she said, still not really expecting any reply, but Ayne smiled up at her, climbed down off her lap and, on very unsteady feet, walked inside. Curious at what she was up to, Lovoa followed her inside and saw her by a box on the floor in the general room, trying unsuccessfully to open it because the lid was too heavy for her. Lovoa leaned down and pulled the lid up and inside was a collection of toys. Ayne shrieked with delight and picked up a very worn doll. Closing the box again, Lovoa picked her up and took her back outside. If she was still suffering from yesterday as her mother thought, then the best thing for her was the sun, though Lovoa noticed that while her own injuries were almost completely gone now, Anye's seemed to be healing much more slowly. Perhaps faster healing came with age, Lovoa thought.

Putting Ayne on the ground, Lovoa sat down next to

her so that she was on the same level and wondered what to do next. Ayne had no such problem as she began happily playing and telling Lovoa what she wanted her to do. Soon Lovoa relaxed into the game the child was playing and was laughing along with her.

She sensed people near her but disregarded them. Kesli lived so close to other people that there always seemed to be others close by, which was rather overwhelming, but anyway, who would know she was here? Consequently, she did not worry about it until they were next to her and casting shadows over both her and Ayne. Lovoa turned and looked up, expecting to see curious peasants wondering who she was, but instead she saw several men in a circle around them, and she recognised them by their dress as Ovato's guards from yesterday.

'Protector Ovato wants to talk to you,' the nearest guard said, 'you need to come with us now.'

'Why? I've done nothing wrong.'

'Yes you have, you attacked the protector.'

'No, I defended myself against him,' Lovoa replied.

'You will come with us whether you want to or not.'

Lovoa jumped to her feet, only too aware that she was at a disadvantage on the ground, but before she could pick Ayne up, one of the other guards took hold of her and she started to scream and kick out, but with no success. If there were other people still about, they were hiding from the guards, not wanting to get involved.

'Do not hurt her,' Lovoa said and started to move towards the guard but before she could take more than a step, she was grabbed from behind by two others. 'Let me go,' she screamed at them. She started to pull in energy, ready to strike them.

'Stop that or the girl dies,' the leader of the group said. Lovoa paused and glared at him. 'Do you really think you could take all of us before one of my men could kill the girl? Are you willing to take the risk?' he asked, and Lovoa let the energy dissipate. 'Smart girl,' he said.

'Please leave her alone,' Lovoa pleaded.

'If you come along nice and quiet, I will not hurt her.' Lovoa looked at him distrustfully and he laughed. 'You think the protector or I are interested in a peasant child? Her only use as far as I'm concerned is ensuring your co-operation. Come along nice and quiet and she will not be harmed, do you understand me?'

'Yes.'

'Well, what is it going to be?'

'I will come with you.'

The guard smiled in triumph.

'But if I find out you lied and she gets hurt, I will make you sorry,' she added.

'Of course you will,' he replied and nodded his head slightly.

Lovoa knew no more as everything went black and she slumped to the ground at the feet of a guard holding a wooded club.

'That was easier than I thought it would be,' the leader said.

'What do you want to do with the girl?' the guard holding her asked.

'Leave her here,' he replied.

'Sir?' he asked.

'She's a child and is hardly a threat. Her mother will feel her distress soon enough and come for her. What benefit would there be in harming her?'

'Yes Sir,' he replied and put the girl back on the ground where she continued to scream hysterically. One of the other guards picked Lovoa up and dragged her to a nearby cart, covered her, then they left quickly, worried about the peasants after yesterday.

Chapter 15

KESLI paused in her work again and looked towards her home. For a while now she had been feeling uneasy, convinced something was very wrong with Ayne.

'What's wrong?' her mate asked when he saw her stop.

'Something's not right with Ayne.'

'I don't feel anything, you worry too much – Ayne is with a protector who can easily look after her.'

'I know, I keep telling myself it's just anxiety after yesterday.'

'Ayne is fine, and we have too much to do,' he said.

'You're right,' Kesli said, turning back to work with a sigh, but after a few minutes she had stopped again.

'Kesli,' her mate said.

'I'm sorry, I have to go,' she said then dropped her tools and started to run home as fast as she could.

She heard it first; the sound of her daughter's hysterical crying. As she got nearer, she saw Ayne lying on the ground in front of their home, of Lovoa there was no sign. Kesli ran as fast as she could, skidded to a stop by her daughter and scooped her up into her arms as she sobbed. Recognising her mother, Ayne clung desperately to her and Kesli tried to sooth her and check her for any injury, but she could detect nothing new. Slowly Ayne started to calm down, more from exhaustion, Kesli thought, than anything else.

She carried Ayne inside. The cabin looked exactly as it had when she had left for the fields. Taking her daughter into the bedroom, she tried to get her to lie down but

Ayne just clung to her with as much strength as she had left.

'It's all right now,' she tried to reassure her, but Ayne still clung to her and would not let go. Kesli stood again and walked back outside, hoping that the sun would help and to try and find a clue as to what had happened and how long ago. She was angry with herself, she should have returned as soon as she felt something was wrong.

Where was Lovoa? There was no sign of her in the cabin and Kesli was sure that she would not just have left Ayne alone after risking so much yesterday and volunteering to look after her today.

As she walked outside, Kesli saw something on the floor and picked it up. It was Ayne's favourite doll, the one her father had made for her, smashed. Looking further, she saw a dark patch on the soil. She bent down as best she could with Ayne in her arms and touched it; it was wet and stuck to her fingers, she realised it was blood. Oh Hannoki!

❉

Brelsa looked at Solvan briefly then smiled. 'But of course,' she responded, indicating that he should follow her out of the room. 'If you want to follow me, I will show you where they are.' As she turned her back on him, Solvan paused, suspicious, everyone else had found an excuse not to take him there. The main reasons were that they did not know how to get there or they required permission from Protector Ovato to go onto the battlements. They had all remained adamant on this point, even when he had informed them that he, as first protector, had greater authority.

Solvan followed Brelsa out of the room and as she led him down the corridor, she started to talk constantly and every sentence seemed to start with, 'My father says...' It was not long before Solvan started to get really irritated with her, but if she was going to take him to the battlements, he would listen, or so he thought until she started talking about the 'ridiculous' rumour that was circulating about the traders' return. Solvan decided that he had had enough.

'How can you say that?' he asked her. 'Pesline and Gilcan are here and must have told you what happened at their collective – you must have felt what happened, you look powerful enough.'

'Yes, but father says they made it up because they are weak and lost control so they had to say something to save embarrassment. As for what I felt, I was just unwell, it was nothing.'

'If you honestly believe that then you are a fool and this collective will be an easy target for skinning when the traders come here.'

'But they don't exist, have you not been listening to my father?' she said.

Solvan clenched his fists in frustration. How could these people not see the danger that is coming? He did not see the point in arguing with Brelsa any more, it was clear that if she did not hear it from her father, then she would not listen to anyone else. What sort of hold did Ovato have over everyone to make them believe in him so completely?

Solvan continued to follow Brelsa for a while as she led him through a series of corridors. She talked constantly, but he had stopped listening to what she was saying as he had no interest in Ovato's arrogance, when she suddenly stopped and went into a set of chambers.

'As I was saying, these rooms...' she started. Solvan looked around him, wondering why they had stopped here. There were no stairs to the top of the building, strangely there were not even any windows, only the door by which they had entered, then he heard what Brelsa was saying and realised that she was telling him about the importance of the chambers and why her family was so proud of them.

'Why are you showing me these?' Solvan asked.

'Were you not listening?' she said and started again with the lecture.

'No!' Solvan exclaimed, cutting over her. 'I told you to take me to the battlements, not give me another tour of the castle.'

'My father said to show you the interesting parts of the castle,' she said.

'I told you to take me to the battlements,' Solvan repeated.

'But father said...'

'Let me make myself very clear to you: I don't care what your father told you, I outrank your father and you will take me to the battlements now.'

Brelsa went silent for the first time and started to shake slightly, and Solvan realised that she was terrified of Ovato.

'Take me to the battlements and if he is angry with you, you can always tell him that I forced you, and if he doesn't like it, I will be more than happy to give him another demonstration of how much stronger than him I am.' Solvan watched Brelsa take a deep breath as she considered her options. She walked to the door and after checking there was no one outside, closed it.

'If I ask you something, will you promise not to tell Father?'

'I will not tell him anything that would get you into trouble.'

'They will not let Protector Gilcan near me or my brothers and sisters, but I have heard what people are saying and you mentioned it just now, about the traders.'

'You want to know what happened?' When Brelsa nodded, Solvan continued, 'The traders attacked their collective, but instead of staying and defending the people, they fled and everyone that remained was skinned alive. That is the truth, no matter what your father tells you. The traders are real and they will be coming soon.'

'Thank you, I will show you to the battlements,' and she led him out of the room. They did not talk again until they arrived at the bottom of a flight of stairs.

'They're up there,' and she walked up, with Solvan following her.

Once at the top, she stood aside so that Solvan could walk past her. She stood by the exit and watched him as he walked around them, inspecting them. She did not know what he was thinking. She could see that they needed repair, they always had, but she did not know what they were supposed to look like.

'You are disappointed with them, aren't you?' Brelsa queried.

'Yes, they are more or less useless as they are now.'

'So if the traders came now, there would be nothing we could do to defend ourselves or the peasants,' she said.

'No, you could still defend yourself and your people but the battlements offer protection for the protectors against the traders. The old documents we have say that they have powerful weapons and if you were standing up high and exposed, they could still attack and kill you from the ground.'

'So what needs to be done to fix the battlements?'

'Why the sudden interest?'

'I don't want to die.' she said simply.

'Why do you believe, when no one else on this collective seems to?' Solvan asked.

'As you said, a few days ago I felt like I was being skinned alive. Both Mother and Father said it was nothing, I was just imagining things because of all the rumours that the first protectors were spreading and that I was not to talk of it again. Then shortly afterwards, Protector Gilcan arrived and I was not allowed to see him or his family, but I heard what people were saying, that the traders had destroyed everything.'

'And your father still doesn't believe?' Solvan asked.

'I don't know what he believes, he tells us what he wants us to know and that is all.'

'Why are you telling me all this now?'

'Partly because you gave me no choice about bringing you up here – Father is going to be furious even if he has to accept that I'm not strong enough to stop you – but also because I want to know the truth.'

'The truth is that it's only a matter of time until the traders come here, and with the battlements in this state and with your father's attitude, this collective will end up like Gilcan's.'

'What can I do? Father would never listen to anything I said.'

'You could start by rebuilding the battlements and learning what to do when the traders come.'

'I couldn't, Father would never allow it.'

'If I dealt with your father?'

'You could do that?'

'I could.'

'Then I would do my best, but I have never tried to do anything like this before.'

'Thank you, I will explain everything that needs to be done later, but now I'm afraid that I have to leave you.'

'Where are you going?'

'Sorry, I really can't tell you that in case your father finds out from you. Please tell him that I gave you no choice and you couldn't stop me,' and with that Solvan stood at the edge of the battlements, spread his wings, jumped into the air and flew away.

❋

Was Lovoa still alive?

Kesli stood and looked around her but saw no one. Examining the ground, she saw several sets of footprints and clear drag marks as well. She followed them and after a short way noticed groves made by wheels. Whoever had taken Lovoa had been prepared and had left her daughter unharmed. They obviously had not been interested in Ayne but would they come back? Perhaps later, when they knew that she and her mate would be back from the fields? She should go now and find her mate so they could think about what best to do, to leave if necessary. Shifting her daughter into a more comfortable hold, she turned and started to walk back towards the fields when a shadow passed over her. She looked up but the sky was clear of any clouds, then behind her she heard a scuffing noise. Startled, she turned and looked back. There he stood, looking at her as he calmly folded his wings gracefully behind him.

As Kesli stared at him, taking in the extensive patterning all over his body, terror filled her. This male was as strong as Lovoa and could overpower her. Was he here to punish her and her family? Kesli's grip on her daughter tightened and Ayne protested.

Solvan felt the mother's fear wash over him and he realised that if he did not get her to trust him quickly, she never would, and she would not tell him what he needed to know unless he forced her.

'Please, I'm not here to harm you or your child.'

She eyed him suspiciously, confused over his behaviour.

'Then why are you here?' she asked.

'I'm looking for someone who is here.'

'There is no one here apart from me and my daughter,'

Kesli said, 'and my mate is in the fields with the others,' she added as an afterthought, as she wanted him to know that there would be someone to miss them if anything happened.

'There was someone else here, a young female?'

Kesli made no reply, she did not know what to say. If this protector had not taken Lovoa, who had? Could she trust him? He had not threatened or harmed her yet, but that did not mean he would not if he did not get the answers he wanted.

'She was here, wasn't she?' he questioned. When she still did not reply, he continued, 'I promise you, you can tell me the truth. I will not harm you or your family and I do not intend to harm the girl either, but it is very important that I find her.'

'She was here, but now she has gone, but I don't know what happened,' Kesli said finally.

'Tell me what you know.'

'If Protector Ovato finds out, we will be in so much trouble.'

'He will not find out from me and if he should threaten you, I can deal with him. I will not let him harm you.'

'Why do you want her?'

'I can help her.'

'She saved my daughter,' Kesli said suddenly, as if she would lose confidence if she did not explain quickly. 'I'll not do anything to hurt her.'

'I promise you I only want to help her, if I can.'

'Yesterday, when the fire started, Ayne got separated from us and knocked to the ground. Lovoa went to help her and saved her from the blasts that Protector Ovato and the other protector were firing at us. When it was all over, she collapsed and we brought her here.'

'But she is not here now?' Solvan asked, again looking around him, checking, both visually and mentally, that he had not missed anything.

'No, this morning she offered to look after Ayne for us so we could work in the fields – we had a lot of work to catch up on and Ayne was still so unsettled...' Kesli stopped talking.

'So what happened then? Where did she go?'

'I don't know. I felt that Ayne was upset and I returned to find her crying and on her own, and I don't know where Lovoa has gone. I was about to return to the fields when you arrived. I don't know any more.'

'As I flew over, you were looking at something on the ground. What were you looking at?'

'There, by your feet,' Kesli pointed, 'are tracks and over there by our cabin, it looks like there was a scuffle and there is a small patch of blood on the ground.' Solvan looked down and saw the marks. Before following them back to the cabin, he knelt down and touched the darker patch.

'Whose is it?'

'I don't know, it's not Ayne's,' she said.

'No one else was here?'

'No, not that I know of. As I said, everyone else is at the fields. Lovoa was looking after Ayne.'

Solvan looked at the child, still crying quietly in her mother's arms. He could feel how upset and scared she was and unlike her mother, her fear had nothing to do with him.

'May I?' Solvan said, putting out his hand and taking a step closer. Kesli took a step back, still distrustful. 'I just want to see if she saw anything that could help me. I promise you I will not hurt her.'

'How do you do it?'

'I just want to touch her. If she saw anything, then I will be able to see it as well, and it might also help to calm her before she makes herself sick.'

'You promise it will not hurt her?' Kesli said. She knew she was being slightly foolish: if he wanted to do it, he could and there would be nothing she could do to stop him, but Ayne was her daughter.

'I promise,' Solvan said. Kesli took a step towards him and Solvan gently placed his hand on the child's head.

Solvan immediately felt how scared the child was. He gently placed the question of what had happened to Lovoa into her mind. He saw the girl playing with her outside, and then someone had grabbed her and held her tight, while others had taken hold of Lovoa. There had been talk but she did not understand what they were saying. Then they had hit Lovoa over the head, picked her up and taken her away, and just dropped her onto the ground and left. Solvan mentally reassured her, telling her she was safe now with her mother and that everything was all right, and how she was such a good and brave girl for showing him. She responded well and began to calm down. Solvan removed his hand and looked at the child, she would sleep soon, he had no doubt, having exhausted herself.

'Thank you,' he said.

'What happened?' Kesli asked tentatively.

'She was taken by Ovato's men,' Solvan replied.

'Kesli!' a male voice shouted. She turned around and saw her mate running towards them. When he joined them, he looked at Solvan with the same suspicion and fear as his mate had. What did Ovato do to his people that everyone lives in fear? Solvan asked himself. 'You were gone for so long I was worried,' he said, putting a defensive arm around her. She smiled up at him.

'I'm fine,' she assured him.

'Where has Lovoa gone?' he asked, noticing her absence as he looked around.

'That's what we were trying to work out,' Kesli said.

'When I got back she had gone and Ayne was on her own, crying.'

'And then I arrived looking for her,' Solvan finished for her. 'Ayne here has answered the mystery of where Lovoa has gone: Ovato's men took her.'

'She is all right?' he said, checking his daughter, who had started to fall asleep in her mother's arms.

'She's fine,' Kesli reassured him.

'Why did they not take Ayne as well, to punish us? Will they come back?' he asked.

'I don't know if Lovoa is all right. Ayne couldn't understand what was said, but Ovato will not be back for you,' Solvan reassured them.

'We pray to Hannoki that he won't, but how can you know that?'

'Because I am First Protector Solvan, and Ovato will do as I say if he wants to keep his collective.' He smiled at them.

'Thank you,' Kesli said.

'Ayne will be fine, you all will,' Solvan promised before launching himself back into the air and flying away. He was furious with himself for letting Ovato get there before him. He was going to have to challenge him again and, if he had to, would even cross a boundary and read his mind, but he was going to find out where Lovoa was. A smile tugged at the corner of his mouth – at least he now knew her name.

Chapter 16

AS they neared the castle, the suns were both high in the sky. Melka turned to the other guards. 'One of you go ahead and inform the protector that we have the girl,' he ordered. 'Ask him what he would like us to do with her when we arrive, I would like to know what his plans are as soon as we get back to the castle.' They all glanced nervously at the cart they were pulling. No one needed to say it – if she woke now, they would not be able to recapture her. He wondered if he had been wise to leave the child behind, but he had feared for her life if they had brought her with them.

'I will go,' one of his men volunteered and he went ahead as quickly as possible before any of the others could stop him. Melka wished he could have gone with him, because though everyone normally dreaded an audience with the protector, at this moment it seemed preferable to being with the girl.

Melka was also concerned about the peasants. Even though they had to pass by some of the fields where people were working, most eyed them with fear, scared that he and his men were there to punish those who had, or were assumed to have had, revolted yesterday, and he noticed the look of relief as they passed by. Melka knew the protector would punish them eventually, but not today. He would want to savour it, let them wait and possibly start to relax when nothing happened, and then he would choose a method that would make them fear ever doing it again. He was more worried about the ones within the fortifications of the castle, there were a lot more of them in a smaller area, and they were a lot angrier and had a lot less to lose. Finally, the castle came into sight, and when Melka saw the guard return, he hoped the man had been able to see the protector and get a sensible answer from him for once.

'Well?' he asked as the guard came to a stop in front of him.

'The protector has ordered for the girl to be placed in one of the lightless cells in the dungeon as soon as we get there. When she is safely secured, he wants to be informed.' The lightless cells, Melka shivered at the thought of them, no one permanently imprisoned there survived for long.

As they walked in through the outer fortifications, Melka told them all to be on their guard, so they each gripped their weapons tighter and closed in around the cart. They were going to have to walk past the steward's burnt-out house to get to the inner fortifications and Melka could still feel the anger and hatred from these people. Several, he knew, had been dragged away and imprisoned and the remainder had returned to the fields, reducing the number within the fortifications, but as he passed them, most stopped what they were doing to stare and he knew that if they were given the chance, they would attack again. 'Hannoki, please do not let her wake up,' he prayed. Some of the peasants were following them, and as the steward's smoking home came into sight, he saw that word must have spread and several more peasants were standing in the square watching them. Then the big, heavy doors of the inner fortifications opened and another troop of guards came out to meet them and all the peasants dispersed as quickly as possible. Melka let out a sigh of relief. He had expected the hostility, but he had not thought that they would be ready to fight again so soon. Melka nodded his thanks to the other troop and went straight through the doors. As soon as they were all on the other side, they slammed the doors closed behind them.

Melka led them straight to the entrance to the dungeons. Once outside, he ordered the door to the cells be opened and the route down to be checked to make sure it was clear. Once he uncovered the girl, she would recover quickly in the sunlight so he wanted nothing to stop them getting her out of the cart and into the dungeon as quickly as possible. When it was confirmed that the path was clear, the door was open and the cell was ready for her, he pulled the cloth back to reveal the unconscious girl lying in the back. He pushed her shoulder but got no response, the only sign of life was the steady rise and fall of her chest. He breathed a sigh of relief and walked to the back of the cart, grabbed her ankles and pulled her forward until she was mostly out of the cart and he was able to grab one of her arms. He looked up and realised that no one had come forward to help him.

'Someone get the other arm, I can't carry her on my own and the sooner we get her into that cell, the better.' Finally, one of the others came forward and took hold of her other arm and together they were able to lift her out of the cart and carry her inside. She was not heavy but the way down to the cells was a narrow, winding staircase that had been roughly cut out of the ground. It was not long until the sun could no longer penetrate and they were reliant on the flickering light of the torches carried by the guards behind them, causing the shadows to dance in front of them. Though the conditions made it harder for them to see, it did at least mean that she could no longer use the sun. On the way down, the other guard missed his footing on the step and stumbled, causing him to lose his grip on the girl. Having suddenly had to take all the weight, Melka also lost his hold and the girl fell to the bottom of the stairs.

Melka cursed and made his way down as quickly as possible. When he got to the bottom of the staircase, he saw that she had rolled when she hit the bottom and was now lying next to the cell door. He moved her onto her back and sighed in relief when she groaned.

'Well, that was an easier way than carrying her. We should have thought about that sooner,' the other guard said.

'If she had broken her neck on the way down, I would've let you explain it to the protector,' Melka replied, annoyed. 'Give me a hand to drag her into the cell,' and with one guard on each arm, they dragged her into the cell and left her lying on the cold, filthy floor.

The guards left the cell, closed the door and locked it behind them.

'Stay here,' Melka said to two of his men.

'Why? She's not going anywhere,' came the protest.

'What if anything happens to her – do you want to explain to the protector that she was left unguarded?'

'No, but there is no light, what can she do?'

'You saw her, how much energy do you think she could have stored?'

'I don't know.'

'Neither do I, which is why she must be watched.'

'We can't see here, there is no light.'

'Then have the torches left here.'

'It's not the same.'

Melka knew what he meant, the darkness felt as though it was closing in, even at night it was never this dark as there was always some light from the moon or stars.

'We will rotate every hour, but until the protector orders us differently, she will be guarded continually. We will need one of the torches to get out of here, but keep the others,' he said and slowly began to make his way back up the stairs. As he reached the top and the sunlight could be seen, he breathed a sigh of relief to be out of that place, very thankful that the cell was hardly ever used.

'Stay at the top of the stairs, I will be back soon,' he told another guard, before walking off to inform Protector Ovato.

Melka hurried to the castle, entered and looked about him. Seeing a servant, he asked him where the protector was and was directed to his personal rooms. As he approached, he saw a guard standing outside the door.

'I have come to make my report to Protector Ovato,' he said. The guard only nodded in response and knocked on the door. When a shout came to enter, the guard opened the door for him and stood back. Melka entered and saw that the protector was with his steward, going over scrolls that were spread over a desk. Briefly he wondered where the steward was now living, since his previous home was a burnt-out shell that could only be pulled down, but then he dismissed the thought as it was neither his concern nor problem.

Protector Ovato looked up as Melka entered. 'Well?' he asked.

'My Protector, as requested, she is in the lightless cell and under guard.'

'Did you have any trouble with her?'

'No, my Protector, we took her by surprise.'

'No trouble at all? Are you sure you have the right peasant?'

'Yes, my Protector.'

'I will see for myself, take me to her,' Protector Ovato said. 'We will come back to this,' he informed the steward and walked out of the room, with Melka respectfully following behind him.

They made their way to the dungeons and Ovato shivered as he walked down the stairway, clearly uncomfortable in the darkness. There was a guard in front of him and one behind, both holding torches, which did little to dispel his unease. As he reached the bottom of the staircase, he saw more light then noticed the additional torches and two men guarding the door. When they saw him, they straightened to attention.

'Has she given you any trouble?' he asked.

'No, my Protector.'

'Open the door,' he ordered.

As the door swung open, Protector Ovato walked in, closely followed by the guards. In the dark, it took a moment to see her lying on the floor where she had been left. He walked up to her and looked down in disgust.

'She had better be alive,' Ovato said.

'She was, my Protector,' replied Melka.

Ovato nudged her with his foot and she groaned with the movement. He took a torch from one of the guards and bent over her. Hair covered her face and he brushed it away to get a better look at her, and even in the poor light he could see the markings covering her whole face and the bruising that was coming through. At least he now knew why they had not had any problems with her. He smiled to himself – he had told them by any means, and this might have been crude but it had been very effective.

He stood up. 'Tell me immediately when she wakes up, and make sure the guards stay in place at all times. If there are any problems with her, I want to know immediately,' he ordered, then taking the torch, left the cells and headed as fast as he could back to the sunlight.

＊

'Have you seen her?' Welra asked as Ovato walked into

the room.

'I have. She is more powerful than I expected her to be.'

'More so than Solvan?'

'I don't know, she was dirty and the cell was very dark, so I can't say for sure, but her face has clear markings.'

'Will the cell even hold her? How many guards are on her? What could she do if she got out?' she asked, clearly panicked.

'Calm down, she will be safe enough in the cell.'

'How can I calm down? You need to kill her now,' she demanded.

'You know what the repercussions would be if I did that.'

'It could take too long for the lack of sun to kill her naturally, and if she were able to get out of the cell, she could cause a massive amount of damage.'

'No, for the moment she is not going to cause problems. She is unconscious, injured, and without the sun she cannot heal quickly or well.'

Welra took a deep breath to calm herself down. 'So what do you plan to do with her? Just wait it out and hope nothing happens when she recovers consciousness?'

'If she had stored energy, she would have healed by now. Without any stored power, she would only have her physical strength until she had access to sunlight again.'

'She makes me feel very uncomfortable, being so close.'

'I know, but having seen her, I was wondering if I'm being very short-sighted in wanting to kill her.'

'What are you taking about?'

'She is young, injured and very powerful. Without light, she has no way to heal effectively and she will get weaker and weaker until she finally has the choice of dying or mating with one of our sons, preferably Isslac.'

'You are insane.'

'You are being blind. If she mates with one of our sons, their child, our grandchild, could be powerful enough to rival the first protectors.'

'The first protectors have no power now, what do I care about them?'

'They have no authority because they have never fought for it, but with the strength of our collective behind them, we can change that, we can get dominance over all the others.' He paused and took a sip of his drink. 'Just think about it,' he told her.

'We need to talk to Isslac.'

Chapter 17

LOVOA became aware of the cold and the pain and reached out her hand and felt the solid, rough surface. She opened her eyes and saw nothing then slowly pulled herself up into a sitting position and gripped her head as the throbbing intensified. She turned her head gently, trying to see anything, but with no luck. Was she blind? Even at night she could see something; she had never known such darkness.

'Hello!' she shouted. 'Is anyone there?' She heard a sound nearby. 'Hello!' she shouted again but got no reply.

Slowly she got to her feet, her whole body was a mass of aches and pains. She was so tired of hurting, it felt as if she had gone from injury to injury for the last few days, never getting the chance to heal fully. She walked forward cautiously, with her hands out in front of her, until she felt cold, damp rock. She ran her hands over it as far as she could reach and then started to walk along until she came to a corner, and then continued. Then suddenly the surface felt different. It was still cold but it was smooth, and she felt her way along for about a metre before the rock wall resumed. She went back to the smooth surface, and running her hands down the side, she felt a very narrow gap around it. Was it a door? She hit it as hard as she could but it made no difference. Where was she? What was the last thing she remembered?

Ayne.

Protector Ovato's men had come to Kesli's home and

that was the last thing she remembered. The men had taken hold of Ayne so she would not attack them. Had they hurt her? Had they waited for Kesli and her mate to return? Were they here, locked up somewhere else? She could not sense them anywhere nearby.

'Let me out,' she screamed and she hit the door again. She tried to pull in energy around her but there was nothing, nothing to draw on. Lovoa hit the door again and again, screaming to be let out.

✳

When the guards first heard her shout, they tensed up. 'I'll go and inform the protector,' one of them said.

'You can't leave, what happens if she blasts the door and gets out?'

'You saw her, how could we stop her? The sooner the protector gets here, the better,' and he grabbed one of the torches and left as quickly as possible. At the top of the stairs he saw two other men guarding the entrance to the cells and told them that the prisoner was awake and they might be needed, before running as fast as he could across the yard and into the main building, hoping the girl would not get out by the time they got back. A servant directed him to the protector and he stopped outside the door, where his friend was standing guard.

'Is Protector Ovato inside?'

'He is. He has informed me that he does not want to be disturbed, for all but one reason.'

'I have news about the prisoner, she has woken up,' he said. The guard nodded and as he raised his hand to knock, they could both hear the raised voices inside.

'Are you mad? She would never agree,' Isslac was saying.

'Just think of what it would mean for you and the rest of the family,' was the reply. Quickly the guard knocked on the door and received the order to come in. When he entered, he saw Protector Ovato with his mate and son, Isslac, who was not looking happy.

'This had better be important,' Welra snapped, clearly unhappy at the interruption.

'I'm sorry, my Protectors, but I was ordered to inform Protector Ovato as soon as the girl woke up.'

'Fine, we will finish this later,' Ovato said to his son and left with the guard straightaway.

'He is joking, isn't he?' Isslac asked his mother as the door closed behind his father.

'No, he's not, and neither am I. Just think of the power she would give you,' she said.

'But a mate who had only agreed because it was that or death! That would be a very destructive relationship for both of us.'

'Don't be too quick to discount the idea. Think about it, maybe see her before you make your mind up,' she said.

'Fine, if it will make you happy, I'll think about it, but I will not promise anything,' he said.

'Don't worry, if you refuse, your brothers might agree – the pairing would guarantee them the collective over you.'

'Not if they have any sense, they will not, collective be damned,' he replied.

⚜

Solvan normally found flying with the wind beneath his wings relaxing and a chance to think clearly, but this time he was so furious both with himself and with Ovato that he could not enjoy the flight. He had known that Ovato would be looking for the person who had knocked him unconscious, but he had thought he had time and, to avoid arguments, he had played Ovato's game and had lost. Either one of the guards had seen what had happened at the steward's house and recognised Kesli and her mate, or one of his peasants had decided to use the information to try to avoid the inevitable punishment and so had told them everything they knew.

He pushed himself harder, aware that the guards were considerably ahead of him, they could even have made it back before he had left the castle. He had to circle the battlements to slow down before landing. By the looks of it, Brelsa had left. Solvan stormed off the battlements and headed straight for Ovato's rooms, walking straight past anyone who tried to talk or stop him. He realised that one of the advantages of the tours he had been subjected to was that he did not need to ask for directions but knew the rooms where Ovato was most likely to be found.

Solvan saw the guard standing outside the rooms and felt sure he had guessed correctly. He was glad that he had not had to resort to searching for Ovato mentally, which could have forewarned him.

'No one is allowed to enter,' Solvan was informed as he approached the door.

'I'm here to speak with Ovato.'

'He is not in there.'

'I'm sure he is not,' Solvan said, not believing the guard, and as he went to push the door open, the guard blocked his way.

'Please, First Protector, my orders are for no one to enter,' the guard pleaded. Solvan could feel that the guard feared punishment if he allowed him to enter and he struggled to keep his anger against Ovato under control.

'You could not stop me from entering,' Solvan stated.

'I know, First Protector,' replied the guard.

'Then tell Ovato any story you like, but I will enter, with or without force,' he said.

'Thank you, First Protector,' the guard said, clearly

relieved, and he stood back and allowed Solvan to push the door open and walk in.

As soon as he entered, Solvan saw that the guard had been right: Ovato was not in the room. Welra and Isslac were, however, and it appeared that he had interrupted an argument between them.

'How dare you come in here?' Welra demanded. 'I gave strict instructions that we were not to be disturbed.'

'So your guard at the door informed me. However, I need to speak to Ovato urgently and so disregarded your wish.'

'He did not even try to stop you?'

'He tried and failed, but I doubt that you could physically stop me, so what chance did he have?' he pointed out.

Welra took a deep breath in an attempt to control herself. She was so furious, she did not know what to say, and they just stared at each other.

'How can we help you, First Protector?' Isslac asked. Solvan turned away from Welra, breaking the tension, and gave his attention to Isslac.

'I need to talk to your father immediately. Do you know where he is?'

'No,' Welra said.

'Yes,' Isslac said at the same time. Solvan looked from one to the other.

'Isslac is mistaken, he doesn't know where Protector Ovato is. An urgent message came for him, so he left and did not inform us of where he was going. I'm sorry, but we can't help you.'

'I find it impossible to believe that you can't locate your mate, Welra. Is there something wrong?'

Welra glared at him. Of course she could locate Ovato with a thought, and he knew that. Silence ruled for a few moments. 'He made it clear that he did not want to be disturbed by anyone,' she said at last.

'I don't care what he wants; I want to know where he is,' Solvan said.

'I will take you to him,' Isslac said.

'You would disobey your father?' Welra asked her son.

'Yes,' he replied simply. 'First Protector, if you follow me, I will show you where my father is.'

'Thank you,' and they both walked out of the room.

'Isslac!' he heard his mother calling him as he walked out, but did not acknowledge her.

He was disgusted with his parents, Solvan realised. Whatever they had been arguing about, it was enough to cause him to completely disobey them.

'He is obsessed, you know,' Isslac said as he led Solvan out of the castle and into the courtyard.

'Do you know what is going on?' Solvan asked him.

Isslac stopped walking and looked around him, and when he was sure that there was no one close enough to hear in the courtyard, he replied, 'Not everything, I can guess a lot, though. I saw you fly off in the direction from which the guards returned a short while ago, so I believe you are looking for the same thing, or should I say, the same someone, a girl.'

'Your father told you about her?' he asked, surprised. He would have thought that Ovato would want as few people as possible to know.

'Oh yes, his great plan is to try and get us to mate to increase the power of the family.'

'Force a mating? Is he mad?' Solvan asked, horrified.

'That's what I was arguing with my parents about,' Isslac said.

'What do they plan to do if you refuse?'

'I have brothers.'

'Madness! Have you seen her?' Solvan asked.

'Not yet, have you?' he asked, curious.

'Briefly. Does your father have a plan for how to make

someone as powerful as this girl mate against her will?'
Solvan was amazed that Ovato honestly thought he
could make someone as strong as Lovoa do anything she
did not want to do.

'He believes that she will agree after time in the
lightless cells.'

'Please tell me this is not what I think it is?' Solvan
asked, disgusted.

'Yes, they are located underground so there is no
sunlight, ever.'

'If anyone was left down there, it would be a torturous
death.'

'Father uses them as a form of punishment and to
instil fear in the people.'

'That explains how he can restrain her: without
sunlight, she has got nothing to draw on.'

'She could use stored energy.'

'That is if she has any left after yesterday,' Solvan
pointed out. 'Take me there now. I will talk to Ovato later.'

'That is where I'm taking you. A guard came to say
she had woken up so I assume he is down in the cells
with her,' Isslac informed him and started to walk
again, now in silence. They went to the furthest point
from the castle, to a building Solvan had never been to.
Outside were several guards armed with staffs. 'This is
the guards' barracks, the cells are also here, including
the lightless ones. Unfortunately, I just know that they
are here, but not where.' Isslac paused. 'I am sorry, I
can't have a confrontation with my father just yet, and
certainly not there in the cells.'

'I understand. You have helped me a great deal.'

'More than you expected from my family?' he queried.

'Much,' Solvan replied, and Isslac turned and walked
back to the castle, leaving Solvan to go ahead on his own.

As he approached the guards, they immediately tried

to stop him. 'This is a restricted area,' he was informed.

'I'm here to speak with Ovato. I was reliably informed that he was inside.'

'I won't be able to comment on that, but as I said, this is a restricted area and you are not allowed to enter.'

'I'm finding that this mix of blind devotion and blind fear that Ovato instils in his people is becoming very boring. I am a First Protector and I don't care what is restricted and what is not, and I don't care what Ovato's orders are, I am entering,' he stated and stepped forward.

The guard lowered his staff in front of him, blocking Solvan's way.

'Do you honestly think you can stop me?' Solvan asked.

'There are a lot more of us than you and we have weapons.'

'As I said, I am finding this very boring.' He put his hand out and touched the staff and as he did so, pulled in some energy from around him. The staff immediately caught alight and the guard dropped it quickly to avoid being burnt. 'Look at me, I am a lot stronger that you, I am twice as strong as Ovato. You can try to stop me, but I guarantee you will get hurt if you do.'

The guards all looked at each other, clearly trying to decide what to do, then one stood back and the rest followed.

'Wise choice,' Solvan said and he walked forward and opened the door. 'Can you point me in the direction of the lightless cells? ' No one replied. 'I could tear this place apart until I find them,' Solvan pointed out, frustrated.

'As you enter, it is the door straight in front of you. There should be another guard at the entrance and more at the bottom of the staircase,' one of the guards replied. Others glared at him, but he just shrugged, 'He would have found it easily enough.'

'Thank you,' Solvan said. He walked in and right in

front of him was the door, with another guard in front of it. Solvan sighed in frustration: the arguments with Ovato's guards were getting tedious.

The guard looked at him as he approached, then just handed him a torch, stood aside and let him through. 'I saw what you did to the steward's house and heard what you said outside. I do not intend to argue with you.'

'I assume you are guarding the lightless cells.'

'Yes, First Protector. Have you ever been without light?' he asked.

'Not total darkness,' he admitted.

'It's not natural. You tire quickly and try to pull energy in around you, but there is nothing and you start to panic. It's like you can't breathe. It's not like night, where light is limited, there is nothingness and emptiness.'

'Thank you for the warning,' Solvan said.

'I have a daughter her age,' the guard said, 'and these cells are pure torture, if he found out I had warned you...'

'He won't,' Solvan promised. He stood in front of the guard for a few moments as he pulled in more energy and stored it inside himself. He was sure that, knowing these cells, Ovato would have done the same and that these cells would be the only place where Ovato could ever have the advantage over him. When he thought he had sufficient, he stepped forward and through the door the guard was holding open for him.

Solvan walked forward cautiously. In front of him was a winding, narrow staircase. He took a deep breath and went forward into the dark.

Chapter 18

BRELSA had been listening to the argument between her mother and brother. Curiosity had got the better of her when she had heard that both of her parents wanted to talk to Isslac in private. Frustrated that she could not get close enough to hear because of the guard at the door, she waited and watched from around the corner. She was about to give up and leave, intending to try and get the information out of Isslac later, when she heard the sound of someone running. Brelsa peered around the corner and saw another guard, slightly out of breath and clearly agitated, approach the door. He spoke briefly with his colleague and was allowed to enter.

Very interesting, she thought. Whatever news he carried, her father had expected and wanted it, and a few moments later both her father and the guard left. She wondered if she should follow them to see where they were going, but she was afraid they might see her and then she would be in trouble. She decided she would wait for a little longer and was rewarded when she saw Solvan approach the guard. She had not realised he had returned. She heard his demand to enter to talk to Ovato and the argument with the guard, and she smiled as he had to point out that the guard could not stop him, and it was not long before he walked into the room. She had been tempted to tell him that her father had left with another guard only a short time ago, but then the guard would tell her parents she had been trying to spy on them, and he would find out quickly enough on his own.

She would wait until he left and was well away from anyone who could hear them before she spoke to him again. Eagerly she waited for him to leave and wished so much she could hear what was going on in the room. She was not strong or skilled enough to listen in mentally without being discovered, as her parents had never considered it important to train her, too disappointed in her strength to bother. It was not long before Solvan left with Isslac, and Brelsa looked on in surprise at seeing her brother with the first protector and hearing her mother shouting behind them, which they ignored. This was a new development, she thought. Was Isslac defying their parents as well? She would have to try to find out, she decided. Brelsa waited a few moments before she walked around the corner and approached the guard.

'Is my mother in the room?'

'She is,' the guard confirmed.

'Is she alone? May I enter to see her?'

'She does not wish to be disturbed,' the guard said.

'Who is out there now?' a voice shouted from inside.

'It's just me mother, Brelsa,' she shouted back.

'Send her in,' Welra ordered and the guard opened the door and held it for her to walk through.

'Why is there a guard on the door?' she asked as she walked in.

Welra was standing by the window, looking out. 'I was with your father and brother and we did not wish to be disturbed. With Pesline and her family here, there is never any peace, and then there is the first protector looking into matters in which he has no business interfering.'

'You are upset,' hope stirred inside her, maybe she had an ally in her brother. When her mother did not immediately reply, she coaxed, 'why don't you sit down and tell me all about it,' and she settled herself down.

'It's your brother, Isslac, he's being so ungrateful. Your father has presented him with a once-in-a-lifetime opportunity and he doesn't want it and then, to make matters worse, Solvan arrived and Isslac openly defied his father in front of me ... *me*.' She paused for a moment, then, 'You were supposed to be keeping Solvan busy, keeping him away from us,' she accused her daughter.

'I tried, is it my fault that he took to the sky and flew off?'

'You should have tried harder. If he had not shown up when he did, I had every hope of talking your brother around to our way of thinking, but now it's too late.'

'I promise you, Mother, that I was my sweetest. After all, you must realise that it is to my advantage as well – do you think I have not noticed how powerful he is and still unmated? Why do you think I volunteered to keep him distracted? Anyway, I sent word to Father as soon as he took off.'

'I'm sorry, you're right, you did the best you could.' She came forward and sat in the chair opposite her daughter, 'Though I hate to say it my dear, there are other, stronger females for Solvan to choose from.'

'I can hope,' she said. Her mother's lack of support made her angry so she changed the subject, 'What is this opportunity of which you spoke? If Isslac doesn't want it, I do.'

'I can't tell you, but it's not something you could have taken advantage off, but it is all too late now and it's gone, thanks to your brother. What did I ever do to deserve such a disobedient child?' she asked. Brelsa did not trust herself to answer that question with all the thoughts that were going around and around in her head.

'Go, I need time to think,' Welra said, waving Brelsa away.

Brelsa got up and walked out of the door as quickly as

possible in case her mother changed her mind. It would seem that Isslac had his own ideas about their parents' actions. Would he have the same ideas as her, though? She was going to have to talk to him and hope he did, because if not, she might end up in a lightless cell when her parents found out what she was doing. She had no idea where Isslac had gone or when he would be back, and she wondered what the great opportunity he had been offered was. She started to make her way to her father's study, and hoped that he was not there, so she could look for the plans of the castle's battlements. She was so absorbed with what she planned to do that she did not see Isslac until she walked into him and he had to grab her before she stumbled to the floor.

'Sorry, I wasn't looking where I was going,' she said.

'Don't worry about it,' he replied as he pushed her away and started to walk down the corridor.

'Wait!' she shouted out and went after him. 'I really need to talk to you.'

'Now is not a good time,' he said and kept on walking.

'I know something happened today with you and our parents.'

'How do you know that?'

'I was spying, I saw you walk off with the first protector in defiance of Mother.'

'So, what do you plan to do with that information? I'm sure Mother will tell Father soon enough without your interference.'

'Nothing, I was hoping we could talk and I really hope you feel the same way I do about how the people are treated, about the traders, about everything. Right now I'm hoping I can trust you because if I can't, what I'm going to say will probably get me a place in the lightless cells.'

'You believe the traders will return?'

'Yes,' she said simply.

'I'm going to Gilcan's rooms to talk with him; you are welcome to join me.'

'Why are you going there?'

'I want to discuss with him everything you just said you want to talk about, and to try to work out what to do. He is not allowed out of his rooms, so I need to go to him.'

'I'll come with you,' and together they walked in silence through the corridors.

As they approached the rooms Gilcan had been given, they saw another guard standing outside the door.

'Do you think he will report us?' Brelsa asked her brother.

'I don't know, but I would expect so. I just hope we have enough time to talk to Gilcan before we are disturbed – you don't have to come as well.'

'Yes, I do.'

Together they walked up to the guard.

'Is Gilcan in?' Isslac asked.

'Yes sir,'

'We want to talk to him,' Isslac said, hoping his father had not given orders to refuse all visitors. He knew why there was a guard: Gilcan had been making his thoughts too public for his parents' comfort and they wanted to keep an eye on him as a result, but he and Brelsa knew the details so hoped they would not be barred.

The guard said nothing as he opened the door for them and they proceeded in. Gilcan was staying in a suite of rooms in which the whole family had been placed when they had first arrived, but the others had moved out to get away from his 'poisonous views' and had been allowed more freedom to move around. There was no indication of which room he was in as the suite was quiet and all the doors were shut. Brelsa and Isslac looked at each other, shrugged and started to search for him. Each went to a door, knocked and entered. Isslac found him in the second room he tried; he was sitting at a desk, writing. He looked up as Isslac walked in and a look of surprise crossed his face at the visit.

'Brelsa, I have found him!' Isslac shouted as he walked further into the room and was very soon followed by his sister.

'Visitors, to what do I owe the pleasure of this visit?' Gilcan asked sarcastically.

'I need the truth,' Brelsa said.

'Your advice,' Isslac said at the same time.

Gilcan looked at them and pushed his work away from him, suddenly looking serious. 'One at a time would be better,' he said and indicated that they should sit down.

'I don't believe Father when he says there are no traders. The first protectors would not be pushing so hard about repairing the battlements if it were just a rumour,' Brelsa said. 'I want you to tell me what happened at your collective, what you saw.'

'And you?' he asked Isslac.

'The same, I want the truth of what happened. I need to know that I'm doing the right thing in going against my parents.'

'Why now?'

'If what I felt the other day was the traders attacking, I want to know. I don't want it to happen again, especially not here, so I need to know if what I felt was real or not,' Brelsa said.

'You felt it too?' Isslac asked her, suprised.

'Yes, I think we should have talked a while ago.'

'Well, we are all talking now,' Gilcan said. 'I confess that when the first protectors came to me telling me about the traders returning, I didn't believe them. I thought, as everyone did, that this was a ploy for them to try and regain their strength and influence over the collectives. Much of this, I think for us, was inspired by a jealously and mistrust of Solvan, and my mate's own prejudices. You are too young to remember but, for the last few generations, the first protectors have not been much stronger than the protectors on the collectives. To many, Essac and Bahia were placed in the postion to stop a consolidation of power as their mating would have meant taking over two collectives and was necessary for stability. There had been no trader attacks in generations making everyone think that the first protectors were redundant. We stopped listening to them and they, in turn, became more and more withdrawn, until now. When Solvan first came, I don't think anyone had seen anyone so powerful for generations, and it was thought that he was just trying to make the role of first protector strong again.'

'So what changed?' Brelsa prompted him.

'I started to have dreams, nightmares, and the occasional stabbing pain. Pesline had them as well but she just said they were bad dreams brought on by the first protectors continually talking about the traders and nothing more, but I wasn't convinced. Much to her horror, I even started looking at repairing the battlements. The day they came, I tried to get her to come to the battlements with me – I grabbed her, prepared to drag her there if need be, and that is the last thing I remember. She admitted later that she and Cardoc had knocked me unconscious. I regained consciousness in the tunnels under the castle after there had been some kind of blast. The air was full of dust and grit and the servants were hurt because they were at the back and my children were terrified, but that was nothing to what I could feel was happening to my people, it was like I was being ripped apart again and again. Eventually, once the pain had subsided, we made it out of the tunnels and back into the light and I went to see what had happened. The castle was a ruin, destroyed, I believe by the energy sent by the first protectors for me to direct onto the traders. On what little I could see of the fields were piles of bodies, and walking between them were these things, they were bigger than us and the sun glinted off them. There was this big vessel that took off and disappeared into the sky...' He paused. 'That's the brief account of what happened. So, are you going to call me mad now, like my family, like your parents?'

'No, we were always taught that the traders come from the sky, everyone knows that, that's why the first protectors are on the biggest mountain, so they can feel them sooner,' Brelsa said. 'I admit I'm scared to believe that what you say is true, because of what it will mean for all of us, of how complacent and ignorant we have become. What of Pesline and Cardoc, what do they think now?'

'They think I was deranged for wanting to stay and help no matter what the cost. They are convinced that they did the right thing in leaving our people to their fate. Pesline will always do what is best for Pesline and Cardoc will follow her. While your parents have the authority here, they will do as they want,' Gilcan said. 'Now that I have told you, what is it you want?'

'For you to help me rebuild the battlements here and work out how to defend the collective,' Brelsa said.

Gilcan laughed. 'Is that all?'

'I know it will be difficult, but I don't want to die and I don't want the people here to die either. If I can't do it, at least I will know I tried,' she said.

'I would need to look at the battlements. I knew how to fix mine, so if yours are similar, then yes, I can help you. How we can get around your father, though, I have no idea.'

'After what I have just told Solvan, I think father will

have a lot of his own problems,' Isslac said.

'What did happen today? What were you arguing with our parents over? Mother mentioned a wonderful opportunity which you refused, but she wouldn't tell me anything else other than it was something that couldn't be of advantage to me.'

'They were right, yesterday, when the people started to revolt and Father, Pesline and Cardoc stared to fire on them, someone stopped Father, knocked him unconscious and seriously winded Pesline and Cardoc as well.'

'I remember, he was furious, but what of it? Surely it was Solvan who did that?'

'No, he arrived a short time later. It was a peasant girl who did that.'

'Are you sure?' both Gilcan and Brelsa said at the same time, both shocked that there was someone else out there who could possibly be as powerful as Solvan.

'Yes, but Father caught her and is holding her in a lightless cell. He told me that, from what he could see through the dirt, her markings are equal to Solvan's.'

'Why did he tell you about her? Surely the fewer who know about her, the better?' Brelsa said.

'Solvan was also surprised that father had told me about her, but then he had to, for the great opportunity. He wants to force her to mate with me or, if I refuse, then with one of my brothers, in order to increase the power of the family.'

'He is mad! We have to get her out now – Hannoki only knows what he will do to her,' said Gilcan, already pulling himself up from the chair.

'That was the open disobedience of which I am guilty: I told Solvan everything and took him to the cells.'

'That was well done,' Gilcan said, 'but in those cells, Solvan will not have the advantage of his strength and

Ovato will have his guards.'

'I'm willing to bet that Solvan can store more energy than Father and his guards put together.'

'Why would he have thought to do it, though? Does he fully understand what the lightless cells are?' Gilcan asked. 'Remember that he has been living up on a mountain his whole life so he might not realise what they are.'

'I warned him of what to expect,' Isslac said.

'I think our first course of action should be to make sure Solvan and the girl have got out of the lightless cells, because without them, anything else we did would be pointless.'

'Thank you for helping us,' Brelsa said.

'I don't want what happened at my collective to ever happen again. We might have problems with the guard out front, he has instructions to follow me everywhere I go.'

'I can deal with him,' Isslac said as they all stood and walked out of the room.

⁕

She heard the clink then a grating noise and scrambled away from the sound. It had seemed like a lifetime since she had been locked up in this cold, dark place. No one had answered her, no matter how hard she had hit the door or how loud she had shouted. She had reached out again and again but there was no energy to grasp, what little she had stored had gone in healing the worst of her injuries. She had nothing left. Finally she had collapsed onto the floor and cried. Now someone was here, someone was coming to see her, and the possibility of getting out and seeing sunlight filled her with relief.

As the door opened outwards she saw a slight flicker of light. She moved forward thinking that she could get out, but as she got to the door she was roughly pushed back into the cell, and she stumbled with the force and fell against the back wall.

'You still have some fight in you, I see,' a male voice said. Lovoa looked up and saw three men enter. The one who spoke walked in first with the other two on either side of him, both holding torches. She glanced away as, after being in the dark, the light hurt her eyes.

'Who are you? Where am I? How long have I been here?' she asked.

'I am not here to answer your questions. You will, however, listen to me and answer any questions that I have, is that understood?' When Lovoa made no reply, he continued, 'Where have you come from?'

Lovoa turned her head and looked at him, her eyes getting used to the light, but she gave no reply.

'I said, where have you come from? You are not from my collective.' When he was met by more silence, he got angry that anyone should dare defy him. He walked forward and grabbed her by her hair, pulled her to her feet and twisted her head back so he could look her straight in the face. 'I know you can understand me,' he said. 'It will be easier for you if you co-operate.' Lovoa glared at him, but still gave no reply. 'Answer me!' he shouted and slammed her into the wall.

'Ouch,' escaped from between her lips as the air was forced out of her lungs with the impact.

'If you had any energy stored, you would have used it by now. My guess is that you do not, which means that the longer you are down here, the weaker you will get, and any injuries you already have, or will sustain while here, will not heal. Do you understand what I'm saying? Answer my questions, do as I say, and you will see sunlight again; continue to defy me and I will leave you to die down here.'

'If you wanted me dead, you would have killed me already,' she spat at him in defiance.

Ovato laughed. 'Are you really that stupid? You should know I can't kill you outright because if you died a sudden death, everyone would feel it and everyone would know what I had done. I could, however, let you die a slow, painful, natural death and although some would still feel it, they would not question it the same way, and I will if you do not start doing as I want.' He slammed her against the wall again as hard as he could before letting her go and watching as her legs collapsed beneath her and she slid down the wall to the floor, gasping for breath.

Slowly she turned her head so that she faced him again. 'I think I'm dead whether I answer your questions or not, so why make it easy for you?'

Ovato kicked her where she lay and was gratified with her grunt of pain. 'No matter, I fully expect that you will change your mind shortly. However, in answer to one of your earlier questions, you have not been here for very long, and perhaps when I come back tomorrow, you will be more willing, or perhaps I will go and get those peasant friends of yours as well. I hear they have a lovely little girl – how do you think they will fare down here with you?'

'You bastard!' she shouted and launched herself up off the floor towards him, but suddenly she found herself being thrown back into the wall with considerable force and her stomach felt as if it was on fire.

'I, however, did store some energy before I came down here, so if you think you could physically take me, you are very much mistaken. Perhaps some more pain would make you start to reflect on what would make you more amenable for when I return.' He walked forward and pinned her to the floor with his foot. Slowly he created a ball of energy above his hand and Lovoa could do nothing but look in horror as it gradually grew bigger and bigger. 'Let us see how you like this,' he said as he pulled his arm back. Lovoa closed her eyes, not wanting to see the blow as it came. Then nothing. The weight of Ovato's foot lifted, followed by a thud next to her, and she opened her eyes to see Ovato slumped on the floor. Startled, she looked around her and saw that another male had entered and stood between two surprised and terrified-looking guards.

'Are you all right?' he asked as he walked forward. Lovoa watched him with caution. She could not see him clearly in the dark, as at this distance his face was in the shadow of the torches, so as he came closer she tried to move back, but could not because of the wall. The male stopped a metre from her and crouched down next to her.

'Who are you?' she whispered.

'Don't you recognise me?' he asked and created his own light so she could see him clearly. She took a sudden gasp of breath and he smiled. 'You know me,' he stated.

'You were by the pool and in my dreams,' she replied, 'you told me I could trust you.'

'And you can. My name is Solvan and I'm one of the first protectors.'

'I'm Lovoa and my parents were peasants,' she replied.

'It is a pleasure to meet you properly at last,' he said and extended his hand to her. She immediately placed hers in his and let him help her to her feet. As she straightened up, she winced in pain, whether from the blast or the kick Ovato had dealt her she was not sure. Solvan heard and felt her pain. 'Can you walk out of here?' he asked.

'Yes, even if it kills me.'

'You are stubborn.'

'So my parents always complained,' she replied, then

shuddered as she remembered what had happened to them before taking a deep breath and controlling herself.

'What about him and the guards?' she suddenly asked, turning to look at the male who was still slouched, unconscious, on the floor.

'Any energy he has stored will go to healing him so he will probably regain consciousness soon. He can stay down here until you are safely away from here. It will be unpleasant for him but it will not hurt him to stay here for a few hours. As for the guards, I think they are quickly learning that I don't take orders from Ovato,' he said, looking at them, but they still looked terrified at how easily their protector had been overcome. 'He is to stay down here until Isslac or Brelsa gives word that he can be released – and only them, do not accept orders from anyone else, including Welra or any of his other children, do you understand?' he asked them and had the satisfaction of watching them nod in bewilderment. 'Good,' he said.

Chapter 19

THEY saw them coming out of the guard barracks.

'There!' Isslac said and pointed towards them, and the others looked in the direction he was indicating. Solvan had just exited the building and was supporting another smaller, dirty person. Guards stood nearby, watching them, but none tried to stop them from leaving. Isslac ran forward towards Solvan with Brelsa and Gilcan following close behind him.

Solvan saw them coming quickly towards him. He had been surprised by the support of both Isslac and Brelsa, but how far would they go against their parents? And Gilcan? He knew he was here but had not spoken to him since he had let his collective fall. The guards were obeying him for the moment but if he were challenged by Isslac, Brelsa and Gilcan, he was worried that they would take their side and he would not be able to get Lovoa out of the collective because he expected her to be too weak to fly on her own at the moment, and he had to consider the possibility that she had never learnt to fly. The guards had tensed on seeing their protector's son and daughter approach at speed and their grip on their weapons tightened. Yes, he could definitely be in for a fight if he were challenged.

'Solvan, you are all right,' Isslac said as he stopped in front of him. 'I'm sorry, it was not until I was talking to Gilcan that I realised that I had not made sure you fully understood the impact of the lightless cells – I take it you knew.'

Solvan smiled slightly. 'No, but I had some help,' he said. As he spoke he felt Lovoa sag slightly against him. She had made it up the stairs with his support but it had taken a lot out of her and she was tired, drained and hurt. Solvan had noticed that the guards had relaxed slightly once they heard the conversation, but he would still prefer to get away from the barracks as soon as possible to somewhere Lovoa could recover some of her strength. 'Is there anywhere I can take Lovoa where she will be safe while she recovers?'

'Of course,' Isslac said, and he looked at the girl holding on to Solvan for the first time. She was slight and so covered in dirt it was hard to see her properly. She kept her head bent so her hair fell across her face, and the only indication that she was awake and listening to the conversation was the strength with which she was holding on to Solvan. He could see nothing special about her as she was, but when she was clean? He had to admit that he was curious as to exactly how extensive her markings were to make Solvan and his father so desperate to have her. 'There are the balconies, I can show you to one of those, they are on all sides so one of them will always get full sunlight during the day.'

'But they are open,' Brelsa said.

'That is the point,' Isslac replied, 'for access to the sun.'

'No, I mean that all the balconies are off main rooms and there are only shutters to close them off during the storms, so anyone could get onto them.'

'She's right, you can't barricade yourself on to one. You might just as well stay here, at least we can clearly see anyone approach.'

'What about the battlements?' Gilcan asked. 'They are designed to restrict access from the castle, though obviously they are accessible by flight, which would, I imagine, greatly limit the number of people who could try to attack you. I haven't seen the condition of the battlements here, but there should be areas which would make defending your position easier – after all, that is their purpose.'

'He's right, obviously Mother and Father could fly up there, as well as the rest of our family and, Gilcan's as well,' Isslac said and glanced over at him to see him nod. 'I assume most of the guards would be capable. It would be difficult to defend, but not impossible bearing in mind that most of those able to fly to the battlements are children. Where is Father?' Isslac asked suddenly. 'I thought he was down in the cells.'

'He was and still is,' Solvan said. 'He did not seem open to listening to reason.'

'You locked him in the lightless cell?' Isslac asked, shocked. 'Are you going to let him out?'

'I gave orders that he is to be released on your or Brelsa's order only, after we have left. I will leave it entirely up to you how you deal with your father.'

'Thank you, we will give you whatever support you need.'

'All right then, one less problem to deal with,' Brelsa said, slightly taken aback at the news but relieved that her father could not interfere. 'Right, now let us get you to the battlements and fetch water to wash off all that dirt.'

'Thank you, Brelsa,' Solvan said and he took a firmer hold of Lovoa. 'Will you be able to fly to the battlements?' he asked her.

'No, I don't think so, but I can walk,' she said and he felt her take more of her own weight.

'Good, we will take it at your pace,' Solvan said, he was tempted to pick her up and fly her there, but knew it was important to her to have some control.

'Follow Isslac, I will meet you up there with water and

anything else I can find that will be useful.'

'All right,' Isslac said and started to head back to the castle. The going was slow and once or twice they had to stop briefly for Lovoa to rest. 'We can carry you,' Isslac said when they stopped the second time, but she just shook her head and continued. Once they were inside the castle, though, and out of the sunlight, Lovoa all but collapsed. Gilcan grabbed her before she hit the floor and had to help Solvan support her until they got to the stairs that led to the battlements, but there was not enough room for both Gilcan and Solvan to support her up them.

'Thank you, Gilcan, I have this now,' Solvan said and when Gilcan was happy that Solvan had a firm hold of the girl, he let go. She briefly slumped without the extra support before Solvan swung her up into his arms. She did not protest at being carried, but relaxed into his arms, totally exhausted. 'After you, Isslac,' Solvan said and Isslac went quickly up the stairs and opened the door at the top. Solvan followed close behind and once they were standing on the battlements, glanced around him and placed Lovoa in direct sunlight.

'Do not close the door,' a shout came as Gilcan had been about to swing it closed behind them, and Brelsa came through carrying a large bowl of water and a bag slung over her back. She walked straight over to Solvan and Lovoa and placed the bowl down in front of the girl. Carefully, she leaned forward and pulled Lovoa's hair away from her face and saw the dirt and bruises that covered her face, but beneath it all she could just make out her markings. 'She will feel better quickly once all this dirt is washed off,' she said, and taking some cloth out of the bag, wet it and carefully put it to Lovoa's face. On feeling the cold, Lovoa jerked back sharply. 'It's all right,' Brelsa said as she looked into Lovoa's now open eyes.

'You have the same markings as the protector here,' Lovoa said.

'I am Brelsa. I'm Protector Ovato's oldest daughter but I promise I mean you no harm,' she said, but as she tried again to clean Lovoa's face, the girl pulled away.

'It's all right, no one here means you any harm, you are safe with us,' Solvan reassured her and he reached out and took the cloth from Brelsa. 'See, it is just a cloth, and once you are clean, you will feel better, you know that,' he said.

Lovoa took a deep breath and said, 'Yes, I'm sorry,' and very gently Solvan started to wipe the dirt from her face. As he got to the bruise, Lovoa winced but said nothing.

Brelsa wet a second cloth. 'May I?' she asked and Lovoa nodded. Just as gently, Brelsa took the arm closest to her and began to clean it.

'At home, I always used to wash in a pool near where I lived. The water was always cold, but so clean, and the currents moved around you.'

'I know it well,' said Solvan. Lovoa's lips twitched into a smile but she said nothing further, she just leaned back against the wall and closed her eyes.

'That sounds nice, we have nothing like that here, this is the best we have.' Brelsa said looking at the cloth and quickly growing dirty water.

Gilcan and Isslac stood a short distance away and watched in silence as the dirt was wiped away, revealing the extent of the girl's markings.

'I don't think we can wash much more off with what we have,' Solvan said after a while as he placed the cloth back into the bowl of now very dirty water.

'Even with all the remaining dirt, I can see that she has more markings than I have on my entire body,' Brelsa commented.

Solvan stood up and looked down at Lovoa. She was relaxed, lying back against the wall, and he thought that she had fallen asleep, but without probing her mind he could not say for sure. Slowly he turned and joined Gilcan and Isslac where they had been watching a short distance away. Brelsa followed him.

'I don't recognise the patterning, who is she?' Gilcan asked.

'She is the daughter of a peasant family who lived on an independent farm just outside of Buxus's collective until a few days ago.'

'You knew about her? Buxus knew about her? No, he won't have tolerated her and her family anywhere near his collective,' Gilcan said, trying to get his mind around the girl's existence. 'I don't understand how I did not know about her.'

'No one knew about her; her parents kept her well hidden.'

'The mating flight must have been seen.'

'It was. My father searched for the couple but never found them, and he never heard that anyone else had found them either.'

'So, what do we do now?'

'I appreciate your help Gilcan, but you let your people die and your collective has been destroyed. Your mate and son have sided with Ovato and helped him assault his people and Lovoa directly. Though your support just now was welcome, how can I trust you? How do I know that you are not just helping now so you can give this information to Ovato in return for somewhere to live?'

'We went to Gilcan for help. Father had placed him under guard shortly after he arrived as he didn't like what he was telling people,' Isslac explained.

'I did not let my people die, I was going to help them but Pesline and Cardoc stopped me.'

'You expect me to just believe you?' Solvan said.

'You believed us, Isslac and myself, you took us at our word that you had our help and support,' Brelsa said.

Solvan paused, she was right, he had accepted both her and her brother's help without question, but he could not think of anything they had to gain by their actions.

'Let me show you,' Gilcan said and he held out his hands, 'let me show you what happened and what I believe.'

'You would do that?' Solvan said, shocked, and looked at Gilcan's outstretched hands.

'There is no time for distrust, so yes, I am sure.'

'I could see everything.'

'I have nothing to hide.'

Solvan gripped Gilcan's hands and reached out with his mind to find that Gilcan had opened his mind fully to him; everything was there for him to see and feel, the pain, the guilt and, most of all, the anger at his mate and son for what they had done.

'I am sorry, Gilcan,' Solvan said, letting go of his hands.

'I need to help, I need to try and repay the debt,' he said simply. Solvan nodded, too shocked by what he had seen to say anything.

'We all want to help,' Isslac corrected, 'so if you need to see my thoughts to trust me, then you are welcome.'

'And me, we know our father is wrong, and we want to help in any way we can, but we need direction on what to do,' Brelsa added.

Solvan looked at them, brother and sister, and wondered how a couple like Ovato and Welra could produce children like them. They both stood there, with their hands held out as Gilcan had, but he could feel the emotion coming off them. They might need the tactile contact for the reading they were willing to allow, but he did not. Gilcan had been different, with him he had wanted to see everything that had happened, and now he had the truth and it horrified him. He had decided not to take their hands, but then realised that they did not fully understand what he could do and not accepting what they offered could cause a rift between the new alliance of Gilcan and the siblings, so he reached out and took their hands one at a time and had his understanding of them reinforced.

'Thank you,' Solvan said, and for a while they all just stood there in silence.

'Then tell us what you need us to do,' Gilcan said, breaking the uneasiness.

'But first, can you tell us more about her? If her parents were sought and never found, how did you know she was here, now?'

'I only found out about her a few days ago when I encountered her by chance at a pool near where she lived. I have been looking for her ever since.'

'I wondered what you found so amusing about that comment.'

'Exactly. However, when she saw me, she ran and I lost her in the forest.'

'How were you able to lose her? Could you not sense her?'

'I don't know what training she has had, but she is very good at closing off her mind. It's my belief that she learnt to do this from a very early age, which is why no one has ever sensed her,' Solvan explained. 'I know that she was living on an independent farm, so it was easy for her parents to keep her isolated from everyone, but other than that, I know very little.'

'I take it you went to the farm, so what explanation did her parents give?' Gilcan asked.

'I went there and found only dead bodies,' Solvan said.

'What happened?' Brelsa asked.

'Strange things came; they were big and shone in the sun. I arrived too late, my parents were lying on the ground, skinned.' As one, they all turned and looked at Lovoa. She was still leaning against the wall, but she sat up straighter and was looking at them.

'I saw their bodies when I went there looking for you,' Solvan said, walking towards her. 'Did you see what happened?' He sat down in front of her so they were face to face, then the others followed him so they were all sitting in a circle.

'I knew there was something wrong when the feeling ripped through me, but I was too late. When I got home, I saw my parents dead, skinned. There were things there that I had never seen before. I think they were talking because they were making this noise, but I couldn't understand them. One of them grabbed me and he was so hard, and I tried kicking him but it was like kicking a smooth rock. He threw me to the floor and started to come towards me. I knew he was going to kill me, as he had my parents. I put my hands up to stop him and something went through me and the next thing I knew, the thing was lying in front of me, in two parts, and I just got up and ran away before the others followed me,' Lovoa said and she started to shake as she remembered. 'What were they?' she asked.

'They were the traders,' Solvan said.

'Where do they come from? Why did they do that to my parents? They wouldn't have hurt anyone.'

'You must have heard all the stories about the traders?' Gilcan said.

'My parents mentioned them the night before they died, but I was upset and wouldn't listen to them. We were going to talk again that night but...' She could not continue.

'The traders have left us alone for many generations, so

I don't have all the answers,' Solvan explained. 'What we do know is that they come from the sky and they take our skins and wings, but I don't know why they want them. Several small farms, like your parents', were attacked first and they have attacked one collective as well.'

'Will they be back?'

'Yes,' he said simply.

'How do we stop them?'

'That is what we were about to discuss,' Solvan said. 'Can I introduce to you Protector Gilcan, and Brelsa and Isslac, who are Protector Ovato's oldest son and daughter.' Solvan felt her tense up next to him. 'I can assure you that they don't support their father in any way. If it were not for Isslac's assistance, I would not have found you when I did.' She looked at them with suspicion but accepted their presence, although Gilcan and his collective meant nothing to her.

'Then I thank you,' she said.

'You're welcome,' Isslac replied.

'So how do we stop them?' Lovoa asked again. She looked around her and did not recognise anything, 'Where are we? Are we safe?'

'We are on the battlements of Ovato's collective, and yes, we are safe,' he reassured her, not wanting to go into all the details, 'do you trust me?' he asked. He was not sure whether she did, as for the first time he was confronted with someone he could not read at all. She looked at him for a while, as if thinking everything through, then slowly she nodded her head. 'How we can stop them is hard to explain, so it would be easier to show you. Will you come back with me?' Solvan asked.

'Back where?'

'To Hannoki.'

'The mountain? There is nothing there.'

'My home is there, there are chambers on the peak.

You can fly?' he asked suddenly.

'Yes,' Lovoa confirmed, 'but just around the farm. I have never tried to fly up a mountain before,' she admitted, somewhat worried. She tried to move and winced in pain: she hurt everywhere.

'You need to rest some more; the bruising will ease quickly in the sunlight.' Lovoa leaned back against the wall again with a sigh. 'We will not leave until you are ready,' he promised her.

'You seem convinced I will go with you?' Lovoa questioned.

'If you want to stop the traders, you will come with me. My parents are doing the best they can at the moment, but you and me! We could blast them from the sky.'

'You sound very sure,' she said.

'That is because I am. We need each other, but you need to rest now.' He stood up and started to walk away.

'Where are you going?' Lovoa asked suddenly, afraid to be left alone here.

'Just to talk to Gilcan, Isslac and Brelsa about what they need to do. We will not leave the battlements without you,' he promised.

Solvan watched her and after a moment she closed her eyes and relaxed. It was hard to tell what was the remaining dirt and what was bruising. He knew that she had taken a beating from Ovato, and just hoped that she would recover quickly, as the sooner they could leave here, the better.

'How was Father even able to capture someone as strong as her?' Isslac asked as Solvan approached them.

'I'm not sure, but she is exhausted and injured and not all of the injuries were caused by your father. She has been through a lot these last few days,' Solvan said.

'Maybe he took her by surprise and knocked her over the head,' Brelsa suggested.

'Why do you say that?' her brother asked.

'Because there is extensive bruising to her face and blood in her hair, with a big lump underneath it,' she told him.

'How Ovato got hold of her is not important at present, but what we do next is,' Solvan said.

'I have had a quick look at the battlements. From what I can see, they are in a better state than my own were and they follow the same design. With the correct materials, tools and enough help, they could be fixed reasonably quickly,' Gilcan informed them.

'Good, what about your father?' Solvan asked Isslac and Brelsa.

'I don't know, but he is going to have to be taken out of the lightless cell sometime soon,' Isslac said.

'He is going to be mad when he comes out,' Brelsa pointed out.

'We could keep him under guard in one of the other cells where the light is very limited,' Isslac pondered. 'The guards have proved to have more loyalty to me than to him, they were more than happy to follow Brelsa's and my lead in letting you and Lovoa go and I have heard rumours spreading about the destruction of Gilcan's collective. No matter how hard Father has tried to stop them, I think a lot of people are afraid that they could be next.'

'Mother will not stand for it when she finds out,' Brelsa pointed out.

'She will have to put up with it. I can talk to the guards and try to get them to follow me rather than Mother. I don't think we will have problems from our other brothers and sisters since they hid to avoid being forced to attack our people, so I believe they will support us. Together we are more than enough to hold against both Mother and Father.'

'I'm not sure what Pesline and Cardoc will do, but I doubt they would do anything unless it is guaranteed to be of advantage to them,' Gilcan stated.

'It sounds as if you are confident you can hold against your parents, but once I have got Lovoa home, I will ask my parents to come and make sure you are all right,' Solvan said.

'Thank you, the extra support would be helpful,' Isslac said.

'Well, these battlements won't fix themselves,' Gilcan said. 'Come on Isslac, show me where everything is kept,' and with a nod to Solvan, they walked off to start work. Solvan went back to where Lovoa was sitting against the wall, saw that she was totally relaxed and saw how shallow her breathing was: she had fallen into an exhausted sleep. He settled himself on the floor next to her and waited.

Chapter 20

CAL would have preferred a small, private affair, but that had been impossible, too many people had wished to pay their last respects to a popular and much-admired leader. His father had been cremated an hour before in a moving ceremony in the Old Catholic style, as this had been his religion. The church had been crowded and the streets outside had been closed off because of the volume of people wanting to mourn. The whole service had been filmed and shown on screens all over the united planets. Cal had not wanted that, but everyone had insisted, saying that the people expected it, that they had the right to say their farewells, but to Cal it seemed like macabre voyeurism, these people had not known his father.

As he had left the church and been driven away, he had seen the pavements lined with people dressed in black and crying. Such grief for someone they had never met seemed unreal. What would they think if they knew the truth about his father's death? Cal wondered. Would they become an angry mob, but after enough time had passed, would they even care?

The further they got from the church, the fewer people he saw, but when they reached his father's home, they found more people waiting at the gate and security had to clear them out of the way to let the cars pass safely through. At least everyone coming to the wake had been invited, he thought. As the car drove through the gates and pulled up outside the mansion, Cal looked up at it.

He had rarely visited his father since he had left home, work and other interests had always taken precedence and he had always thought there would be more time. He had an apartment near enough to the Capitol that when he had business here he rarely had to stay over, and on the rare occasions when it had been necessary, he had taken a hotel room, telling his father he would be working very late and did not want to disturb him. He had been here, of course, since his father had died to talk to some of the staff and make the necessary arrangements, but he and Jane had been staying at a nearby hotel.

A hand took hold of his and squeezed it. 'Are you ready?' Jane asked him.

With a deep breath, he squeezed Jane's hand back and let it go. 'Let's get this over with,' he said and opened the car door. As he climbed out, the mansion doors were thrown open by the staff, all ready to receive the arriving guests. He looked towards them and realised that he did not know any of them, he did not know which had been employed by his father or which had been hired for the wake. He moved to the other side and helped Jane out of the car, and together they walked up the stairs and inside, ready to greet all the guests.

Caterers had been hired to arrange the food. In fact, Cal had taken no part in organising the wake at all, and he did not even know for sure who would be attending. Jane had offered to do it, but he had not wanted her attention taken from investigating why his father had died, so he had left it all to his father's personal assistant, telling him that he and his staff were in a better position to know who should be invited and, if in doubt, the state department would tell them who needed to be on the guest list and which catering companies would be acceptable. He had told them that he could not cope with arranging everything, and whether they had believed him or not, had accepted the excuse and taken on the arrangements without complaint, leaving Cal free to further investigate who had killed his father.

Cal stood alone and received the guests because as far as everyone was concerned, Jane was just his PA, and she had moved into the living rooms where the wake was being held. He kept his face neutral and thanked everyone for coming. The faces and names blurred together and it was not long before he was acting on instinct, but luckily no one was expecting anything from him. Most of the guests arrived together, having followed them from the church, and once they had passed through, he felt he could leave his welcoming position and join the wake.

Looking around the room, Cal recognised his father's board, other people he knew from the media, and politicians and prominent social figures, but he was disturbed by how many people he did not know at all. Over the course of the evening he spoke with as many people as possible, and when he did not know them, he asked how they knew his father, trying to build up a picture of to whom he had been most connected. Most were happy to talk to him about his father, curious about the son everyone knew the chairman had, but whom they had never met, but always the conversation was general and always ended with the same thing, 'I'm so sorry for your loss,' and, 'What a tragic accident,' and he politely thanked them and moved on – what more was there to say?

'Cal, may I offer you my deepest condolences,' a very familiar voice said behind him. Turning, he saw a very welcome face.

'Thank you, Admiral,' Cal said, 'I'm so glad you could make it.'

'Your father was a very old friend of mine, of course I would be here,' he replied. 'I would very much like to meet tomorrow, to catch up on old times and to talk about your father, about his life.'

'I would like that very much,' Cal replied.

'How about breakfast in my office, is 8.00am too early?'

'No, that will be fine.'

'Good, I will see you tomorrow then,' and he moved away to make room for others trying to get Cal's attention.

Cal slowly started to walk around the room again, having a few words with guests, being a good host, even though he did not want all these people here. He could see that Jane was also moving from group to group.

'Have you seen the new season?' he heard one of the board member's wives, Mrs Alver, say. 'I have never seen anything like it, I've already placed an order.'

'It's true then, these new coats can really change colour with your mood?'

'Oh yes, I saw one that was already reserved at Gloria's, and she's expecting a bigger delivery any day now.'

Cal moved on, this conversation bringing clearly to mind what Jane had told him about the skins that had been harvested. He moved around the room, making his way towards Jane, and as she saw him, she said something to the people she was talking to and came towards him.

'How are you doing?' she asked him.

'Holding up. I need you to talk to Mrs Alver, I've just overheard her talking about a new coat that changes colour with the wearer's mood.'

'Like before?'

'Possibly. I didn't ask for details because my asking fashion questions would be regarded as strange.'

'I'll see what I can find out for you,' she said and moved past him to talk to Mrs Alver.

Eventually the last of the guests were leaving and soon, Cal thought, he would be alone with Jane. He had seen her talking with Mrs Alver for some time, and when he had glanced over, their conversation seemed to be going well, with their heads close together as if sharing secrets, but his duty as host had not allowed him to talk to Jane again.

As Cal closed the door on the last person, he walked back into the living room and saw all the staff busy tidying away the rubbish and glasses.

'Why don't we have a brandy in your father's study?' Jane said as she came up to him, holding two glasses and a bottle in her hands, 'let the staff clear up here without us getting underfoot.'

'A brandy sounds wonderful,' he said and he cupped Jane's elbow, led her out of the room and down the corridor. He paused outside a solid oak door, 'I haven't been in his office since I left home.'

'He would want you to use it,' Jane said, understanding his feeling about invading his father's privacy, 'but there are plenty of other rooms.'

'No, here is a good place to talk.'

Cal put his hand out, turned the handle and pushed the door open. Part of him was surprised, he had expected the room to be locked, and he walked in. The office was more or less as he remembered it; the furniture was the same, even down to the old and worn comfortable chair in the corner and the solid oak desk which had been in the family for generations. Walking around, he saw that the room had been upgraded, noted the security at the windows which would allow his father to secure himself inside if necessary. He sat at the desk and ran his hands over the smooth surface and down to the drawers. He tried pulling at the handles and smiled, they were locked. Cal noticed that no computers or files had been left out; he guessed that everything was locked in the desk. He would have to see if he could get into it soon, but found that he did not have the strength to do it tonight. He was annoyed with himself for not having thought to check sooner whether there were written documents here, he had assumed that Jane would find that everything his father had been working on by hacking into his computer.

He looked up and saw that she had sat down opposite him and was pouring two generous measures before picking up one of the glasses and handing it to him. He accepted it gratefully and took a long swallow, then put the glass down and leaned back in the chair.

'Did you find out anything useful?' Cal asked finally.

'Most people were telling me about how they knew your father and their favourite stories about him, or they were indulging in gossip. I'm sorry, I wasn't able to get anything that would help find out who killed him. However, Mrs Alver and her friends were different, she was more than happy to talk about fashion and her recent order, and she described it in extensive detail.'

'And are the coats what I think they are?'

'It sounds like it, yes.'

'It's only been days – how could they have got the skins into the shops already?'

'They must have started earlier than we thought, before your father died.'

'So how many are already dead?'

'I don't know. Mrs Alver was boasting about how exclusive the coats were, how much they cost and how long she had to wait for one. I couldn't find out anything more than that.'

'I didn't find out anything either,' Cal admitted. 'The only useful thing from the wake was a meeting arranged for early tomorrow with the admiral.'

'What time and where?' she asked.

'Tomorrow at 8.00am at his office.'

Jane looked at the time, 'It's getting late, do you want to

head back to the hotel?'

'No,' Cal said, 'I'm going to stay here tonight. If you wish to go back, I will arrange a lift for you,' but as he spoke he reached over and took hold of her hand in a silent request.

'I can stay,' Jane said.

⁎

The next morning, just before 8.00am, both Cal and Jane arrived at the naval base, and were met at the entrance by a member of the admiral's staff. After introducing himself and checking their identity, he led them in silence through numerous corridors to the admiral's office. Cal thought his father had had a lot of security, but there was even more here, and their escort had to have his pass scanned several times before they were allowed to proceed, and a palm reader was used at the final check. Cal and Jane walked into an office with several desks on either side and another set of doors at the end, which opened as they made their way towards them.

'Cal, on time as always,' Admiral Johnson said as he came towards them. He held his hand out and Cal took it. 'I'm sorry to drag you all the way over here to catch up, but unfortunately things are so busy these days, breakfast was the only free time I had this week.'

'That's fine, I'm just glad we were able to find a mutual time,' Cal said, following his lead that this was just a social call.

'Simon is fine, Cal, we don't need to be so formal.' He led them across the room and closed the solid doors behind them. 'I don't think we are acquainted,' Simon said, looking at Jane.

'I'm sorry,' Cal said, 'Admiral Simon Johnson, this is Jane Keyworth. She has been my PA for the last five years and is also my partner. Jane, this is my godfather,

Admiral Simon Johnson.'

'A pleasure to meet you, my dear,' he said, then turned to Cal. 'I thought you would be coming on your own.'

'Jane is fully aware of everything I know so far. In fact, she found out most of it herself. She is fully trustworthy.'

The admiral sighed and looked at Jane, clearly trying to make up his mind about her.

'Admiral, if we want to find out everything that is happening, we are going to have to trust each other. If I'm honest, I don't know you at all and I was reluctant to involve you, especially as someone close to Cal's father must be involved, but Cal has told me I can trust you, and I trust Cal,' Jane said simply.

'All right,' he said after a moment's pause, 'it would look strange if my godson's girlfriend was told she had to leave when you are here on a social visit. At best, people would say I disapprove, but it would still bring more attention our way, but I want a promise that whatever is discussed in this room stays in this room.'

'Of course, I would ask the same as well,' Jane said.

'Agreed. Please take a seat and tell me what you want to eat so we can get it delivered and not be disturbed.' He indicated to where two sofas were placed on either side of a low table. Cal and Jane took one and the admiral sat opposite them. 'So what do you want?' he asked and once they had given him their choices, he called the order through to someone. 'It will be here shortly,' he told them. 'I did as you asked and have been informed of the results. I'm hoping you will tell me why you needed this done.'

'Admiral, I would but...' Cal started to say in denial.

'Trust is trust,' Jane said over him, 'you asked him to trust you when you asked for the favour, at risk to his career, and he's just told you he has done it. You've asked him to trust me and I'm still sitting here.'

'I know, but someone close to my father betrayed him,' Cal said.

'And if it were the admiral, don't you think he would already know we are on to something with your request?' Jane pointed out. She took hold of his hand, 'I know you're struggling with trusting people, you were never good at it even before your father was killed, but you need to trust him or I don't think we will ever get all answers. You told me to trust him when I was unsure about contacting him, so I'm telling you now to follow that instinct and trust him with everything or we might as well leave now.'

'I'm not sure what your father's accident had to do with the space co-ordinates you gave me, but I would never betray either you or your father,' the admiral reassured him.

A knock on the door broke the tense silence and Admiral Johnson called for the person to come in. As expected, it was their food, the staff officer came in, placed it on the table between them and was dismissed.

'I'm not sure how much time you have this morning, but if you want to know everything, it will take a while,' Cal said as the door closed, sealing them in the room again.

'I'm getting the feeling I'll be clearing my schedule today,' he replied.

Jane smiled slightly, leaned forward and picked up the cafetière. 'Coffee anyone?' she asked and when both men looked at her, she said, 'What, I'm hungry and in need of coffee. I always think better on a full stomach and caffeine fix, I don't know about you,' and the strain left the room as Cal started to laugh at the comment.

'Thank you, I would love some.'

Jane served the drinks and as they settled down to their breakfast, Cal started to explain everything they knew so far.

'When I was told about my father's death, I wanted answers, I wanted to know how, with all the security, the accident could have happened. Had he taken a different car from normal? So, I came home and waited for the report to come through, hoping it would answer the questions going around and around in my head, but it didn't. If anything, it created more. I asked Jane to get me an appointment to see the car and to meet with the officials who wrote the report, but she could do neither. I also tried using some of my connections, but still had no luck, so we decided to just go and look at the car.'

'You're saying that after refusing to make a formal appointment for you to see the car, they just let you in when you showed up?'

'Not exactly, we didn't call during office hours,' Cal admitted.

'I'm thinking that *how* you got in should remain your business,' the admiral said. 'Did you find anything out?'

'Oh yes, the car he was in was not his, it was the same make and model and had the same identification tags, but it was not his car.'

'So he changed his car, what does that prove?'

'The car he was in had no shields and none of the extra security I had created. In was, in fact, just a basic car. My father was very security conscious; he would never have got into that car if he had known. This raised the question of the crash and how accidental was it? Jane started to look through computer records and found out that the head technician had gone missing before the crash and his deputy was heavily in debt. The deputy had recently been paid a large sum of money, and we believe it was to switch the cars. Having gone to so much trouble, they could not leave anything to chance and the accident was deliberately orchestrated. How exactly this was done I'm still unclear, but what we do know is that it was not a teenager, as reported in the news. The person in the car was the missing technician and, according to the coroner's report, was already dead when the accident happened.'

'What you're telling me is that you believe your father was murdered!' the admiral stated. He had gone white and his hands shook slightly as he took a sip of coffee. 'Are you sure about these facts?'

'Yes,' Cal said.

'Who is responsible? Why?'

'We don't know who is responsible yet, though we have our suspicions. Clearly it has to be someone close to him to know his movements and with enough authority to cover it up.'

'Do you know the why?'

'I believe we do know, which is also why we asked you to check out that section of space,' Cal said. 'We started looking through my father's files to see if there was anything people would want to keep quiet. In his files was research into a new trade deal which was being changed at the time of his death. The deal would take ships through a restricted area of space, and an appeal had been filed to unrestrict the area, which would cut travelling times for supply ships.'

'Why would anyone want to do that? Areas are normally restricted because it is dangerous to travel through them, so why would he want to change anything?'

'It was not restricted due to any space hazards; it was restricted because of the planet in this area and the people who live there. According to the records, the people, though sentient, were not technically advanced and were killed for their skins and wings. The practice was stopped and the scandal was covered up. I can only guess that the area was closed off to stop others finding them and the same thing happening again.'

'Why not just say the truth, this is where the items came from, and it would have stopped without all this secrecy?'

'I believe it was covered up because of *who* was involved. This is a scandal that could only have occurred with support from the FWN and would only have affected people with money and, most likely, a lot of influence.'

'So, say you're right about your history, how does this affect the now?' the admiral asked.

'We thought that with my father finding out about this, others did as well and decided to start the trade again. Of course, Father would have known where these products came from, and that allowing other ships near the restricted area would have increased the likelihood of rogue ships being seen to enter and exit an area where they were not meant to be.'

'It seems to be a great leap to assume all of this.'

'I know, that's why I asked for you to check into the area, to see if there was anything going on,' Cal said.

'Also, at the wake yesterday,' Jane continued, 'we found out that a new fashion sensation is coming into the stores, coats that change colour with the wearer's mood. There is lots of speculation on how they can do it. The description I was given matches the one given in the first chairman's files, which is why we now think that this started before Cal's father died.'

'Now you know what has been happening, what we believe, what did your checks of the area show?' Cal asked.

'No ships were seen, but there is evidence that at least one has been in that area of space recently,' the admiral said. 'It will be impossible for you to prove anything with what you have, and from what you are not telling me, I gather some of it was gained illegally, so how do you propose to prove any of this?'

'By going to the planet and getting the evidence of the trade so we can expose it,' Cal said.

'You think it would be that easy? If you are correct, this knowledge got your father killed,' he said, getting angry and frustrated with Cal.

'I know that, but other than you, no one knows how much we have found out, and if we expect trouble, we can take precautions against it,' Cal argued.

'You honestly think that just because you sneaked in to look at your father's car, these people haven't noticed that you have been pulling off all his files on this?'

'You know when you said some of it was "gained illegally", well actually, most of it. They won't know about the information I've gained from his computer,' Jane admitted.

'I honestly don't know what to say to that.'

'Cal was shocked too, and I think a little scared of what else I might have looked at,' she said jokingly, and the tension in the office relaxed slightly.

'How are you planning to get to this planet? You can't just hire a ship to take you there, and what happens when you get there? I expect these people would be hostile towards you, or worse, what if the people you are after are there? They would be well armed.'

'I was hoping you could help us with that,' Cal admitted.

'Right, I can just give you a ship and crew to go into an area of space that is restricted without explanation, because I won't be able to do so without announcing everything we know,' he replied sarcastically.

'I didn't think it would be easy, but you were able to get a ship to go to the location.'

'They patrolled the restricted area – it's not uncommon for us to show a presence where ships are not allowed to go. Let me think on it, but it won't be easy, especially with the growing problems with the Urigans, and I'll contact you.'

'Thank you.'

Chapter 21

LOVOA woke with a start, memories of being trapped somewhere dark and cold scared her for a moment before she registered the warmth of the sun. She opened her eyes and remembered where she was. People were moving around and talking nearby. Slowly she pulled herself to her feet and found that she did not hurt as much as she had expected. How long had she been sleeping?

'I'm glad you are awake,' a voice stated from behind her and she turned to see the male who had got her out of the cell. 'Do you remember what happened? Who I am?' he asked her.

'You are Solvan, one of the first protectors. How long have I been asleep?' Lovoa asked.

'A few hours. How do you feel?'

'Much stronger and less sore. What are they doing?'

'Looking at how best to repair the battlements in case the traders attack here.'

'Do you think they will?'

'I think they will definitely come again soon, but I don't know which collective they will go to next. This is one of the largest and we have shown no resistance to them, so I think it's likely it will be attacked soon.'

'We showed no resistance,' she repeated, taking in his words. 'They have already destroyed one, haven't they? I dreamt of so many piles of dead bodies, and you were there.'

'They went to Gilcan's collective a few days ago and

skinned everyone there. I dreamt of the bodies, you somehow found your way into my dream while I was remembering what I saw when I visited there.'

'Is there no way to stop them? You talk of repairing the battlements, is that why they killed everyone, because the battlements were in ruins?'

'No, we can stop them, and the battlements are necessary to protect the protectors as they fight the traders, but the protectors didn't believe that they would come because it has been so long since they last attacked and so didn't prepare and learn what they had to do when the traders descended.'

'Do they believe now?'

'Some do, as you can see, but no, not everyone believes. Some of the protectors are no longer strong enough to feel the deaths as we did.'

'How is that possible? I'm a peasant and I felt them die. Why am I so important to you? Why was Protector Ovato so keen to get hold of me?'

'Your parents may have been peasants, but that doesn't always mean they wouldn't have a powerful child, and it is because of your strength that I need your help and Ovato fears you.'

Lovoa laughed. 'Fears me?'

'The law states that the collective goes to the most powerful person born on that collective. Being a protector is not a right of birth, though normally the protector's family is by far the most powerful so it does tend to pass from family member to family member, so your existence would be a threat to him.'

'The night before they died, my parents said that I was strong, that I was different, but I didn't know what they meant by that, they didn't explain it. Are you saying that what my parents said is true?' Lovoa asked.

'Yes, they told you the truth.'

'How do you know I am powerful? I don't even know what I can do.'

'I know just by looking at you, everyone would know by looking at you,' Solvan said and he took her hand in his and traced the markings across her palm. 'These patterns make you strong, the more of them you have, the more power you have. Have you never wondered why you look different?'

'I only ever knew my parents, they wouldn't let me meet anyone else. I was sometimes able to spy on them when Protector Buxus came to the collective, but until I saw you at the pool, I never met anyone else. I did start to notice I look different to others over the last few days, and Kesli kept referring to me as a protector.'

'They told you nothing else other than that you are strong?'

'My parents tried to explain more, but I got upset and left. We were going to talk again the following night, but they died that day.'

'You have a lot to learn then.'

'I am discovering that. Is it because I'm strong that you have been looking for me too?'

'Yes, that is why I was hoping you will agree to come back to Hannoki with me and help me fight back against the traders.'

'How do we fight them? You still have not explained.'

'It is difficult to explain. It would be a lot easier for me to show you, but please believe me, when everything has been made clear to you, if you can't bring yourself to do what is required, no one will make you and you can go wherever you want, with my support.'

Lovoa was silent for a while as she thought. 'All right,' she said finally.

'You will come?'

'Yes, I will come. When do you want to leave?'

'Now.'

'What about the work here? What about Protector Ovato?'

'Gilcan, Isslac and Brelsa have everything under control here and my father will come to help support them.'

'You mentioned flying to get there. I have only ever flown close to the ground, around the farm and where the spaces in the forest allowed. I don't know if I can make it all the way to the peak.'

'Then I will help you, I will not let you fall,' Solvan promised. Squeezing her hand, he led her to the edge of the battlements, climbed up onto the wall surrounding them and helped her to climb up next to him.

'Isslac,' Solvan turned his head and shouted back, 'we are leaving now. I will ask my father to come and assist you.'

'My thanks, Solvan. I will wait until he arrives before I release father from the cells – I don't think I can keep him under control and work up here at the same time. Good luck to you both and Hannoki protect you.'

'Hannoki protect you, Brelsa and Gilcan,' Solvan responded.

'Are you ready?' he asked, turning back to Lovoa and as she nodded, he let go of her hand and took a step away from her to make room for him to spread his wings slightly.

Lovoa looked down at the drop in front of her and felt a thrill of excitement go through her. This is what she was made for, she thought. She spread her wings and felt the wind in them and it felt so good. She looked at Solvan and smiled and, without saying anything, went with her instincts and jumped off the building, letting the wind catch beneath her wings before beating them to gain altitude.

Solvan was taken by surprise when Lovoa launched herself into the air and quickly gained height. Like him, she flew as if she were born to it. He followed and quickly joined her. She acknowledged him with a smile and a nod of her head and let him lead her to where they needed to go.

She felt free and exhilarated as she flew. It was not as tiring as she had feared and the vastness that she could see amazed her. She seemed to cover the distances she had walked to Ovato's collective in an instant as she soared through the air. As they approached the forest area where she used to live, Lovoa saw her small farm and realised that the bodies that had been left lying on the ground had been removed, and she wondered where had they gone.

'I buried them,' Solvan shouted at her, as if he could read her thoughts, 'it did not seem right to leave them.'

'Thank you,' Lovoa said, feeling guilty that she had not done so, she had just left them to rot.

'We need to start to climb,' Solvan said as they started to fly over the forest. 'How are you doing?'

'Good,' she replied, and she was. The higher they climbed, the colder it got, but the intensity of the sun increased and continually replaced the energy she used. Having spent most of her life hidden away inside, she had never felt so invigorated and a lot of the soreness she had felt on waking was also easing off. Lovoa found it harder to keep up with Solvan as he started to climb on the approach to Hannoki. The winds started to come down the mountain and tried to push her away. Solvan, she noticed, was moving from left to right, right to left, as he flew. He turned around and saw that she had fallen behind and he slowed and flew directly in front of her, shielding her from the worst of the wind. He shouted something down but it was lost, and Lovoa shook her head, indicating that she could not hear him.

'*You need to fly around the gusts,*' he said, and she could hear him in her head. '*Follow where I go.*' Lovoa was so shocked at hearing him in her head that she missed a beat of her wings but caught it again quickly. She did as Solvan said, and as she flew she understood what he meant as he went around the strong, downward currents. Even following him, Lovoa felt herself starting to tire. They were now going straight up against the rock of the mountain and she did not want to think about how high they were. She was starting to wonder how much longer she could keep going when everything started to narrow and she realised that she had reached the peak. Just ahead of her she could see a large opening, the chamber, she thought, and saw Solvan fly straight into it. Lovoa followed him. As soon as she went in, she lost control as she had not anticipated the lack of wind. She tried to compensate by beating her wings less, but ended up falling to the floor.

'I'm sorry,' Solvan said, helping her to her feet, 'I forgot to warn you about that.'

Lovoa looked around her. She could not make out much as the only light came from the entrance she had just flown through, but on first sight it was just a large cavern. 'This is where you live?' she asked, looking around.

'This is normally how we enter when the winds are high, we need the bigger space to land. I live above this cavern with my parents, I will show you,' and taking her hand, he led her across the chamber. As they neared the back, Lovoa could see an exit with stairs leading up. It was dark as no light penetrated this far in, and for a moment she hesitated, remembering the cells and how she had felt with the lack of light and how difficult the dark stairs had been on her way out. Solvan felt her pause and understood her fear. 'It opens out into the light after a very short climb,' he reassured her. Lovoa nodded and, taking a deep breath, allowed herself to be taken up the stairs, but it was just as he had said and it was not long before light from above could be seen and she sighed with relief.

As she walked into the room above, Lovoa saw what she would have expected to see when she landed. It was a large room full of tables and chairs, and one side had been opened up and looked straight off the side of the mountain, with a balcony running around the side to stop people from falling off, she guessed. Lovoa could also see large wooden shutters which she assumed would be pulled over when needed to protect the room against strong winds. The table was covered in papers where people had been working. It looked like a home.

'Solvan,' a female voice called out. Lovoa turned in the direction from which it had come but could only see a closed door.

'My mother,' he whispered to her, 'she is next door in the general room. Mother!' he shouted back, and the door opened. An older woman entered the room, followed by a male with the same markings, and Lovoa recognised him from the pool.

'I thought I felt your return,' she said as she walked in, then she paused. 'I'm sorry, I didn't realise you had company. I am First Protector Bahia and this is my mate, Essac.'

'It is a pleasure to meet you both. I'm Lovoa.'

'You were at the pool,' Essac said.

'Yes,' Lovoa replied, nervous.

'We have been looking for you for a very long time, I think,' he said.

'A few days is not a long time, sir,' Lovoa corrected.

'No, it's not, but that is not when I started to look for

you. Your parents were very resourceful in hiding you,' he said with a smile on his face.

'Lovoa has come here so I can explain everything to her,' Solvan said.

'Then welcome, my dear, and I hope you will agree to help us,' Bahia said.

'It is a difficult flight if you're not used to it, do you want to rest first?' Solvan asked.

'No, I have rested enough for today. I need to know what is happening.'

'Then we will start in a moment,' he said to her before turning to Essac. 'Father, I'm sorry but I need you to go to Ovato's collective and offer Isslac and Brelsa your support against their father.'

'Why? What has happened there? Have the people stopped revolting? You never did report back.'

'I know, but everything got complicated. I'm not sure what the people are planning, if anything. There is a great feeling of unrest but after Ovato's attack on them, I don't know if they will do anything else soon. That aside, Ovato has been locked temporarily in a lightless cell and must be released soon. Brelsa and Isslac are at present trying to rebuild the battlements with the aid of Gilcan. If they are going to get everything set to rights and control their father, they will need help.'

'Sounds like you have had an interesting time of it,' Essac said.

'Very much so. It's a long story, however, and they can give you more details when you get there.'

'I will go now, but if there is any indication that the traders are returning, call me immediately.'

'I promise, though that dark, alien feeling is still absent and has been for the last day or so.'

'We noticed that too; do you think they have gone?'

'No, just preparing for the next attack. I do think it

gives us a little time to prepare, though.'

'I agree. I will see what I can do at Ovato's and, again, if you feel them returning, call me.'

'I will,' Solvan promised. 'Lovoa, if you're ready, I will show you around and explain everything so you will understand what has been happening and why you are so important,' and with a farewell nod to his parents, he led her out of the room.

When the door had closed behind them, Bahia turned to her mate. 'Hannoki! She is powerful.'

'I know, I only caught a glimpse of her at the pool but she is stronger than I expected her to be.'

'Do you think she will help?'

'I don't know. It will depend on whether she can trust Solvan enough to mate with him. I think it's a positive sign that he was able to bring her here,' Essac said, 'but what happens here is for you to manage, as it appears I must go and help Isslac out on Ovato's collective.'

'We must hope there is not another attack while you are away,' Bahia worried.

'I wouldn't worry, the nightmares have stopped for now. Solvan was able to feel the traders coming long before we could, so we must trust him to warn me quickly enough if they do return.'

'I know. Go and sort them out quickly so you can get back here,' Bahia said.

'I will do my best,' he promised, and he leaned in close and kissed her farewell.

⁜

Solvan led Lovoa through more rooms and up several more staircases. She was learning that though the rooms were large and open to the sun on one side, all the staircases were enclosed and she quickly got over her nervousness of them. At the bottom of one, Solvan stopped and turned to her.

'At the top of this staircase is the peak of Hannoki and though it is well built up on either side so you can't fall off and is shielded from a lot of the wind, it is fully open from above so be careful as you step off the stairs.'

'I understand,' she said, though she was slightly confused at the warning, and followed him up. As she walked out, the feel of the sun was so intense on her skin and she got such a rush of power that it made her gasp.

'We are a lot higher here, so the suns are stronger,' Solvan explained and led her across the plateau. Lovoa could see some strange device in front of them. It was shielded on three sides by rock and on the floor were strange grooves that ran from the device outwards. Solvan stopped in front of it.

'This is what we use to stop the traders,' he said. 'Luckily there were documents left behind explaining how to use it, otherwise we won't have had a clue.'

Lovoa looked at it. She had never seen anything like it before. She reached out and touched it, and found that the surface was cold and very smooth under her fingers. There were two chairs with circular objects on either side and in the centre, but she had no idea what you were supposed to do to operate it.

'I have never seen anything like this. Where did it come from? What is it made of?' she asked.

'We don't know,' he replied honestly. 'All the documents just say that it has always been here, there is nothing written about who built it or how, or even how to repair it should it ever break.'

'How could there be nothing about it?'

'They either must not have thought it necessary for us to know, or the accounts were lost over time. We know it was here during Hannoki's time as his granddaughter, Prela, documented his life and started the first records.'

'The records on how to use it remain, though,' Lovoa stated.

'Yes, several first protectors documented how they used it, so luckily we had numerous accounts to follow. Traditionally, the first protectors would train those who were going to succeed them, but my parents took over the position after the previous couple had died so were never trained in the role.'

'If you know how to use it, why have you not done so?' she accused him. 'All those people on Gilcan's collective, my parents and, judging by the pains and nightmares I have been having, I'm sure there have been many more.'

'There were. Several independent farms were attacked before Gilcan's collective was. However, this machine does not alert us to the traders' coming, and because of the way it works, we could not help the small farmers. When they targeted the small farms, we also felt it too late to do anything to prevent it, so I always got there too late.'

'What about Gilcan's collective?'

'We tried. This machine increases our power and sends it out to where it is needed, but we can't target what we cannot see, so we are unable to hit the traders directly, but we know where the collectives are so we can send the power there so the protectors on the battlements can then direct it towards the traders to destroy them. When the traders attacked Gilcan's collective my parents sent the energy out but the protectors were not on the battlements to receive it. Instead they fled and the energy hit the castle and destroyed it, there was nothing to stop the traders landing and skinning all the people.'

'So this machine is useless unless the protectors stand and fight?'

'That is what all the accounts we have found say, yes,' Solvan admitted.

'How many protectors believe in the traders? How many will stand and fight as they are meant to?'

'Before the attack on the collective, a few listened to us when we said the traders had returned but were still reluctant to act; now I don't know. I know Ovato still will not listen but his children do believe and have taken control of their collective. I can't say what is happening elsewhere because I have been trying to find you and my parents didn't want to leave Hannoki in case the traders attacked again.'

'Why waste your time looking for me? I still don't understand why I'm so important to you. You say I am strong, but what good is that to you when I don't know how to use my strength?' she pleaded with him.

'This takes two people to operate, two of equal power, which means I cannot use it at the moment. My parents used it when Gilcan's collective was attacked. They are strong but they have been relying on me to warn them when I sense the traders and they struggled to control the machine.' He took a deep breath and said, 'I can't use this until I have mated, so I was looking for you in the hope that you would help me.'

After a moment thinking over what he had said, Lovoa confirmed what he had tried to say, 'You want me to mate with you.'

'Yes,' Solvan said.

'What happens if I say no?'

'Then I go back to what I had planned before I ever knew you existed and mate with Erle, the girl from the pool.'

'She is nowhere near as strong as you; you said a mated couple of equal power was needed, so what would happen if you mated with her?'

'I would lose power and hers would increase, but we would still be stronger than my parents.'

'Why did you choose her?'

'Other than you, she is the strongest female that I know of.'

'You do not care for her. I felt that from you as I watched you at the pool, you were disgusted by her.'

'You're right, I don't like her, but if I am to use this, I need to mate, and soon. I don't have the luxury of forming an attachment first.'

'What makes you think she would still have you after you ran off, chasing me?'

'As I said, I would make her stronger than she had ever dreamed possible and she is desperate for that.'

'Does she believe the traders are back again?'

'When I last saw her, no, she did not, but once we mate, she will know everything that I know and she will have to accept that they have returned.'

'It would make this so much easier if there were a way to know everything now. So much has happened since I saw you at the pool, I'm struggling to make sense of it all, and the only thing I *do* know is that there is so much that I *do not* know.'

'There is a way I can clarify and teach you a lot very quickly: I can allow you to read my mind.'

'Would you be able to read mine?'

'Only if you let me.'

'You would let me do that? You would let me see everything?'

'If you mated with me, you would know it all anyway, so why not let you see it all now? I need you to trust me,' he said.

'How does it work? I can read minds but not well. I only know what I was able to work out for myself by reading my parents' minds.'

'I will allow you in so there will be no barriers to stop you seeing what you want to see. If you take my hands, it will enforce the connection and make it easier for you. If you ask a question, it will allow me to think of the information you want so you will not have to find it yourself,' Solvan said, holding his hands out to her. Lovoa hesitated and looked at him. 'If you do not want to do this, that's fine, but this could answer all your questions and help you decide what you want to do.'

'If I get this wrong, could I hurt you?' she asked.

'No, you will not be able to hurt me. Try it, if it doesn't work, then I will answer your questions the normal way and will just have to hope and pray to Hannoki that you will trust me enough to give you honest answers. This way I cannot lie to you.'

Lovoa smiled, took his hands in hers and, taking a deep breath, relaxed. Solvan closed his eyes and dropped all the shields he had around his mind and allowed her in. He felt her mind tentatively pushing at his as if still unsure of its welcome, and when no resistance was offered, fully came into his. Though he and his parents regularly read surface thoughts and spoke to each other on a telepathic level, he had never allowed anyone fully into his mind. He had always thought that allowing someone to know everything would be a huge violation, and when Gilcan and the others had all allowed it, he had known the extent of their commitment. Lovoa was different, her mind felt strangely familiar to him. She was gentle as she sought out the answers that she so desperately needed from him, and he gave them up freely to her, and suddenly she was gone and he felt the loss.

She pulled her hands out of his and he opened his eyes and looked at her. 'Did you find out everything you need?' he asked her.

'Yes, we have made it easy for them, haven't we? I saw your memories from Gilcan's collective, the piles of dead bodies rotting in the sun, and you think they will just keep coming.' Lovoa was shaking from the images she had seen. She had thought her dreams had been vivid, but those memories were so much worse.

'They will be stopped. The other protectors will fight back when they see that the traders are real.'

'You would have mated with her to ensure you could fight,' Lovoa stated. 'She saw me at the pool. I wondered what Protector Buxus was doing back at the farm again so soon. She must have told him about me and he knew where to go, he knew of my existence, or suspected it, and he went to the farm to see my parents. That is why I was not there when the traders came. "Hide," they told me, "always hide," so I did and they died.'

'I am so sorry,' Solvan said as he saw the repercussions of that day.

'For what? I was not supposed to be at the pool, they had told me again and again not to go there, but they had gone to visit another farmer and I needed to get out, I needed to feel the sun. When I got home and saw Protector Buxus, I could have stayed close to the farm until he had left as well, but then I did as I had been told and I hid, and now they are gone. If I had listened to them, I would have hidden on the farm as usual and I would have been there when the traders came.'

'Their deaths were not your fault; you had no way of knowing that they would be killed.'

'I know their deaths were not my fault, but I will have to accept that I could have saved them if I had done as I was meant to and been there,' Lovoa said, 'but I will not hide any more.'

'Does that mean you will mate with me?' Solvan asked.

'Yes, I don't want anyone else to die because I would not do everything I could to stop them.'

'Then the sooner we do, the better,' Solvan said, and Lovoa just stood there in silence. After a few minutes, he continued, 'We can't afford to wait for long, the traders could return at any moment. I know that nothing about this situation is normal, and that couples normally know each other well first to make sure they are compatible. We can spend a few days getting to know each other so you can be sure that this is what you want.'

'No, I know you now from your mind, and a few days will not change that, but mother never explained to me what to do,' she admitted, embarrassed.

Solvan pulled her close and ran his hand through her hair, trying to reassure her. 'We will find my mother, I'm sure she will answer any questions you have.'

'She doesn't know me; I do not know her.'

'She will want to get to know you,' he assured her and he took her hand and led her back down the stairs to the living compartments.

Lovoa and Bahia spent some time in private discussion, and eventually Solvan and Lovoa stood together on the plateau of Hannoki's Peak, hand in hand.

'Are you ready? Mother explained everything?' Solvan asked.

'She was very helpful.'

'There is still time to change your mind.'

'No, I'm ready,' Lovoa reassured him. 'You?'

'I'm sure, let us do this,' he said and together they climbed the wall protecting the peak. The wind was powerful and tried to knock them off balance. 'Ready?' Solvan shouted over the wind.

'Yes, let us light up the sky,' Lovoa replied and together they jumped into the air.

⁂

Bahia stood on the balcony and watched as the couple fell past her. Already they were starting to generate light, and she smiled. She had spoken to Lovoa for some time explaining what she had to do and what to expect. It was evident that Lovoa's mother had never spoken to her about this or anything else. From what she had gathered, her parents had been too busy hiding her from everyone. She was hopeful for them. Lovoa was of a very similar strength to Solvan and she was as determined to defeat the traders as they were. Even after a short meeting, Bahia knew that Lovoa was a better match than Erle could ever have been. The rest would be discovered in time, but for now she did not expect them to return for several hours.

She left the balcony as they were moving fast and, other than a rainbow of colours streaking the sky, there was no longer anything to see.

'*Essac*,' she called out to her mate.

'*Is everything all right? Are the traders coming?*'

'*Not that I am aware of. Lovoa has agreed to mate with Solvan*,' she told him.

'*That is good news, how long are they going to wait?*'

'*They are not. If you look up to the sky, you should be able to see them lighting it up.*'

✳

Essac was on the battlements with Gilcan and Brelsa when his mate spoke to him. He turned and looked towards Hannoki's Peak and, sure enough, there in the distance the sky was changing colour. He pointed it out to the others and together they watched as the sky slowly turned red, blue, yellow and green.

'I have never seen anything like it,' Brelsa whispered.

✳

'Have you seen the sky?' Misca demanded as she walked into the room where her mate and daughter were sitting.

'Of course not, we have been in here. What is so important about the sky?' Protector Buxus replied. He and Erle had been discussing what move they should make next, as nothing further had been heard from Solvan since he had brought Erle back a few days ago. Buxus had returned to the farm but had found only graves, and he was sure that the girl was not one of the dead bodies as he would have felt her passing. 'What's wrong with the sky?'

'You must see it for yourself,' she said and led them to the balcony.

'I don't believe it!' Buxus exclaimed.

'What does it mean?' Erle asked as she looked up at the colourful sky. She had never seen anything like it.

'It appears that Solvan has found the girl,' Buxus said, and Erle started to scream her frustration.

Chapter 22

'I thought the admiral said that he would not be able to get us a ship,' Jane said as she climbed into the car next to Cal.

'He did.'

'So where did he get this one from?'

'I don't know, all he said was, "Don't ask and don't hack," – I think the last part was aimed at you.'

'And you didn't ask. Don't you want to know? Don't you want me to find out for you?'

'I would love to know, but I also appreciate that if you or I dig around to satisfy our curiosity, it might raise unwanted questions in unwanted places, so please behave and do as the admiral has asked. You never know, when we get there, all our questions might be answered.'

'So, no hacking?'

'No hacking,' Cal confirmed.

'Fine,' Jane replied and lapsed into silence. She turned her head and watched as the car pulled away from Cal's father's home and sped towards the spaceport. The surroundings slowly changed from rows of mansions to expensive high rises with small boutique shops beneath them, and these gave way to less and less exclusive properties until eventually they entered an industrial area. Jane did not know where she was and had to trust the driver the admiral had sent. All around her now were large, shapeless buildings. She was about to ask Cal which spaceport they were going to when the car stopped briefly at a navel security checkpoint before passing through.

Cal did not know what favours the admiral had had to cash in to arrange all of this and he hoped that he was not grossly mistaken in his theories. The admiral had contacted him early that morning and told him to pack quickly as a car would be picking them up in an hour to take them to a ship that would be leaving very soon. He had stressed that if they were not ready when the car arrived, then tough luck as the vessel would not wait for them. Jane had been grumpy when he woke her but had packed both quickly and efficiently. He looked at her as she gazed out of the car window and wondered what she thought about it; she always liked to have all the answers, so this mystery must be killing her.

The driver got them through all the security quickly and easily and continued for a short while longer before he eventually stopped at a terminal. He got out of the car and opened the passenger door for Cal and Jane to get out.

'This is your terminal sir, ma'am,' the driver said. They were met by an ensign who took their bags and stowed them on a shuttle, and made sure they were correctly strapped in before taking off. On landing in a docking bay, the hatch was released and they were told that the captain was waiting for them, and when they walked out they were met by a tall, athletic man dressed in a captain's uniform.

'Cal, so glad to see you again. Jane, I'm pleased to meet you. I'm so glad you were able to join me aboard the FWN *London*. Cal, it's been such a long time since we had the chance to catch up,' he said, walking forward with his hand outstretched. Cal had no idea who the captain was but guessed he was meant to play along.

'Thank you so much for having us,' he said and took the captain's hand.

'It's a pleasure to meet you at last,' Jane said.

'Stay close and watch where you walk here, we're just finishing some major repairs,' he warned as he led them through the ship.

'Isn't there something about asking permission to come aboard?' Cal asked.

'I think you can both take it as read that you have my permission,' the captain replied. 'I will take you to your cabin – I'm sorry it is small but it's the best that I can offer.'

'I'm sure it will be fine,' Cal replied as they followed the captain through numerous corridors. There were people working everywhere, until they changed levels and suddenly it was deserted.

'This level is mainly living quarters and recreational facilities for the crew. At the moment everyone will either be working, preparing for our departure or sleeping for the later shifts,' he explained. After a short walk, he stopped outside a door, swiped a card and it swung open. 'This is where you will be staying,' he told them and indicated that they should go in. The room was very cramped compared to the luxury suites that Cal was used to, but was a very generous size for a military ship. The bed took up most of the room but there was also a small washing unit and a table and chairs.

'Thank you,' Cal said.

'Your luggage should be here very soon. I need to make sure everything is ready for launch and then get us onto our course. For your safety, I need you to stay in here until we are underway, it won't be safe for you to be wandering around the corridors and I don't need to be worrying about you.'

'We promise to say put,' Cal said.

'Good. As soon we are on our way, I will come and talk to you and catch up,' the captain promised, then turned and left them in the cabin.

When they were alone and the door had closed behind them, Jane turned to Cal. 'Do you have any idea who the captain is?'

'None whatsoever.'

'Probably a silly question to ask now, but since we are on a ship that we can't easily get off, do you trust him?'

'I don't think we have a choice. I trust the admiral and I just have to trust his plan for us.'

'So, what do we do now?'

'Sit and wait for him...' Cal said as the doorbell rang and their bags were delivered, 'and unpack?' he suggested.

'Why couldn't the captain just have told you what was happening?' Jane asked, ignoring his comment about unpacking.

'No idea,' Cal said as he settled himself into one of the chairs and opened the computer he had carried on board, 'why don't you ask him when he comes back?'

'How long do you think he will be?'

'No idea, I've never been on a military ship before. He will come back when he comes back.' Jane just stood there and looked at him. 'You're not going to unpack our things?'

'I'll unpack my things when I know how long this trip will take,' she replied.

'Fine, then sit down and unlock your computer so we can get some work done while we wait.'

It was several hours later and both Cal and Jane were engrossed in the files they had brought with them when the door chimed, causing Jane to jump. Cal opened the door.

'Sorry for the wait,' the captain said as he walked into the room and closed the door behind him.

'I take it we are safely underway?' Cal asked.

'Of course,' he replied. Jane stood up to allow the

captain to take her seat at the table and she perched on the edge of the bed as the captain continued, 'I bet you have several questions to ask me, but first I think proper introductions are in order. I am Captain Alex Wilhelm.'

'It's a pleasure to meet you, but when I met with Admiral Johnson, he said it would be impossible to get passage to where we need to go, and why the assumption that we know each other?'

'I have a personal interest in the area of space to which you wish to travel, and where possible I make sure I'm notified of anyone else paying attention to it. When I found out that the admiral had made enquiries about it, I approached him. We're not sure who else is paying attention, so we decided that the easiest way to explain why you were coming on board was to pretend that we are friends and I'm doing you a favour. Once we are deeper into space, the admiral will change my orders and send us to Lismar, greatly reducing the chance of being found out and stopped.'

'How much did the admiral tell you?'

'Everything he knew, which just got me up to speed since I have been deployed away. I know a lot more of the history than he did.'

'How?' Jane asked.

'Why are you so interested?' Cal spoke at the same time.

'Luckily the answer to both questions is the same. As you have discovered, over seventy years ago an alien race was being skinned alive and having their wings harvested for industry. This was discovered by my grandfather, David Wilhelm.'

'We knew about the use of skins, but we did not read anything about the wings.'

'The wings are very lightweight and incredibly strong, and that was where the real money was being made, the clothing was a nice sideline. Once the trade had been discovered and stopped, many businesses went bankrupt. My grandfather believed that corruption in the FWN had allowed the trade.'

'I thought people were held to account over it?'

'Some were, the obvious targets, others fled the Federation of Worlds, never to be heard of again, but the main suspect, Admiral Mathers, very conveniently committed suicide. Granddad always believed the real players were never brought to account, and that frustrated the hell out of him. He always feared that because the scandal was buried, there was always a risk of it starting again. From what I've been told, it appears he was correct.'

'It's too soon to know for sure, but it would appear so,' Cal said.

'Have you spoken to your grandfather?' Jane asked.

'No, he died many years ago in a shuttle accident, but he made sure all his children knew what had happened and my father told me.'

'Do you know anything that could help us?'

'I'm not sure if it will help, but it is certainly interesting if you want to hear it.'

'Definitely,' Cal and Jane said together.

⁕

Solvan and Lovoa had made it back several hours ago and had collapsed, exhausted, in Solvan's rooms. Bahia had not seen them when they had returned but had been informed by a servant. Now she was getting impatient to see what the effects of the mating had been on them both. She was also concerned that with both of them sleeping, would they sense a trader attack or were they all very vulnerable with Essac still at the collective with Isslac?

'Stop worrying,' Essac told her, 'if either of them had any indication that a trader attack was imminent, I am sure they would have waited before they mated and I would have been called back.'

'I know, I know, Solvan would not have taken any unnecessary chances, but it is not just that, we do not know anything about Lovoa, so we don't know how this mating will have affected him.'

'Consider what choices there were. He could have chosen not to mate and trust we could cope; he could have mated with Erle and lost a great deal of his strength, and possibly picked up a few undesirable personality traits; or he could have mated with Lovoa. We may not know much about her but we do know that she cared enough to defend the people against Ovato's attack, and Solvan will have lost none of his strength. Do not worry until there is something to worry about.'

'I will do my best,' she assured her mate. 'How goes it at the collective?'

'Much better than I had hoped. Ovato has been released from the lightless cell and he immediately tried to regain control, but was quickly put into a normal cell where the sunlight is restricted so he will not get the chance to store any significant amount of power. I think it was a considerable shock to discover that his guards were happily following his son and daughter rather than him. Welra tried to get him out and rally support for her mate but quickly found she had none and has been confined under guard to the same rooms in which Gilcan had previously been confined. Isslac now has all his siblings, excluding Brelsa, helping with the battlements and hopefully they will be completed in good time.'

'Sounds like things are going well, but what is Brelsa doing? I thought she was one of our biggest supporters, so why is she not helping with the battlements?'

'She and Gilcan have left. She said that I'm needed here as I outrank her father and my support is vital if Isslac is going to be able to maintain his authority here, and she has decided to try to get the other protectors to listen to what happened at Gilcan's collective and to convince them that this is a real threat.'

'I wish her luck.'

'She is very determined; I am sure she will succeed.' Essac paused for a moment, and Bahia felt that his attention had been distracted. *'I'm going to have to go, I will talk to you soon,'* and with that he withdrew his mind.

∗

All her limbs felt heavy as she tried to move, and at first she felt as though she had just stacked the whole barn. As she turned over she groaned, her entire body protesting at the movement. The ache felt good, really good, as if she had been pulled apart but put back together again, only better than before. Opening her eyes slowly, she saw that she was in a room that she did not recognise, but the sunlight flooded in. Pulling herself up into a sitting position, she looked around her at the heavy, worn furnishings and something about the room tugged at her memory.

Movement next to her caught her attention and she turned to see a male lying next to her. She was startled and started to move away from him. His back was turned to her but she did not recognise the markings that covered him. With a groan, he also turned around and she gasped in surprise when she saw his face. She recognised the face as belonging to Solvan, but he had changed.

'Good morning,' he said as he opened his eyes, looked at her and smiled, 'at least, I think it's morning,' and he started to pull himself into a sitting position.

'You look different,' she stated.

Solvan looked at his hands and arms and then at her. 'So do you,' he pointed out. Lovoa looked at herself for the first time and realised that her markings had changed – they were now the same as Solvan's.

'I'm sorry, I knew this would happen,' Lovoa said as she examined herself. 'My brain feels so full, nothing is making sense, it is all jumbled up.'

'I feel the same, but it should pass soon. Everything I know, you now know, and the same for me. It will just take time for us to process it.'

Lovoa stood up and walked out onto the balcony and lifted her face to the sun. She heard Solvan coming out to join her.

'This is your room,' she stated. 'I have never been here but I feel that I know it well.'

'Yes,' he replied.

'Do you know how long we were asleep?'

'I'm not sure, several hours at least, judging by the suns. We should really go and find mother and find out if anything has happened,' he said, and together they walked out of the room. Lovoa looked around her as they walked through various corridors and rooms, and realised that the place no longer felt alien to her; it felt like home and she knew where they would find Solvan's mother. Was Solvan comparing everything to her memories of her home? Would he be judging her parents for the way they had hidden her, for not teaching what she so desperately needed to know?

'No,' he surprised her by saying, 'in keeping you hidden they kept you safe.' He noticed the shock on her face. 'Sorry, I just heard what you were thinking.'

'Is that normal, that you should be able to do that so easily?'

'I don't know,' he said honestly. They walked into the

room where Lovoa had first met Solvan's parents, and there was his mother, sitting at the table looking at the papers in front of her.

She looked up as she heard them enter and stood up. 'Look at you both, it looks like it went well. How do you both feel?'

'Sore and confused,' Solvan said.

Bahia chuckled. 'I'm not surprised, there is a lot to process after a mating flight.'

'I have lots of memories that are not mine. I know that this is normal but it's disorienting trying to remember what I experienced and what Lovoa experienced.'

'If I recall correctly, it took your father and me several days to sort everything out in our minds, but it will all settle after time, and you knew that would be the case. Is there anything else you are worrying about?'

'As we walked here just now, I read Lovoa's surface thoughts – I was not even trying to, yet they were just there in my head,' Solvan told her.

'Between a mated couple it is always easier to communicate mind to mind. You have become one, and you will find that if you just think about your partner, you will be able to sense them. But reading surface thoughts without intending to? Your father and I were never that close,' Bahia admitted.

'Does it mean anything is wrong?' Solvan asked.

'I don't think so. Both you and Lovoa are so much stronger than us, which is possibly a factor, or you are so well matched. If a couple are not compatible or are resisting each other, it will affect how they sense each other,' Bahia explained. 'Your father and I discovered that, with practice, you can shield against each other as and when you wish, so you will not have to be permanently in each other's minds when you do not want to be.'

'Is there anything else of which we should be aware?'

Solvan asked.

'Possibly for you, Lovoa,' she admitted. 'If we had had the luxury of time, I would have advised that you spend time learning how to use your strength first. I am sorry, my dear, but you suddenly have the knowledge of how to use your abilities and possibly the confidence that Solvan has, but you have never tried to use your powers for yourself. I don't know what will happen when you do use them; you might have perfect control or you might not. I would advise you to be careful until you do know what will happen.'

'Am I going to be dangerous?' Lovoa asked.

'Less so than you were before,' Bahia said. 'Before you mated with Solvan, you used your powers on instinct, with no real concept of how strong you really are. You could have caused a lot of damage without meaning to, but now you have Solvan's knowledge and know how to store energy and use it.'

'Why didn't you say anything before?' Solvan asked.

'I didn't think it was something that you needed to consider when making your decision about mating. Lovoa, you were always going to need to be taught how to use your abilities. The only reason you have not been dangerous is because you were not told anything about what you could do, so never tried until your survival depended on it.'

'How much of a risk is there?' Solvan asked as Lovoa sat down in the nearest chair, feeling very shaken.

'If you have the time to practise, none, I would have thought. If you had mated someone considerably weaker, then they would have had the same problem.'

'Like the girl at the pool?' Lovoa asked.

'Yes, like Erle,' she confirmed.

'What would you recommend now?' Solvan asked.

'As I have already said, practise, while you have the

chance.'

'We do not have the time,' Solvan said in frustration, 'we need to get back to Isslac. Then there are the other protectors to talk to as well, to make sure they are doing as they have been instructed. I cannot allow another collective to fall.'

'Solvan, your father and Isslac have Ovato's collective well in hand. Brelsa and Gilcan have gone to talk to the other protectors. Lovoa needs to understand her powers and you both need to learn how to work together, as a team. Your job now is to get yourselves ready for the next attack.'

'It sounds like they have all been busy,' Solvan mused.

'Your father may not be as strong as you but he has been first protector since before you were born. He knows better than you what needs to be done, so leave him to bring in the protectors and you two get yourselves ready.'

'Yes Mother,' Solvan said, having truly been put in his place. 'Are you ready for this?' he asked Lovoa.

'A bit late if I'm not,' Lovoa replied.

'That's true,' Solvan agreed. He stood up, took hold of Lovoa's hand and gently pulled her to her feet. 'Time to learn how to use all that knowledge in your head.'

'Where can we go? I don't want to accidentally hurt anyone or destroy anything.'

'The plateau, there is nothing up there apart from the machine, so it should be fine.'

'Lead the way,' and after excusing themselves to Bahia, they left.

Lovoa gasped as she walked back out onto the plateau, revelling in the sunlight. Solvan smiled as he felt her pleasure and paused next to her. He had been up here so often that he was used to the intensity of it and he wondered if she would become so used to it as well.

'It would be a shame if I did,' she responded to his unspoken thought, then turned and smiled at him.

'Your parents did not teach you anything,' Solvan stated.

'No, if they ever knew what I could do, they never said and I learnt to block them out of my mind when I was very young. With the traders and Ovato, I acted without understanding what I was doing.'

'If you remember what you did and then think about what you now know from me, do you understand what you did?'

Lovoa closed her eyes and thought. There was so much information in her mind but as she thought about what she wanted, it came to her. 'Yes,' she said, 'I know what I did.'

'Good, then we will work from there.'

Chapter 23

'DON'T you ever pick anything up?' Jane asked in exasperation as she again tidied away after Cal.

'You never minded before.'

'I probably just didn't notice before as you have a large apartment and a housekeeper, but in this very small space, trust me, I notice.'

'This from the person who didn't want to unpack to start with.'

'I unpacked.'

'Only when you knew we would be here for a while.'

'What would be the point if we were only going to be here for a few days?'

'You are the one obsessed with having everything in the correct place.'

'Why you...' Jane started but was cut off as the communicator buzzed. She walked up to it and pressed the receive button. There was only one person who ever called them. 'Captain, how can we help you?' she asked.

'I need you both to come to the bridge immediately.'

'Of course, is anything wrong?'

'I will explain what is happening when you both get here,' and he cut the communication.

'That doesn't sound good,' Jane said, turning to Cal. They had dined with Alex regularly, and as far as everyone else was concerned, they were old friends catching up. If anyone was suspicious, then a search of the media sites would confirm the old friendship between their families, compliments of Jane. Alex used the dinners to

get as much information as possible out of them about
the head chairman's death and why Cal believed it was
murder, in return he told them more about what his
father had told him about the Lismarians and the skin
trade and about what his sources had been telling him.
These conversations always happened when he had
finished his tour for the day. When he was working, he
expected Cal and Jane to keep to their quarters and
the communal rooms, and they had not seen any of the
operational areas or met any of the other officers; Alex
had kept the boundaries clear.

'No,' Cal agreed and together they made their way
as quickly as possible to the bridge. As they entered
they saw Captain Wilhelm and paused in the doorway,
suddenly worried about protocol. He turned then, saw
them and waved them forward.

'Thank you for coming here, please follow me,' and he
led them to an office just off the bridge. Once they were
inside and the door closed, he continued, 'The senior
crew are aware that we are going to investigate illegal
activity in this area of space, but a ship has been picked
up heading towards Lismar.'

'You think they are going there to attack the people?'

'I can't think of any other reason, and since it's likely
that we will end up in a battle with them, I'm going to
tell my senior officers everything. I just wanted to let
you know what I intend to do out of courtesy. You are
welcome to come and join me, answer any questions
that they might have that I can't.'

'Of course, whatever you think best,' Cal said.

'Thank you. If you will follow me to the conference
room, they are waiting for us.'

Cal and Jane were led through to another room where
several people were sitting around a boardroom table
and talking, but on seeing them and the captain, they fell

respectfully silent.

'Callum Everson, Jane Keyworth, may I introduce you to my senior staff? This is my Executive Officer, Lieutenant Commander Duval Bastian; Gunnery Officer, Lieutenant Commander James Samuels; Weapons Officer, Lieutenant Commander Pheir Langish; Head Engineer, Lieutenant Maria Mendoza; and my Navigation Officer, Lieutenant Ari Xhia.'

'Pleasure to meet you,' Cal responded.

'As you all know, we are a day away from our destination and we have picked up a ship ahead of us, a ship that I believe is heading to a planet called Lismar. My bridge crew know that we are going to investigate illegal activity in this area, but what you don't know is the significance of this planet and the type of illegal activity we believe is going on.'

'With due respect Captain, we thought it strange when you suddenly decided to take these two on board. You clearly have a bigger picture of what is happening than we do, but you have never led us wrong in all the years I've worked with you,' Lieutenant Commander Bastian replied.

'Thank you, Duval. You are correct, there is more to this mission than you have been told. There is a lot of history, and we intend to fill you in, but when we started on this assignment it was to confirm whether an old illegal trade had restarted. With that ship ahead of us, we have to assume that it has and the risk has gone from standard to high. Both Callum and I have personal interest in this mission and we will now brief you on what we know.'

The tension in the room suddenly increased as they all realised the escalation in risk, but all were willing to hear their captain out before passing comment.

'With respect, Captain, I think it would be best if I

started with how we got involved and our enquiries.'

'Please do.'

'My late father was the head chairman of the Federation of Worlds. When he died in a car crash, I could not believe it because it should not have been possible. I was told there was a mechanical failure with his car that caused the security and autopilot to fail, but having built them myself, I couldn't understand how that had happened, so I started to investigate. I found out that his car had been swapped with another vehicle and engineers paid off to write the report. I still can't work out how the switch was made, but Jane and I also started to look at why. I believe that my father was murdered because of what he had discovered.' Cal paused and his hands clenched. Jane knew that he still struggled to deal with his father's death. Those around the table waited patiently for him to continue. 'Jane looked through my father's records and saw that he had started to look at this area of space and at why it was restricted. It's not because there are any dangers, but because there is a planet inhabited by a species that years ago were killed for their skins and wings, so the restriction was to protect them from further interference from us. However, my father believed that this horrific trade had started again and he had started to investigate it, and we believe that the perpetrators are also behind his death.'

'What happened the last time this trade occurred?' James asked.

'That is where I think I should take over,' Captain Wilhelm said. 'What I know was told to my father by his father, who died before I was born, so the reliability can't be verified. My grandfather, David, worked as a solo scout during his twenties. During one of his scouting missions, he was fired upon and crashed onto an uncharted planet. He would have died if one of the inhabitants had not helped him. I'm sure most of you know that my grandfather, like me, was a telepath, as were the population of the planet, and he used those skills to communicate with his rescuer and learnt from him what was happening to the people. David was able to fix his shuttle and return to Europa, where he briefed an admiral over his findings, but the admiral then died and the investigation stopped. My grandfather returned to the planet and stayed there, helping the people to learn how to help themselves, before he returned to Federation space. He was arrested and held for some time before he was released and was able to sneak back to Lismar. What happened next has never been properly explained, but a FWN ship looking for him found a rogue ship with damage to the hull, with skins and wings on board. They traced the route the ship had travelled and found that it had come from Lismar. I don't know how that ship sustained the damage, but it is believed that the Lismarian people had discovered some way to protect themselves or, more likely, my grandfather had taken technology there illegally.'

'I have never heard of this before,' Duval said.

'It was covered up, but it could only have happened with the knowledge and approval of high-ranking personnel in both the FWN and government. Those believed to be involved either committed suicide or fled the Federation of Worlds, so no one was ever brought to account. My grandfather never got over the lack of action taken and the secrecy around it.'

'Why didn't he blow the whistle on what had happened?' Duval asked.

'It was deemed to come under the Federation Secrets Act, so if he had spoken out, he would have been imprisoned for life. The trade had stopped and safeguards were put in place, and in keeping silent, he could continue to investigate, but as far as I'm aware, he never found out who was ultimately behind it.'

'Do you know what risk the Lismarian people and those who are attacking them pose to us?'

'There is no known risk from the people on the planet – when my grandfather was there, they had no technology at all and I doubt that they have progressed much since then. The ship en route to the planet is another matter. Previously they were heavily armed and I would expect the same to apply this time as well.'

'Why are these skins and wings so important to the people who traded them?'

'My grandfather believed that the skins were a perk, they brought in a nice, additional profit when sold as clothing. The real value was in the wings, described as being very lightweight and strong. When the trade stopped, new ground-breaking inventions suddenly stopped and companies that had been booming suddenly went bankrupt because, it was believed, the wings were the vital component and there was no known substitute.'

'Are we thinking that there are still people in the FWN involved in this?'

'We're not ruling anything out at this time.'

'So, what do you plan to do now?' Cal asked.

'For the moment, we will keep our distance and watch them. They may bypass the planet altogether or change course at the last minute. Should they decide to stop and attack, it would be helpful to have a strategy in place, so I want to start looking at our tactical options now. That is where our collective knowledge will come in useful,' Alex said, looking around the table.

✳

She woke up in a panic, gasping for breath and shaking. Next to her, Solvan sat up suddenly, in a cold sweat.

'You felt that too?' Lovoa asked him, trying control herself.

'Yes,' he said and rubbed his face as if trying to rub away the shock, 'we need to get to the plateau now!' He swung his legs onto the floor and stood up. Together they left the room and went towards the stairs.

'It feels different to what I felt before; from your memories, it's stronger,' Lovoa said as she emerged outside into the sun.

'I know. It might be that now we have mated and our experiences and senses have merged, we have become more aware of them, but once we are in the machine, we will be much more focused.'

Together they sat down on the chairs. 'Do you remember what to do?' Solvan asked.

'Of course – do you?' she replied. Solvan had never used the machine against the traders either, though he had read the ancient instructions in more detail than her. They had been working with Bahia on how to use the machine and had even practised sending energy to Isslac on his collective the day before. They both started to draw in the suns' energy, and relaxed and let their minds merge before pushing their consciousness up into the sky. It took them only moments to find the ship in orbit around them. '*I think it is bigger than the one described by Bahia,*' Lovoa said.

'*I think you are right, I can feel so many minds inside the ship.*'

'*Could they be preparing to attack a larger collective?*' Lovoa asked.

'*That's very possible, yes, and there is another one behind them.*'

'*I don't think it is the same, it feels different.*'

'*Possibly, but it is too far away to know for sure.*'

'*We need to start warning everyone that they could be*

attacked.'

'*Mother, Father,*' Solvan called out.

'*Yes Solvan,*' they both replied in his mind, and as Lovoa was still merged with him she could hear everything that was said.

'*The traders have returned. They are above us, though their vessel is bigger than you described,*' and he pulled what he could see and feel above him to the front of his mind.

'*It is a lot bigger,*' Essac confirmed.

'*We need to warn everyone that an attack is imminent.*'

'*I will tell Isslac and pass it on to Gilcan and Brelsa. Hopefully with their support all the protectors in their area will be persuaded that this is real.*'

'*Then I will take the protectors to the south-east,*' said Bahia.

'*And we will take the northern protectors,*' Solvan informed them.

'*If you are struggling to talk to them all, let us know and we will take over contacting everyone in the north,*' Bahia told them. '*You need to keep an eye on the traders and track them as they come down, and when we can determine their course, we can give the relevant protectors more information.*'

'*We will do, good luck,*' and Solvan closed his mind to his parents. '*Are you ready to start talking with the protectors?*' Solvan asked Lovoa. '*Do not get into arguments with them, just tell them that the traders are back, they need to be getting ready for an attack and we will be back in contact if we sense them approaching their collectives. They will try to argue and question why they should listen to you, so once you have told them, cut the communication and move on or we will not have time to tell everyone.*'

'*I understand,*' she said, and drawing on the knowledge

she had gained as a result of the mating, started to call the various protectors.

Lovoa was talking to Protector Drela when she sensed the movement above her. She quickly passed on the information and cut him off as he was trying to put her in her place. She turned her full attention to the sky above her and saw that several smaller vessels had left the main ship and were now heading down to the surface.

'*Solvan,*' she called to draw his attention to what was happening above them, and they followed the vessels' path down to the planet.

'*This is it,*' he said, '*all we can do now is wait and see where they are heading and be prepared.*' He called out to his parents, '*They are coming!*'

'*Where are they heading?*' Essac asked.

'*We don't know yet, they are still some distance away. I will keep you updated.*'

'*They are splitting up,*' Lovoa said, breaking in on Solvan's communication with his parents.

He looked upwards again and saw that Lovoa was right.

'*Solvan, Lovoa, what is happening?*' Essac asked.

'*Solvan?*' his mother questioned.

'*They are splitting up.*'

'*What do you mean?*'

'*The vessels are going in different directions; it looks like they are going to attack two collectives at the same time,*' Solvan said.

'*Can we spilt the energy to defend two collectives?*' Lovoa asked.

'*I don't think so.*' Solvan's voice was filled with the dread he felt. '*I think we can only defend one of them.*'

'*So which one do we defend?*' Lovoa asked.

'*The biggest? The one most prepared? I do not know,*' Solvan replied.

'The first one to be attacked,' Lovoa suggested, 'that way we might still have time to help the second one.'

'Would you have the energy left for two? Your father and I were exhausted after we used it to try and help Gilcan's collective,' Bahia exclaimed.

'But they are a lot stronger than us,' Essac pointed out.

'We won't know until we try,' Lovoa said.

'One group of vessels appears to be heading towards either you, Father, or Protector Veran's collective; the others are heading north and are still too far away to know where they will attack.'

'I am contacting Veran now,' Essac said and, after a pause, 'he does not believe us but is willing to humour us and is going to the battlements now. He hopes we are proved wrong but will be in position if the traders do attack him.'

'I do not care whether he believes us or not, just as long as he fulfils his duties when the time comes,' Solvan said.

'I still cannot say where the others are going,' Lovoa said.

'The first vessels are definitely going to Veran's collective,' Solvan confirmed. 'Protector Veran, are you receiving?' he called.

'First Protector Solvan,' Protector Veran acknowledged.

'The first trader vessels are on a direct course for your collective – are you ready?'

'We are, my mate and I are on the battlements.'

'I still don't know where the others are going to land,' Lovoa said in frustration.

'We will defend Protector Veran's collective and then do what we can for the north afterwards. Mother, Father, can you contact the protectors in the north and let them know that trader vessels are heading to them and instruct everyone to be ready?'

'Doing it now,' they both replied.

'Are you ready?' Solvan said, turning to Lovoa.

'As I will ever be,' she replied and turned to smile at him. Together they started to draw in as much energy as they could from the sun until they felt that they could not absorb any more, then gripped the cold circular panels in the middle and on either side of the chairs. They felt the machine vibrate through them and increase the power that they had stored. Lovoa had lost sight of the vessel as it had gone in to land but could feel Protector Veran's fear as he stood on his battlements watching it land on his collective. Just as she felt she would explode with the energy she contained, Solvan shouted '*NOW!*' and she let go, sending everything that had been building up inside her towards Protector Veran, while uttering a prayer to Hannoki that Veran would be able to divert the energy they sent him towards the traders. As the last of it left her, she slumped forward, totally drained.

✵

Protector Veran stood on the battlements looking out at his collective. The first protector said that the traders were coming, but did he believe him? A few weeks ago, he would have said no, that it was all lies, but he had since heard tales about Protector Gilcan's collective having been destroyed and all the peasants skinned alive. He had felt pain and had had nightmares at the time that the attack had supposedly happened, the result being that he was now standing on the battlements with his mate, not quite believing that anything would happen. The sky started to light up with a blaze of colour as if it had been set on fire, and a strange, shining object started to come down from the sky.

'By Hannoki!' Veran cursed.

'What is that?' his mate asked.

'I think it is the traders,' he replied. None of the stories he had ever heard prepared him for what he was seeing now.

'*NOW!*' the first protector's voice shouted in his head so he grabbed his mate's hand and together they braced themselves. They saw it coming, a bright light from the Hannoki mountain range. Veran knew that they could not absorb it and it would be suicide to try, they needed to divert it towards the vessels that had caused the sky to burn. Veran merged his mind with his mate's so they thought as one and when the energy arrived, they shielded against it and then aimed it straight at the traders' vessels, staggering under the force of the energy they were directing. They managed to hit them all and watched as the sky seemed to explode and rain pieces of wreckage down on everyone below it, and they hoped that those on the ground would be able to get away from the falling debris.

⚜

As the energy left them and went flying towards Protector Veran, both Solvan and Lovoa slumped back in their seats. Bahia had started to make her way to Solvan and Lovoa as soon as the communication had ended and came running onto the plateau in time to see them both collapse.

'Solvan!' she shouted as she raced towards him. She shook him and again shouted his name, but got no response.

'*How are they?*' Essac asked.

'*I cannot rouse Solvan,*' she said. '*I think something went wrong, they should not have collapsed and there is a smell of burning from the machine.*'

'*What about Lovoa?*'

'*I don't know – give me a moment,*' and she moved to Lovoa, shook her and shouted her name.

Lovoa groaned and opened her eyes. 'Were they destroyed?' she managed to ask.

'I don't know,' Bahia admitted, 'I was so worried about you both that I did not check.'

Lovoa closed her eyes and concentrated on Veran's collective. She tried to call him but there was no reply. 'I can just about sense him but he is not responding. I don't think he is conscious but I feel no deaths,' she told Bahia.

'Where are the other vessels?' Solvan asked, and they turned to look at him. His eyes were open and his head had turned to look in their direction but he was still leaning back on the chair, needing its support.

'I only know that it was coming down onto one of the northern collectives,' Lovoa said, 'then I lost it when we went to help Veran.'

Solvan pulled himself up in the chair and sent his mind out. 'It has landed on Protector Uslac's collective, we have to do something about it *now*.' He put his hands back onto the panels, and Lovoa did the same.

'Can you do it a second time?' Bahia asked, worried.

'We won't know until we try,' Solvan said. Both he and Lovoa frantically tried to pull in as much energy as they could as quickly as possible when they saw a shaft of light coming down from the sky towards Protector Uslac's collective.

'What in Hannoki was that?' Solvan asked.

※

Cal and Jane were in the conference room again with Alex and his senior officers, but had to admit they had little extra to add to their previous meeting. Jane had been up all night on the computer trying to dig deeper to see if there were any further accounts, but this far into space made every search extremely slow. Cal, meanwhile, trawled through the records to see if there was anything they had missed. They could not find anything that the captain had not already briefed them on. Compared to what the captain knew, the lack of records screamed of a high-level cover up. Going forward, they could only assume the worst as the call came through for them to come to the bridge.

'The long-range scans confirm that there is no technology on the planet,' Ari Xhia said as they all walked onto the bridge.

'That doesn't mean that they don't have any, just that we are too far away,' Pheir Langish challenged.

'I know, but at the moment there is nothing, not even basic industry. There might be something when we can get close enough, but I doubt it,' Ari replied.

'Thank you, Ari. Pheir, I understand your concern over the inaccuracy of the long-range scans but at present they are all we have to work on. Do we know anything about the ship ahead of us?'

'We have been able to get some scans without risking detection. The ship is large and dense, and I would have to say that it's heavily armoured. If the Lismarian people have no defence, why have they sent such a ship? They have been given no indication that the FWN is aware of what they are doing, but are they assuming they might be challenged by us?' asked Pheir.

'We know nothing about the Lismarian people other than what they look like. There have been scans and surveys from orbit, but as far as I'm aware, no one other than the pirates and David Wilhelm have ever landed on the planet. How do we know they don't have some sort of ability to defend themselves?' Jane asked.

'What are you suggesting? That these people can blow shuttles up on their own? That's science fiction,' said James Samuels.

'If you go back far enough, space travel was science

fiction, telepaths were science fiction; just because we haven't encountered something before doesn't mean it isn't possible,' Cal challenged.

'It's not the same. Telepathic capability always existed even though we didn't understand it. What you are suggesting is pure fantasy,' argued James.

'Enough,' Alex shouted and silence fell across the bridge. 'It's more likely that they were able to defend themselves with weapons provided by my grandfather.'

'Which would now be old and easy to defend against,' countered Jane.

'I'm sorry to disturb you Captain, but the ship has settled into orbit around the planet,' Ensign Conner reported.

'Move us closer to the planet, but keep us out of range of the ship's sensors.'

'Aye Captain,' then a few minutes later, 'they are sending shuttles down to the planet.'

'Track those shuttles, I want to know where they are heading – and get security ready to deploy down to the planet.'

'Aye Captain.'

'Captain, if we get much closer, we risk being detected,' said Ari.

'Understood, move us closer and arm the missiles.'

'The shuttles are separating; they will be landing at different locations,' Conner informed them.

'How much longer until we are close enough to open fire on them?'

'Five minutes for the nearest of the shuttles, and we are coming into firing range now for the main ship,' James said.

'There is a strange build-up of energy from the planet,' Conner reported.

'What's causing it?'

'Unknown, the sensors are registering the energy, but not what's causing it,' and as she spoke, the monitors lit up. 'Wow!'

'What's happened?'

'I don't know, stand by,' Conner said as she worked on the terminal. 'The shuttles heading to the south hemisphere have been destroyed.'

'How?'

'I don't know. Whatever that energy was, it hit the shuttles and destroyed them.'

'Where are the others?'

'They are still on course.'

'Is the energy building again?'

'Negative,' Pheir said, 'the shuttles are still on course to land on the planet.'

'Move us closer and as soon as we are in range, fire at the shuttles,' Alex said.

'Captain, if we do that they will definitely know we are here, and now we are closer, I can tell you that that ship is very heavily armed. We will be out-gunned,' Pheir informed Alex.

'Then we had better hope that our tactics are better than theirs,' he replied. 'Send an emergency transmission to the nearest FWN base telling them our location and that pirates are attacking a restricted planet.'

'Communications are down, Captain.'

'We are in firing range.'

'Fire!' Captain Wilhelm ordered.

'Direct hit sir, the shuttles have been destroyed.'

'The ship is opening fire on us.'

'Raise the shields and return fire.'

'We have taken a direct hit. The shields are holding but they are firing again.' The report came in as the whole ship shuddered under the impact and warning lights started to flash.

'What was that?' the captain asked.

'I don't know sir, our sensors do not recognise the type of weapon they just used.'

'How is that possible?' the captain asked Pheir.

'It shouldn't be,' he replied as the ship shuddered under a second impact.

'Keep firing.'

'Their shields are holding against us; no damage recorded,' Conner said, 'but our shields are weakening under the attack. We won't be able to maintain this for long.'

'Can you move us out of here?'

'I will try, Captain.'

'They're moving to block our withdrawal.'

'Direct hit again; our shields won't take much more.'

*

'What was that?' Solvan asked.

'It came from above us,' Lovoa said.

'Where did it hit? Is this another form of attack?' Bahia questioned them.

'*First Protector,*' a voice called to Solvan, breaking through the conversation.

'*Yes, Protector Uslac,*' he acknowledged.

'*What just happened? Those vessels were coming in to land, then something hit them and they exploded. I thought you had to send the energy to me to direct?*'

'*It was not us, we do not know what just happened,*' he admitted. '*We had just sent the energy to Protector Veran and were preparing to do the same for you when we saw the light come from the sky. Can you confirm that you do not need anything from us now?*'

'*That is correct, there is only a hole in the ground where the vessels were.*'

'*Then we will try to find out what happened, and will*

keep you informed.'

'That was Protector Uslac, the other vessels have been destroyed,' Solvan informed his mother, knowing that Lovoa would have heard it for herself as their minds were still linked.

'It must have come from the other large vessel you sensed.'

'But I thought that only traders have ever come here. Do you think there are others that can travel here?' Lovoa asked.

'Why not? We don't know what is out there, so if the traders can get here, then why not others? But there is only one way to find out,' and together Solvan and Lovoa closed their eyes and concentrated on the space above them.

'Oh Hannoki!' Solvan swore as their minds soared. He saw both ships and they appeared to be fighting each other. They saw the missiles fly between the ships and the explosions as they hit.

'What do you sense?' Bahia asked, frustrated that she could not see what was going on. 'What is happening?'

'They appear to be attacking each other,' Solvan informed her.

'I am not sensing anything from them, but I think the second vessel is losing,' Lovoa said.

'Yes, I think you are right, it does seem to be sustaining damage.'

'We should try to help them,' Lovoa said.

'Why? It is one less vessel to attack us,' Bahia said.

'I don't think they did – they feel different to the other vessels that have come here. What if they are being attacked now because they helped us by destroying the others?'

'But you don't know if it was them.'

'I can't believe the attackers were blown up by their

own vessel and it was not us, or anyone else on the planet, so who else could it have been?' Lovoa asked.

'Lovoa is right, and if we don't do something soon, it will be too late.'

'But what can you do?' Bahia asked.

'Can we send energy up?' Lovoa asked.

'It has never been done before,' Solvan said.

'Has it ever been tried?' Lovoa questioned.

'Not that I know of,' Bahia admitted.

'We can try,' Solvan said. 'If we fail, we have lost nothing – the other vessel will be destroyed soon anyway if we don't do anything.'

'I agree,' Lovoa said and together they again started to pull in as much energy as they could, as quickly as they could, and then released it into the sky above them towards the trader vessel.

∗

'Captain, the shields can't take another direct hit,' Ari said.

'Get us out of here,' Alex ordered.

'Doing my best Captain, but the engines have been damaged and are not capable of much speed.'

'They have locked on to us again,' James said.

'I can't shake them, Captain,' Ari told him.

'Get the crew to the life pods,' the captain ordered.

'Captain, there is another massive energy reading coming from the planet and it's heading our way,' and even as James spoke, the light filled up the screen in front of him, hurtling upwards at incredible speed, and hit the pirates' ship. They all watched as the ship exploded in front of them, their shields protected them from the worst of the explosion before they failed.

'Impressive for a race with no technology,' Pheir stated.

'This could get interesting; are there any more power

surges from the planet?' the captain asked.

'No sir.'

'Start repairs immediately – the shields and engines are the main priority.'

Chapter 24

THEY had all watched from the bridge as the ship they had thought was about to destroy them had blown up in front of them. They had tried to communicate with the planet below to see if all the reports were incorrect and the Lismarians did have technology, but no reply had come back. When there hadn't been another energy build-up, the captain had asked all his senior bridge crew to meet in the conference room to decide what to do next.

'What do you mean, you think we should go down to the planet?' Duval Bastian demanded of Cal. 'Are you mad? Didn't you just see what they did to the pirate ship?'

'Of course I did, they blew the ship up just before it destroyed us. They saved us. Your shields were about to fail and then the pirates were blasted out of space by someone or something from the planet. We should go down and talk to them.'

'And if they take us as a threat and blast at us?'

'If they think that, then why haven't they destroyed us since we are still in their orbit? We can't even move out of the way until the engines are fixed.'

'The conditions on the planet have also got to be taken into consideration if you're thinking of going down,' Ari added.

'What do you mean?' Jane said.

'The planet has two suns so the temperature on the surface is extremely high and we would burn immediately. Consequently, we would need to wear environmental suits on the surface.'

'That's a minor consideration; we have the training and the equipment to deal with the environment,' Alex said.

'If we did go to the planet, where would we land? Who would we talk to? How would we communicate with them? Their language will not be programmed into our translators,' Duval argued.

'Could you take scans of the planet, try to get as much information as possible to answer these questions?' Cal pushed.

'No amount of scanning is ever going to allow us to communicate and say "Hey, we're friends and want to help," before they kill us,' Duval mocked.

'I think that if they intended to harm us, they would have done so by now. You said yourself that we can't move anywhere at the moment. If they had wanted to attack us, they would have done so.'

'I wouldn't be willing to bet my life or the lives of this crew on that until we know more. For a people without technology, they have destroyed shuttles and a heavily armoured and shielded spaceship, a ship we could not destroy. How the hell did they do that?' Duval asked.

'That is what we need to go down and find out,' Cal argued.

'I'm sorry Cal, but we can still protect the planet from orbit while our engines are fixed, and once communications are back up we can ask for assistance from other ships, but until we know that we wouldn't be destroyed as soon as we have landed, it's too dangerous for us to try. It's also against the law to make contact with a planet that isn't capable of space travel as we could hinder their natural development. We've already interfered more than we should when we destroyed those shuttles. They have to be left alone for now until authority comes from the Head Chairman of the Federation of Worlds.'

'There isn't one at the moment,' Cal snapped, 'he got murdered.'

'Cal,' Alex's voice was hard, 'until I have orders, we are not going down to the planet.'

'If we can't go down, why are you trying to communicate with them? What would you say to them if they replied?' Jane asked.

'If they could hear us from here then they would have advanced communications and would give us more of an argument to go down to the planet. As to how we would communicate, there are set programs in the system to assist with that.'

The intercom buzzed and Alex answered it. 'I'm sorry to bother you, Captain, but I think you need to come back to the bridge.'

'Are they getting ready for another attack?'

'No Captain, I think they are trying to communicate.'

※

Their minds followed the energy as it soared above them and watched as it hit the vessel, causing it to explode. Suddenly their minds were pulled back into their bodies with a force that made them gasp.

'What happened?' Lovoa was able to ask and in the background they heard a pop followed by a hissing noise. Turning in the direction of the noise, smoke could be seen coming out of the machine.

'I think it's broken,' Solvan replied.

'Are you both all right?' Bahia asked. 'Did it work?'

'We are, and yes, the vessel has been destroyed.'

'But at what cost?' Bahia asked, also looking at the machine.

'I gather that it hasn't done that before,' Lovoa stated.

'Not that we are aware of, no,' Bahia replied.

'It might still be all right,' Solvan said hopefully, 'we

could test it by putting a small amount of energy into it and see what happens.'

'It's worth a try,' Bahia agreed.

Solvan and Lovoa looked at each other and, as one, they again started to pull in a small amount of energy but when they tried to feed it into the machine, nothing happened.

'Oh Hannoki,' Solvan cursed, 'this can't be good.'

'Can you fix it?' Lovoa asked, looking at Bahia. 'Do you know what is wrong with it?'

'No, I don't know any more than Solvan does about how it works. The writings never mentioned how to fix it, they only describe how to use it.'

'Maybe it just needs time to recover, as we do between attacks. Perhaps we just acted too quickly for it?' Lovoa asked hopefully, though she knew, as did Solvan and Bahia, that this was most probably not the case. They sat in silence for a few minutes contemplating the impact that not having the machine would have on their planet.

'We will wait for a while, then try again,' Solvan said, and the three of them sat in an anxious silence and watched as the smoke continued to belch out of the side of the machine.

'How long do we wait?'

'Until the smoke stops?' Bahia suggested.

'Should we look and see what is causing the smoke and stop it?'

'All the records advise that we should not tamper with the machine,' Bahia warned.

'I know, but nothing describes what is happening now,' Solvan reminded her.

'If it has broken, then surely looking can't hurt it any more. Smoke means a fire and if it is not put out, more damage would be caused,' Lovoa reasoned.

'I don't think it can hurt to look,' Solvan said and pulled

himself up off the seat. Lovoa followed him and watched as he went to where the smoke was coming from and pulled off the panel. Solvan moved back suddenly as a hot black cloud of smoke escaped from behind the panel as it was released. It cleared, revealing a black surface. Solvan guessed that it should have been smooth but the heat had caused sections of it to warp. He did not know what was behind it and could see no easy way to find out. None of them understood what they were seeing.

'What do we do now?' Bahia asked, realising that whatever had gone wrong, they were unable to fix it. 'What do we do when the traders come back again?'

'We could get the protectors to attack them once they have landed.' Lovoa suggested. 'They can be killed – I proved that.'

'It would be a possibility,' Solvan agreed, 'but we don't know how many there are, or what weapons they could use against us. When the traders attacked your family, there were only a few of them, nowhere near the number that landed on Gilcan's collective, and we don't know what would happen if they expected to be attacked on the ground.'

'What about the vessel that helped us? Could we try asking them for help?' Lovoa asked.

'How do you plan to communicate with them? They are all the way up there,' Bahia said.

'I know, but this vessel felt different from the start. With the traders, I just felt their hostility towards us, but the others were different and when they were under attack, I knew that they thought they were going to die. I think there is someone on that vessel we could try to talk with on a telepathic level,' Lovoa said.

'Can you reach that far for coherent communication without the machine?' Bahia queried.

'Even if we can reach that far, you said you could not

understand what they were saying when they attacked you, so how are we going to make ourselves understood?'

'By projecting emotions and images to them.'

'Do you think it will work?' Bahia asked her son.

'I have no idea,' he replied.

'What happens if they are hostile, that they were just fighting off the competition? Then we would just have helped them,' his mother said, worried.

'I did not feel that from them, and if I'm wrong, then we will know sooner rather than later,' Lovoa responded.

'It's worth a try, we have nothing to lose and a lot to gain,' Solvan said, having come to a decision.

'*Let them give it a go,*' Essac said. '*At best it could end this threat forever but it is unlikely to make anything worse. Whoever is on that vessel knows that we are here, so why not try to talk to them?*'

Together Solvan and Lovoa merged their minds and again went up to the vessel, but this time they took their time. Without the machine to increase their abilities, they had to be careful not to over-extend themselves and continually pulled in more energy as they went. When their minds arrived at the vessel, they slowly scanned every consciousness. Most were closed to them, they felt one or two others but could not make themselves heard, then finally found one mind that was stronger than the rest.

❉

'Are you all right, Ensign?'

'I'm fine sir,' Conner said as she sat there rubbing her temples. All the tension and emotion of the battle was obviously getting to her. She was annoyed with herself: she should be able to close out the other minds around her better than this. Taking a few deep breaths, she concentrated on the minds around her, trying to find and block out the ones that were giving her this headache.

'Oh my God,' she said, sitting bolt upright on her chair. 'Sir!' she shouted as she held her head.

'What is it Ensign, are you sure you are not ill – you've gone very white.'

'No sir, but I think they are trying to communicate with *me.*'

'I beg your pardon?'

'Someone, or more correctly some two, from the planet are trying to communicate with me.'

'Are you saying that they are responding to the message you sent out? That they do have technology?'

'No sir, they are trying to communicate with me, they are telepaths. What do you want me to do?'

'Wait, I'll call the captain.'

'How are they communicating?' Alex asked as he walked back onto the bridge a few moments later with the rest of the senior officers, Cal and Jane following close behind.

'Ensign Conner says they are trying to communicate direct to her, sir.'

Alex looked over at the young officer slumped forward in her chair, holding her head. She was pale and sweating. 'Ensign, what makes you think that the people on the planet below are trying to communicate with you? What are you receiving?'

'It is faint but persistent, and is aimed directly at me. As the strongest telepath on the ship, it could be that I'm the only one they can reach. I feel like my brain is straining to hear as it's coming from so far away, and I can't understand anything they're trying to say. It's not a language I recognise but the emotions are warm.'

'Have you tried to respond?'

'No sir, not yet.'

'Can you try, try and get across that we mean them no

harm?'

'Yes sir,' and after a few moments pause, 'I think they realise that we don't understand and have started to send me images – oh God!' she cried.

'Ensign?'

'They are showing me pictures of lots of skinned bodies, there are so many of them. Now it has changed, I think they're showing me what just happened, of them destroying the shuttles and now I'm seeing our missile coming through the atmosphere to destroy the others. They could see the fight we had with the pirates and they helped us. I feel that they want to be friends, that they know that we helped them.'

'Can you communicate back that we want the same thing?' Alex asked.

'I'll do my best.'

'Captain, the situation is still the same, they are not at the requisite technological level for us to open communications,' said Duval.

'No it's not,' Cal said. 'We didn't open up the communication, they did, they are trying to talk to us. If they thought we were a danger, they would just have fired at us and we would be debris in the atmosphere by now.'

'I have to agree with Cal, these people have been attacked by pirates, they have saved us and are now trying to talk to us. As long as we don't pass any technology over to them, what further damage would we do? We might put them in more danger if we ignore them now and do nothing,' Alex said. 'Ensign, can you indicate that we would like to meet?'

'I will do my best, sir.'

'Duval, if we don't talk to them, they might assume that everyone who came near the planet would be hostile towards them, which could cause a major cultural mindset which could be devastating in the future for any ship that gets near the planet.'

'Captain,' Conner said, 'I think they understood the request. They are showing me a mountain with a large plateau, and I think they're telling us to land there.'

'Any idea which mountain they are showing us?'

'I believe so, sir. Scans show that the highest mountain has a large plateau at the top. It's also where the energy build-ups came from.'

'Can you say we will go down tomorrow?'

'Yes sir.' After a moment's pause, 'They have acknowledged and now they have gone,' Conner said and she slumped even further into the chair.

'Ensign, are you all right?'

'I'm sorry sir, communicating was very difficult and now I have a splitting headache.'

'Report to the sick bay. Ensign Alders, go with her and make sure she is all right,' Alex said.

'Yes sir.'

As Conner stood up, she staggered and Ensign Alders took her arm and they left together.

⁜

'Well?' Bahia asked when Solvan and Lovoa broke the connection.

'We now know we can reach that far but it was not easy,' Solvan said.

'What did they say?' she pushed, impatient to find out what had happened.

'We found one that could hear us, but we could not understand what she was thinking so we sent images, which they seemed to be able to interpret, and they sent others to us. They want to come down and talk to us but are afraid. We reassured them and they will come tomorrow morning, judging by the position of the suns they gave us.'

'We told them to land here,' Lovoa said, 'that way they will not scare everyone and possibly be attacked.'

'I am coming back,' Essac said, *'just in case.'*

✢

The shuttle broke through the atmosphere, heading towards the planet. Everyone on board was silent as the mountains came into range. Only a skeleton crew was on board and all had volunteered to go, Captain Wilhelm had not been prepared to order anyone, just in case they were proved wrong and the shuttle was fired upon. Cal and Jane were at first told that it was too dangerous for them to go, but were granted permission after a long argument in which they pointed out that if things turned violent, no amount of training was going to save anyone, and though their knowledge was not vast, no one knew more about the Lismarian people than them. Ensign Conner had also wanted to go, and when objections were raised because of her health after her visit to the sick bay, she asked how they planned to communicate with the people without her. Captain Wilhelm had stayed behind, aware that leaving his ship and crew without a captain could prove disastrous should anything happen. Lieutenant Commander Pheir Langish was the senior officer on the shuttle, as he had stated that he was just too curious as to how a people with no technology had been able to blow a ship out of orbit.

'Sir, we are approaching the plateau.'

'Take us in slowly,' Pheir ordered and they all watched as the shuttle gently touched down. Pheir picked up his helmet and sealed it in place, and the others followed suit. Once Cal and Jane's helmets were on and another member of the crew had checked that they were properly connected, the hatch was opened and they left the shuttle. Both suns were in the sky, making everything very bright, even through the tinted helmets.

'There.' Jane pointed to two people approaching them. They were small and thin and the patterning on their skin was identical and extensive. They stopped a short distance from the landing party.

'It's the same minds as before, and I'm sensing calm and peace from them,' Conner informed her colleagues. Then they all watched as the pair looked at each other, startled. 'They are surprised, very surprised,' Conner said.

'In a good way?' Pheir asked.

'I don't know,' she said.

The male walked forward and stopped in front of them.

'How can we understand you?' he asked. 'Your thoughts make no sense, yet we can understand the words you say.'

'Bloody hell,' one of the crew said.

'It's just the translators working,' Jane said.

'How can that be? No one has ever landed on this planet before to communicate with the people, and I can't believe the pirates would have taken the time to learn their language and program it into the FWN translators.'

'The captain's grandfather? He came here,' Cal suggested.

'For now, let's just count it as a blessing,' Pheir said, then turning to the male standing in front of him, who looked even more confused, said, 'we have translators that are programmed with many different languages, but they can only translate the spoken word.'

'I don't understand what you mean by translators, but it does make this easier. My name is Solvan, I am first protector, and this is my mate, Lovoa,' he said, indicating behind him, then the female walked up to stand beside the male.

'I am Lieutenant Commander Pheir Langish, this is Ensign Conner, with whom you communicated yesterday, and Ensign Phelps, Cal Everson and Jane Keyworth.'

'It is good to meet you all, and we thank you for trusting us and coming down,' Lovoa said.

'You, or someone down here, saved us so we had no reason to distrust you.'

'You helped us first; the favour was repaid,' Solvan said. 'We wanted to meet as we are curious. We have only known the traders' attacks, so we did not know that there were others who could travel as well.'

'We were also curious as to how you were able to destroy the traders' ship,' Pheir said, using their word for the pirates, 'we could detect no technology here at all.'

'I do not understand the word "technology",' Solvan said.

'Do you have any weapons, computers, machines?'

'We have a machine,' Solvan said, 'it magnifies our abilities. It is here,' and he led them to it.

'You sure you are doing the right thing?' Bahia said into his mind. *'How do you know that you can trust them?'*

'I don't feel anything negative from them. They are as curious as we are and they might be able to help us. Something went wrong with the machine when we fired into space and we have no idea how to fix it, but perhaps they do.'

'But to show them that we are weak and vulnerable?'

'It would not take them long to work it out if they decided to attack us,' Solvan replied as he showed them the machine.

'Oh my God!' Cal said as he bent down and examined it, 'we have definitely been here before – this is our technology.'

'You're kidding. If it *is* our technology, why didn't our sensors pick it up?'

'It's old, but there would be no energy signature until it was used. It conducts and increases any power put into it, but without energy input, there is no energy reading, which is why your sensors didn't pick it up.'

'Do you know where this came from?' Cal asked Solvan.

'No, it has always been here since the time of Hannoki, who first fought the traders. There is no account of where it came from.'

'May I have a closer look?' he asked, and Solvan nodded and watched as he removed sections.

'It's broken,' he said after a few moments.

'Yes,' Solvan admitted.

'So you weren't using this when you fired on the traders?' Pheir asked.

'We were, but we had to put a lot more energy into it than we normally would to get the range we needed, and afterwards there was nothing.'

'It overloaded,' Cal said. 'Too much was fed into it and it couldn't take it. To be honest, I'm surprised it was working at all with how old it is.'

'Can it be fixed?' Lovoa asked.

'I don't know, I would need to see the extent of the damage, but it's unlikely, I'm afraid.'

'Did you know that this would happen when you helped us?' Pheir asked.

'We did not even know that we would be able to destroy the vessel from so great a distance. As far as we knew, no one had ever tried to destroy the traders while they were in space.'

'How much energy did you put through this thing?' Cal asked.

'A lot.'

'I get that, but how much? How many petawatts, for example, and where does it come from? We detected no energy signatures until just before you fired.'

'I do not understand petawatts, we just collect the energy and put it into the machine,' Solvan explained.

'But collect it from where?'

'The sun,' he said, as if it were obvious.

'You mean you have solar panels?'

'I do not know what they are, so probably not.'

'We pull in the energy,' Lovoa said.

'How? I'm sorry, I don't understand what you are trying to say,' Cal said, confused, looking around him for further technology, but seeing none.

Solvan and Lovoa looked at each other. 'Watch,' she said and started to pull in the energy around her, stretching her arm out and releasing it in a bright blast over the mountain range. 'That is how.'

'Bloody hell!' Cal said. Pheir was also cursing behind him and Jane coughed while mumbling something that sounded like, 'Told you,' behind her hand.

They heard a bleeping sound, then, 'Is everything all right down there, Lieutenant Commander? We registered an energy surge in your area.'

'Yes sir, they were just giving us a demonstration,' he replied. 'That was our captain,' he explained to Solvan and Lovoa when he saw that they looked agitated by the unknown voice, 'we can communicate with our ship using other machines.'

'So you can pull in the solar energy around you and convert it?' Jane asked.

'Yes,' Lovoa confirmed.

'Can everyone do this?'

'Everyone can pull in energy, but some can pull in more than others.'

'Unbelievable.'

'You find this surprising?' Lovoa asked.

'Very, we have encountered numerous different people

but never anyone who could do that,' Pheir explained.

'Would you like to come off the plateau?' Lovoa asked. 'We have food and drink, although I do not know if we have anything that you can eat...' she paused, 'or if you eat.'

'We eat, yes, but we can't while we wear these suits,' Pheir explained.

'You do not normally look like that?'

'No, your suns are too strong for us and would cause us serious harm, so these suits protect us from them.'

'Then come in, you may find it more comfortable,' Lovoa said, leading the way.

Lovoa led them into the main living area where Essac, Bahia and Brelsa were waiting for them. When Essac had contacted Brelsa and told her that he was returning to the mountain and the reason why, and that she or Gilcan may have to return to support Isslac, she had asked to come as well. Solvan introduced them all.

Pheir then got right to the point, 'The people who have been attacking you, that you call traders, how long has this been going on? How many have they killed? What is it that they do once they have killed one of your people?'

'At present, they have not been coming for very long, though the damage they have done has been great. Most of what we know we had to relearn from our histories as it has been so long since they last came here,' Bahia explained. 'It is hard to say how many they have killed as they attacked small, isolated farms first before moving on to a large collective farm where they skinned everyone alive. If I had to give an estimate, possibly two thousand, though Gilcan would be in a better position to answer that. What do they do with the bodies? They just leave them to rot in the sun.'

Silence followed this announcement, then, 'Are you sure?' as if he did not quite believe what he had heard.

'We are, as you know, telepathic and between family members this is much stronger than with anyone else. I felt my parents' pain as they were skinned alive; the pain was so great that it debilitated me and I was not able to get to them until it was too late to save them,' Lovoa explained. 'So yes, I am sure of what they do.'

'Christ!'

'Do you know what they do when they leave? Why they want your skins and wings?' Cal asked.

'No, we just know that they come and if we do not stop them, they kill many of us,' Solvan said. 'Why are you here now? Do you know how we can stop them for good?' Solvan said. 'I'm sorry, I have so many questions for you.'

'It is probably easiest if I start at the beginning as it will explain how we found out what was happening and how we all got involved. If you need me to explain further, let me know,' and Cal started to tell them everything that had occurred since his father's death. He had to try to explain a few points more clearly as they had no concept of cars or computers. When he had finished, there was silence in the room.

'They used us for clothing?' Bahia said in shock. 'Something to be used for their pleasure?'

'Yes. However, only the people involved would know where the skins came from, no one buying them would know, they would assume they were made from other materials.'

'How can you be so sure?' Lovoa asked.

'Because what they are doing is a crime and they would be executed if caught.'

'Then why do it if you can make clothing?'

'I don't fully understand everything that I read, but from what I can gather, the skins change colour depending on the mood of the wearer, which is something that we can't replicate, but people liked the uniqueness of it without understanding how it works,' Jane said.

'If we are not careful, we change colour depending on how we feel,' Lovoa told them.

'So why aren't you changing now?' Conner asked. 'I can feel how upset you are but nothing has visibly changed.'

Solvan and Lovoa exchanged looks and, as if an agreement had been reached, Lovoa's skin turned green. 'We can control it. Showing your emotions either demonstrates that you cannot control yourself or, if you do it deliberately, is considered rude,' Lovoa said and then brought her skin back to its normal colour.

'Can you stop them?' Essac asked. 'Can you tell people what the traders are doing?'

'I don't know. Last time the origin of the coats was discovered, the trade was stopped and the authorities tried to cover everything up, which has allowed it to start up again now. We don't even know who is involved in it, and who would listen and help or who would try to silence us,' Pheir said.

'What would happen if one of you came back with us?' Jane asked.

'What good would that do?' Pheir asked.

'Then we would not need to explain and try to get others at home to prove it; we could just say, "Look at where your clothes come from," preferably in front a big, influential audience, then it would be very difficult to stop us and they couldn't cover it up.'

'It would certainly stir everything up – there would have to be an investigation because of the public outcry,' Cal said. 'How reliant are you on the sun? You said you can draw it in but if there were no sun, what would happen to you?'

'We would die,' Solvan said. 'How long it would take would depend on how strong each person was, how much energy they had stored and how much they expended.'

'Could you last a few weeks?'

They all looked at each other. 'I don't know, I have never been without it,' Solvan said. 'I don't think anyone has ever been without sunlight for that long.'

'Yes, we can if we have stored energy and do not expend it.' Brelsa spoke for the first time.

'How would you know?' Essac said.

'From how long people have survived in my father's lightless cells,' she replied. 'If anyone is going, I want to be the one.'

'No, you have done so much already,' Lovoa said.

'Then who would you suggest? You, Essac, Bahia? You are all mated which means that if this goes wrong, we lose two people instead of one, and I would hope that with everything I have done, you could trust me to do this.'

'We would take good care of her,' Cal said.

'We are forgetting one very important point here,' Pheir said.

'What? It seems like a great idea,' Cal said.

'Unless the captain agrees to this, nothing is going to happen.'

'Oh, guess we need to go and talk to him,' Cal said. He addressed Brelsa, 'If you are willing to come with us, we will go and speak to our captain, our boss, and ask him if he will agree to our plan.'

'I will come with you if he agrees,' Brelsa said.

Chapter 25

DRAWING in as much of the suns' energy as she could, Brelsa walked up the ramp, with Ensign Conner next to her. She paused at the top and looked in cautiously.

'It's all right,' Conner reassured her. Talking a deep breath, Brelsa walked in, gasped at the sudden lack of sunlight and felt a moment of panic. 'Brelsa, if you can't do this, then we will think of something else – it's not a problem.'

'No, I will be fine' she said. As her eyes adjusted to the slightly darker interior, she was amazed; she had never seen anything like it. Everything was different shades of grey and as she reached out and touched the surfaces, she found them to be cold and smooth. At the front of the vessel, two other men were sitting in front of a panel where different coloured lights were flickering.

'You will need to sit down as we take off,' Conner said and indicated the seats on her left. Once Brelsa was seated, Conner helped her strap in before sitting next to her.

'They keep calling you Ensign, but that is a position, I think, and indicates what you do but is not your name,' Brelsa said.

'Yes, with the exception of Cal and Jane, we all belong to the Federation of Worlds Navy, or FWN, and we all have ranks. My rank is Ensign.'

'As I'm not part of this FWN, what is your name, what can I call you?'

'Ann,' she replied, 'my name is Ann Conner.'

'What did your captain say to my coming with you?' she asked.

'I don't know, I wasn't in the meeting.'

'But your lieutenant commander was, so what did you sense from him afterwards?'

'Nothing, it would have been an unforgivable intrusion,' Conner replied. 'I just know that he has agreed, otherwise you would not be coming. You will meet him when we get on board, though.'

Brelsa nodded her understanding. The crew had not had to leave the planet to talk to the captain, as Brelsa had expected, instead they had used their technology. They had described it as a conference call, but she hadn't understood what that meant, though it did mean that a decision had been made quickly. Brelsa watched the two men up front as their hands moved over the lights. Conner told her that they were the 'pilots' and they were responsible for flying them back to the main ship. Everything was so different and confusing, but she was fascinated by it all.

'When Lieutenant Commander Langish and Mr Everson return, we will be leaving. You will feel pressure when the shuttle takes off; this is normal but if you have any questions, please just ask.'

As if on cue, both men walked back into the shuttle and took the seats opposite. 'How are you doing, Brelsa?' Cal asked her.

'Nervous,' she admitted.

'Are you sure you can manage the flight?'

'I will survive it, though I expect it to be very uncomfortable.'

'You will do just fine,' Jane reassured her.

'If need be, we can experiment with the solar lamps in hydroponics,' Cal suggested.

'What is that?' Brelsa asked.

'Every deep-range ship has hydroponics which is where fresh food is grown. If it is to grow, it needs sunlight, so solar lamps were created to replicate the sun's energy. Unfortunately, with no knowledge of how you absorb and break down the energy, I don't know if the lamps would help you or not.'

'It would be interesting to see if they work,' Brelsa said.

'Ensign, we are good to go,' Pheir called down to the pilots after he had reassured himself that everyone was correctly strapped in.

'Yes sir,' he said, and started up the engines.

The trip was short and the silence was broken only by the pilots communicating with each other, then suddenly, 'FWN *London*, this is Shuttle 2, permission to dock?'

'Shuttle 2 from FWN *London*, permission granted, please proceed to Docking Bay 1.'

A few moments later, one of the pilots turned around and said, 'Sir, we have now docked.'

'Please release the hatch, Ensign.'

'Yes sir,' and there was a hissing noise as the door opened.

'Officially, the captain greets people as they come aboard, but let me just say "Welcome aboard, Brelsa",' Pheir said as he unbuckled himself and walked off the shuttle.

'Are you ready?' Conner asked her. She nodded and together they walked out into the ship. As she exited, she saw several people standing nearby. They all looked different to the people she had already met and then she saw both Pheir and Conner pull at something around their necks and remove their helmets, and she realised that they were all the same.

'Brelsa,' Pheir said, 'may I introduce you to Captain Wilhelm; Sir, this is Brelsa, daughter of Protector Ovato and personal friend to the first protectors.'

'It is a pleasure to meet you Brelsa, and to welcome you aboard the FWN *London*.'

'Thank you, sir,' she replied.

'Are you all right?' Conner asked Brelsa, feeling her confusion.

'I am sorry, but you look very different without your suits on – I did not expect you to look as you do – and it is not very bright in here,' she said.

'I hope we don't look too bad to you and, of course, we should have thought about the light before you landed. I understand that we consider your planet to be very bright. Are you able to see well enough to move around freely?' Alex asked.

'Oh yes, it does get darker than this when both of the suns set, it will just take a few moments to get used to it.'

'Good, then if you feel up to it, let me show you where you will be staying and the areas you are allowed to go,' Alex said. 'I have also assigned Ensign Conner to assist you in anything that you need.'

'Thank you.'

'If you would like to follow me,' and he showed her off the docking bay. Brelsa followed him down the corridors, constantly looking around her, unable to fully take in everything she saw. She was shown to a small room with a bed in it and immediately started to feel very closed in. 'This will be your room,' Alex explained. 'Cal and Jane are in the room next to you should you need anything from them and Ensign Conner is on the deck below, but if you want her nearer, she can move while you are here.'

'It looks very nice.'

'Are you all right Brelsa?' Conner asked.

'Yes, it's just strange. There are no windows, all our rooms have windows, the bigger the better, to allow the light in. I have never been anywhere where there is no light.'

'Will you be able to make it to Europa?' the captain asked, concerned.

'Yes, I stored as much energy as I could before we left, it will just be an uncomfortable trip.'

'There are solar lamps in hydroponics so I will take you there and see if they make you any more comfortable.'

'Thank you.'

'This way,' and he led her through several corridors and up to the top deck. 'I should warn you before you go in that while most areas have no outside view, hydroponics does and it unnerves some people.'

Brelsa nodded her understanding and followed him in. In front of her was row upon row of greenery above which were huge lamps covering the plants with light. As she walked into the light she felt a slight relief from the agitation, and although she did not know if the lamps would be enough for a very long trip, she thought that they would be sufficient for this one.

※

'Did Alex need much persuading to have Brelsa on board?' Jane asked. Cal had sat in on the call but Jane had stayed with the Lismarians trying to learn as much of their history as she could in the short time they could stay on the planet.

'He is very concerned over the repercussions for him and his crew as it's against the law even to allow her aboard the ship, let alone take her to another planet. The doctor was concerned about medical implications for both her and us, but Alex pointed out that the FWN regularly lands on unknown planets so he didn't consider that a problem as protocols are in place should she be ill.'

'If he could get into so much trouble, why did he agree?'

'I think, to a great extent, because of his grandfather and how much he cared for these people. Aside from that, laws are there to protect people of other planets and allow them to develop at their own pace. The pirates have already made the Lismarians aware that there are other species, that there is space travel. Alex is afraid that in the time it takes us to get back and get the right people to listen, more pirates could have gone back to the planet and killed again. We can't stay here because while the engines will get us back to Europa, the weapons, shields and long distance communications will take longer to fix, and though Alex can't protect the people by remaining, he thinks he can by showing Brelsa to everyone.'

⁜

'Ensign, how is our guest coping?' Alex asked the next day. He had called her to a meeting in the conference room with the other senior officers and Cal and Jane.

All right, I think. She is more or less living in hydroponics, though – the lamps seem to make her less nervous.'

'She just sits there?'

'No sir, she is fascinated by the range of vegetables and fruit that we have. I gather that their diet is very limited, only a few crops grow on their planet due to excessive heat and lack of water.'

'Is she able to eat any of it?' the medical officer asked. 'She brought some food aboard but not much and, as I understand it, she has yet to eat any of it.'

'I've asked her several times if she needs me to get any food for her but she always declines.'

'Captain, I'm concerned that she hasn't eaten anything since coming aboard. I'm also worried that I know nothing about their biology, so I would like to run scans and tests so I would have some idea of how to help her should she become sick or get injured.'

'You may talk to her but under no circumstances are

you to do anything without her express permission.'

'But Captain, if anything should go wrong...'

'Doctor, as you said, we know nothing about them, so this might be perfectly normal for them. She came aboard this ship as a massive sign of trust and I will not have that betrayed. Also, on a serious safety issue, if Brelsa were to get upset and think we were attacking her, she could blow a hole in our hull and I'm not willing to risk it. I appreciate your concerns with regard to her health, but she is fully aware of the risks, as are the leaders on her planet.'

'Yes sir.'

'Ensign, you will introduce the doctor to Brelsa.'

'Yes sir.'

⁂

'Brelsa!' Ann Conner called as they entered the hydroponics bay.

'Here,' was the reply and, turning, they saw her talking to one of the gardeners and went over to them.

'Brelsa, may I introduce Doctor Jenkins to you; Doctor Jenkins, this is Brelsa.'

'Pleased to meet you,' she responded. 'How can I help you?'

'Brelsa,' the doctor started, 'I'm in charge of everyone's health on board this ship and it has been brought to my attention that you have not eaten while you have been on board.'

'I thought I had only been on board for a day,' Brelsa said, 'though I find it hard to tell without suns.'

'You have.'

'Then I do not understand, I ate before I left, I brought extra food in case there were any delays or I got hungrier without the suns.'

'But you have not eaten,' the doctor stressed again.

'Brelsa, we eat three times a day, ideally at the start of the day, in the middle and at the end. Since you came aboard, I have eaten three times. The doctor is worried that you haven't.'

'You eat three times a day?' Brelsa was shocked. 'The workers on the collectives would eat once a day at the very most. I can go several days between meals.'

'Why is there a difference?'

'The more markings you have, the more energy you can take in, and the more energy you take in, the less you need to eat. The workers have very few markings on them. They also eat more to store the food so if it runs short over the summer, then hopefully they can keep going until the winter months and the next harvest.'

'Amazing. I have met and studied the biology of several different races in my career, but I have never heard of anyone being able to do that,' the doctor said. 'I know nothing about how your body works and I would love the chance to examine you to try to understand how your bodies absorb and use the energy. It also worries me that if you became sick or got injured, I wouldn't be able to treat you, so I was hoping that you would allow me to run some tests so I know what is healthy for you.'

'We heal very well when injured so I'm not concerned about that, but what do you mean by if I get "sick"?' she asked.

'When you are unwell and not because you are hurt,' the doctor explained.

'Brelsa, it might be easier if I show you what the doctor means – may I?' Conner said, realising that Brelsa did not understand the doctor. Nodding in agreement, Brelsa opened her mind to the images that Conner sent her.

'We do not get sick,' Brelsa said, breaking the connection.

'You don't understand, you may have been lucky and

not been ill before, but you are going to another planet where there will be lots of illnesses which you won't have encountered before, and your system may not be able to fight them.'

'I appreciate your concern doctor, but I'm not saying that I do not get sick; I'm saying that we as a people do not get sick – we can be hurt, yes, but not sick in the way you mean it. The nearest we come to it is when we get old and our ability to take in the suns' energy deteriorates so our bodies start to break down. So no, I will stay here with the lamps for the trip and I will eat when I am hungry, and I will not have any tests done.'

'How is that possible?' the doctor said. 'If you would just let me...'

'I said no,' Brelsa said. 'I'm here to try and help my people and to stop your kind from killing us. You will understand that with what you have taken from us, I am not very trusting towards you and do not want to give you any other advantage over us. Please leave.'

'I'm sorry,' and with the captain's words in her head about how Brelsa could blow a hole in the hull if she got upset, Conner and the doctor left.

⁜

The voyage was uneventful and soon they were back at the spaceport they had left just over a week before. Brelsa had done exactly as she had said and stayed in hydroponics for the whole voyage, and had caused few problems. Conner spent a couple of hours a day with her, as did Cal and Jane. Most of the other crew members kept their distance, though a few let their curiosity get the better of them. The majority of these were also telepaths who wanted to learn more about such an alien mind, and Brelsa was happy to learn as much as she could from them as they were from her.

The difficult part was what was going to happen next. Jane had been back on her computer before the ship had even left orbit, trying to find a way to show Brelsa to everyone and reveal the trade. It didn't take her long to find the fashion show on Cornucopia as it was so well publicised. Tickets for the event were exclusive, but it would be broadcast for anyone who wanted to see it, so Jane worked on trying to find a way in.

'It's the perfect opportunity,' she argued, 'the audience is by invitation only, which can only mean it will be full of the rich and powerful, but it's also going to be broadcast all over different planetary networks. The show is to promote the clothes made from the Lismarian skins, so if we can get in and say what we need to say, there will be no hiding it, too many people will have heard about it. Even if they think there's nothing to it, imagine the outcry for an investigation, even if only to try and disprove what you have said.'

'It would be a very good public arena for our purpose,' Alex agreed, 'but if it's that exclusive, how do you plan to get in?'

'I can get tickets for the event that will get Cal and guest in and, hopefully, once in, we can help get the rest of you in.'

'I thought you said the tickets were by invitation only? How would I suddenly be invited to one of these events?' Cal asked.

'Don't be daft, I can hack the system and add your name to the guest list and show us travelling from Europa to Cornucopia.'

'Could you add others?' Cal asked, thinking that some of the crew could get in as well.

'I could, but if I add too many people who are not well known in the elite social circles, the organisers would know, or at least suspect, that their systems had been hacked. You might not have an interest in fashion, but you are of the correct social standing and could argue that your partner had wanted you to ask for the tickets.'

'Point taken.'

'I should have remembered, the admiral warned me about you,' Alex said.

'Yes, he is a wise man,' Jane said. 'Also, during my search I just happened to find the layout for the event and the security arrangements,' and she showed them the printout with a smile.

'God help us.'

'Don't worry, I haven't gone into any of your systems, I would never have done anything so rude as we are your guests.'

'Thank you so much, that relieves my mind no end,' Alex said.

Chapter 26

'SIR, the majority of people who were sent invitations to the show have sent a positive response.'

'Very good – can I see the list?' and the computer with the details was turned towards him. 'Cal Everson is coming. I didn't realise he had been invited.'

'He wasn't originally, but apparently his female companion wished to attend so he requested an invitation.'

'It still seems strange, he's not known for his interest in fashion or keeping company with those who are. What is the name of his guest?'

'There is no name listed.'

'Look into what he has been up to since his father died. I want to know if he's up to anything, or if this is just a coincidence.'

'Yes, sir.'

⁂

'Spaceport Cornucopia from FWN *London* receiving,' Alex hailed as they approached orbit.

'FWN *London*, this is spaceport Cornucopia, how can we help you? We have no record of your arrival.'

'No, unfortunately we encountered some heavily armed pirates shortly after we departed and they damaged our engines and long-range communications. We need emergency docking for repairs. Can you assist us?'

'Stand by.' There was silence on the communication link, then, 'Proceed to Dock 6.'

'Many thanks spaceport, FWN *London* out,' Alex said. 'Ensign, bring us in to Dock 6.'

'Yes, sir.'

'What will they think about the ship suddenly turning up?' Cal asked.

'They would have scanned us before giving us the docking bay, and would have seen the damage consistent with a firefight and know we urgently need repairs. Questions will be asked over the battle we had with the pirates, but they should wait for my report first, so we have a day or two.'

#

'What do you have to report?'

'I'm not sure what to make of Mr Everson's actions. He was pushing hard to see the report, and when he read it he made it clear that he was unhappy with the level of investigation and demanded to see the car. He was refused repeatedly and then he stopped asking and just seemed to accept it.'

'What do you mean he "just seemed to accept it" – what did he do?'

'Nothing as far as I can tell, he made no attempt to force his way in. He hasn't even been to his father's office, the staff there packed up his personal items and sent them on, and his computer and files are still there as far as I can tell.'

'Where is he now?'

'Either at his apartment or his father's home, there are no records of him travelling anywhere since his father's death, until he came here.'

'That's it? He hasn't been going through his father's files, asking questions about his death?'

'Not that I can see, no. It doesn't mean that he hasn't, all I can go by is his bank transactions, but if he paid by credit, I would have no way of tracing it.'

'Keep monitoring him. If he does anything out of character, I want to know.'

'Problems?' a new voice asked as he came into the room.

'I don't think so. Cal Everson is coming to the show, so I had his recent activities looked into, but he seems to have been keeping to himself and accepted the official report.'

'Good, he is so antisocial, we never did know how he would react. Obviously the reports that he was not close to his father were correct, but keep watching him, just in case.'

'That's what I plan to do.'

'No, I mean watch him. Send someone round to where he is staying.'

✳

Cal climbed out of the car and held out his hand to help Jane. After the FWN *London* had docked they had disembarked and Cal had booked them into the top hotel before leaving with her for a shopping trip.

'What's wrong with what I wear?' Jane had complained.

'Nothing as far as I'm concerned, but if we're going to this show, you need the perfect dress.' This is what had led to an afternoon in the top retail stores, buying not just the dress but the accessories to go with it. Now they returned to the hotel having sent the bags ahead and walked in hand in hand, unaware that they were being watched.

✳

Cal walked towards the entrance of the show with Jane on his arm, her dress flowing around her as she walked. Cal gave their names to the security guard at the door and they were allowed through.

'First step passed,' he whispered to her.

'How many more have we got?'

'Just take them one at a time,' he advised as they walked towards the other guests.

'Cal,' an acquaintance cried, 'I'm so glad you were able to make it. How are you?'

'I'm doing well, thank you. May I introduce you to my partner, Jane Keyworth.'

'A pleasure, my dear,' and they shook hands. After some polite conversation, they moved on to another group and another round of introductions.

'Please excuse me for a moment,' Jane said as she slipped away and walked towards the ladies, their shadow watched her as she approached the door, then turned their attention back to Cal. At the last moment Jane walked right past the ladies door and went towards the rear fire exit, having memorised the override code for the alarm system. No one paid any attention to her as she walked past various groups of other guests and slipped out of the public area. She got to the door and started to input the code. If there had been a fire, the system would have released the doors immediately, indeed there was once a time when these doors would have opened from the inside with no locks, but after a series of terrorist attacks, fire safety and security had to be balanced.

'What do you think you are doing? Stand away from the door.' Jane turned around to see a male in a security uniform, his hand hovering over his gun.

'I'm sorry, I was just looking for a place to get some air.'

'Not through there you don't, come away from the door,' he ordered again. Jane's finger hit the last button and the door clicked open. The guard pulled his gun just as Alex and his crew came through the door, but did not get the chance to fire before Alex and Pheir put him on the ground.

'Are you all right?' Alex turned and asked her.

'I am now, thank you,' and in the background they could hear the show starting.

⁜

In front of the cameras broadcasting live across the Federation of Worlds, models walked up and down the catwalk displaying the new coats. The show had been running for the last half an hour to the approval and applause of the audience, which was full of the Federation's wealthy and influential. The number of orders had increased as the show progressed, with the waiting lists now months long.

'What has Cal been doing?'

'Nothing, he has just been talking to the other guests.'

'Are you sure he hasn't been doing anything else?'

'I'm sure.'

'Good. When is the next shipment due to arrive?'

'Any day now.'

'As soon as they have off-loaded it, I want them back out there as soon as possible for another load.'

'Are you sure? If we wait, the exclusivity will drive the price up.'

'I know, we can always hold the skins back from sale, but I'm worried that if we make them too difficult to get hold of, people won't bother waiting and will move on to the next fashion trend. Besides, our associates are demanding more wings and I don't want to upset them.'

'I'll talk to them when they get back.'

'Good, now I need to get back to the show, the finale is about to happen,' and with that the lights went out.

'What the fuck!' he swore.

'I take it this is not part of the show.'

'No, find out what's wrong,' and in the dim glow of the

emergency lighting, he made his way back to the stage area where he could hear the audience whispering among themselves in anticipation of what would come next, as they were assuming that this was part of the show.

'Ladies and gentlemen,' a voice rang out, and a spotlight came on and shone down upon the speaker, 'can I please have your full attention. Many of you may know me personally or at least by reputation. My name is Cal Everson and I am the son of the late Head Chairman Richard Everson who was murdered last month.' He paused as he let his words sink in and he listened to the shocked whispering in the audience. 'You can imagine my horror and disgust when I found he had been murdered over a fashion item, the fashion item you have all come here today to see and buy.'

The men slipped quietly out of the building; they did not need to hear any more.

'This is ridiculous,' someone shouted, 'everyone knows that your father died in a car crash, and why would anyone want to kill him over clothes? This is foolishness.' Several others could be heard shouting their agreement while others were telling them to shut up and urging Cal to explain further.

'My father discovered where these coats came from. He wanted to stop the trade and punish those involved for genocide.' He paused, waiting for his words to sink in, then there were shouts of disagreement from the audience. 'I can hear that many of you think I've lost my mind, so may I introduce you to the source of your coats,' and onto the stage walked a small, cloaked figure protected on all sides by armed men. The figure stopped next to Cal and when it pulled the cloak off, there was a collective gasp of shock and the sound of urgent whispers. 'I present to you Brelsa from Lismar.

Her people are being skinned alive for the coats that you wear in the name of fashion.'

Silence followed the announcement, then, 'Are you telling me that what I'm wearing came from someone who used to be alive?'

'That is exactly what I'm saying.'

'No, that can't be right, they just copied the patterning.'

'No, I went to Lismar to see if what I had learnt was true, and in orbit was a pirate ship collecting more skins. A ship that now won't be returning.'

'You still don't believe what he says,' Brelsa said. 'I come here before you, to show you what I am, but many of you still will not accept it, so here is my proposal: my people are telepaths and I can sense that there are telepaths among you, and if you want proof, I will show you what has been happening on my planet, what they have done to my people. I felt them die, I saw through them what was being done as they were slowly being stripped of their skin. All that was left behind were piles of dead bodies rotting in the suns.'

Silence followed the offer, then, 'Show me,' a female said and a shadowy figure in the audience stood up and began to walk towards the stage.

'Mother, this is absurd.'

'No, they have come here making these horrific allegations, which I can't comprehend in this age. I say show me the evidence,' and with that she climbed up and stood next to Cal.

'Lady Dorrington,' Cal said to the elderly female in front of him, the matriarch of one of the oldest and richest families in the Federated Planets.

'So, show me, my dear,' she instructed Brelsa.

'Perhaps you want to sit down for this?' Cal suggested.

'Don't patronise me, my boy. Are you going to show me or not?'

Brelsa closed her eyes, drowned out the noise around her and pulled the memories of that day to her mind, the day she had so wished had been a nightmare, and the later ones when she had left her collective with Gilcan and asked to see the remains on his collective before going with him to argue with the other protectors. With them in the forefront of her mind, she searched for and found Lady Dorrington's mind and slowly, so as not to overwhelm it, pushed the images towards her.

'Stop it, stop it, oh God, stop!' Lady Dorrington started to shout, her hands going to her head, and Brelsa immediately broke the connection.

'Mother!' someone shouted and people could be heard rushing to the stage. 'What have you done to her?'

'She showed me the truth,' Lady Dorrington said as she struggled to get control of herself. 'Oh God!' she said again as she realised what she was wearing. She stripped off the coat and held it in her shaking hands, looking at it. 'I don't know what to do with it, how to honour your dead?'

'We bury where possible or burn if not,' Brelsa said. 'If you would give it to me, I will take it home.'

'Of course,' she said and held it out, and Brelsa took it from her. Lady Dorrington turned to the audience and announced, 'What Cal has said is the truth, these coats came from living people,' then she turned and left, shaking and very white, so shocked by what she had been shown that she collapsed into the arms of her family.

Someone in the audience walked up to the stage and laid her coat at Brelsa's feet, then another and another as the reality of what they had been told sank in.

Cal gripped Brelsa's shoulder in support as she watched the slowly growing pile of coats in front of her.

*

'Well, you certainly created a massive outcry,' Admiral Johnson said. After their disclosure, the FWN had moved in as the outraged elite had demanded an immediate investigation into how the sale of these coats had ever been allowed. Admiral Johnson had volunteered to go as the senior FWN representative. As soon as he arrived, he had made his way to where Cal and Jane were staying. Cal filled him in on everything that had occurred while they waited for Alex Wilhelm to join them, which he did shortly. 'Why didn't you tell me what you were planning on doing? Didn't you trust me?' he demanded as the captain walked in.

'No, I was trying to protect you. We broke so many laws in the last few days that I don't know why I'm not under arrest at present or how this is all going to end. If you didn't know, you can't be regarded as an accessory.'

'I got Cal and Jane onto your ship – if I'd been worried about myself, I wouldn't have got involved,' he said, frustrated.

'I know, but if this had all gone wrong, you would have been the only person who knew what had been going on,' Alex pointed out. 'If they had taken us all down, there would have been no one left to continue to fight.'

'I don't like it but I will accept your argument.'

'So what has been happening?' Cal asked. 'The news just keeps playing the fashion show over and over again and Jane is worried about hacking into systems at the moment due to the now very active investigation.'

'Battleships have been ordered to Lismar to patrol their space, but not too close in case they are seen as a threat. There is an absolute outcry and demands everywhere for a full investigation. I heard from a friend that the organisers of the show have all been arrested to try to find out if they were involved and who hired them, but they are all swearing that they didn't know anything about where the coats came from.'

'Do you think we'll find out who was behind it all?' Cal said.

'It's early in the investigation, but I hope so,' the admiral said.

'I would like to know who was responsible for killing my father, and at least he would be happy that they have been stopped.'

'He would be proud, Cal.'

'Do you know the one thing that confuses me the most about all of this,' Jane said.

'There is only one?' Cal retorted, and Jane playfully slapped him.

'The old reports say that last time the wings were taken and used in various industries. They would still be an extremely valuable commodity today, but I couldn't find any indication that they are being used anywhere. Lovoa and Solvan both confirmed that the wings were removed from the bodies, but why take them if you're not going to sell them?'

'Maybe they hadn't found a buyer for them yet.'

'I can't see that they were even looking.'

'I don't know, but let's not worry about it now. The trade has stopped, those responsible are being hunted, I think we can say that we've won this round,' Cal said.

'Speaking of the Lismarians, where is she? I assume she's here somewhere,' the admiral asked.

'On the roof, she dislikes being inside. We can go up there, if you like.'

'That's another problem, we still have to get her home,' Alex pointed out, 'she can't say here.'

'I know, I've been trying to arrange for you to take her back but, as you know, there will have to be an inquiry into your actions. People higher up than me are very unhappy that you brought an unknown species into the

Federation without permission. Also, your crew can give evidence on this matter so they may be unwilling to let you go, it might have to be someone else. I won't know for a few days.'

'I would only be gone for a week or so, her planet is not far away,' Alex protested.

'Would we at least be allowed to return with her? I promised I would try to fix something for them,' Cal asked, and Alex looked at him suspiciously, having had the report from Pheir about the machine.

'I will try my best to get you on board any ship leaving for the area.'

'If Alex can't go, you just have to make sure it's a deep-space ship.'

'For a trip that will only take a week?' the admiral asked.

'Solar lamps admiral, there must be solar lamps,' and Cal and Alex laughed at the look on his face.

Epilogue

'HOW could you have allowed this to happen?' he demanded of the man stitting in front of him.

'It appears that Cal was very clever at covering up what he was doing, there was no indication that he was investigating his father's death at all.' The deputy head chairman said. 'This is the preliminary report. It appears that Cal had been meeting with his godfather, Admiral Johnson, and left for Lismar on the ship captained by Alex Wilhelm, grandson of David Wilhelm, but Cal was never recorded as a passenger.' The man picked it up and started to read it. 'We can only go by the records we can get from the computers; it appears the good admiral covered up the visit because we could find no record of it.'

'What is done is done, we can't change the fact that the existence of the Lismarians is now well known. The question now is, what are you going to do to fix this mess?'

'Nothing.'

'What do you mean, nothing? This is a disaster.'

'And yours to resolve. You wanted the wings, I provided them for you; you wanted the head chairman out of the way, it was done.'

'It was your idea to make a personal fortune out of the skins, not ours, and it was those skins that started people looking up the old records. All I can hope is that we got enough for our needs.'

'If my involvement comes out, I will be ruined. If they

are going to execute me, I will tell them everything, including your involvement in this.'

'Are you threatening me?'

'Just stating the facts.'

'I will help you avoid the investigation.'

'I knew you would see it my way,' the man then walked forward to stand next to the deputy head chairman, and placed the report back on his desk. There was a quiet popping noise and he slumped over the desk, blood coming from his temples. The man wiped the gun and put it into the dead man's hand before typing, 'I am sorry,' onto his computer and leaving.